THE NEW HUGO WINNERS VOLUME III

Presented
by

CONNIE WILLIS

BAEN

THE NEW HUGO WINNERS, VOLUME III

This is a work of fiction. All the characters and events portrayed in this book are fictional, and any resemblance to real people or incidents is purely coincidental.

A Baen Books Original

Baen Publishing Enterprises
P.O. Box 1403
Riverdale, N.Y. 10471

ISBN: 0-671-87604-X

Cover art by Bob Eggleton

Printed in the United States of America

Contents

Credits

INTRODUCTION
by Connie Willis

I shouldn't be doing this. Isaac Asimov edited the first Hugo Winners volume in 1962, and all the ones after that (*The Hugo Winners, Volumes Two through Five*, and *The New Hugo Winners, Volumes One and Two*) and he was terrific at it—he not only knew everything about the stories, but all about the field and the World Science Fiction Conventions and the history of the Hugo Awards, and he was funny and charming besides. As he said himself, in his introduction to *The Hugo Winners, Volume Three*, "For the Hugo winner anthologies . . . any other editor but myself is unthinkable—at least, I can't think of any . . ."

I can't either. But now that Isaac's gone, somebody has to, and for now the job of editing has fallen to me. Following in his footsteps is out of the question—they are too wide and deep—but I like to feel that I was chosen to limp along after him because of what we had in common.

Isaac and I shared two things: our love of science fiction and how much the Hugos meant to us. Isaac was alternately boastful and deprecating about his, doing a sort of Bob Hope schtick about never winning and claiming he was "filled with righteous indignation against all those who had perpetrated this injustice by accepting the awards" and saying he used the *Hugo Winners* introductions to "denounce the Establishment" and insult the authors.

When he did win for "The Bicentennial Man," (he had already won the Best Novel award for *The Gods Themselves* in 1972 and *Foundation's Edge* in 1982 and special Hugos for his science columns and for Best All-Time Series for the *Foundation* trilogy) he announced the fact with "unconfined glee" as a chance to brag and boost his career.

The truth was the awards mattered terribly to him. He was surprised and thrilled each time he won, and displayed the awards proudly. He saw them as the ultimate tribute from the people who loved science fiction as much as he did.

For me, winning the Hugo was the culmination of a lifelong dream. When I was nominated the first time, at the Boston Worldcon in 1980, I sat next to my editor Charlie Ryan and watched the authors I'd read since I was a teenager coming in, unable to believe I was really sitting there with them. "I used to read about the Hugo Awards when I was a kid," I told Charlie, "and I used to dream about winning one, I told myself I *was* going to win one, but I didn't *really* think it was something that could happen."

At that point, Robert Silverberg—Robert Silverberg!—who was sitting in front of us, turned around and said to me—to me!—, "I felt exactly the same way." It was the most wonderful moment of my life.

I've loved science fiction since I first read Heinlein's *Have Space Suit, Will Travel*, which didn't win a Hugo Award, though *I* think it should have (he won for *Double Star, Starship Troopers, Stranger in a Strange Land*, and *The Moon is a Harsh Mistress*), and I've always read the novels that had "Hugo Award Winner" on them.

The Hugo Awards are presented annually by the membership of the World Science Fiction Convention. Their official name, the Science Fiction Achievement Awards, is almost never used, and they are known simply as the

Hugos, after Hugo Gernsback, the publisher and editor of the first science fiction magazine and the winner of a Hugo Award himself in 1960 for being "The Father of Science Fiction."

The Hugo Award for Best Novel was started in 1953, dropped for a year (maybe because the first winner, Alfred Bester's *The Demolished Man*, was such a tough act to follow), and has been given annually ever since, but awards for short fiction weren't given in the three present categories—novella, novelette, and short story—until 1973. The winners have varied from Larry Niven's "Neutron Star" to Samuel Delaney's "Time Considered as a Helix of Semi-Precious Stones" to James Tiptree, Jr.'s "Houston, Houston, Do You Read?"

The stories in this volume, the winners of the Hugo Awards from the Forty-seventh to the Forty-ninth World Science Fiction Conventions, are just as varied and astonishing. They represent science fiction, the field that Hugo Gernsback started, at its best. Isaac would have loved them.

1989
47th Convention
Boston

Kirinyaga
by Mike Resnick

Schrödinger's Kitten
by George Alec Effinger

The Last of the Winnebagos
by Connie Willis

Over the years, science fiction has explored the effect of technology on society in a number of ways. Sometimes it's been delighted at future possibilities, showing us hovercars and domed cities. At others, as in George Orwell's *1984* and J. G. Ballard's "Build-up," it shows the darker side of progress. Whichever tack it takes, however, it's usually our own society we're looking at. In "Kirinyaga," though, Mike Resnick has brought together space technology and an African tribe to bring up some disturbing new questions about science and society, and the impact they have on each other.

Mike Resnick has written a number of moving and perceptive stories about Kenya and the Kikuyu tribe, including Paradise: A Chronicle of a Distant World, *and* "Bwana." *He won the Hugo for Best Short Story for* "Kirinyaga" *in 1989, his first Hugo Award. Another of his stories about the Kikuyu tribe,* "The Manamouki," *also in this volume, won the Hugo for Best Novelette two years later, and three others were Hugo finalists.*

—Connie Willis

Kirinyaga

by Mike Resnick

In the beginning, Ngai lived alone atop the mountain called Kirinyaga. In the fullness of time, he created three sons, who became fathers of the Maasai, the Kamba, and the Kikuyu races; and to each son he offered a spear, a bow, and a digging stick. The Maasai chose the spear, and was told to tend herds on the vast savannah. The Kamba chose the bow, and was sent to the dense forests to hunt for game. But Gikuyu, the first Kikuyu, knew that Ngai loved the earth and the seasons, and chose the digging stick. To reward him for this, Ngai not only taught him the secrets of the seed and the harvest, but gave him Kirinyaga, with its holy fig tree and rich lands.

The sons and daughters of Gikuyu remained on Kirinyaga until the white man came and took their lands away; and even when the white man had been banished, they did not return, but chose to remain in the cities, wearing Western clothes and using Western machines and living Western lives. Even I, who am a *mundumugu*—a witch doctor—was born in the city. I have never seen the lion or the elephant or the rhinoceros, for all of them were extinct before my birth; nor have I seen Kirinyaga as Ngai meant it to be seen, for a bustling, overcrowded city of 3 million inhabitants covers its slopes, every year approaching closer and closer to Ngai's throne at the summit. Even the Kikuyu have forgotten its true name, and now know it only as Mount Kenya.

To be thrown out of Paradise, as were the Christian Adam and Eve, is a terrible fate, but to live beside a debased Paradise is infinitely worse. I think about them frequently, the descendants of Gikuyu who have forgotten their origin and their traditions and are now merely Kenyans, and I wonder why more of them did not join with us when we created the Eutopian world of Kirinyaga.

True, it is a harsh life, for Ngai never meant life to be easy; but it is also a satisfying life. We live in harmony with our environment; we offer sacrifices when Ngai's tears of compassion fall upon our fields and give sustenance to our crops; we slaughter a goat to thank Him for the harvest.

Our pleasures are simple: a gourd of *pombe* to drink, the warmth of a *boma* when the sun has gone down, the wail of a newborn son or daughter, the footraces and spear throwing and other contests, the nightly singing and dancing.

Maintenance watches Kirinyaga discreetly, making minor orbital adjustments when necessary, assuring that our tropical climate remains constant. From time to time they have subtly suggested that we might wish to draw upon their medical expertise, or perhaps allow our children to make use of their educational facilities, but they have taken our refusal with good grace, and have never shown any desire to interfere in our affairs.

Until I strangled the baby.

It was less than an hour later that Koinnage, our paramount chief, sought me out.

"That was an unwise thing to do, Koriba," he said grimly.

"It was not a matter of choice," I replied. "You know that."

"Of course you had a choice," he responded. "You could have let the infant live." He paused, trying to control his anger and his fear. "Maintenance has never set foot on Kirinyaga before, but now they will come."

"Let them," I said with a shrug. "No law has been broken."

"We have killed a baby," he replied. "They will come, and they will revoke our charter!"

I shook my head. "No one will revoke our charter."

"Do not be too certain of that, Koriba," he warned me. "You can bury a goat alive, and they will monitor us and shake their heads and speak contemptuously among themselves about our religion. You can leave the aged and the infirm out for the hyenas to eat, and they will look upon us with disgust and call us godless heathens. But I tell you that killing a newborn infant is another matter. They will not sit idly by; they will come."

"If they do, I shall explain why I killed it," I replied calmly.

"They will not accept your answers," said Koinnage. "They will not understand."

"They will have no choice but to accept my answers," I said. "This is Kirinyaga, and they are not permitted to interfere."

"They will find a way," he said with an air of certainty. "We must apologize and tell them that it will not happen again."

"We will not apologize," I said sternly. "Nor can we promise that it will not happen again."

"Then, as paramount chief, *I* will apologize."

I stared at him for a long moment, then shrugged. "Do what you must do," I said.

Suddenly I could see the terror in his eyes.

"What will you do to me?" he asked fearfully.

"I? Nothing at all," I said. "Are you not my chief?" As he relaxed, I added: "But if I were you, I would beware of insects."

"Insects?" he repeated. "Why?"

"Because the next insect that bites you, be it spider or mosquito or fly, will surely kill you," I said. "Your blood will boil within your body, and your bones will melt. You will want to scream out your agony, yet you will be unable to utter a sound." I paused. "It is not a death I would wish on a friend," I added seriously.

"Are we not friends, Koriba?" he said, his ebon face turning an ash gray.

"I thought we were," I said. "But my friends honor our traditions. They do not apologize for them to the white man."

"I will not apologize!" he promised fervently. He spat on both his hands as a gesture of his sincerity.

I opened one of the pouches I kept around my waist and withdrew a small polished stone, from the shore of our nearby river. "Wear this around your neck," I said, handing it to him, "and it shall protect you from the bites of insects."

"Thank you, Koriba!" he said with sincere gratitude, and another crisis had been averted.

We spoke about the affairs of the village for a few more minutes, and finally he left me. I sent for Wambu, the infant's mother, and led her through the ritual of purification, so that she might conceive again. I also gave her an ointment to relieve the pain in her breasts, since they were heavy with milk. Then I sat down by the fire within my *boma* and made myself available to my people, settling disputes over the ownership of chickens and goats, and supplying charms against demons, and instructing my people in the ancient ways.

By the time of the evening meal, no one had a thought for the dead baby. I ate alone in my *boma*, as befitted my status, for the *mundumugu* always lives and eats apart from his people. When I had finished, I wrapped a blanket around my body to protect me from the cold and walked down the dirt path to where all the other *bomas* were clustered. The cattle and goats and chickens were penned up for the night, and my people, who had slaughtered and eaten a cow, were now singing and dancing and drinking great quantities of *pombe*. As they made way for me, I walked over to the caldron and took a drink of *pombe*, and then, at Kanjara's request, I slit open a goat and read its entrails and saw that his youngest wife would soon conceive, which was cause for more celebration. Finally the children urged me to tell them a story.

"But not a story of Earth," complained one of the taller boys. "We hear those all the time. This must be a story about Kirinyaga."

"All right," I said. "If you will all gather around, I will tell you a story of Kirinyaga." The youngsters all moved closer. "This," I said, "is the story of the Lion and the Hare." I paused until I was sure that I had everyone's attention, especially that of the adults. "A hare was chosen by his people to be sacrificed to a lion, so that the lion would not bring disaster to their village. The hare might have run away, but he knew that sooner or later the lion would catch him, so instead he sought out the lion and walked right up to him, and as the lion opened his mouth to swallow him, the hare said, 'I apologize, Great Lion.'

" 'For what?' asked the lion curiously.

" 'Because I am such a small meal,' answered the hare. 'For that reason, I brought honey for you as well.'

" 'I see no honey,' said the lion.

" 'That is why I apologized,' answered the hare. 'Another lion stole it from me. He is a ferocious creature, and says that he is not afraid of you.'

"The lion rose to his feet. 'Where is this other lion?' he roared.

"The hare pointed to a hole in the earth. 'Down there,' he said, 'but he will not give you back your honey.'

" 'We shall see about that!' growled the lion.

"He jumped into the hole, roaring furiously, and was never seen again, for the hare had chosen a very deep hole indeed. Then the hare went home to his people and told them that the lion would never bother them again."

Most of the children laughed and clapped their hands in delight, but the same young boy voiced his objection.

"That is not a story of Kirinyaga," he said scornfully. "We have no lions here."

"It *is* a story of Kirinyaga," I replied. "What is important about the story is not that it concerned a lion and a hare, but that it shows that the weaker can defeat the stronger if he uses his intelligence."

"What has that to do with Kirinyaga?" asked the boy.

"What if we pretend that the men of Maintenance, who have ships and weapons, are the lion, and the Kikuyu are the hares?" I suggested. "What shall the hares do if the lion demands a sacrifice?"

The boy suddenly grinned. "Now I understand! We shall throw the lion down a hole!"

"But we have no holes here," I pointed out.

"Then what shall we do?"

"The hare did not know that he would find the lion near a hole," I replied. "Had he found him by a deep lake, he would have said that a large fish took the honey."

"We have no deep lakes."

"But we do have intelligence," I said. "And if Maintenance ever interferes with us, we will use our intelligence to destroy the lion of Maintenance, just as the hare used his intelligence to destroy the lion of the fable."

"Let us think how to destroy Maintenance right now!" cried the boy. He picked up a stick and brandished it at an imaginary lion as if it were a spear and he a great hunter.

I shook my head. "The hare does not hunt the lion, and the Kikuyu do not make war. The hare merely protects himself, and the Kikuyu do the same."

"Why would Maintenance interfere with us?" asked another boy, pushing his way to the front of the group. "They are our friends."

"Perhaps they will not," I answered reassuringly. "But you must always remember that the Kikuyu have no true friends except themselves."

"Tell us another story, Koriba!" cried a young girl.

"I am an old man," I said. "The night has turned cold, and I must sleep."

"Tomorrow?" she asked. "Will you tell us another tomorrow?"

I smiled. "Ask me tomorrow, after all the fields are planted and the cattle and goats are in their enclosures and the food has been made and the fabrics have been woven."

"But girls do not herd the cattle and goats," she protested. "What if my brothers do not bring all their animals to the enclosure?"

"Then I will tell a story just to the girls," I said.

"It must be a long story," she insisted seriously, "for we work much harder than the boys."

"I will watch you in particular, little one," I replied, "and the story will be as long or as short as your work merits."

The adults all laughed, and suddenly she looked very uncomfortable, but then I chuckled and hugged her and patted her head, for it was necessary that the children learn to love their *mundumugu* as well as hold him in awe, and finally she ran off to play and dance with the other girls, while I retired to my *boma*.

Once inside, I activated my computer and discovered that a message was waiting for me from Maintenance, informing me that one of their number would be visiting me the following morning. I made a very brief reply—"Article II, Paragraph 5," which is the ordinance forbidding intervention—and lay down on my sleeping blanket, letting the rhythmic chanting of the singers carry me off to sleep.

I awoke with the sun the next morning and instructed my computer to let me know when the Maintenance ship had landed. Then I inspected my cattle and my goats—I, alone of my people, planted no crops, for the Kikuyu feed their *mundumugu*, just as they tend his herds and weave his blankets and keep his *boma* clean—and stopped by Simani's *boma* to deliver a balm to fight the disease that was afflicting his joints. Then, as the sun began warming the earth, I returned to my own *boma*, skirting the pastures where the young men were tending their animals. When I arrived, I knew the ship had landed, for I found the droppings of a hyena on the ground near my hut, and that is the surest sign of a curse.

I learned what I could from the computer, then walked outside and scanned the horizon while two naked children took turns chasing a small dog and running away from it. When they began frightening my chickens, I gently sent them back to their own *boma*, and then seated myself beside my fire. At last I saw my visitor from Maintenance, coming up the path from Haven. She was obviously uncomfortable in the heat, and she slapped futilely at the flies that circled her head. Her blonde hair was starting to turn gray, and I could tell by the ungainly way she negotiated the steep, rocky path that she was unused to such terrain. She almost lost her balance a number of times, and it was obvious that her proximity to so many animals frightened her, but she never slowed her pace, and within another ten minutes she stood before me.

"Good morning," she said.

"*Jambo, Memsaab,*" I replied.

"You are Koriba, are you not?"

I briefly studied the face of my enemy; middle-aged and weary, it did not appear formidable. "I am Koriba," I replied.

"Good," she said. "My name is—"

"I know who you are," I said, for it is best, if conflict cannot be avoided, to take the offensive.

"You do?"

I pulled the bones out of my pouch and cast them on the dirt. "You are Barbara Eaton, born of Earth," I intoned, studying her reactions as I picked up the bones and cast them again. "You are married to Robert Eaton, and you have worked for Maintenance for nine years." A final cast of the bones. "You are forty-one years old, and you are barren."

"How did you know all that?" she asked with an expression of surprise.

"Am I not the *mundumugu*?"

She stared at me for a long minute. "You read my biography on your computer," she concluded at last.

"As long as the facts are correct, what difference does

it make whether I read them from the bones or the computer?" I responded, refusing to confirm her statement. "Please sit down, *Memsaab* Eaton."

She lowered herself awkwardly to the ground, wrinkling her face as she raised a cloud of dust.

"It's very hot," she noted uncomfortably.

"It is very hot in Kenya," I replied.

"You could have created any climate you desired," she pointed out.

"We *did* create the climate we desired," I answered.

"Are there predators out there?" she asked, looking out over the savannah.

"A few," I replied.

"What kind?"

"Hyenas."

"Nothing larger?" she asked.

"There *is* nothing larger anymore," I said.

"I wonder why they didn't attack me?"

"Perhaps because you are an intruder," I suggested.

"Will they leave me alone on my way back to Haven?" she asked nervously, ignoring my comment.

"I will give you a charm to keep them away."

"I'd prefer an escort."

"Very well," I said.

"They're such ugly animals," she said with a shudder. "I saw them once when we were monitoring your world."

"They are very useful animals," I answered, "for they bring many omens, both good and bad."

"Really?"

I nodded. "A hyena left me an evil omen this morning."

"And?" she asked curiously.

"And here you are," I said.

She laughed. "They told me you were a sharp old man."

"They are mistaken," I replied. "I am a feeble old man who sits in front of his *boma* and watches younger men tend his cattle and goats."

"You are a feeble old man who graduated with honors

from Cambridge and then acquired two postgraduate degrees from Yale," she replied.

"Who told you that?"

She smiled. "You're not the only one who reads biographies."

I shrugged. "My degrees did not help me become a better *mundumugu*," I said. "The time was wasted."

"You keep using that word. What, exactly, is a *mundumugu*?"

"You would call him a witch doctor," I answered. "But in truth the *mundumugu*, while he occasionally casts spells and interprets omens, is more a repository of the collected wisdom and traditions of his race."

"It sounds like an interesting occupation," she said.

"It is not without its compensations."

"And *such* compensations!" she said with false enthusiasm as a goat bleated in the distance and a young man yelled at it in Swahili. "Imagine having the power of life and death over an entire Eutopian world!"

So now it comes, I thought. Aloud I said: "It is not a matter of exercising power, *Memsaab* Eaton, but of maintaining traditions."

"I rather doubt that," she said bluntly.

"Why should you doubt what I say?" I asked.

"Because if it were traditional to kill newborn infants, the Kikuyu would have died out after a single generation."

"If the slaying of the infant arouses your disapproval," I said calmly, "I am surprised Maintenance has not previously asked about our custom of leaving the old and the feeble out for the hyenas."

"We know that the elderly and the infirm have consented to your treatment of them, much as we may disapprove of it," she replied. "We also know that a newborn infant could not possibly consent to its own death." She paused, staring at me. "May I ask why this particular baby was killed?"

"That *is* why you have come here, is it not?"

"I have been sent here to evaluate the situation," she

replied, brushing an insect from her cheek and shifting her position on the ground. "A newborn child was killed. We would like to know why."

I shrugged. "It was killed because it was born with a terrible *thahu* upon it."

She frowned. "A *thahu*? What is that?"

"A curse."

"Do you mean that it was deformed?" she asked.

"It was not deformed."

"Then what was this curse that you refer to?"

"It was born feet-first," I said.

"That's it?" she asked, surprised. "That's the curse?"

"Yes."

"It was murdered simply because it came out feet-first?"

"It is not murder to put a demon to death," I explained patiently. "Our tradition tells us that a child born in this manner is actually a demon."

"You are an educated man, Koriba," she said. "How can you kill a perfectly healthy infant and blame it on some primitive tradition?"

"You must never underestimate the power of tradition, *Memsaab* Eaton," I said. "The Kikuyu turned their backs on their traditions once; the result is a mechanized, impoverished, overcrowded country that is no longer populated by Kikuyu, or Maasai, or Luo, or Wakamba, but by a new, artificial tribe known only as Kenyans. We here on Kirinyaga are true Kikuyu, and we will not make that mistake again. If the rains are late, a ram must be sacrificed. If a man's veracity is questioned, he must undergo the ordeal of the *githani* trial. If an infant is born with a *thahu* upon it, it must be put to death."

"Then you intend to continue killing any children that are born feet-first?" she asked.

"That is correct," I responded.

A drop of sweat rolled down her face as she looked directly at me and said: "I don't know what Maintenance's reaction will be."

"According to our charter, Maintenance is not permitted to interfere with us," I reminded her.

"It's not that simple, Koriba," she said. "According to your charter, any member of your community who wishes to leave your world is allowed free passage to Haven, from which he or she can board a ship to Earth." She paused. "Was that baby you killed given such a choice?"

"I did not kill a baby, but a demon," I replied, turning my head slightly as a hot breeze stirred up the dust around us.

She waited until the breeze died down, then coughed before speaking. "You do understand that not everyone in Maintenance may share that opinion?"

"What Maintenance thinks is of no concern to us," I said.

"When innocent children are murdered, what Maintenance thinks is of supreme importance to you," she responded, "I am sure you do not want to defend your practices in the Eutopian Court."

"Are you here to evaluate the situation, as you said, or to threaten us?" I asked calmly.

"To evaluate the situation," she replied. "But there seems to be only one conclusion that I can draw from the facts that you have presented to me."

"Then you have not been listening to me," I said, briefly closing my eyes as another, stronger, breeze swept past us.

"Koriba, I know that Kirinyaga was created so that you could emulate the ways of your forefathers—but surely you must see the difference between the torture of animals as a religious ritual and the murder of a human baby."

I shook my head. "They are one and the same," I replied. "We cannot change our way of life because it makes you uncomfortable. We did that once before, and within a mere handful of years, your culture had corrupted our society. With every factory we built, with every job we created, with every bit of Western technology we accepted, with every Kikuyu who converted to

Christianity, we became something we were not meant to be." I stared directly into her eyes. "I am the *mundumugu*, entrusted with preserving all that makes us Kikuyu, and I will not allow that to happen again."

"There are alternatives," she said.

"Not for the Kikuyu," I replied adamantly.

"There *are*," she insisted, so intent upon what she had to say that she paid no attention to a black-and-gold centipede that crawled over her boot. "For example, years spent in space can cause certain physiological and hormonal changes in humans. You noted when I arrived that I am forty-one years old and childless. That is true. In fact, many of the women in Maintenance are childless. If you will turn the babies over to us, I am sure we can find families for them. This would effectively remove them from your society without the necessity of killing them. I could speak to my superiors about it; I think that there is an excellent chance that they would approve."

"That is a thoughtful and innovative suggestion, *Memsaab* Eaton," I said truthfully. "I am sorry that I must reject it."

"But why?" she demanded.

"Because the first time we betray our traditions, this world will cease to be Kirinyaga, and will become merely another Kenya, a nation of men awkwardly pretending to be something they are not."

"I could speak to Koinnage and the other chiefs about it," she suggested meaningfully.

"They will not disobey my instructions," I replied confidently.

"You hold that much power?"

"I hold that much respect," I answered. "A chief may enforce the law, but it is the *mundumugu* who interprets it."

"Then let us consider other alternatives."

"No."

"I am trying to avoid a conflict between Maintenance and your people," she said, her voice heavy with frustration.

"It seems to me that you could at least make the effort to meet me halfway."

"I do not question your motives, *Memsaab* Eaton," I replied, "but you are an intruder representing an organization that has no legal right to interfere with our culture. We do not impose our religion or our morality upon Maintenance, and Maintenance may not impose its religion or morality upon us."

"It is not that simple."

"It is precisely that simple," I said.

"That is your last word on the subject?" she asked.

"Yes."

She stood up. "Then I think it is time for me to leave and make my report."

I stood up as well, and a shift in the wind brought the odors of the village: the scent of bananas, the smell of a fresh caldron of *pombe,* even the pungent odor of a bull that had been slaughtered that morning.

"As you wish, *Memsaab* Eaton," I said. "I will arrange for your escort." I signaled to a small boy who was tending three goats and instructed him to go to the village and send back two young men.

"Thank you," she said. "I know it's an inconvenience, but I just don't feel safe with hyenas roaming loose out there."

"You are welcome," I said. "Perhaps, while we are waiting for the men who will accompany you, you would like to hear a story about the hyena."

She shuddered involuntarily. "They are such ugly beasts!" she said distastefully. "Their hind legs seem almost deformed." She shook her head. "No, I don't think I'd be interested in hearing a story about a hyena."

"You will be interested in *this* story," I told her.

She stared at me curiously and shrugged. "All right," she said. "Go ahead."

"It is true that hyenas are deformed, ugly animals," I began, "but once, a long time ago, they were as lovely and graceful as the impala. Then one day a Kikuyu chief gave a hyena a young goat to take as a gift to Ngai, who lived atop the holy mountain Kirinyaga. The hyena took the goat between his powerful jaws and headed toward the distant mountain—but on the way he passed a settlement filled with Europeans and Arabs. It abounded in guns and machines and other wonders he had never seen before, and he stopped to look, fascinated. Finally an Arab noticed him staring intently, and asked if he, too, would like to become a civilized man—and as he opened his mouth to say that he would, the goat fell to the ground and ran away. As the goat raced out of sight, the Arab laughed and explained that he was only joking, that of course no hyena could become a man." I paused for a moment, and then continued. "So the hyena proceeded to Kirinyaga, and when he reached the summit, Ngai asked him what had become of the goat. When the hyena told him, Ngai hurled him off the mountaintop for having the audacity to believe he could become a man. He did not die from the fall, but his rear legs were crippled, and Ngai declared that from that day forward, all hyenas would appear thus—and to remind them of the foolishness of trying to become something that they were not, He also gave them a fool's laugh." I paused again, and stared at her. "*Memsaab* Eaton, you do not hear the Kikuyu laugh like fools, and I will not let them become crippled like the hyena. Do you understand what I am saying?"

She considered my statement for a moment, then looked into my eyes. "I think we understand each other perfectly, Koriba," she said.

The two young men I had sent for arrived just then, and I instructed them to accompany her to Haven. A moment later they set off across the dry savannah, and I returned to my duties.

I began by walking through the fields, blessing the scarecrows. Since a number of the smaller children followed me, I rested beneath the trees more often than was necessary, and always, whenever we paused, they begged me to tell them more stories. I told them the tale of the Elephant and the Buffalo, and how the Maasai *elmoran* cut the rainbow with his spear so that it never again came to rest upon the earth, and why the nine Kikuyu tribes are named after Gikuyu's nine daughters; and when the sun became too hot, I led them back to the village.

Then, in the afternoon, I gathered the older boys about me and explained once more how they must paint their faces and bodies for their forthcoming circumcision ceremony. Ndemi, the boy who had insisted upon a story about Kirinyaga the night before, sought me out privately to complain that he had been unable to slay a small gazelle with his spear, and asked for a charm to make its flight more accurate. I explained to him that there would come a day when he faced a buffalo or a hyena with no charm, and that he must practice more before he came to me again. He was one to watch, this little Ndemi, for he was impetuous and totally without fear; in the old days, he would have made a great warrior, but on Kirinyaga we had no warriors. If we remained fruitful and fecund, however, we would someday need more chiefs and even another *mundumugu,* and I made up my mind to observe him closely.

In the evening, after I ate my solitary meal, I returned to the village, for Njogu, one of our young men, was to marry Kamiri, a girl from the next village. The bride-price had been decided upon, and the two families were waiting for me to preside at the ceremony.

Njogu, his face streaked with paint, wore an ostrich-feather headdress, and looked very uneasy as he and his betrothed stood before me. I slit the throat of a fat ram that Kamiri's father had brought for the occasion, and then I turned to Njogu.

"What have you to say?" I asked.

He took a step forward. "I want Kamiri to come and till the fields of my *shamba,*" he said, his voice cracking with nervousness as he spoke the prescribed words, "for I am a man, and I need a woman to tend to my *shamba* and dig deep around the roots of my plantings, that they may grow well and bring prosperity to my house."

He spit on both his hands to show his sincerity, and then, exhaling deeply with relief, he stepped back.

I turned to Kamiri.

"Do you consent to till the *shamba* of Njogu, son of Muchiri?" I asked her.

"Yes," she said softly, bowing her head. "I consent."

I held out my right hand, and the bride's mother placed a gourd of *pombe* in it.

"If this man does not please you," I said to Kamiri, "I will spill the *pombe* upon the ground."

"Do not spill it," she replied.

"Then drink," I said, handing the gourd to her.

She lifted it to her lips and took a swallow, then handed it to Njogu, who did the same.

When the gourd was empty, the parents of Njogu and Kamiri stuffed it with grass, signifying the friendship between the two clans.

Then a cheer rose from the onlookers, the ram was carried off to be roasted, more *pombe* appeared as if by magic, and while the groom took the bride off to his *boma*, the remainder of the people celebrated far into the night. They stopped only when the bleating of the goats told them that some hyenas were nearby, and then the women and children went off to their *bomas* while the men took their spears and went into the fields to frighten the hyenas away.

Koinnage came up to me as I was about to leave.

"Did you speak to the woman from Maintenance?" he asked.

"I did," I replied.

"What did she say?"

"She said that they do not approve of killing babies who are born feet-first."

"And what did *you* say?" he asked nervously.

"I told her that we did not need the approval of Maintenance to practice our religion," I replied.

"Will Maintenance listen?"

"They have no choice," I said. "And *we* have no choice, either," I added. "Let them dictate one thing that we must or must not do, and soon they will dictate *all* things. Give them their way, and Njogu and Kamiri would have recited wedding vows from the Bible or the Koran. It happened to us in Kenya; we cannot permit it to happen on Kirinyaga."

"But they will not punish us?" he persisted.

"They will not punish us," I replied.

Satisfied, he walked off to his *boma* while I took the narrow, winding path to my own. I stopped by the enclosure where my animals were kept and saw that there were two new goats there, gifts from the bride's and groom's families in gratitude for my services. A few minutes later I was asleep within the walls of my own *boma*.

The computer woke me a few minutes before sunrise. I stood up, splashed my face with water from the gourd I keep by my sleeping blanket, and walked over to the terminal.

There was a message for me from Barbara Eaton, brief and to the point:

It is the preliminary finding of Maintenance that infanticide, for any reason, is a direct violation of Kirinyaga's charter. No action will be taken for past offenses.

We are also evaluating your practice of euthanasia, and may require further testimony from you at some point in the future.

Barbara Eaton

A runner from Koinnage arrived a moment later, asking me to attend a meeting of the Council of Elders, and I knew that he had received the same message.

I wrapped my blanket around my shoulders and began walking to Koinnage's *shamba*, which consisted of his *boma* as well as those of his three sons and their wives. When I arrived, I found not only the local elders waiting for me, but also two chiefs from neighboring villages.

"Did you receive the message from Maintenance?" demanded Koinnage, as I seated myself opposite him.

"I did."

"I warned you that this would happen!" he said. "What will we do now?"

"We will do what we have always done," I answered calmly.

"We cannot," said one of the neighboring chiefs. "They have forbidden it."

"They have no right to forbid it," I replied.

"There is a woman in my village whose time is near," continued the chief, "and all of the signs and omens point to the birth of twins. We have been taught that the firstborn must be killed, for one mother cannot produce two souls—but now Maintenance has forbidden it. What are we to do?"

"We must kill the firstborn," I said, "for it will be a demon."

"And then Maintenance will make us leave Kirinyaga!" said Koinnage bitterly.

"Perhaps we could let the child live," said the chief. "That might satisfy them, and then they might leave us alone."

I shook my head. "They will not leave you alone. Already they speak about the way we leave the old and feeble out for the hyenas, as if this were some enormous sin against their God. If you give in on the one, the day will come when you must give in on the other."

"Would that be so terrible?" persisted the chief. "They have medicines that we do not possess; perhaps they could make the old young again."

"You do not understand," I said, rising to my feet. "Our society is not a collection of separate people and customs and traditions. No, it is a complex system, with all the pieces as dependent upon each other as the animals and vegetation of the Savannah. If you burn the grass, you will not only kill the impala who feeds upon it, but the predator who feeds upon the impala, and the ticks and flies who live upon the predator, and the vultures and maribou storks who feed upon his remains when he dies. You cannot destroy the part without destroying the whole."

I paused to let them consider what I had said, and then continued speaking: "Kirinyaga is like the savannah. If we do not leave the old and feeble out for the hyenas, the hyenas will starve. If the hyenas starve, the grass eaters will become so numerous that there is no land left for our cattle and goats to graze. If the old and feeble do not die when Ngai decrees it, then soon we will not have enough food to go around."

I picked up a stick and balanced it precariously on my forefinger.

"This stick," I said, "is the Kikuyu people, and my finger is Kirinyaga. They are in perfect balance." I stared at the neighboring chief. "But what will happen if I alter the balance and put my finger *here*?" I asked, gesturing to the end of the stick.

"The stick will fall to the ground."

"And here?" I asked, pointing to a spot an inch away from the center.

"It will fall."

"Thus is it with us," I explained. "Whether we yield on one point or all points, the result will be the same: the Kikuyu will fall as surely as the stick will fall. Have we learned nothing from our past? We *must* adhere to our traditions; they are all that we have!"

"But Maintenance will not allow us to do so!" protested Koinnage.

"They are not warriors, but civilized men," I said, allowing a touch of contempt to creep into my voice. "Their chiefs and their *mundumugus* will not send them to Kirinyaga with guns and spears. They will issue warnings and findings and declarations, and finally, when that fails, they will go to the Eutopian Court and plead their case, and the trial will be postponed many times and reheard many more times." I could see them finally relaxing, and I smiled confidently at them. "Each of you will have died from the burden of your years before

Maintenance does anything other than talk. I am your *mundumugu*; I have lived among civilized men, and I tell you that this is the truth."

The neighboring chief stood up and faced me. "I will send for you when the twins are born," he pledged.

"I will come," I promised him.

We spoke further, and then the meeting ended and the old men began wandering off to their *bomas*, while I looked to the future, which I could see more clearly than Koinnage or the elders.

I walked through the village until I found the bold young Ndemi, brandishing his spear and hurling it at a buffalo he had constructed out of dried grasses.

"*Jambo*, Koriba!" he greeted me.

"*Jambo*, my brave young warrior," I replied.

"I have been practicing, as you ordered."

"I thought you wanted to hunt the gazelle," I noted.

"Gazelles are for children," he answered. "I will slay *mbogo*, the buffalo."

"*Mbogo* may feel differently about it," I said.

"So much the better," he said confidently. "I have no wish to kill an animal as it runs away from me."

"And when will you go out to slay the fierce *mbogo*?"

He shrugged. "When I am more accurate." He smiled up at me. "Perhaps tomorrow."

I stared at him thoughtfully for a moment, and then spoke: "Tomorrow is a long time away. We have business tonight."

"What business?" he asked.

"You must find ten friends, none of them yet of circumcision age, and tell them to come to the pond within the forest to the south. They must come after the sun has set, and you must tell them that Koriba the *mundumugu* commands that they tell no one, not even their parents, that they are coming." I paused. "Do you understand, Ndemi?"

"I understand."

"Then go," I said. "Take my message to them."

He retrieved his spear from the straw buffalo and set off at a trot, young and tall and strong and fearless.

You are the future, I thought, as I watched him run toward the village. *Not Koinnage, not myself, not even the young bridegroom Njogu, for their time will have come and gone before the battle is joined. It is you, Ndemi, upon whom Kirinyaga must depend if it is to survive.*

Once before, the Kikuyu had to fight for their freedom. Under the leadership of Jomo Kenyatta, whose name has been forgotten by most of your parents, we took the terrible oath of Mau Mau, and we maimed and we killed and we committed such atrocities that finally we achieved Uhuru, for against such butchery civilized men have no defense but to depart.

And tonight, young Ndemi, while your parents are asleep, you and your companions will meet me deep in the woods, and you in your turn and they in theirs will learn one last tradition of the Kikuyu, for I will invoke not only the strength of Ngai but also the indomitable spirit of Jomo Kenyatta. I will administer a hideous oath and force you to do unspeakable things to prove your fealty, and I will teach each of you, in turn, how to administer the oath to those who come after you.

There is a season for all things: for birth, for growth, for death. There is unquestionably a season for Utopia, but it will have to wait.

For the season of Uhuru is upon us.

In the Good Old Days of science fiction, the argument goes, it was easy to tell the "hard science" science fiction stories from everything else. They were about physics and astronomy (and, once in a great while, chemistry), and they usually involved the solving of some problem—the space ship was falling out of orbit, PeeWee's spacesuit was running out of air—with a slide rule and Newton's laws.

Things have gotten blurrier in recent years. Stories like Pamela Zoline's "The Heat Death of the Universe" and Ed Bryant's "Particle Theory" have no slide rules or formulas in them, but seem nevertheless to be about science, and science itself has gotten more difficult to define, straying into regions of uncertainty and chaos where Heisenberg, not Newton, reigns, regions of butterfly effects and dragging clocks and cats that are neither alive nor dead. And in this shimmering story by George Alec Effinger, which has no slide rules in it but is very much about science, a world of infinite alternate probabilities.

"Schrödinger's Kitten" is George Alec Effinger's first Hugo. His hard-edged novel, When Gravity Fails, was a finalist for the Hugo for Best Novel in 1987. He is the author of What Entropy Means to Me, A Fire in the Sun, and the wonderful alternate history Civil War novella, "Look Away."

—Connie Willis

Schrödinger's Kitten
by George Alec Effinger

The clean crescent moon that began the new month
hung in the western sky across from the alley. Jehan was
barely twelve years old, too young to wear the veil, but
she did so anyway. She had never before been out so
late alone. She heard the sounds of celebration far away,
the three-day festival marking the end of the holy month
of Ramadan. Two voices sang drunkenly as they passed
the alley; two others loudly and angrily disputed the price
of some honey cakes. The laughter and the shouting
came to Jehan as if from another world. In the past,
she'd always loved the festival of Îd-el-Fitr; she took no
part in the festivities now, though, and it seemed somehow odd to her that anyone else still could. Soon she
gave it all no more of her attention. This year she must
keep a meeting more important than any holiday. She
sighed, shrugging: The festival would come around again
next year. Tonight, with only the silver moon for company, she shivered in her blue-black robe.

Jehan Fatima Ashûfi stepped back a few feet deeper
into the alley, farther out of the light. All along the street,
people who would otherwise never be seen in this quarter were determinedly amusing themselves. Jehan shivered again and waited. The moment she longed for
would come at dawn. Even now the sky was just dark

enough to reveal the moon and the first impetuous stars. In the Islamic world, night began when one could no longer distinguish a white thread from a black one; it was not yet night. Jehan clutched her robe closely to her with her left hand. In her right hand, hidden by her long sleeve, was the keen-edged, gleaming, curved blade she had taken from her father's room.

She was hungry and wished she had money to buy something to eat, but she had none. In the Budayeen there were many girls her age who already had ways of getting money of their own; Jehan was not one of them. She glanced about and saw only the filth-strewn, damp, and muddy paving stones. The reek of the alley disgusted her. She was bored and lonely and afraid. Then, as if her whole sordid world suddenly dissolved into something else, something wholly foreign, she saw more.

Jehan Ashûfi was twenty-six years old. She was dressed in a conservative dark gray woolen suit, cut longer and more severely than fashion dictated but appropriate for a bright young physicist. She affected no jewelry and wore her black hair in a long braid down her back. She took a little effort each morning to look as plain as possible while she was accompanying her eminent teacher and adviser. That had been Heisenberg's idea: In these days who believed a beautiful woman could also be a highly talented scientist? Jehan soon learned that her wish of being inconspicuous was in vain. Her dark skin and her accent marked her as a foreigner. She was clearly not European. Possibly she had Levantine blood. Most who met her thought she was probably a Jew. This was Göttingen, Germany, and it was 1925.

The brilliant Max Born, who had first used the expression *quantum mechanics* in a paper written two years before, was leading a meeting of the university's physicists. They were discussing Max Planck's latest proposals concerning his own theories of radiation. Planck had developed some basic ideas in the emerging field of quantum physics, yet he had used classical Newtonian mechanics to describe the interactions of light and matter. It was clear that this approach was inadequate, but as yet there was no better system. At the Göttingen conference, Pascual Jordan rose to introduce a compromise solution; but before Born, the department chairman, could reply, Werner Heisenberg fell into a violent fit of sneezing.

"Are you all right, Werner?" asked Born.

Heisenberg merely waved a hand. Jordan attempted to continue, but again Heisenberg began sneezing. His eyes were red, and tears crept down his face. He was in obvious distress. He turned to his graduate assistant. "Jehan," he said, "please make immediate arrangements; I must get away. It's my damned hay fever. I want to leave at once."

One of the others at the meeting objected. "But the colloquium—"

Heisenberg was already on his feet. "You can tell Planck to go straight to hell and to take De Broglie and his matter waves with him. The same goes for Bohr and his goddamn jumping electrons. I can't stand any more of this." Heisenberg took a few shaky steps and left the room. Jehan stayed behind to make a few notations in her journal. Then she followed Heisenberg back to their apartments.

There were no minarets in the Budayeen, but in the city all around the walled quarter there were many mosques. From the tall, ancient towers, strong voices called the faithful to morning devotions. "Come to prayer, come to prayer! Prayer is better than sleep!"

Leaning against a grimy wall, Jehan heard the chanted cries of the muezzins, but she paid them no mind. She stared at the dead body at her feet, the body of a boy a few years older than she, someone she had seen about the Budayeen but whom she did not know by name. She still held the bloody knife that had killed him.

In a short while three men pushed their way through a crowd that had formed at the mouth of the alley. The three men looked down solemnly at Jehan. One was a police officer; one was a qadi, who interpreted the ancient Islamic commandments as they applied to modern life; and the third was an imam, a prayer leader who had hurried from a small mosque not far from the east gate of the Budayeen. Within the walls the pickpockets, whores, thieves, and cut-throats could do as they liked to each other. A death in the Budayeen didn't attract much attention in the rest of the city.

The police officer was tall and heavily built, with a thick black mustache and sleepy eyes. He was curious only because he had watched over the Budayeen for fifteen years, and he had never investigated a murder by a girl so young.

The qadi was young, clean-shaven, and quite plainly deferring to the imam. It was not yet clear to those in attendance if this matter should be the responsibility of the civil or the religious authorities.

The imam was tall, taller even than the police officer, but thin and narrow shouldered; yet it was not asceticism that made him so slight. He was well-known for two things: his common sense concerning the conflicts of everyday affairs and the high degree of earthly pleasures he permitted himself. He, too, was puzzled and curious. He wore a short, grizzled gray beard, and his soft brown eyes were all but hidden within the reticulation of wrinkles that had slowly etched his face. Like the police officer, the imam had once worn a brave black mustache, but the days of fierceness had long since passed for him. Now he appeared decent and kindly. In truth, he was neither; but he found it useful to cultivate that reputation.

"O my daughter," he said in his hoarse voice. He was very upset. He much preferred explicating obscure passages of the glorious Qur'an to viewing such tawdry matters as blatant dead bodies in the nearby streets.

Jehan looked up at him, but she said nothing. She looked back down at the unknown boy she had killed.

"O my daughter," said the imam, "tell me, was it thou who hath slain this child?"

Jehan looked back calmly at the old man. She was concealed beneath her kerchief, veil, and robe; all that was visible of her were her dark eyes and the long thin fingers that held the knife. "Yes, O Wise One," she said, "I killed him."

The police officer glanced at the qadi.

"Prayest thou to Allah?" asked the imam. If this hadn't been the Budayeen, he wouldn't have needed to ask.

"Yes," said Jehan. And it was true. She had prayed on several occasions in her lifetime, and she might yet pray again sometime.

"And knowest thou there is a prohibition against taking of human life that Allah hath made sacred?"

"Yes, O Wise One."

"And knowest thou further that Allah hath set a penalty upon those who breaketh this law?"

"Yes, I know."

"Then, O my daughter, tell us why thou hath brought low this poor boy."

Jehan tossed the bloody knife to the stone-paved alley. It rang noisily and then came to rest against one leg of the corpse. "I killed him because he would do me harm in the future," she said.

"He threatened you?" asked the qadi.

"No, O Respected One."

"Then—"

"Then how art thou certain that he would do thee harm?" the imam finished.

Jehan shrugged. "I have seen it many times. He would throw me to the ground and defile me. I have seen the visions."

A murmur grew from the crowd still cluttering the mouth of the alley behind Jehan and the three men. The imam's shoulders slumped. The police officer waited patiently. The qadi looked discouraged. "Then he didst not offer thee harm this morning?"

"No."

"Indeed, as thou sayest, he hath *never* offered thee harm?"

"No, I do not know him. I have never spoken with him."

"Yet," said the qadi, clearly unhappy, "you murdered him because of what you have seen? As in a dream?"

"As in a dream, O Respected One, but more truly as in a vision."

"A dream," muttered the imam. "The Prophet, mayest blessings be on his name and peace, didst offer no absolution for murder provoked only by dreams."

A woman in the crowd cried out, "But she is only twelve years old!"

The imam turned and pushed his way through the rabble.

"Sergeant," said the qadi, "this young girl is now in your custody. The Straight Path makes our duty clear."

The police officer nodded and stepped forward. He bound the young girl's wrists and pushed her forward through the alley. The crowd of fellahin parted to make way for them. The sergeant led Jehan to a small, dank cell until she might have a hearing. A panel of religious elders would judge her according to Shari'a, the contemporary code of laws derived from the ancient and noble Qur'an. Jehan did not suffer in her noxious cell. A lifetime in the Budayeen had made her familiar with deprivation. She waited patiently for whatever outcome Allah intended.

She did not wait long. She was given another brief hearing, during which the council asked her many of the same questions the imam had asked. She answered them all without hesitation. Her judges were saddened but compelled to render their verdict. They gave her an opportunity to change her statement, but she refused. At last the senior member of the panel stood to face her. "O young one," he said in the most reluctant of voices, "the Prophet, blessings be on his name and peace, said, 'Whoso slayeth a believer, his reward is hell forever.' And elsewhere, 'Who killeth a human being for other than

manslaughter or corruption in the earth, it shall be as if
he killed all mankind.' Therefore, if he whom you slew
had purposed corruption upon you, your act would have
been justified. Yet you deny this. You rely on your
dreams, your visions. Such insubstantial defense cannot
persuade this council otherwise than that you are guilty.
You must pay the penalty as it is written. It shall be
exacted tomorrow morning just before sunrise."

Jehan's expression did not change. She said nothing.
Of her many visions, she had witnessed this particular
scene before also. Sometimes, as now, she was con-
demned; sometimes she was freed. That evening she ate
a good meal, a better meal than most she had taken
before in her life of poverty. She slept the night, and
she was ready when the civil and religious officials came
for her in the morning. An imam of great repute spoke
to her at length, but Jehan did not listen carefully. The
remaining acts and motions of her life seemed mechani-
cally ordered, and she did not pay great heed to them.
She followed where she was led, she responded dully
when pressed for a reply, and she climbed the platform
set up in the courtyard of the great Shimaal Mosque.

"Dost thou feel regret?" asked the imam, laying a gentle hand on her shoulder.

Jehan was made to kneel with her head on the block.
She shrugged. "No," she said.

"Dost thou feel anger, O my daughter?"

"No."

"Then mayest Allah in His mercy grant thee peace."
The imam stepped away. Jehan had no view of the headsman, but she heard the collective sigh of the onlookers
as the great ax lifted high in the first faint rays of dawn,
and then the blade fell.

Jehan shuddered in the alley. Watching her death always made her exceptionally uneasy. The hour wasn't
much later; the fifth and final call to prayer had sounded
not long before, and now it was night. The celebration
continued around her more intensely than before. That

her intended deed might end on the headsman's block did not deter her. She grasped the knife tightly, wishing that time would pass more swiftly, and she thought of other things.

By the end of May 1925 they were settled in a hotel on the tiny island of Helgoland some fifty miles from the German coast. Jehan relaxed in a comfortably furnished room. The landlady made her husband put Heisenberg's and Jehan's luggage in the best and most expensive room. Heisenberg had every hope of ridding himself of his allergic afflictions. He also intended to make some sense of the opaque melding of theories and countertheories put forward by his colleagues back in Göttingen. Meanwhile the landlady gave Jehan a grim and glowering look at their every meeting but said nothing. The Herr Doktor himself was too preoccupied to care for anything as trivial as propriety, morals, the reputation of this Helgoland retreat, or Jehan's peace of mind. If anyone raised eyebrows over the arrangement, Heisenberg certainly was blithely unaware; he walked around as if he were insensible to everything but the pollen count and the occasional sheer cliffs over which he sometimes came close to tumbling.

Jehan was mindful of the old woman's disapproval. Jehan, however, had lived a full, harsh life in her twenty-six years, and a raised eyebrow rated very low on her list of things to be concerned about. She had seen too many people abandoned to starvation, too many people dispossessed and reduced to beggary, too many outsiders slain in the name of Allah, too many maimed or beheaded through the convoluted workings of Islamic justice. All these years Jehan had kept her father's bloodied dagger, packed now beneath her shetland wool sweaters and still as deadly as ever.

Heisenberg's health improved on the island, and there was a beautiful view of the sea from their room. His mood brightened quickly. One morning, while walking along the shoreline with him, Jehan read a passage from the glorious Qur'an. "This sura is called 'The Earthquake,' " she said. " 'In the name of Allah, the Beneficent, the Merciful. When Earth is shaken with her final earthquake, and Earth yields up her burdens and man saith: What aileth her? That day she will relate her chronicles, because thy Lord inspireth her. That day mankind will issue forth in separate groups to be shown their deeds. And whoso doeth good an atom's weight will see it then. And whoso doeth ill an atom's weight will see it then.' "

And Jehan wept, knowing that however much good she might do, it could never outweigh the wrongs she had already performed. But Heisenberg only stared out over the gray, tumbling waves of the ocean. He did not listen closely to the sacred verses, yet a few of Jehan's words struck him. " 'And whoso doeth good an atom's weight will see it then,' " he said, emphasizing the single word. There was a small, hesitant smile quivering at the corners of his mouth. Jehan put her arm around him to comfort him because he seemed chilled, and she led him back to the hotel. The weather had turned colder, and the air was misty with sea spray; together they listened to the cries of the herring gulls as the birds dived for fish or hovered screeching over the strip of beach. Jehan thought of what she'd read, of the end of the world. Heisenberg thought only of its beginning, and its still closely guarded secrets.

They liked their daily peaceful walk about the island. Now, more than ever before, Jehan carried with her a copy of the Qur'an, and she often read short verses to him. So different from the biblical literature he'd heard all his life, Heisenberg let the Islamic scriptures pass without comment. Yet it seemed to him that certain specific images offered their meanings to him alone.

Jehan saw at last that he was feeling well. Heisenberg took up again full-time the tangled knot that was the current state of quantum physics. It was both his vocation and his means of relaxation. He told Jehan the best scientific minds in the world were frantically working to cobble together a slipshod mathematical model, one that might account for all the observed data. Whatever approach they tried, the data would not fit together. *He,* however, would find the key; he was that confident. He wasn't quite sure how he'd do it, but, of course, he hadn't yet really applied himself thoroughly to the question.

Jehan was not amused. She read to him: " 'Hast thou not seen those who pretend that they believe in that which is revealed unto thee and that which was revealed before thee, how they would go for judgment in their disputes to false deities when they have been ordered to abjure them? Satan would lead them far astray.' "

Heisenberg laughed heartily. "Your Allah isn't just talking about Göttingen there," he said. "He's got Bohr in mind, too, and Einstein in Berlin."

Jehan frowned at his impiety. It was the irreverence and ignorant ridicule of the kaffir, the unbeliever. She wondered if the old religion that had never truly had any claim on her was yet still part of her. She wondered how she'd feel after all these years, walking the narrow, crowded, clangorous ways of the Budayeen again. "You mustn't speak that way," she said at last.

"Hmm?" said Heisenberg. He had already forgotten what he'd said to her.

"Look out there," said Jehan. "What do you see?"

"The ocean," said Heisenberg. "Waves."

"Allah created those waves. What do *you* know about that?"

"I could determine their frequency. I could measure their amplitude."

"Measure!" cried Jehan. Her own long years of scientific study were suddenly overshadowed by an imagined insult to her heritage. "Look here," she demanded. "A handful of sand. Allah created this sand. What do *you* know about it?"

Heisenberg couldn't see what Jehan was trying to tell him. "With the proper instruments," he said, a little afraid of offending her, "in the proper setting, I could take a single grain of sand and tell you—" His words broke off suddenly. He got to his feet slowly, like an old man. He looked first at the sea, then down at the shore, then back out at the water. "Waves," he murmured, "particles, it makes no difference. All that counts is what we can actually measure. We can't measure Bohr's orbits, because they don't really *exist*! So the spectral lines we see are caused by transitions between two states. Pairs of states, yes; but that will mean a new form of mathematical expression just to describe them, referencing tables listing every possible—"

"Werner." Jehan knew that he was now lost to her.

"Just the computations alone will take days, if not weeks."

"Werner, *listen* to me. This island is so small, you can throw a stone from one end to the other. I'm not going to sit on this freezing beach or up on your bleak and dreary cliff while you make your brilliant breakthrough, whatever it is. I'm saying good-bye."

"What? Jehan?" Heisenberg blinked and returned to the tangible world.

She couldn't face him any longer. She was pouring one handful of sand through the fingers of her other hand.

It came suddenly to her mind then: If you had no water to perform the necessary ablution before prayer in the direction of Mecca, you were permitted to wash with clean sand instead. She began to weep. She couldn't hear what Heisenberg was saying to her—if indeed he was.

It was a couple of hours later in the alley now, and it was getting even colder. Jehan wrapped herself in her robe and paced back and forth.

She'd had visions of this particular night for four years, glimpses of the possible ways that it might conclude. Sometimes the young man saw her in the alley shortly after dawn, sometimes he didn't. Sometimes she killed him, sometimes she didn't. And, of course, there was the open question of whether her actions would lead to her freedom or to her execution.

When she'd had the first vision, she hadn't known what was happening or what she was seeing. She knew only the fear and the pain and the terror. The boy threw her roughly to the ground, ripped her clothing, and raped her. Then the vision passed. Jehan told no one about it; her family would have thought her insane. About three months later, the vision returned; only this time it was different in subtle ways. She was in the alley as before, but this time she smiled and gestured to the boy, inviting him. He smiled in return and followed her deeper into the alley. When he put his hand on her shoulder, she drew her father's dagger and plunged it into the boy's belly. That was as much as the vision showed her then. It terrified her even more than the rape scene had.

As time passed, the visions took on other forms. She was certain now that she was not always watching *her* future, *the* future, but rather a future, each as likely to come to pass as the others. Not all the visions could possibly be true. In some of them, she saw herself living into her old age in the city, right here in this filthy quarter of the Budayeen. In others she moved about strange places that didn't seem Islamic at all, and she spoke languages definitely not Arabic. She did not know if these conflicting visions were trying to tell her or warn her of something. Jehan prayed to know which of these versions she must actually live through. Soon after, as if to reward her for her faith, she began to have less violent visions: She could look into the future a short way and find lost objects or warn against unlucky travel plans or predict the rise and fall of crop prices. The neighbors, at first amused, began to be afraid of her. Jehan's mother counseled her never to speak of these "dreams" to anyone, or else Jehan might be locked away in some horrible institution. Jehan never told her father about her visions, because Jehan never told her father about anything. In that family, as in the others of the Budayeen—and the rest of the city, for that matter—the father did not concern himself very much with his daughters. His sons were his pride, and he had three strong sons whom he firmly believed would someday vastly increase the Ashûfi prestige and wealth. Jehan knew he was wrong, because she'd

already seen what would become of the sons—two would
be killed in wars against the Jews; the third would be a
coward, a weakling, and a fugitive in the United States.
But Jehan said nothing.

A vision: It was just past dawn. The young man—
whose name Jehan never learned—was walking down the
stone-paved street toward her alley. Jehan knew it without even peering out. She took a deep breath. She
walked a few steps toward the street, looked left, and
caught his eye. She made a brief gesture, turned her
back, and went deeper into the shadowy seclusion of the
alley. She was certain that he would follow her. Her
stomach ached and rumbled, and she was shaking with
nervous exhaustion. When the young man put his hand
on her shoulder, murmuring indecent suggestions, her
hand crept toward the concealed knife, but she did not
grasp it. He threw her down roughly, clawed off her
clothing, and raped her. Then he left her there. She was
almost paralyzed, crying and cursing on the wet, foul-
smelling stones. She was found sometime later by two
women who took her to a doctor. Their worst fears were
confirmed: Her honor had been ravaged irredeemably.
Her life was effectively over, in the sense of becoming a
normal adult female in that Islamic community. One of
the women returned to Jehan's house with her, to tell
the news to Jehan's mother, who must still tell Jehan's
father. Jehan hid in the room she shared with her sisters.
She heard the violent breaking of furniture and shrill
obscenity of her father. There was nothing more to be
done. Jehan did not know the name of her assailant. She
was ruined, less than worthless. A young woman no
longer a virgin could command no bride price. All those
years of supporting a worthless daughter in the hopes of
recovering the investment in the marriage contract—all
vanished now. It was no surprise that Jehan's father felt
betrayed and the father of a witless creature. There was
no sympathy for Jehan; the actual story, whatever it
might be, could not alter the facts. She had only the

weeping of her sisters and her mother. From that morning on, Jehan was permanently repudiated and cast out from her house. Jehan's father and three brothers would not even look at her or offer her their farewells.

The years passed ever more quickly. Jehan became a woman of the streets. For a time, because of her youth and beauty, she earned a good living. Then as the decades left their unalterable blemishes upon her, she found it difficult even to earn enough for a meal and a room to sleep in. She grew older, more bitter, and filled with self-loathing. Did she hate her father and the rest of her family? No, her fate had been fixed by the will of Allah, however impossible it was for her to comprehend it, or else by her own timidity in the single moment of choice and destiny in the alley so many years before. She could not say. Whatever the answer, she could not benefit now from either insight or wisdom. Her life was as it was, according to the inscrutable designs of Allah the Merciful. Her understanding was not required.

Eventually, she was found dead, haggard and starved, and her corpse was contorted and huddled for warmth coincidentally in the same alley where the young man had so carelessly despoiled any chance Jehan had for happiness in this world. After she died, there was no one to mourn her. Perhaps Allah the Beneficent took pity on her, showing mercy to her who had received little enough mercy from her neighbors while she lived among them. It had always been a cold place for Jehan.

For a while estranged from Heisenberg, Jehan worked with Erwin Schrödinger in Zurich. At first Schrödinger's ideas confused her because they went against many of Heisenberg's basic assumptions. For the time being, Heisenberg rejected any simple picture of what the atom was like, any model at all. Schrödinger, older and more conservative than the Göttingen group, wanted to explain quantum phenomena without new mathematics and elusive imagery. He treated the electron as a wave function but a different sort of wave than De Broglie's. The properties of waves in the physical world were well-known and without ambiguity. Yet when Schrödinger calculated how a change in energy level affected his electron wave, his solutions didn't agree with observed data.

"What am I overlooking?" he asked.

Jehan shook her head. "Where I was born they say, 'Don't pour away the water in your canteen because of a mirage.'"

Schrödinger rubbed his weary eyes. He glanced down at the sheaf of papers he held. "How can I tell if this water is worth keeping or something that belongs in a sewer?" Jehan had no reply to that, and Schrödinger set his work aside, unsatisfied. A few months later several papers showed that after taking into account the relativistic effects, Schrödinger's calculations agreed remarkably well with experimental results after all.

Schrödinger was pleased. "I knew in my heart that quantum physics would prove to be a sane world, not a realm populated by phantoms and governed by ghost forces."

"It seems unreal to me now," said Jehan. "If you say the electron is a wave, you are saying it is a phantom. In the ocean, it is the water that is the wave. As for sound, it is the air that carries the wave. What exists to be a wave in your equations?"

"It is a wave of probability, Bohr says. I do not wholly understand that yet myself," he said, "but my equations explain too many things to be illusions."

"Sir," said Jehan, frowning, "it may be that in this case the mirage is in your canteen and not before you in the desert."

Schrödinger laughed. "That might be true. I may yet have to abandon my mental pictures, but I will not abandon my mathematics."

It was a breathless afternoon in the city. The local Arabs didn't seem to be bothered by the heat, but the small party of Europeans was beginning to suffer. Their cruise ship had put ashore at the small port, and a tour had been arranged to the city some fifty miles to the south. Two hours later the travelers concluded that the expedition had been a mistake.

Among them was David Hilbert, the German mathematician, a lecturer at Göttingen since 1895. He was accompanied by his wife, Käthe, and their maid, Clärchen. At first they were quite taken by the strangeness of the city, by the foreign sights and sounds and smells; but after a short time, their senses were glutted with newness, and what had at first been exotic was now only deplorable. As they moved slowly through the bazaars, shaded ineffectually by awnings or meager arcades of sticks, they longed for the whisper of a single cool breeze. Arab men dressed in long white *gallebeyas* cried out shrilly, all the while glaring at the Europeans. It was impossible to tell what the Arabs were saying. Some dragged little carts loaded with filthy cups and pots—water? Tea? Lemonade? It made no difference. Cholera lingered at every stall; every beggar offered typhus as he clutched at sleeves.

Hilbert's wife fanned herself weakly. She was almost overcome and near collapse. Hilbert looked about desperately. "David," murmured the maid Clärchen, the only one of Hilbert's amours Frau Hilbert could tolerate, "we have come far enough."

"I know," he said, "but I see nothing—nowhere—"

"There are some ladies and gentlemen in that place. I think it's an eating place. Leave Käthe with me there and find a taxi. Then we shall go back to the boat."

Hilbert hesitated. He couldn't bear to leave the two unprotected women in the midst of this frantic heathen marketplace. Then he saw how pale his wife had become, how her eyelids drooped, how she swayed against Clärchen's shoulder. He nodded. "Let me help," he said. Together they got Frau Hilbert to the restaurant, where it was no cooler but at least the ceiling fans created a fiction of fresh air. Hilbert introduced himself to a well-dressed man who was seated at a table with his family, a wife and four children. The mathematician tried three

languages before he was understood. He explained the
situation, and the gentleman and his wife both assured
Hilbert that he need not worry. Hilbert ran out to find
a taxi.

He was soon lost. There were no streets here, not in
the European sense of the word. Narrow spaces between
buildings became alleys, opened into small squares,
closed again; other narrow passages led off in twisting,
bewildering directions. Hilbert found himself back at a
souk; he thought at first it was where he'd begun and
looked for the restaurant, but he was wrong. This was
another souk entirely; there were probably hundreds in
the city. He was beginning to panic. Even if he managed
to find a taxi, how could he direct it back to where his
wife and Clärchen waited?

A man's hand plucked at him. Hilbert tried to shrug
the long fingers away. He looked into the face of a lean,
hollowcheeked man in a striped robe and a blue knitted
cap. The Arab kept repeating a few words, but Hilbert
could make no sense of them. The Arab took him by the
arm and half-led, half-shoved Hilbert through the crowd.
Hilbert let himself be guided. They crossed through two
bazaars, one of tinsmiths and one of poultry dressers.
They entered a stone-paved street and emerged into an
immense square. On the far side of the square was a
huge, many-towered mosque, built of pink stone. Hilbert's first impression was awe; it was as lovely an edifice
as the Taj. Then his guide was pushing him again through
the throng or hurrying in front to hew a path for Hilbert.
The square was jammed and choked with people. Soon
Hilbert could see why—a platform had been erected in
the center, and on it stood a man with what could only
be an executioner's ax. Hilbert felt his stomach sicken.
His Arab guide had thrust aside everyone in their way
until Hilbert stood at the foot of the platform. He saw
uniformed police and a bearded old man leading out a
young girl. The crowd parted to allow them by. The girl
was stunningly lovely. Hilbert looked into her huge, dark
eyes—"like the eyes of a gazelle," he remembered from

reading Omar Khayyám—and glimpsed her slender form undisguised by her modest garments. As she mounted the steps, she looked down directly at him again. Hilbert felt his heart lurch; he felt a tremendous shudder. Then she looked away.

The Arab guide screamed in Hilbert's ear. It meant nothing to the mathematician. He watched in horror as Jehan knelt, as the headsman raised his weapon of office. When the fierce, bellowing cry went up from the crowd, Hilbert noticed that his suit was now spattered with small flecks of red. The Arab screamed at him again and tightened his grip on Hilbert's arm until Hilbert complained. The Arab did not release him. With his other hand, Hilbert took out his wallet. The Arab smiled. Above him, Hilbert watched several men carry away the body of the decapitated girl.

The Arab guide did not let him go until he'd paid an enormous sum.

Perhaps another hour had passed in the alley. Jehan had withdrawn to the darkest part and sat in a damp corner with her legs drawn up, her head against the rough brick wall. If she could sleep, she told herself, the night would pass more quickly; but she would not sleep, she would fight it if drowsiness threatened. What if she should slip into slumber and waken in the late morning, her peril and her opportunity both long since lost? Her only companion, the crescent moon, had abandoned her; she looked up at fragments of constellations, stars familiar enough in their groups but indistinguishable now as individuals. How different from people, where the opposite was true. She sighed; she was not a profound person, and it did not suit her to have profound thoughts. These must not truly be profound thoughts, she decided; she was merely deluded by weariness. Slowly she let her head fall forward. She crossed her arms on her knees and cradled her head. The greater part of the night had already passed, and only silence came from the street.

There were perhaps only three more hours until dawn. . . .

Soon Schrödinger's wave mechanics was proved to be equivalent to Heisenberg's matrix mechanics. It was a validation of both men's work and of the whole field of quantum physics as well. Eventually Schrödinger's simplistic wave picture of the electron was abandoned, but his mathematical laws remained undisputed. Jehan remembered Schrödinger predicting that he might need to take just that step.

Jehan had at last returned to Göttingen and Heisenberg. He had "forgiven her petulance." He welcomed her gladly, because of his genuine feelings for her and because he had much work to do. He had just formally developed what came to be known as the Heisenberg uncertainty principle. This was the first indication that the impartial observer could not help but play an essential, active role in the universe of subatomic particles. Jehan grasped Heisenberg's concept readily. Other scientists thought Heisenberg was merely making a trivial criticism of the limitations of their experiments or the quality of their observations. It was more profound than that. Heisenberg was saying that one can never hope to know both the position and momentum of an electron at the same time under *any* circumstances. He had destroyed forever the assumption of the impartial observer.

"To observe is to disturb," said Heisenberg. "Newton wouldn't have liked any of this at all."

"Einstein still doesn't like it right this very minute," said Jehan.

"I wish I had a mark for every time he's made that sour 'God doesn't play dice with the universe' comment."

"That's just the way he sees a 'wave of probability.' The path of the electron can't be known unless you look; but once you look, you change the information."

"So maybe God doesn't play dice with the universe," said Heisenberg. "He plays vingt-et-un, and if He does not have an extra ace up His sleeve, He creates one—

first the sleeve, then the ace. And He turns over more natural twenty-ones than is statistically likely. Hold on, Jehan! I'm not being sacrilegious. I'm not saying that God cheats. Rather, He invented the rules of the game, and He *continues* to invent them; and this gives Him a rather large advantage over poor physicists and their lagging understanding. We are like peasants watching the card tricks of someone who may be either genius or charlatan."

Jehan pondered this metaphor. "At the Solvay conference, Bohr introduced his complementarity idea, that an electron was a wave function until it was detected, and then the wave function collapsed to a point, and you knew where the electron was. Then it was a particle. Einstein didn't like that, either."

"That's God's card trick," said Heisenberg, shrugging.

"Well, the noble Qur'an says, 'They question thee about strong drink and games of chance. Say: In both is great sin, and some usefulness for men; but the sin of them is greater than their usefulness.' "

"Forget dice and cards, then," said Heisenberg with a little smile. "What kind of game *would* it be appropriate for Allah to play against us?"

"Physics," said Jehan, and Heisenberg laughed.

"And knowest thou there is a prohibition against taking of human life that Allah hath made sacred?"

"Yes, O Wise One."

"And knowest thou further that Allah hath set a penalty upon those who breaketh this law?"

"Yes, I know."

"Then, O my daughter, tell us why thou hath brought low this poor boy."

Jehan tossed the bloody knife to the stone-paved alley. It rang noisily and then came to rest against one leg of the corpse. "I was celebrating the Îd-el-Fitr," she said. "This boy followed me, and I became afraid. He made filthy gestures and called out terrible things. I hurried away, but he ran after me. He grabbed me by the shoulders and pressed me against a wall. I tried to escape, but I could not. He laughed at my fear, then he struck me many times. He dragged me along through the narrowest of streets, where there were not many to witness; and then he pulled me into this vile place. He told me that he intended to defile me, and he described what he would do in foul detail. It was then that I drew my father's dagger and stabbed him. I have spent the night in horror of his intentions and of my deed, and I have prayed to Allah for forgiveness."

The imam put a trembling hand on Jehan's cheek. "Allah is All-Wise and All-Forgiving, O my daughter. Alloweth me to return with thee to thy house, where I may put the hearts of thy parents at ease."

Jehan knelt at the imam's feet. "All thanks be to Allah," she murmured.

"Allah be praised," said the imam, the police officer, and the qadi together.

More than a decade later, when Jehan had daughters of her own, she told them this story. But in those latter days children did not heed the warnings of their parents, and the sons and daughters of Jehan and her husband did many foolish things.

Dawn slipped even into the narrow alleyway where Jehan waited. She was very sleepy and hungry, but she stood up and took a few wobbling steps. Her muscles had become cramped, and she could hear her heart beating in her ears. Jehan steadied herself with one hand on the brick wall. She went slowly to the mouth of the alley and peered out. There was no one in sight. The boy was coming neither from the left nor the right. Jehan waited until several other people appeared, going about the business of the new day. Then she hid the dagger in her sleeve once more and departed from the alley. She hurried back to her father's house. Her mother would need her to help make breakfast.

Jehan was in her early forties now, her black hair cut short, her eyes framed by clumsy spectacles, her beauty

stolen by care, poor diet, and sleeplessness. She wore a
white lab coat and carried a clipboard, as much a part
of her as her title, Fräulein Professor Doktor Ashûfi. This
was not Göttingen any longer; it was Berlin, and a war
was being lost. She was still with Heisenberg. He had
protected her until her own scientific credentials became
protection of themselves. At that point, the Nazi officials
were compelled to make her an "honorary" Aryan, as
they had the Jewish physicists and mathematicians whose
cooperation they needed. It had been only Jehan's long-
standing loyalty to Heisenberg himself that kept her in
Germany at all. The war was of little concern to her;
these were not her people, but neither were the British,
the French, the Russians, or the Americans. Her only
interest was in her work, in the refinement of physics,
in the unending anticipation of discovery.

She was glad, therefore, when the German atomic
bomb project was removed from the control of the German army and given to the Reich Research Council. One
of the first things to be done was the calling of a research
conference at the Kaiser Wilhelm Institute of Physics in
Berlin. The conference would be conducted under the
tightest security; no preliminary list of topics would be
released in advance, so that no foreign agents might see
such terms as *fission cross sections* and *isotope enrich-
ment*, leading to speculation on the long-term goals of
these physicists.

At the same time, the Reich Research Council decided
to hold a second conference for the benefit of the government's highest officials on the same day. The idea
was that the scientists speaking at the Kaiser Wilhelm
Institute's meeting could present short, elementary sum-
maries of their work in plain language so that the political
and military leaders could be briefed on the progress
that was being made toward a nuclear weapon. Then,
following the laymen's presentation, the physicists could
gather and discuss the same matters in their more technical jargon.

Heisenberg thought it was a good idea. It was 1942,

and material, political support, and funding were getting more difficult to find. The army wanted to put all available research resources into the rocketry program; they argued that the nuclear experiments were not showing sufficient success. Heisenberg was a theoretical physicist, not an engineer; he could not find a way to tell the council that the development of the uranium bomb must necessarily be slow and methodical. Each new step forward in theory had to be tested carefully, and each experiment was expensive in both time and money. The Reich, however, cared only for positive results.

One evening Jehan was alone in an administrative office of the Reich Research Council, typing her proposal for an important test of their isotope-separation technique. She saw on the desk two stacks of papers. One stack listed the simple synopses the physicists had prepared for the Reich ministers who had little or no background in science. She took those papers and hid them in her briefcase. The second stack was the secret agenda for the physicists' own meeting: "Nuclear Physics as a Weapon," by Professor Dr. Schumann; "The Fission of the Uranium Atom," by Professor Dr. Hahn; "The Theoretical Basis for the Production of Energy from the Fission of Uranium," by Heisenberg; and so on. Each person attending the technical seminar would be given a program after he entered the lecture hall and he would be required to sign for it. Jehan thought for a long while in the quiet office. She remembered her wretched childhood. She recalled her arrival in Europe and the people she had come to know, the life she had come to lead here. She thought about how Germany had changed while she hid in her castle of scientific abstractions, uninvolved with the outside world. At last she thought about what this new Germany might do with the uranium bomb. She knew exactly what she must do.

It took her only a few moments to take the highly technical agendas and drop them into the already-addressed envelopes to be sent to the Third Reich's leaders. She had guaranteed that the brief introductory discussion would be attended by no one. Jehan could easily imagine the response the unintelligible scientific papers would get from the political and military leaders—curt, polite regrets that they would not be in Berlin on that day, or that their busy schedules prevented them from attending. It was all so easy. The Reich's rulers did not hear the talks, and they did not learn how close Germany was to developing an atomic bomb. Never again was there any hope that such a weapon could be built in time to save the Reich—all because the wrong invitations had been slipped into a few envelopes.

Jehan awoke from a dream and saw that the night had grown very old. It would not be long before the sun began to flood the sky with light. Soon she would have a resolution to her anxiety. She would learn if the boy would come to the alley or stay away. She would learn if he would rape her or if she would find the courage to defend herself. She would learn if she would be judged guilty or innocent of murder. She would be granted a glimpse of the outcome to all things that concerned her.

Nevertheless, she was so tired, hungry, and uncomfortable that she was tempted to give up her vigil. The urge to go home was strong. Yet she had always believed that her visions were gifts granted by Allah, and it might offend Him to ignore the clear warnings. For Allah's sake, as well as her own, she reluctantly chose to wait out the rest of the dying night. She had seen so many visions since last evening—more than on any other day of her life—some new, some familiar from years past. It was, in a small, human way, almost comparable to the Night of Power that was bestowed upon the Prophet, may Allah's blessings be on him and peace. Then Jehan felt guilty and blasphemous for comparing herself to the Messenger that way.

She got down on her knees and faced toward Mecca and addressed a prayer to Allah, reciting one of the later suras from the glorious Qur'an, the one called "The Morning Hours," which seemed particularly relevant to her situation. " 'In the name of Allah, the Beneficent, the Merciful. By the morning hours, and by the night when it is stillest, thy Lord hath not forsaken thee nor doth He hate thee, and verily the latter portion will be better for thee than the former, and verily thy Lord will give unto thee so that thou wilt be content. Did He not find thee an orphan and protect thee? Did He not find thee wandering and direct thee? Did He not find thee destitute and enrich thee? Therefore the orphan oppress not, therefore the beggar drive not away, therefore of the bounty of thy Lord be thy discourse.' " When she finished praying, she stood up and leaned against the wall. She wondered if that sura prophesied that soon she'd be an orphan. She hoped that Allah understood that she never intended anything awful to happen to her parents. Jehan was willing to suffer whatever consequences Allah willed, but it didn't seem fair for her mother and father to have to share them with her. She shivered in the damp, cold air and gazed up to see if there was yet any brightening of the sky. She pretended that already the stars were beginning to disappear.

The square was jammed and choked with people. Soon Hilbert could see why—a platform had been erected in the center, and on it stood a man with what could only be an executioner's ax. Hilbert felt his stomach sicken. His Arab guide had thrust aside everyone in their way until Hilbert stood at the very foot of the platform. He saw uniformed police and a bearded old man leading out a young girl. The crowd parted to allow them by. The girl was stunningly lovely. Hilbert looked into her huge, dark eyes—"like the eyes of a gazelle," he remembered from reading Omar Khayyám—and glimpsed her slender form undisguised by her modest garments. As she mounted the steps, she looked down directly at him again. Hilbert felt his heart lurch; he felt a tremendous shudder. Then she looked away.

The Arab guide screamed in Hilbert's ear. It meant nothing to the mathematician. He watched in horror as

Jehan knelt, as the headsman raised his weapon of office. Hilbert shouted. His guide tightened his grip on the outsider's arm, but Hilbert lashed out in fury and threw the man into a group of veiled women. In the confusion, Hilbert ran up the steps of the scaffold. The imam and the police officers looked at him angrily. The crowd began to shout fiercely at this interruption, this desecration by a European kaffir, an unbeliever. Hilbert ran to the police. "You must stop this!" he cried in German. They did not understand him and tried to heave him off the platform. "Stop!" he screamed in English.

One of the police officers answered him. "It cannot be stopped," he said gruffly. "The girl committed murder. She was found guilty, and she cannot pay the blood price to the victim's family. She must die instead."

"Blood price!" cried Hilbert. "That's barbarous! You would kill a young girl just because she is poor? Blood price! *I'll* pay your goddamn blood price! How much is it?"

The policeman conferred with the others and then went to the imam for guidance. Finally the English-speaking officer returned. "Four hundred *kiam*."

Hilbert took out his wallet with shaking hands. He counted out the money and handed it with obvious disgust to the policeman. The imam cried a declaration in his weak voice. The words were passed quickly through the crowd, and the onlookers grew more enraged at this spoiling of their morning's entertainment. "Take her and go quickly," said the police officer. "We cannot protect you, and the crowd is becoming furious."

Hilbert nodded. He grasped Jehan's thin wrist and pulled her along after him. She questioned him in Arabic, but he could not reply. As he struggled through the menacing crowd, they were struck again and again by stones. Hilbert wondered what he had done, if he and the girl would get out of the mosque's courtyard alive. His fondness for young women—it was an open joke in Göttingen—had that been all that had motivated him? Had he unconsciously decided to rescue the girl and take her back to Germany? Or was it something more laudable? He would never know. He shocked himself: While he tried to shield himself and the girl from the vicious blows of the crowd, he thought only of how he might explain the girl to his wife, Käthe, and Clärchen, his mistress.

In 1957 Jehan Fatima Ashûfi was fifty-eight years old and living in Princeton, New Jersey. By coincidence, Albert Einstein had come here to live out the end of his life, and before he died in 1955 they had many pleasant afternoons at his house. In the beginning, Jehan wanted to discuss quantum physics with Einstein; she even told him Heisenberg's answer to Einstein's objection to God playing dice with the universe. Einstein was not very amused, and from then on their conversation concerned only nostalgic memories of the better days in Germany, before the advent of the National Socialists.

This afternoon, however, Jehan was sitting in a Princeton lecture hall, listening to a young man read a remarkable paper, his Ph.D. thesis. His name was Hugh Everett, and what he was saying was that there was an explanation for all the paradoxes of the quantum world, a simple but bizarre way of looking at them. His new idea included the Copenhagen interpretation and explained away all the objections that might be raised by less open-minded physicists. He stated first of all that quantum mechanics provided predictions that were invariably correct when measured against experimental data. Quantum physics *had* to be consistent and valid, there was no longer any doubt. The trouble was that quantum theory was beginning to lead to unappetizing alternatives.

Schrödinger's cat paradox—in which the cat in the box was merely a quantum wave function, not alive and not dead, until an observer looked to see which state the cat was in—was eliminated. Everett showed that the cat was no mere ghostly wave function. Everett said that wave functions do not "collapse," choosing one alternative or the other. He said that the process of observation chose one reality, but the other reality existed in its own right, just as "real" as our world. Particles do not choose at random which path to take—they take every path, in a separate, newly branched world for each option. Of course, at the particle level, this meant a huge number of branchings occurring at every moment.

Jehan knew this almost-metaphysical idea would find a chilly reception from most physicists, but she had special reasons to accept it eagerly. It explained her visions. She glimpsed the particular branch that would be "real" for her and also those that would be "real" for other versions of her, her own duplicates living on the countless parallel worlds. Now, as she listened to Everett, she smiled. She saw another young man in the audience, wearing a T-shirt that said, WIGNER: DO YOU THINK YOUR FRIEND COULD FEED MY CAT? HEISENBERG WASN'T SURE. THANKS, SCHRÖDINGER. She found that very amusing.

When Everett finished reading, Jehan felt good. It wasn't peace she felt; it was more like the release one feels after an argument that had been brewing for a long while. Jehan thought back over the turns and sidetracks she had taken since that dawn in the alley in the Buda-yeen. She smiled again, sadly, took a deep breath, and let it out. How many things she had done, how many things had happened to her! They had been long, strange lives. The only question that still remained was, How many uncountable futures did she still have to devise, to fabricate from the immaterial resources of this moment? As she sat there—in some worlds—Jehan knew the futures went on without her willing them to, needing nothing of her permission. She was not cautious of when tomorrow came but *which* tomorrow came.

Jehan saw them all, but she still understood nothing. She thought, *The Chinese say that a journey of a thousand li begins with a single step. How shortsighted that is! A thousand journeys of a thousand li begin with each step. Or with each step not taken.* She sat in her chair until everyone else had left the lecture hall. Then she got up slowly, her back and her knees giving her pain, and she took a step. She pictured myriad mirror-Jehans taking that step along with her, and a myriad that didn't. And in all the worlds across time, it was another step into the future.

At last there was no doubt about it: It was dawn. Jehan fingered her father's dagger and felt a thrill of excitement. Strange words flickered in her mind. "The Heisenty uncertainberg principle," she murmured, already hurrying toward the mouth of the alley. She felt no fear.

One of science fiction's finest traditions is destroying the world. SF writers have done it from almost the very beginning, starting with H. G. Wells' The War of the Worlds, and coming up with all sorts of methods of destruction, from nuclear war (Nevil Shute's On the Beach) to epidemics (George R. Stewart's Earth Abides) to natural disasters (J. G. Ballard's The Wind from Nowhere) and everything in between (Robert Silverberg's "When We Went to See the End of the World"). These endings are almost always all-consuming, with only a few survivors left amid the wreckage of civilization.

When I wrote "The Last of the Winnebagos," I was thinking of the end of the world on a smaller, more personal scale. Like the disaster in the village of Aberfan, Wales, where the slag heap came down on the school and killed all the children. The village wasn't destroyed, business went on pretty much as usual. It wasn't the end of the world. It just felt like it.

"The Last of the Winnebagos" was my second Hugo. I won my first for my novelette, "Fire Watch," in 1983. Both stories meant a great deal to me, and so did both awards.

—Connie Willis

The Last of the Winnebagos
by Connie Willis

On the way out to Tempe I saw a dead jackal in the road. I was in the far left lane of Van Buren, ten lanes away from it, and its long legs were facing away from me, the squarish muzzle flat against the pavement so it looked narrower than it really was, and for a minute I thought it was a dog.

I had not seen an animal in the road like that for fifteen years. They can't get onto the dividers, of course, and most of the multiways are fenced. And people are more careful of their animals.

The jackal was probably somebody's pet. This part of Phoenix was mostly residential, and after all this time, people still think they can turn the nasty, carrion-loving creatures into pets. Which was no reason to have hit it and, worse, left it there. It's a felony to strike an animal and another one to not report it, but whoever had hit it was long gone.

I pulled the Hitori over onto the center shoulder and sat there awhile, staring at the empty multiway. I wondered who had hit it and whether they had stopped to see if it was dead.

Katie had stopped. She had hit the brakes so hard she sent the jeep into a skid that brought it up against the ditch, and jumped out of the jeep. I was still running toward him, floundering in the snow. We made it to him almost at the same time. I knelt beside him, the camera dangling from my neck, its broken case hanging half open.

"I hit him," Katie had said. "I hit him with the jeep."

I looked in the rearview mirror. I couldn't even see over the pile of camera equipment in the back seat with the eisenstadt balanced on top. I got out. I had come nearly a mile, and looking back, I couldn't see the jackal, though I knew now that's what it was.

"McCombe! David! Are you there yet?" Ramirez's voice said from inside the car.

I leaned in. "No," I shouted in the general direction of the phone's mike. "I'm still on the multiway."

"Mother of God, what's taking you so long? The governor's conference is at twelve, and I want you to go out to Scottsdale and do a layout on the closing of Taliesin West. The appointment's for ten. Listen, McCombe, I got the poop on the Amblers for you. They bill themselves as 'One Hundred Percent Authentic,' but they're not. Their RV isn't really a Winnebago, it's an Open Road. It *is* the last RV on the road, though, according to Highway Patrol. A man named Eldridge was touring with one, also *not* a Winnebago, a Shasta, until March, but he lost his license in Oklahoma for using a tanker lane, so this is it. Recreation vehicles are banned in all but four states. Texas has legislation in committee, and Utah has a full-divided bill coming up next month. Arizona will be next, so take lots of pictures, Davey boy. This may be your last chance. And get some of the zoo."

"What about the Amblers?" I said.

"Their name *is* Ambler, believe it or not. I ran a lifeline on them. He was a welder. She was a bank teller. No kids. They've been doing this since eighty-nine when he retired. Nineteen years. David, are you using the eisenstadt?"

We had been through this the last three times I'd been on a shoot. "I'm not *there* yet," I said.

"Well, I want you to use it at the governor's conference. Set it on his desk if you can."

I intended to set it on a desk, all right. One of the desks at the back, and let it get some nice shots of the rear ends of reporters as they reached wildly for a little clear air-space to shoot their pictures in, some of them holding their vidcams in their upstretched arms and aiming them in what they hope is the right direction because they can't see the governor at all, let it get a nice shot of one of the reporter's arms as he knocked it face-down on the desk.

"This one's a new model. It's got a trigger. It's set for faces, full-lengths, and vehicles."

So great. I come home with a hundred-frame cartridge full of passersby and tricycles. How the hell did it know when to click the shutter or which one the governor was in a press conference of eight hundred people, full-length or face? It was supposed to have all kinds of fancy light-metrics and computer-composition features, but all it could really do was mindlessly snap whatever passed in front of its idiot lens, just like the highway speed cameras.

It had probably been designed by the same government types who'd put the highway cameras along the road instead of overhead so that all it takes is a little speed to reduce the new side-license plates to a blur, and people go faster than ever. A great camera, the eisenstadt. I could hardly wait to use it.

"Sun-co's very interested in the eisenstadt," Ramirez said. She didn't say goodbye. She never does. She just stops talking and then starts up again later. I looked back in the direction of the jackal.

The multiway was completely deserted. New cars and singles don't use the undivided multiways much, even during rush hours. Too many of the little cars have been squashed by tankers. Usually there are at least a few obsoletes and renegade semis taking advantage of the Patrol's being on the dividers, but there wasn't anybody at all.

I got back in the car and backed up even with the jackal. I turned off the ignition but didn't get out. I could see the trickle of blood from its mouth from here. A tanker went roaring past out of nowhere, trying to beat the cameras, straddling the three middle lanes and crushing the jackal's rear half to a bloody mush. It was a good thing I hadn't been trying to cross the road. He never would have even seen me.

I started the car and drove to the nearest off-ramp to find a phone. There was one at an old 7-Eleven on McDowell.

"I'm calling to report a dead animal on the road," I told the woman who answered the Society's phone.

"Name and number?"

"It's a jackal," I said. "It's between Thirtieth and Thirty-Second on Van Buren. It's in the far right lane."

"Did you render emergency assistance?"

"There was no assistance to be rendered. It was dead."

"Did you move the animal to the side of the road?"

"No."

"Why not?" she said, her tone suddenly sharper, more alert.

Because I thought it was a dog. "I didn't have a shovel," I said, and hung up.

I got out to Tempe by eight-thirty, in spite of the fact that every tanker in the state suddenly decided to take Van Buren. I got pushed out onto the shoulder and drove on that most of the way.

The Winnebago was set up in the fairgrounds between Phoenix and Tempe, next to the old zoo. The flyer had said they would be open from nine to nine, and I had wanted to get most of my pictures before they opened, but it was already a quarter to nine, and even if there were no cars in the dusty parking lot, I was probably too late.

It's a tough job being a photographer. The minute most people see a camera, their real faces close like a shutter in too much light, and all that's left is their camera face, their public face. It's a smiling face, except in the case of Saudi terrorists or senators, but, smiling or not, it shows no real emotion. Actors, politicians, people who have their pictures taken all the time are the worst. The longer the person's been in the public eye, the easier it is for me to get great vidcam footage and the harder it is to get anything approaching a real photograph, and the Amblers had been at this for nearly twenty years. By a quarter to nine they would already have their camera faces on.

I parked down at the foot of the hill next to the clump of ocotillas and yucca where the zoo sign had been, pulled my Nikon longshot out of the mess in the back seat, and took some shots of the sign they'd set up by the multiway: "See a Genuine Winnebago. One Hundred Percent Authentic."

The Genuine Winnebago was parked longways against the stone banks of cacti and palms at the front of the zoo. Ramirez had said it wasn't a real Winnebago, but it had the identifying W with its extending stripes running the length of the RV, and it seemed to me to be the right shape, though I hadn't seen one in at least ten years.

I was probably the wrong person for this story. I had never had any great love for RV's, and my first thought when Ramirez called with the assignment was that there are some things that should be extinct, like mosquitoes and lane dividers, and RV's are right at the top of the list. They had been everywhere in the mountains when I'd lived in Colorado, crawling along in the left-hand lane, taking up two lanes even in the days when a lane was fifteen feet wide, with a train of cursing cars behind them.

I'd been behind one on Independence Pass that had stopped cold while a ten-year-old got out to take pictures of the scenery with an Instamatic, and one of them had tried to take the curve in front of my house and ended up in my ditch, looking like a beached whale. But that was always a bad curve.

An old man in an ironed short-sleeved shirt came out

the side door and around to the front end and began washing the Winnebago with a sponge and a bucket. I wondered where he had gotten the water. According to Ramirez's advance work, which she'd sent me over the modem about the Winnebago, it had maybe a fifty-gallon water tank, tops, which is barely enough for drinking water, a shower, and maybe washing a dish or two, and there certainly weren't any hookups here at the zoo, but he was swilling water onto the front bumper and even over the tires as if he had more than enough.

I took a few shots of the RV standing in the huge expanse of parking lot and then hit the longshot to full for a picture of the old man working on the bumper. He had large reddish-brown freckles on his arms and the top of his bald head, and he scrubbed away at the bumper with a vengeance. After a minute he stopped and stepped back, and then called to his wife. He looked worried, or maybe just crabby. I was too far away to tell if he had snapped out her name impatiently or simply called her to come and look, and I couldn't see his face. She opened the metal side door, with its narrow louvered window, and stepped down onto the metal step.

The old man asked her something, and she, still standing on the step, looked out toward the multiway and shook her head, and then came around to the front, wiping her hands on a dishtowel, and they both stood there looking at his handiwork.

They were One Hundred Percent Authentic, even if the Winnebago wasn't, down to her flowered blouse and polyester slacks, probably also one hundred percent, and the cross-stitched rooster on the dishtowel. She had on brown leather slip-ons like I remembered my grandmother wearing, and I was willing to bet she had set her thinning white hair on bobby pins. Their bio said they were in their eighties, but I would have put them in their nineties, although I wondered if they were too perfect and therefore fake, like the Winnebago. But she went on wiping her hands on the dishtowel the way my grandmother had when she was upset, even though I couldn't see if her face was showing any emotion, and that action at least was authentic.

She apparently told him the bumper looked fine because he dropped the dripping sponge into the bucket and went around behind the Winnebago. She went back inside, shutting the metal door behind her even though it had to be already at least a hundred and ten out, and they hadn't even bothered to park under what scanty shade the palms provided.

I put the longshot back in the car. The old man came around the front with a big plywood sign. He propped it against the vehicle's side. "The Last of the Winnebagos," the sign read in somebody's idea of what Indian writing should look like. "See a vanishing breed. Admission—Adults—$8.00, Children under twelve—$5.00 Open 9 A.M. to Sunset." He strung up a row of red and yellow flags, and then picked up the bucket and started toward the door, but halfway there he stopped and took a few steps down the parking lot to where I thought he probably had a good view of the road, and then went back, walking like an old man, and took another swipe at the bumper with the sponge.

"Are you done with the RV yet, McCombe?" Ramirez said on the car phone.

I slung the camera into the back. "I just got here. Every tanker in Arizona was on Van Buren this morning. Why the hell don't you have me do a piece on abuses of the multiway system by water-haulers?"

"Because I want you to get to Tempe alive. The governor's press conference has been moved to one, so you're okay. Have you used the eisenstadt yet?"

"I told you, I just got here. I haven't even turned the damned thing on."

"You don't turn it on. It self-activates when you set it bottom down on a level surface."

Great. It had probably already shot its 100-frame cartridge on the way here.

"Well, if you don't use it on the Winnebago, make sure you use it at the governor's conference," she said.

"By the way, have you thought any more about moving to investigative?"

That was why Sun-co was really so interested in the eisenstadt. It had been easier to send a photographer who could write stories than it had to send a photographer and a reporter, especially in the little one-seater Hitoris they were ordering now, which was how I got to be a photojournalist. And since that had worked out so well, why send either? Send an eisenstadt and a DAT deck and you won't need an Hitori and way-mile credits to get them there. You can send them through the mail. They can sit unnoticed on the old governor's desk, and after a while somebody in a one-seater who wouldn't have to be either a photographer or a reporter can sneak in to retrieve them and a dozen others.

"No," I said, glancing back up the hill. The old man gave one last swipe to the front bumper and then walked over to one of the zoo's old stone-edged planters and dumped the bucket in on a tangle of prickly pear, which would probably think it was a spring shower and bloom before I made it up the hill. "Look, if I'm going to get any pictures before the turistas arrive, I'd better go."

"I wish you'd think about it. And use the eisenstadt this time. You'll like it once you try it. Even *you'll* forget it's a camera."

"I'll bet," I said. I looked back down the multiway. Nobody at all was coming now. Maybe that was what all the Amblers' anxiety was about—I should have asked Ramirez what their average daily attendance was and what sort of people used up credits to come this far out and see an old beat-up RV. The curve into Tempe alone was three point two miles. Maybe nobody came at all. If that was the case, I might have a chance of getting some decent pictures. I got in the Hitori and drove up the steep drive.

"Howdy," the old man said, all smiles, holding out his reddish-brown freckled hand to shake mine. "Name's Jake Ambler. And this here's Winnie," he said, patting the metal side of the RV, "Last of the Winnebagos. Is there just the one of you?"

"David McCombe," I said, holding out my press pass. "I'm a photographer. Sun-co. Phoenix *Sun*, Tempe-Mesa *Tribune*, Glendale *Star*, and affiliated stations. I was wondering if I could take some pictures of your vehicle?" I touched my pocket and turned the taper on.

"You bet. We've always cooperated with the media, Mrs. Ambler and me. I was just cleaning old Winnie up," he said. "She got pretty dusty on the way down from Globe." He didn't make any attempt to tell his wife I was there, even though she could hardly avoid hearing us, and she didn't open the metal door again. "We been on the road now with Winnie for almost twenty years. Bought her in 1989 in Forest City, Iowa, where they were made. The wife didn't want to buy her, didn't know if she'd like traveling, but now she's the one wouldn't part with it."

He was well into his spiel now, an open, friendly, I-have-nothing-to-hide expression on his face that hid everything. There was no point in taking any stills, so I got out the vidcam and shot the TV footage while he led me around the RV.

"This up here," he said, standing with one foot on the flimsy metal ladder and patting the metal bar around the top, "is the luggage rack, and this is the holding tank. It'll hold thirty gallons and has an automatic electric pump that hooks up to any waste hookup. Empties in five minutes, and you don't even get your hands dirty." He held up his fat pink hands palms forward as if to show me. "Water tank," he said, slapping a silver metal tank next to it. "Holds forty gallons, which is plenty for just the two of us. Interior space is a hundred fifty cubic feet with six feet four of headroom. That's plenty even for a tall guy like yourself."

He gave me the whole tour. His manner was easy, just short of slap-on-the-back hearty, but he looked relieved when an ancient VW bug came chugging catty-cornered up through the parking lot. He must have thought they wouldn't have any customers either.

A family piled out, Japanese tourists, a woman with short black hair, a man in shorts, two kids. One of the kids had a ferret on a leash.

"I'll just look around while you tend to the paying customers," I told him.

I locked the vidcam in the car, took the longshot, and went up toward the zoo. I took a wide-angle of the zoo sign for Ramirez. I could see it now—she'd run a caption like, "The old zoo stands empty today. No sound of lion's roar, of elephant's trumpeting, or children's laughter, can be heard here. The old Phoenix Zoo, last of its kind, while just outside its gates stands yet another last of its kind. Story on page 10." Maybe it would be a good idea to let the eisenstadts and the computers take over.

I went inside. I hadn't been out here in years. In the late eighties there had been a big flap over zoo policy. I had taken the pictures, but I hadn't covered the story since there were still such things as reporters back then. I had photographed the cages in question and the new zoo director who had caused all the flap by stopping the zoo's renovation project cold and giving the money to a wildlife protection group.

"I refuse to spend money on cages when in a few years we'll have nothing to put in them. The timber wolf, the California condor, the grizzly bear, are in imminent danger of becoming extinct, and it's our responsibility to save them, not make a comfortable prison for the last survivors."

The Society had called him an alarmist, which just goes to show you how much things can change. Well, he was an alarmist, wasn't he? The grizzly bear isn't extinct in the wild—it's Colorado's biggest tourist draw, and there are so many whooping cranes Texas is talking about limited hunting.

In all the uproar, the zoo had ceased to exist, and the animals all went to an even more comfortable prison in Sun City—sixteen acres of savannah land for the zebras and lions, and snow manufactured daily for the polar bears.

They hadn't really been cages, in spite of what the zoo director said. The old capybara enclosure, which was the first thing inside the gate, was a nice little meadow with a low stone wall around it. A family of prairie dogs had taken up residence in the middle of it.

I went back to the gate and looked down at the Winnebago. The family circled the Winnebago, the man bending down to look underneath the body. One of the kids was hanging off the ladder at the back of the RV. The ferret was nosing around the front wheel Jake Ambler had so carefully scrubbed down, looking like it was about ready to lift its leg, if ferrets do that. The kid yanked on its leash and then picked it up in his arms. The mother said something to him. Her nose was sunburned.

Katie's nose had been sunburned. She had had that white cream on it, that skiers used to use. She was wearing a parka and jeans and bulky pink-and-white moonboots that she couldn't run in, but she still made it to Aberfan before I did. I pushed past her and knelt over him.

"I hit him," she said bewilderedly. "I hit a dog."

"Get back in the jeep, damn it!" I shouted at her. I stripped off my sweater and tried to wrap him in it. "We've got to get him to the vet."

"Is he dead?" Katie said, her face as pale as the cream on her nose.

"No!" I had shouted. "No, he isn't dead."

The mother turned and looked up toward the zoo, her hand shading her face. She caught sight of the camera, dropped her hand, and smiled, a toothy, impossible smile. People in the public eye are the worst, but even people having a snapshot taken close down somehow, and it isn't just the phony smile. It's as if that old superstition is true, and cameras do really steal the soul.

I pretended to take her picture and then lowered the camera. The zoo director had put up a row of tombstone-shaped signs in front of the gate, one for each endangered species. They were covered with plastic, which hadn't helped much. I wiped the streaky dust off the one in front of me. "Canis latrans," it said, with two green stars after it. "Coyote. North American wild dog. Due to large-scale poisoning by ranchers, who saw it as a threat to cattle and sheep, the coyote is nearly extinct in the wild." Underneath there was a photograph of a ragged coyote sitting on its haunches and an explanation of the stars. Blue—endangered species. Yellow—endangered habitat. Red—extinct in the wild.

After Misha died, I had come out here to photograph the dingo and the coyotes and the wolves, but they were already in the process of moving the zoo, so I couldn't get any pictures, and it probably wouldn't have done any good. The coyote in the picture had faded to a greenish-yellow and its yellow eyes were almost white, but it stared out of the picture looking as hearty and unconcerned as Jake Ambler, wearing its camera face.

The mother had gone back to the bug and was herding the kids inside. Mr. Ambler walked the father back to the car, shaking his shining bald head, and the man talked some more, leaning on the open door, and then got in and drove off. I walked back down.

If he was bothered by the fact that they had only stayed ten minutes and that, as far as I had been able to see, no money had changed hands, it didn't show in his face. He led me around to the side of the RV and pointed to a chipped and faded collection of decals along the painted bar of the W. "These here are the states we've been in." He pointed to the one nearest the front. "Every state in the Union, plus Canada and Mexico. Last state we were in was Nevada."

Up this close it was easy to see where he had painted out the name of the original RV and covered it with the bar of red. The paint had the dull look of unauthenticity. He had covered up the "Open Road" with a burnt-wood plaque that read, "The Amblin' Amblers."

He pointed at a bumper sticker next to the door that said, "I got lucky in Vegas at Caesar's Palace," and had a picture of a naked showgirl. "We couldn't find a decal for Nevada. I don't think they make them anymore. And you know something else you can't find? Steering wheel covers. You know the kind. That keep the wheel from burning your hands when it gets hot?"

"Do you do all the driving?" I asked.

He hesitated before answering, and I wondered if one of them didn't have a license. I'd have to look it up in the lifeline. "Mrs. Ambler spells me sometimes, but I do most of it. Mrs. Ambler reads the map. Damn maps nowadays are so hard to read. Half the time you can't tell what kind of road it is. They don't make them like they used to."

We talked for a while more about all the things you couldn't find a decent one of anymore and the sad state things had gotten in generally, and then I announced I wanted to talk to Mrs. Ambler, got the vidcam and the eisenstadt out of the car, and went inside the Winnebago.

She still had the dishtowel in her hand, even though there couldn't possibly be space for that many dishes in the tiny RV. The inside was even smaller than I had thought it would be, low enough that I had to duck and so narrow I had to hold the Nikon close to my body to keep from hitting the lens on the passenger seat. It felt like an oven inside, and it was only nine o'clock in the morning.

I set the eisenstadt down on the kitchen counter, making sure its concealed lens was facing out. If it would work anywhere, it would be here. There was basically nowhere for Mrs. Ambler to go that she could get out of range. There was nowhere I could go either, and sorry, Ramirez, there are just some things a live photographer can do better than a preprogrammed one, like stay out of the picture.

"This is the galley," Mrs. Ambler said, folding her dishtowel and hanging it from a plastic ring on the cupboard below the sink with the cross-stitch design showing. It wasn't a rooster after all. It was a poodle wearing a sunbonnet and carrying a basket. "Shop on Wednesday," the motto underneath said.

"As you can see, we have a double sink with a hand-pump faucet. The refrigerator is LP-electric and holds four cubic feet. Back here is the dinette area. The table folds up into the rear wall, and we have our bed. And this is our bathroom."

She was as bad as her husband. "How long have you had the Winnebago?" I said to stop the spiel. Sometimes, if you can get people talking about something besides what they intended to talk about, you can disarm them into something like a natural expression.

"Nineteen years," she said, lifting up the lid of the chemical toilet. "We bought it in 1989. I didn't want to buy it—I didn't like the idea of selling our house and going gallivanting off like a couple of hippies, but Jake went ahead and bought it, and now I wouldn't trade it for anything. The shower operates on a forty-gallon pressurized water system." She stood back so I could get a picture of the shower stall, so narrow you wouldn't have to worry about dropping the soap. I dutifully took some vidcam footage.

"You live here full-time then?" I said, trying not to let my voice convey how impossible that prospect sounded. Ramirez had said they were from Minnesota. I had assumed they had a house there and only went on the road for part of the year.

"Jake says the great outdoors is our home," she said. I gave up trying to get a picture of her and snapped a few high-quality detail stills for the papers: the "Pilot" sign taped on the dashboard in front of the driver's seat, the crocheted granny-square afghan on the uncomfortable-looking couch, a row of salt and pepper shakers in the back windows—Indian children, black scottie dogs, ears of corn.

"Sometimes we live on the open prairies and sometimes on the seashore," she said. She went over to the sink and hand-pumped a scant two cups of water into a little pan and set it on the two-burner stove. She took down two turquoise melmac cups and flowered saucers and a jar of freeze-dried and spooned a little into the cups. "Last year we were in the Colorado Rockies. We can have a house on a lake or in the desert, and when we get tired of it, we just move on. Oh, my, the things we've seen."

I didn't believe her. Colorado had been one of the first states to ban recreational vehicles, even before the gas crunch and the multiways. It had banned them on the passes first and then shut them out of the national forests, and by the time I left they weren't even allowed on the interstates.

Ramirez had said RV's were banned outright in forty-seven states. New Mexico was one, Utah had heavy restricks, and daytime travel was forbidden in all the western states. Whatever they'd seen, and it sure wasn't Colorado, they had seen it in the dark or on some unpatrolled multiway, going like sixty to outrun the cameras. Not exactly the footloose and fancy-free life they tried to paint.

The water boiled. Mrs. Ambler poured it into the cups, spilling a little on the turquoise saucers. She blotted it up with the dishtowel. "We came down here because of the snow. They get winter so early in Colorado."

"I know," I said. It had snowed two feet, and it was only the middle of September. Nobody even had their snow tires on. The aspens hadn't turned yet, and some of the branches broke under the weight of the snow. Katie's nose was still sunburned from the summer.

"Where did you come from just now?" I asked her.

"Globe," she said, and opened the door to yell to her husband. "Jake! Coffee!" She carried the cups to the table-that-converts-into-a-bed. "It has leaves that you can put in it so it seats six," she said.

I sat down at the table so she was on the side where the eisenstadt could catch her. The sun was coming in through the cranked-open back windows, already hot. Mrs. Ambler got onto her knees on the plaid cushions and let down a woven cloth shade, carefully, so it wouldn't knock the salt and pepper shakers off.

There were some snapshots stuck up between the ceramic ears of corn. I picked one up. It was a square Polaroid from the days when you had to peel off the print and glue it to a stiff card: The two of them, looking exactly the way they did now, with that friendly, impenetrable camera smile, were standing in front of a blur of orange rock—the Grand Canyon? Zion? Monument Valley? Polaroid had always chosen color over definition. Mrs. Ambler was holding a little yellow blur in her arms that could have been a cat but wasn't. It was a dog.

"That's Jake and me at Devil's Tower," she said, taking the picture away from me. "And Taco. You can't tell from this picture, but she was the cutest little thing. A chihuahua." She handed it back to me and rummaged behind the salt and pepper shakers. "Sweetest little dog you ever saw. This will give you a better idea."

The picture she handed me was considerably better, a matte print done with a decent camera. Mrs. Ambler was holding the chihuahua in this one, too, standing in front of the Winnebago.

"She used to sit on the arm of Jake's chair while he drove and when we came to a red light she'd look at it, and when it turned green she'd bark to tell him to go. She was the smartest little thing."

I looked at the dog's flaring, pointed ears, its bulging eyes and rat's snout. The dogs never come through. I took dozens of picture, there at the end, and they might as well have been calendar shots. Nothing of the real dog at all. I decided it was the lack of muscles in their faces—they could not smile, in spite of what their owners claimed. It is the muscles in the face that make people leap across the years in pictures. The expressions on dogs' faces were what breeding had fastened on them— the gloomy bloodhound, the alert collie, the rakish mutt—and anything else was wishful thinking on the part of the doting master, who would also swear that a

colorblind chihuahua with a brain pan the size of a Mexican
jumping bean could tell when the light changed.

My theory of the facial muscles doesn't really hold
water, of course. Cats can't smile either, and they come
through. Smugness, slyness, disdain—all of those expressions come through beautifully, and they don't have any
muscles in their faces either, so maybe it's love that you
can't capture in a picture because love was the only
expression dogs were capable of.

I was still looking at the picture. "She is a cute little
thing," I said and handed it back to her. "She wasn't
very big, was she?"

"I could carry Taco in my jacket pocket. We didn't
name her Taco. We got her from a man in California
that named her that," she said, as if she could see herself
that the dog didn't come through in the picture. As if,
had she named the dog herself, it would have been different. Then the name would have been a more real
name, and Taco would have, by default, become more
real as well. As if a name could convey what the picture
didn't—all the things the little dog did and was and
meant to her.

Names don't do it either, of course. I had named Aberfan myself. The vet's assistant, when he heard it, typed
it in as Abraham.

"Age?" he had said calmly, even though he had no
business typing all this into a computer, he should have
been in the operating room with the vet.

"You've got that in there, damn it," I shouted.

He looked calmly puzzled. "I don't know any Abraham . . ."

"Aberfan, damn it. Aberfan!"

"Here it is," the assistant said imperturbably.

Katie, standing across the desk, looked up from the
screen. "He had the newparvo and lived through it?" she
said bleakly.

"He had the newparvo and lived through it," I said,
"until you came along."

"I had an Australian shepherd," I told Mrs. Ambler.

Jake came into the Winnebago, carrying the plastic bucket. "Well, it's about time," Mrs. Ambler said, "Your coffee's getting cold."

"I was just going to finish washing off Winnie," he said. He wedged the bucket into the tiny sink and began pumping vigorously with the heel of his hand. "She got mighty dusty coming down through all that sand."

"I was telling Mr. McCombe here about Taco," she said, getting up and taking him the cup and saucer. "Here, drink your coffee before it gets cold."

"I'll be in in a minute," he said. He stopped pumping and tugged the bucket out of the sink.

"Mr. McCombe had a dog," she said, still holding the cup out to him. "He had an Australian shepherd. I was telling him about Taco."

"He's not interested in that," Jake said. They exchanged one of those warning looks that married couples are so good at. "Tell him about the Winnebago. That's what he's here for."

Jake went back outside. I screwed the longshot's lens cap on and put the vidcam back in its case. She took the little pan off the miniature stove and poured the coffee back into it. "I think I've got all the pictures I need," I said to her back.

She didn't turn around. "He never liked Taco. He wouldn't even let her sleep on the bed with us. Said it made his legs cramp. A little dog like that that didn't weigh anything."

I took the longshot's lens cap back off.

"You know what we were doing the day she died? We were out shopping. I didn't want to leave her alone, but Jake said she'd be fine. It was ninety degrees that day, and he just kept on going from store to store, and when we got back she was dead." She set the pan on the stove and turned on the burner. "The vet said it was the newparvo, but it wasn't. She died from the heat, poor little thing."

I set the Nikon down gently on the formica table and estimated the settings.

"When did Taco die?" I asked her, to make her turn around.

"Ninety," she said. She turned back to me, and I let my hand come down on the button in an almost soundless click, but her public face was still in place: apologetic now, smiling, a little sheepish. "My, that was a long time ago."

I stood up and collected my cameras. "I think I've got all the pictures I need," I said again. "If I don't, I'll come back out."

"Don't forget your briefcase," she said, handing me the eisenstadt. "Did your dog die of the newparvo, too?"

"He died fifteen years ago," I said. "In ninety-three."

She nodded understandingly. "The third wave," she said.

I went outside. Jake was standing behind the Winnebago, under the back window, holding the bucket. He shifted it to his left hand and held out his right hand to me. "You get all the pictures you needed?" he asked.

"Yeah," I said. "I think your wife showed me about everything." I shook his hand.

"You come on back out if you need any more pictures," he said, and sounded, if possible, even more jovial, open-handed, friendly than he had before. "Mrs. Ambler and me, we always cooperate with the media."

"Your wife was telling me about your chihuahua," I said, more to see the effect on him than anything else.

"Yeah, the wife still misses that little dog after all these years," he said, and he looked the way she had, mildly apologetic, still smiling. "It died of the newparvo. I told her she ought to get it vaccinated, but she kept putting it off." He shook his head. "Of course, it wasn't really her fault. You know whose fault the newparvo really was, don't you?"

Yeah, I knew. It was the communists' fault, and it didn't matter that all their dogs had died, too, because he would say their chemical warfare had gotten out of hand or that everybody knows commies hate dogs. Or maybe it was the fault of the Japanese, though I doubted that. He was, after all, in a tourist business. Or the Democrats or the atheists or all of them put together, and even that was One Hundred Percent Authentic—portrait of the kind of man who drives a Winnebago—but I didn't want to hear it. I walked over to the Hitori and slung the eisenstadt in the back.

"You know who really killed your dog, don't you?" he called after me.

"Yes," I said, and got in the car.

I went home, fighting my way through a fleet of red-painted water tankers who weren't even bothering to try to outrun the cameras and thinking about Taco. My grandmother had had a chihuahua. Perdita. Meanest dog that ever lived. Used to lurk behind the door waiting to take Labrador-sized chunks out of my leg. And my grandmother's. It developed some lingering chihuahuan ailment that made it incontinent and even more ill-tempered, if that was possible.

Toward the end, it wouldn't even let my grandmother near it, but she refused to have it put to sleep and was unfailingly kind to it, even though I never saw any indication that the dog felt anything but unrelieved spite toward her. If the newparvo hadn't come along, it probably would still have been around making her life miserable.

I wondered what Taco, the wonder dog, able to distinguish red and green at a single intersection, had really been like, and if it had died of heat prostration. And what it had been like for the Amblers, living all that time in a hundred and fifty cubic feet together and blaming each other for their own guilt.

I called Ramirez as soon as I got home, breaking in without announcing myself, the way she always did. "I need a lifeline," I said.

"I'm glad you called," she said. "You got a call from the Society. And how's this as a slant for your story? 'The Winnebago and the Winnebagos.' They're an Indian tribe. In Minnesota, I think—why the hell aren't you at the governor's conference?"

"I came home," I said. "What did the Society want?"

"They didn't say. They asked for your schedule. I told them you were with the governor in Tempe. Is this about a story?"

"Yeah."

"Well, you run a proposal past me before you write it. The last thing the paper needs is to get in trouble with the Society."

"The lifeline's for Katherine Powell." I spelled it.

She spelled it back to me. "Is she connected with the Society story?"

"No."

"Then what is she connected with? I've got to put something on the request-for-info."

"Put down background."

"For the Winnebago story?"

"Yes," I said. "For the Winnebago story. How long will it take?"

"That depends. When do you plan to tell me why you ditched the governor's conference? *And* Taliesin West. Jesus Maria, I'll have to call the *Republic* and see if they'll trade footage. I'm sure they'll be thrilled to have shots of an extinct RV. That is, assuming you got any shots. You did make it out to the zoo, didn't you?"

"Yes. I got vidcam footage, stills, the works. I even used the eisenstadt."

"Mind sending your pictures in while I look up your old flame, or is that too much to ask? I don't know how long this will take. It took me two days to get clearance on the Amblers. Do you want the whole thing—pictures, documentation?"

"No. Just a resume. And a phone number."

She cut out, still not saying goodbye. If phones still had receivers, Ramirez would be a great one for hanging up on people. I highwired the vidcam footage and the eisenstadts in to the paper and then fed the eisenstadt cartridge into the developer. I was more than a little curious about what kind of pictures it would take, in spite of the fact that it was trying to do me out of a job.

At least it used high-res film and not some damn two hundred thousand–pixel TV substitute. I didn't believe it could compose, and I doubted if the eisenstadt would be able to do foreground-background either, but it might, under certain circumstances, get a picture I couldn't.

The doorbell rang. I answered the door. A lanky young man in a Hawaiian shirt and baggies was standing on the front step, and there was another man in a Society uniform out in the driveway.

"Mr. McCombe?" he said, extending a hand. "Jim Hunter. Humane Society."

I don't know what I'd expected—that they wouldn't bother to trace the call? That they'd let somebody get away with leaving a dead animal on the road?

"I just wanted to stop by and thank you on behalf of the Society for phoning in that report on the jackal. Can I come in?"

He smiled, an open, friendly, smug smile, as if he expected me to be stupid enough to say, "I don't know what you're talking about," and slam the screen door on his hand.

"Just doing my duty," I said, smiling back at him.

"Well, we really appreciate responsible citizens like you. It makes our job a whole lot easier." He pulled a folded readout from his shirt pocket. "I just need to double-check a couple of things. You're a reporter for Sun-co, is that right?"

"Photo-journalist," I said.

"And the Hitori you were driving belongs to the paper?"

I nodded.

"It has a phone. Why didn't you use it to make the call?"

The uniform was bending over the Hitori.

"I didn't realize it had a phone. The paper just bought the Hitoris. This is only the second time I've had one out."

Since they knew the paper had had phones put in, they also knew what I'd just told them. I wondered where they'd gotten the info. Public phones were supposed to be tap-free, and if they'd read the license number off one of the cameras, they wouldn't know who'd had the car unless they'd talked to Ramirez, and if they'd talked to her, she wouldn't have been talking blithely about the last thing she needed being trouble with the Society.

"You didn't know the car had a phone," he said, "so you drove to—" He consulted the readout, somehow giving the impression he was taking notes. I'd have bet there was a taper in the pocket of that shirt. "—The 7-Eleven at McDowell and Fortieth Street, and made the call from there. Why didn't you give the Society rep your name and address?"

"I was in a hurry," I said. "I had two assignments to cover before noon, the second out in Scottsdale."

"Which is why you didn't render assistance to the animal either. Because you were in a hurry."

You bastard, I thought. "No," I said. "I didn't render assistance because there wasn't any assistance to be rendered. The—it was dead."

"And how did you know that, Mr. McCombe?"

"There was blood coming out of its mouth," I said.

I had thought that that was a good sign, that he wasn't bleeding anywhere else. The blood had come out of Aberfan's mouth when he tried to lift his head, just a little trickle, sinking into the hard-packed snow. It had stopped before we even got him into the car. "It's all right, boy," I told him. "We'll be there in a minute."

Katie started the jeep, killed it, started it again, backed it up to where she could turn around.

Aberfan lay limply across my lap, his tail against the gear shift. "Just lie still, boy," I said. I patted his neck. It was wet, and I raised my hand and looked the palm, afraid it was blood. It was only water from the melted snow. I dried his neck and the top of his head with the sleeve of my sweater.

"How far is it?" Katie said. She was clutching the steering wheel with both hands and sitting stiffly forward in the seat. The windshield wipers flipped back and forth, trying to keep up with the snow.

"About five miles," I said, and she stepped on the gas pedal and then let up on it again as we began to skid. "On the right side of the highway."

Aberfan raised his head off my lap and looked at me. His gums were gray, and he was panting, but I couldn't see any more blood. He tried to lick my hand. "You'll make it, Aberfan," I said. "You made it before, remember?"

"But you didn't get out of the car and go check, to make sure it was dead?" Hunter said.

"No."

"And you don't have any idea who hit the jackal?" he said, and made it sound like the accusation it was.

"No."

He glanced back at the uniform, who had moved around the car to the other side. "Whew," Hunter said, shaking his Hawaiian collar, "it's like an oven out here. Mind if I come in?" which meant the uniform needed more privacy. Well, then, by all means, give him more privacy. The sooner he sprayed print-fix on the bumper and tires and peeled off the incriminating traces of jackal blood that weren't there and stuck them in the evidence bags he was carrying in the pockets of that uniform, the sooner they'd leave. I opened the screen door wider.

"Oh, this is great," Hunter said, still trying to generate a breeze with his collar. "These old adobe houses stay so cool." He glanced around the room at the developer and the enlarger, the couch, the dry-mounted photographs on the wall. "You don't have any idea who might have hit the jackal?"

"I figure it was a tanker," I said. "What else would be on Van Buren that time of morning?"

I was almost sure it had been a car or a small truck. A tanker would have left the jackal a spot on the pavement. But a tanker would get a license suspension and two weeks of having to run water into Santa Fe instead of Phoenix, and probably not that. Rumor at the paper had it the Society was in the water board's pocket. If it was a car, on the other hand, the Society would take away the car and stick its driver with a prison sentence.

"They're all trying to beat the cameras," I said. "The tanker probably didn't even know it'd hit it."

"What?" he said.

"I said, it had to be a tanker. There isn't anything else on Van Buren during rush hour."

I expected him to say, "Except for you," but he didn't. He wasn't even listening. "Is this your dog?" he said.

He was looking at the photograph of Perdita. "No," I said. "That was my grandmother's dog."

"What is it?"

A nasty little beast. And when it died of the newparvo, my grandmother had cried like a baby. "A chihuahua."

He looked around at the other walls. "Did you take all these pictures of dogs?" His whole manner had changed, taking on a politeness that made me realize just how insolent he had intended to be before. The one on the road wasn't the only jackal around.

"Some of them," I said. He was looking at the photograph next to it. "I didn't take that one."

"I know what this one is," he said, pointing at it. "It's a boxer, right?"

"An English bulldog," I said.

"Oh, right. Weren't those the ones that were exterminated? For being vicious?"

"No," I said.

He moved on to the picture over the developer, like a tourist in a museum. "I bet you didn't take this one either," he said, pointing at the high shoes, the old-fashioned hat on the stout old woman holding the dogs in her arms.

"That's a photograph of Beatrix Potter, the English children's author," I said. "She wrote *Peter Rabbit.*"

He wasn't interested. "What kind of dogs are those?"

"Pekingese."

"It's a great picture of them."

It is, in fact, a terrible picture of them. One of them

has wrenched his face away from the camera, and the other sits grimly in her owner's hand, waiting for its chance. Obviously neither of them liked having its picture taken, though you can't tell that from their expressions. They reveal nothing in their little flat-nosed faces, in their black little eyes.

Beatrix Potter, on the other hand, comes through beautifully, in spite of the attempt to smile for the camera and the fact that she must have had to hold onto the Pekes for dear life, or maybe because of that. The fierce, humorous love she felt for her fierce, humorous little dogs is all there in her face. She must never, in spite of *Peter Rabbit* and its attendant fame, have developed a public face. Everything she felt was right there, unprotected, unshuttered. Like Katie.

"Are any of these your dog?" Hunter asked. He was standing looking at the picture of Misha that hung above the couch.

"No," I said.

"How come you don't have any pictures of your dog?" he asked, and I wondered how he knew I had had a dog and what else he knew.

"He didn't like having his picture taken."

He folded up the readout, stuck it in his pocket, and turned around to look at the photo of Perdita again. "He looks like he was a real nice little dog," he said.

The uniform was waiting on the front step, obviously finished with whatever he had done to the car.

"We'll let you know if we find out who's responsible," Hunter said, and they left. On the way out to the street the uniform tried to tell him what he'd found, but Hunter cut him off. The suspect has a house full of photographs of dogs, therefore he didn't run over a poor facsimile of one on Van Buren this morning. Case closed.

I went back over to the developer and fed the eisenstadt film in. "Positives, one two three order, five seconds," I said, and watched as the pictures came up on the developer's screen. Ramirez had said the eisenstadt automatically turned on whenever it was set upright on a level surface. She was right. It had taken a half-dozen shots on the way out to Tempe. Two shots of the Hitori it must have taken when I set it down to load the car, open door of same with prickly pear in the foreground, a blurred shot of palm trees and buildings with a minuscule, sharp-focused glimpse of the traffic on the expressway. Vehicles and people. There was a great shot of the red tanker that had clipped the jackal and ten or so of the yucca I had parked next to at the foot of the hill.

It had gotten two nice shots of my forearm as I set it down on the kitchen counter of the Winnebago and some beautifully composed still lifes of Melmac with Spoons. Vehicles and people. The rest of the pictures were dead losses: my back, the open bathroom door, Jake's back, and Mrs. Ambler's public face.

Except the last one. She had been standing right in front of the eisenstadt, looking almost directly into the lens. "When I think of that poor thing, all alone," she had said, and by the time she turned around she had her public face back on, but for a minute there, looking at what she thought was a briefcase and remembering, there she was, the person I had tried all morning to get a picture of.

I took it into the living room and sat down and looked at it awhile.

"So you knew this Katherine Powell in Colorado," Ramirez said, breaking in without preamble, and the highwire slid silently forward and began to print out the lifeline. "I always suspected you of having some deep dark secret in your past. Is she the reason you moved to Phoenix?"

I was watching the highwire advance the paper. Katherine Powell, 4628 Dutchman Drive, Apache Junction. Forty miles away.

"Holy Mother, you were really cradle-robbing. According to my calculations, she was seventeen when you lived there."

Sixteen.

"Are you the owner of the dog?" the vet had asked

her, his face slackening into pity when he saw how young
she was.

"No," she said. "I'm the one who hit him."

"My God," he said. "How old are you?"

"Sixteen," she said, and her face was wide open. "I
just got my license."

"Aren't you even going to tell me what she has to do
with this Winnebago thing?" Ramirez said.

"I moved down here to get away from the snow," I
said, and cut out without saying goodbye.

The lifeline was still rolling silently forward. Hacker at
Hewlett-Packard. Fired in ninety-nine, probably during
the unionization. Divorced. Two kids. She had moved to
Arizona five years after I did. Management programmer
for Toshiba. Arizona driver's license.

I went back to the developer and looked at the picture
of Mrs. Ambler. I had said dogs never came through.
That wasn't true. Taco wasn't in the blurry snapshots
Mrs. Ambler had been so anxious to show me, in the
stories she had been so anxious to tell. But she was in
this picture, reflected in the pain and love and loss on
Mrs. Ambler's face. I could see her plain as day, perched
on the arm of the driver's seat, barking impatiently when
the light turned green.

I put a new cartridge in the eisenstadt and went out
to see Katie.

I had to take Van Buren—it was almost four o'clock,
and the rush hour would have started on the divideds—
but the jackal was gone anyway. The Society is efficient.
Like Hitler and his Nazis.

"Why don't you have any pictures of your dog?"
Hunter had asked. The question could have been based
on the assumption that anyone who would fill his living
room with photographs of dogs must have had one of
his own, but it wasn't. He had known about Aberfan,
which meant he'd had access to my lifeline, which meant
all kinds of things. My lifeline was privacy-coded, so I
had to be notified before anybody could get access,

except, it appeared, the Society. A reporter I knew at the paper, Dolores Chiwere, had tried to do a story a while back claiming that the Society had an illegal link to the lifeline banks, but she hadn't been able to come up with enough evidence to convince her editor. I wondered if this counted.

The lifeline would have told them about Aberfan but not about how he died. Killing a dog wasn't a crime in those days, and I hadn't pressed charges against Katie for reckless driving or even called the police.

"I think you should," the vet's assistant had said. "There are less than a hundred dogs left. People can't just go around killing them."

"My God, man, it was snowing and slick," the vet had said angrily, "and she's just a kid."

"She's old enough to have a license," I said, looking at Katie. She was fumbling in her purse for her driver's license. "She's old enough to have been on the roads."

Katie found her license and gave it to me. It was so new it was still shiny. Katherine Powell. She had turned sixteen two weeks ago.

"This won't bring him back," the vet had said, and taken the license out of my hand and given it back to her. "You go on home now."

"I need her name for the records," the vet's assistant had said.

She had stepped forward. "Katie Powell," she had said.

"We'll do the paperwork later," the vet had said firmly.

They never did do the paperwork, though. The next week the third wave hit, and I suppose there hadn't seemed any point.

I slowed down at the zoo entrance and looked up into the parking lot as I went past. The Amblers were doing a booming business. There were at least five cars and twice as many kids clustered around the Winnebago.

"Where the hell are you?" Ramirez said. "And where the hell are your pictures? I talked the *Republic* into a trade, but they insisted on scoop rights. I need your stills now!"

"I'll send them in as soon as I get home," I said. "I'm on a story."

"The hell you are! You're on your way out to see your old girlfriend. Well, not on the paper's credits, you're not."

"Did you get the stuff on the Winnebago Indians?" I asked her.

"Yes, They were in Wisconsin, but they're not any-more. In the mid-seventies there were sixteen hundred of them on the reservation and about forty-five hundred altogether, but by 1990, the number was down to five hundred, and now they don't think there are any left, and nobody knows what happened to them."

I'll tell you what happened to them, I thought. Almost all of them were killed in the first wave, and people blamed the government and the Japanese and the ozone layer, and after the second wave hit, the Society passed all kinds of laws to protect the survivors, but it was too late, they were already below the minimum survival pop-ulation limit, and then the third wave polished off the rest of them, and the last of the Winnebagos sat in a cage somewhere, and if I had been there I would proba-bly have taken his picture.

"I called the Bureau of Indian Affairs," Ramirez said, "and they're supposed to call me back, and you don't give a damn about the Winnebagos. You just wanted to get me off the subject. What's this story you're on?"

I looked around the dashboard for an exclusion button.

"What the hell is going on, David? First you ditch two big stories, now you can't even get your pictures in. Jesus, if something's wrong, you can tell me. I want to help. It has something to do with Colorado, doesn't it?"

I found the button and cut her off.

Van Buren got crowded as the afternoon rush spilled over off the dividers. Out past the curve, where Van Buren turns into Apache Boulevard, they were putting in new lanes. The cement forms were already up on the eastbound side, and they were building the wooden forms up in two of the six lanes on my side.

The Amblers must have just beaten the workmen, though at the rate the men were working right now, leaning on their shovels in the hot afternoon sun and smoking stew, it had probably taken them six weeks to do this stretch.

Mesa was still open multiway, but as soon as I was through downtown, the construction started again, and this stretch was nearly done—forms up on both sides and most of the cement poured. The Amblers couldn't have come in from Globe on this road. The lanes were barely wide enough for the Hitori, and the tanker lanes were gated. Superstition is full-divided, and the old highway down from Roosevelt is, too, which meant they hadn't come in from Globe at all. I wondered how they had come in—probably in some tanker lane on a multiway.

"Oh, my, the things we've seen," Mrs. Ambler had said. I wondered how much they'd been able to see skittering across the dark desert like a couple of kangaroo mice, trying to beat the cameras.

The roadworkers didn't have the new exit signs up yet, and I missed the exit for Apache Junction and had to go halfway to Superior, trapped in my narrow, cement-sided lane, till I hit a change-lanes and could get turned around.

Katie's address was in Superstition Estates, a development pushed up as close to the base of Superstition Mountain as it could get. I thought about what I would say to Katie when I got there. I had said maybe ten sentences altogether to her, most of them shouted directions, in the two hours we had been together. In the jeep on the way to the vet's I had talked to Aberfan, and after we got there, sitting in the waiting room, we hadn't talked at all.

It occurred to me that I might not recognize her. I didn't really remember what she looked like—only the sunburned nose and that terrible openness, and now, fifteen years later, it seemed unlikely that she would have either of them. The Arizona sun would have taken care of the first, and she had gotten married and divorced, been fired, had who knows what else happen to her in fifteen years to close her face. In which case, there had been no point in my driving all the way out here. But Mrs. Ambler had had an almost impenetrable public face, and you could still catch her off-guard. If you got her talking about the dogs. If she didn't know she was being photographed.

Katie's house was an old-style passive solar, with flat black panels on the roof. It looked presentable, but not compulsively neat. There wasn't any grass—tankers won't waste their credits coming this far out, and Apache Junction isn't big enough to match the bribes and incentives of Phoenix or Tempe—but the front yard was laid out with alternating patches of black lava chips and prickly pear. The side yard had a parched-looking palo verde tree, and there was a cat tied to it. A little girl was playing under the tree with toy cars.

I took the eisenstadt out of the back and went up to the front door and rang the bell. At the last moment, when it was too late to change my mind, walk away, because she was already opening the screen door, it occurred to me that she might not recognize me, that I might have to tell her who I was.

Her nose wasn't sunburned, and she had put on the weight a sixteen-year-old puts on to get to be thirty, but otherwise she looked the same as she had that day in front of my house. And her face hadn't completely closed. I could tell, looking at her, that she recognized me and that she had known I was coming. She must have put a notify on her lifeline to have them warn her if I asked her whereabouts. I thought about what that meant.

She opened the screen door a little, the way I had to the Humane Society. "What do you want?" she said.

I had never seen her angry, not even when I turned on her at the vet's. "I wanted to see you," I said.

I had thought I might tell her I had run across her name while I was working on a story and wondered if it was the same person or that I was doing a piece on the last of the passive solars. "I saw a dead jackal on the road this morning," I said.

"And you thought I killed it?" she said. She tried to shut the screen door.

I put out my hand without thinking to stop her. "No," I said. I took my hand off the door. "No, of course I don't think that. Can I come in? I just want to talk to you."

The little girl had come over, clutching her toy cars to her pink T-shirt, and was standing off to the side, watching curiously.

"Come on inside, Jana," Katie said, and opened the screen door a fraction wider. The little girl scooted through. "Go on in the kitchen," she said. "I'll fix you some Kool-Aid." She looked up at me. "I used to have nightmares about your coming. I'd dream that I'd go to the door and there you'd be."

"It's really hot out here," I said and knew I sounded like Hunter. "Can I come in?"

She opened the screen door all the way. "I've got to make my daughter something to drink," she said, and led the way into the kitchen, the little girl dancing in front of her.

"What kind of Kool-Aid do you want?" Katie asked her, and she shouted, "Red!"

The kitchen counter faced the stove, refrigerator, and water cooler across a narrow aisle that opened out into an alcove with a table and chairs. I put the eisenstadt down on the table and then sat down myself so she wouldn't suggest moving into another room.

Katie reached a plastic pitcher down from one of the shelves and stuck it under the water tank to fill it. Jana dumped her cars on the counter, clambered up beside them, and began opening the cupboard doors.

"How old's your little girl?" I asked.

Katie got a wooden spoon out of the drawer next to the stove and brought it and the pitcher over to the table. "She's four," she said. "Did you find the Kool-Aid?" she asked the little girl.

"Yes," the little girl said, but it wasn't Kool-Aid. It was a pinkish cube she peeled a plastic wrapping off of. It fizzed and turned a thinnish red when she dropped it in the pitcher. Kool-Aid must have become extinct, too, along with Winnebagos and passive solar. Or else changed beyond recognition. Like the Humane Society.

Katie poured the red stuff into a glass with a cartoon whale on it.

"Is she your only one?" I asked.

"No, I have a little boy," she said, but warily, as if she wasn't sure she wanted to tell me, even though if I'd requested the lifeline I already had access to all this information. Jana asked if she could have a cookie and then took it and her Kool-Aid back down the hall and outside. I could hear the screen door slam.

Katie put the pitcher in the refrigerator and leaned against the kitchen counter, her arms folded across her chest. "What do you want?"

She was just out of range of the eisenstadt, her face in the shadow of the narrow aisle.

"There was a dead jackal on the road this morning," I said. I kept my voice low so she would lean forward into the light to try and hear me. "It'd been hit by a car, and it was lying funny, at an angle. It looked like a dog. I wanted to talk to somebody who remembered Aberfan, somebody who knew him."

"I didn't know him," she said. "I only killed him, remember? That's why you did this, isn't it, because I killed Aberfan?"

She didn't look at the eisenstadt, hadn't even glanced at it when I set it on the table, but I wondered suddenly if she knew what I was up to. She was still carefully out of range. And what if I said to her, "That's right. That's why I did this, because you killed him, and I didn't have any pictures of him. You owe me. If I can't have a picture of Aberfan, you at least owe me a picture of you remembering him."

Only she didn't remember him, didn't know anything about him except what she had seen on the way to the vet's, Aberfan lying on my lap and looking up at me, already dying. I had had no business coming here, dredging all this up again. No business.

"At first I thought you were going to have me arrested," Katie said, "and then after all the dogs died, I thought you were going to kill me."

The screen door banged. "Forgot my cars," the little girl said and scooped them into the tail of her T-shirt. Katie tousled her hair as she went past, and then folded her arms again.

" 'It wasn't my fault,' I was going to tell you when you came to kill me," she said. " 'It was snowy. He ran right in front of me. I didn't even see him.' I looked up everything I could find about newparvo. Preparing for the defense. How it mutated from parvovirus and from cat distemper before that and then kept on mutating, so they couldn't come up with a vaccine. How even before the third wave they were below the minimum survival population. How it was the fault of the people who owned the last survivors because they wouldn't risk their dogs to breed them. How the scientists didn't come up with a vaccine until only the jackals were left. 'You're wrong,' I was going to tell you. 'It was the puppy mill owners' fault that all the dogs died. If they hadn't kept their dogs in such unsanitary conditions, it never would have gotten out of control in the first place.' I had my defense all ready. But you'd moved away."

Jana banged in again, carrying the empty whale glass. She had a red smear across the whole lower half of her face. "I need some more," she said, making "some more" into one word. She held the glass in both hands while Katie opened the refrigerator and poured her another glassful.

"Wait a minute, honey," she said. "You've got Kool-Aid all over you," and bent to wipe Jana's face with a paper towel.

Katie hadn't said a word in her defense while we

waited at the vet's, not, "It was snowy," or, "He ran right out in front of me," or, "I didn't even see him." She had sat silently beside me, twisting her mittens in her lap, until the vet came out and told me Aberfan was dead, and then she had said, "I didn't know there were any left in Colorado. I thought they were all dead."

And I had turned to her, to a sixteen-year-old not even old enough to know how to shut her face, and said, "Now they all are. Thanks to you."

"That kind of talk isn't necessary," the vet had said warningly.

I had wrenched away from the hand he tried to put on my shoulder. "How does it feel to have killed one of the last dogs in the world?" I had shouted at her. "How does it feel to be responsible for the extinction of an entire species?"

The screen door banged again. Katie was looking at me, still holding the reddened paper towel.

"You moved away," she said, "and I thought maybe that meant you'd forgiven me, but it didn't, did it?" She came over to the table and wiped at the red circle the glass had left. "Why did you do it? To punish me? Or did you think that's what I'd been doing the last fifteen years, roaring around the roads murdering animals?"

"What?" I said.

"The Society's already been here."

"The Society?" I said, not understanding.

"Yes," she said, still looking at the red-stained towel. "They said you had reported a dead animal on Van Buren. They wanted to know where I was this morning between eight and nine A.M."

I nearly ran down a roadworker on the way back into Phoenix. He leaped for the still-wet cement barrier, dropping the shovel he'd been leaning on all day, and I ran right over it.

The Society had already been there. They had left my house and gone straight to hers. Only that wasn't possible, because I hadn't even called Katie then. I hadn't even seen the picture of Mrs. Ambler yet. Which meant they had gone to see Ramirez after they left me, and the last thing Ramirez and the paper needed was trouble with the Society.

"I thought it was suspicious when he didn't go to the governor's conference," she had told them, "and just now he called and asked for a lifeline on this person here. Katherine Powell, 4628 Dutchman Drive. He knew her in Colorado."

"Ramirez!" I shouted at the car phone. "I want to talk to you!" There wasn't any answer.

I swore at her for a good ten miles before I remembered I had the exclusion button on. I punched it off. "Ramirez, where the hell are you?"

"I could ask you the same question," she said. She sounded even angrier than Katie, but not as angry as I was. "You cut me off, you won't tell me what's going on."

"So you decided you had it figured out for yourself, and you told your little theory to the Society."

"What?" she said, and I recognized that tone, too. I had heard it in my own voice when Katie told me the Society had been there. Ramirez hadn't told anybody anything, she didn't even know what I was talking about, but I was going too fast to stop.

"You told the Society I'd asked for Katie's lifeline, didn't you?" I shouted.

"No," she said. "I didn't. Don't you think it's time you told me what's going on?"

"Did the Society come see you this afternoon?"

"No. I told you. They called this morning and wanted to talk to you. I told them you were at the governor's conference."

"And they didn't call back later?"

"No. Are you in trouble?"

I hit the exclusion button. "Yes," I said. "Yes, I'm in trouble."

Ramirez hadn't told them. Maybe somebody else at the paper had, but I didn't think so. There had after all been Dolores Chiwere's story about them having illegal access to the lifelines. "How come you don't have any pictures of your dog?" Hunter had asked me, which meant they'd read my lifeline, too. So they knew we had both lived in Colorado, in the same town, when Aberfan died.

"What did you tell them?" I had demanded of Katie. She had been standing there in the kitchen still messing with the Kool-Aid-stained towel, and I had wanted to yank it out of her hands and make her look at me. "What did you tell the Society?"

She looked up at me. "I told them I was on Indian School Road, picking up the month's programming assignments from my company. Unfortunately, I could just as easily have driven in on Van Buren."

"About Aberfan!" I shouted. "What did you tell them about Aberfan?"

She looked steadily at me. "I didn't tell them anything. I assumed you'd already told them."

I had taken hold of her shoulders. "If they come back, don't tell them anything. Not even if they arrest you. I'll take care of this. I'll . . ."

But I hadn't told her what I'd do because I didn't know. I had run out of her house, colliding with Jana in the hall on her way in for another refill, and roared off for home, even though I didn't have any idea what I would do when I got there.

Call the Society and tell them to leave Katie alone, that she had nothing to do with this? That would be even more suspicious than everything else I'd done so far, and you couldn't get much more suspicious than that.

I had seen a dead jackal on the road (or so I said), and instead of reporting it immediately on the phone right there in my car, I'd driven to a convenience store two miles away. I'd called the Society, but I'd refused to give them my name and number. And then I'd canceled two shoots without telling my boss and asked for the lifeline of one Katherine Powell, whom I had known fifteen years ago and who could have been on Van Buren at the time of the accident.

The connection was obvious, and how long would it take them to make the connection that fifteen years ago was when Aberfan had died?

Apache was beginning to fill up with rush hour overflow and a whole fleet of tankers. The overflow obviously spent all their time driving divideds—nobody bothered to signal that they were changing lanes. Nobody even gave an indication that they knew what a lane was. Going around the curve from Tempe and onto Van Buren they were all over the road. I moved over into the tanker lane.

My lifeline didn't have the vet's name on it. They were just getting started in those days, and there was a lot of nervousness about invasion of privacy. Nothing went online without the person's permission, especially not medical and bank records, and the lifelines were little more than puff bios: family, occupation, hobbies, pets. The only things on the lifeline besides Aberfan's name were the date of his death and my address at the time, but that was probably enough. There were only two vets in town.

The vet hadn't written Katie's name down on Aberfan's record. He had handed her driver's license back to her without even looking at it, but Katie had told her name to the vet's assistant. He might have written it down. There was no way I could find out. I couldn't ask for the vet's lifeline because the Society had access to the lifelines. They'd get to him before I could. I could maybe have the paper get the vet's records for me, but I'd have to tell Ramirez what was going on, and the phone was probably tapped, too. And if I showed up at the paper, Ramirez would confiscate the car. I couldn't go there.

Wherever the hell I was going, I was driving too fast to get there. When the tanker ahead of me slowed down to ninety, I practically climbed up his back bumper. I had gone past the place where the jackal had been hit without ever seeing it. Even without the traffic, there probably hadn't been anything to see. What the Society hadn't taken care of, the overflow probably had, and anyway, there hadn't been any evidence to begin with. If there had been, if the cameras had seen the car that hit it, they wouldn't have come after me. And Katie.

The Society couldn't charge her with Aberfan's death—killing an animal hadn't been a crime back then—but if they found out about Aberfan they would charge her with the jackal's death, and it wouldn't matter if a hundred witnesses, a hundred highway cameras had seen her on Indian School Road. It wouldn't matter if the print-fix on her car was clean. She had killed one of the last dogs, hadn't she? They would crucify her.

I should never have left Katie. "Don't tell them anything," I had told her, but she had never been afraid of admitting guilt. When the receptionist had asked her what had happened, she had said, "I hit him," just like that, no attempt to make excuses, to run off, to lay the blame on someone else.

I had run off to try to stop the Society from finding out that Katie had hit Aberfan, and meanwhile the Society was probably back at Katie's, asking her how she'd happened to know me in Colorado, asking her how Aberfan died.

I was wrong about the Society. They weren't at Katie's house. They were at mine, standing on the porch, waiting for me to let them in.

"You're a hard man to track down," Hunter said.

The uniform grinned. "Where you been?"

"Sorry," I said, fishing my keys out of my pocket. "I thought you were all done with me. I've already told you everything I know about the incident."

Hunter stepped back just far enough for me to get the screen door open and the key in the lock. "Officer Segura and I just need to ask you a couple more questions."

"Where'd you go this afternoon?" Segura asked.

"I went to see an old friend of mine."

"Who?"

"Come on, come on," Hunter said. "Let the guy get in his own front door before you start badgering him with a lot of questions."

I opened the door. "Did the cameras get a picture of the tanker that hit the jackal?" I asked.

"Tanker?" Segura said.

"I told you," I said, "I figure it had to be a tanker. The jackal was lying in the tanker lane." I led the way into the living room, depositing my keys on the computer and switching the phone to exclusion while I talked. The last thing I needed was Ramirez bursting in with, "What's going on? Are you in trouble?"

"It was probably a renegade that hit it, which would explain why he didn't stop." I gestured at them to sit down.

Hunter did. Segura started for the couch and then stopped, staring at the photos on the wall above it. "Jesus, will you look at all the dogs!" he said. "Did you take all these pictures?"

"I took some of them. That one in the middle is Misha."

"The last dog, right?"

"Yes," I said.

"No kidding. The very last one."

No kidding. She was being kept in isolation at the Society's research facility in St. Louis when I saw her. I had talked them into letting me shoot her, but it had to be from outside the quarantine area. The picture had an unfocused look that came from shooting it through a wire mesh–reinforced window in the door, but I wouldn't have done any better if they'd let me inside. Misha was past having any expression to photograph. She hadn't eaten in a week at that point. She lay with her head on her paws, staring at the door, the whole time I was there.

"You wouldn't consider selling this picture to the Society, would you?"

"No, I wouldn't."

He nodded understandingly. "I guess people were pretty upset when she died."

Pretty upset. They had turned on anyone who had anything to do with it—the puppy mill owners, the scientists who hadn't come up with a vaccine, Misha's vet—

and a lot of others who hadn't. And they had handed over their civil rights to a bunch of jackals who were able to grab them because everybody felt so guilty. Pretty upset.

"What's this one?" Segura asked. He had already moved on to the picture next to it.

"It's General Patton's bull terrier Willie."

They fed and cleaned up after Misha with those robot arms they used to use in the nuclear plants. Her owner, a tired-looking woman, was allowed to watch her through the wire-mesh window but had to stay off to the side because Misha flung herself barking against the door whenever she saw her.

"You should make them let you in," I had told her. "It's cruel to keep her locked up like that. You should make them let you take her back home."

"And let her get the newparvo?" she said.

There was nobody left for Misha to get the newparvo from, but I didn't say that. I set the light readings on the camera, trying not to lean into Misha's line of vision.

"You know what killed them, don't you?" she said. "The ozone layer. All those holes. The radiation got in and caused it."

It was the communists, it was the Mexicans, it was the government. And the only people who acknowledged their guilt weren't guilty at all.

"This one here looks kind of like a jackal," Segura said. He was looking at a picture I had taken of a German shepherd after Aberfan died. "Dogs were a lot like jackals, weren't they?"

"No," I said, and sat down on the shelf in front of the developer's screen, across from Hunter. "I already told you everything I know about the jackal. I saw it lying in the road, and I called you."

"You said when you saw the jackal it was in the far right lane," Hunter said.

"That's right."

"And you were in the far left lane?"

"I was in the far left lane."

They were going to take me over my story, point by point, and when I couldn't remember what I'd said before, they were going to say, "Are you sure that's what you saw, Mr. McCombe? Are you sure you didn't see the jackal get hit? Katherine Powell hit it, didn't she?"

"You told us this morning you stopped, but the jackal was already dead. Is that right?" Hunter asked.

"No," I said.

Segura looked up. Hunter touched his hand casually to his pocket and then brought it back to his knee, turning on the taper.

"I didn't stop for about a mile. Then I backed up and looked at it, but it was dead. There was blood coming out of its mouth."

Hunter didn't say anything. He kept his hands on his knees and waited—an old journalist's trick, if you wait long enough, they'll say something they didn't intend to, just to fill the silence.

"The jackal's body was at a peculiar angle," I said, right on cue. "The way it was lying, it didn't look like a jackal. I thought it was a dog." I waited till the silence got uncomfortable again. "It brought back a lot of terrible memories," I said. "I wasn't even thinking. I just wanted to get away from it. After a few minutes I realized I should have called the Society, and I stopped at the 7-Eleven.

I waited again, till Segura began to shoot uncomfortable glances at Hunter, and then started in again. "I thought I'd be okay, that I could go ahead and work, but after I got to my first shoot, I knew I wasn't going to make it, so I came home." Candor. Openness. If the Amblers can do it, so can you. "I guess I was still in shock or something. I didn't even call my boss and have her get somebody to cover the governor's conference. All I could think about was—" I stopped and rubbed my hand across my face. "I needed to talk to somebody. I had the paper look up an old friend of mine, Katherine Powell."

I stopped, I hoped this time for good. I had admitted

lying to them and confessed to two crimes: leaving the scene of the accident and using press access to get a lifeline for personal use, and maybe that would be enough to satisfy them. I didn't want to say anything about going out to see Katie. They would know she would have told me about their visit and decide this confession was an attempt to get her off, and maybe they'd been watching the house and knew it anyway, and this was all wasted effort.

The silence dragged on. Hunter's hands tapped his knees twice and then subsided. The story didn't explain why I'd picked Katie, who I hadn't seen in fifteen years, who I knew in Colorado, to go see, but maybe, maybe they wouldn't make the connection.

"This Katherine Powell," Hunter said, "you knew her in Colorado, is that right?"

"We lived in the same little town."

We waited.

"Isn't that when your dog died?" Segura said suddenly. Hunter shot him a glance of pure rage, and I thought, it isn't a taper he's got in that shirt pocket. It's the vet's records, and Katie's name is on them.

"Yes," I said. "He died in September of eighty-nine." Segura opened his mouth.

"In the third wave?" Hunter asked before he could say anything.

"No," I said. "He was hit by a car."

They both looked genuinely shocked. The Amblers could have taken lessons from them. "Who hit it?" Segura asked, and Hunter leaned forward, his hand moving reflexively toward his pocket.

"I don't know," I said. "It was a hit and run. Whoever it was just left him lying there in the road. That's why when I saw the jackal, it . . . that was how I met Katherine Powell. She stopped and helped me. She helped me get him into her car, and we took him to the vet's, but it was too late."

Hunter's public face was pretty indestructible, but

Segura's wasn't. He looked surprised and enlightened and disappointed all at once.

"That's why I wanted to see her," I said unnecessarily.

"Your dog was hit on what day?" Hunter asked.

"September thirtieth."

"What was the vet's name?"

He hadn't changed his way of asking the questions, but he no longer cared what the answers were. He had thought he'd found a connection, a cover-up, but here we were, a couple of dog lovers, a couple of good Samaritans, and his theory had collapsed. He was done with the interview, he was just finishing up, and all I had to do was be careful not to relax too soon.

I frowned. "I don't remember his name. Cooper, I think."

"What kind of car did you say hit your dog?"

"I don't know," I said, thinking, not a jeep. Make it something besides a jeep. "I didn't see him get hit. The vet said it was something big, a pickup maybe. Or a Winnebago."

And I knew who had hit the jackal. It had all been right there in front of me—the old man using up their forty-gallon water supply to wash the bumper, the lies about their coming in from Globe—only I had been too intent on keeping them from finding out about Katie, on getting the picture of Aberfan, to see it. It was like the damned parvo. When you had it licked in one place, it broke out somewhere else.

"Were there any identifying tire tracks?" Hunter said.

"What?" I said. "No. It was snowing that day." It had to show in my face, and he hadn't missed anything yet. I passed my hand over my eyes. "I'm sorry. These questions are bringing it all back."

"Sorry," Hunter said.

"Can't we get this stuff from the police report?" Segura asked.

"There wasn't a police report," I said. "It wasn't a crime to kill a dog when Aberfan died."

It was the right thing to say. The look of shock on

their faces was the real thing this time, and they looked at each other in disbelief instead of at me. They asked a few more questions and then stood up to leave. I walked them to the door.

"Thank you for your cooperation, Mr. McCombe," Hunter said. "We appreciate what a difficult experience this has been for you."

I shut the screen door between us. The Amblers would have been going too fast, trying to beat the cameras because they weren't even supposed to be on Van Buren. It was almost rush hour, and they were in the tanker lane, and they hadn't even seen the jackal till they hit it, and then it was too late. They had to know the penalty for hitting an animal was jail and confiscation of the vehicle, and there wasn't anybody else on the road.

"Oh, one more question," Hunter said from halfway down the walk. "You said you went to your first assignment this morning. What was it?"

Candid. Open. "It was out at the old zoo. A sideshow kind of thing."

I watched them all the way out to their car and down the street. Then I latched the screen, pulled the inside door shut, and locked it, too. It had been right there in front of me—the ferret sniffing the wheel, the bumper, Jake anxiously watching the road. I had thought he was looking for customers, but he wasn't. He was expecting to see the Society drive up. "He's not interested in that," he had said when Mrs. Ambler said she had been telling me about Taco. He had listened to our whole conversation, standing under the back window with his guilty bucket, ready to come back in and cut her off if she said too much, and I hadn't tumbled to any of it. I had been so intent on Aberfan I hadn't even seen it when I looked right through the lens at it. And what kind of an excuse was that? Katie hadn't even tried to use it, and she was learning to drive.

I went and got the Nikon and pulled the film out of it. It was too late to do anything about the eisenstadt pictures or the vidcam footage, but I didn't think there was anything in them. Jake had already washed the bumper by the time I'd taken those pictures.

I fed the longshot film into the developer. "Positives, one two three order, fifteen seconds," I said, and waited for the image to come on the screen.

I wondered who had been driving. Jake, probably. "He never liked Taco," she had said, and there was no mistaking the bitterness in her voice. "I didn't want to buy the Winnebago."

They would both lose their licenses, no matter who was driving, and the Society would confiscate the Winnebago. They would probably not send two octogenarian specimens of Americana like the Amblers to prison. They wouldn't have to. The trial would take six months, and Texas already had legislation in committee.

The first picture came up. A light-setting shot of an ocotillo.

Even if they got off, even if they didn't end up taking away the Winnebago for unauthorized use of a tanker lane or failure to purchase a sales tax permit, the Amblers had six months left at the outside. Utah was all ready to pass a full-divided bill, and Arizona would be next. In spite of the road crews' stew-slowed pace, Phoenix would be all-divided by the time the investigation was over, and they'd be completely boxed in. Permanent residents of the zoo. Like the coyote.

A shot of the zoo sign, half-hidden in the cactus. A close-up of the Amblers' balloon-trailing sign. The Winnebago in the parking lot.

"Hold," I said. "Crop." I indicated the areas with my finger. "Enlarge to full screen."

The longshot takes great pictures, sharp contrast, excellent detail. The developer only had a five hundred thousand–pixel screen, but the dark smear on the bumper was easy to see, and the developed picture would be much clearer. You'd be able to see every splatter, every grayish-yellow hair. The Society's computers would probably be able to type the blood from it.

"Continue," I said, and the next picture came on the screen. Artsy shot of the Winnebago and the zoo entrance. Jake washing the bumper. Red-handed.

Maybe Hunter had bought my story, but he didn't have any other suspects, and how long would it be before he decided to ask Katie a few more questions? If he thought it was the Amblers, he'd leave her alone.

The Japanese family clustered around the waste-disposal tank. Closeup of the decals on the side. Interiors—Mrs. Ambler in the gallery, the upright-coffin shower stall, Mrs. Ambler making coffee.

No wonder she had looked that way in the eisenstadt shot, her face full of memory and grief and loss. Maybe in the instant before they hit it, it had looked like a dog to her, too.

All I had to do was tell Hunter about the Amblers, and Katie was off the hook. It should be easy. I had done it before.

"Stop," I said to a shot of the salt-and-pepper collection. The black and white scottie dogs had painted, red-plaid bows and red tongues. "Expose," I said. "One through twenty-four."

The screen went to question marks and started beeping. I should have known better. The developer could handle a lot of orders, but asking it to expose perfectly good film went against its whole memory, and I didn't have time to give it the step-by-steps that would convince it I meant what I said.

"Eject," I said. The scotties blinked out. The developer spat out the film, rerolled into its protective case.

The doorbell rang. I switched on the overhead and pulled the film out to full length and held it directly under the light. I had told Hunter an RV hit Aberfan, and he had said on the way out, almost an afterthought, "That first shoot you went to, what was it?" And after he left, what had he done, gone out to check on the sideshow kind of thing, gotten Mrs. Ambler to spill her guts? There hadn't been time to do that and get back.

He must have called Ramirez. I was glad I had locked the door.

I turned off the overhead. I rerolled the film, fed it back into the developer, and gave it a direction it could handle. "Permanganate bath, full strength, one through twenty-four. Remove one hundred percent emulsion. No notify."

The screen went dark. It would take the developer at least fifteen minutes to run the film through the bleach bath, and the Society's computers could probably enhance a picture out of two crystals of silver and thin air, but at least the detail wouldn't be there. I unlocked the door.

It was Katie.

She held up the eisenstadt. "You forgot your briefcase," she said.

I stared blankly at it. I hadn't even realized I didn't have it. I must have left it on the kitchen table when I went tearing out, running down little girls and stewed roadworkers in my rush to keep Katie from getting involved. And here she was, and Hunter would be back any minute, saying, "That shoot you went on this morning, did you take any pictures?"

"It isn't a briefcase," I said.

"I wanted to tell you," she said, and stopped. "I shouldn't have accused you of telling the Society I'd killed the jackal. I don't know why you came to see me today, but I know you're not capable of—"

"You have no idea what I'm capable of," I said. I opened the door enough to reach for the eisenstadt. "Thanks for bringing it back. I'll get the paper to reimburse your way-mile credits."

Go home. Go home. If you're here when the Society comes back, they'll ask you how you met me, and I just destroyed the evidence that could shift the blame to the Amblers. I took hold of the eisenstadt's handle and started to shut the door.

She put her hand on the door. The screen door and

the fading light made her look unfocused, like Misha. "Are you in trouble?"

"No," I said. "Look, I'm very busy."

"Why did you come to see me?" she asked. "Did you kill the jackal?"

"No," I said, but I opened the door and let her in.

I went over to the developer and asked for a visual status. It was only on the sixth frame. "I'm destroying evidence," I said to Katie. "I took a picture this morning of the vehicle that hit it, only I didn't know it was the guilty party until a half an hour ago." I motioned for her to sit down on the couch. "They're in their eighties. They were driving on a road they weren't supposed to be on, in an obsolete recreation vehicle, worrying about the cameras and the tankers. There's no way they could have seen it in time to stop. The Society won't see it that way, though. They're determined to blame somebody, anybody, even though it won't bring them back."

She set her canvas carryit and the eisenstadt down on the table next to the couch. "The Society was here when I got home," I said. "They'd figured out we were both in Colorado when Aberfan died. I told them it was a hit and run, and you'd stopped to help me. They had the vet's records, and your name was on them."

I couldn't read her face. "If they come back, you tell them that you gave me a ride to the vet's." I went back to the developer. The longshot film was done. "Eject," I said, and the developer spit it into my hand. I fed it into the recycler.

"McCombe! Where the hell are you?" Ramirez's voice exploded into the room, and I jumped and started for the door, but she wasn't there. The phone was flashing. "McCombe! This is important!"

Ramirez was on the phone and using some override I didn't even know existed. I went over and pushed it back to access. The lights went out. "I'm here," I said.

"You won't believe what just happened!" She sounded outraged. "A couple of terrorist types from the Society just stormed in here and confiscated the stuff you sent me!"

All I'd sent her was the vidcam footage and the shots from the eisenstadt, and there shouldn't have been anything on those. Jake had already washed the bumper. "What stuff?" I said.

"The prints from the eisenstadt!" she said, still shouting. "Which I didn't have a chance to look at when they came in because I was too busy trying to work a trade on your governor's conference, not to mention trying to track you down! I had hardcopies made and sent the originals straight down to composing with your vidcam footage. I finally got to them half an hour ago, and while I'm sorting through them, this Society creep just grabs them away from me. No warrants, no 'would you mind?,' nothing. Right out of my hand. Like a bunch of—"

"Jackals," I said. "You're sure it wasn't the vidcam footage?" There wasn't anything in the eisenstadt shots except Mrs. Ambler and Taco, and even Hunter couldn't have put that together, could he?

"Of course I'm sure," Ramirez said, her voice bouncing off the walls. "It was one of the prints from the eisenstadt. I never even saw the vidcam stuff. I sent it straight to composing. I told you."

I went over to the developer and fed the cartridge in. The first dozen shots were nothing, stuff the eisenstadt had taken from the back seat of the car. "Start with frame ten," I said. "Positives. One two three order. Five seconds."

"What did you say?" Ramirez demanded.

"I said, did they say what they were looking for?"

"Are you kidding? I wasn't even there as far as they were concerned. They split up the pile and started through them on *my* desk."

The yucca at the foot of the hill. More yucca. My forearm as I set the eisenstadt down on the counter. My back.

"Whatever it was they were looking for, they found it," Ramirez said.

I glanced at Katie. She met my gaze steadily, unafraid. She had never been afraid, not even when I told her she had killed all the dogs, not even when I showed up on her doorstep after fifteen years.

"The one in the uniform showed it to the other one," Ramirez was saying, "and said, 'You were wrong about the woman doing it. Look at this.' "

"Did you get a look at the picture?"

Still life of cups and spoons. Mrs. Ambler's arm. Mrs. Ambler's back.

"I tried. It was a truck of some kind."

"A truck? Are you sure? Not a Winnebago?"

"A truck. What the hell is going on over there?"

I didn't answer. Jake's back. Open shower door. Still life with Sanka. Mrs. Ambler remembering Taco.

"What woman are they talking about?" Ramirez said. "The one you wanted the lifeline on?"

"No," I said. The picture of Mrs. Ambler was the last one on the cartridge. The developer went back to the beginning. Bottom half of the Hitori. Open car door. Prickly pear. "Did they say anything else?"

"The one in the uniform pointed to something on the hardcopy and said, 'See. There's his number on the side. Can you make it out?' "

Blurred palm trees and the expressway. The tanker hitting the jackal.

"Stop," I said. The image froze.

"What?" Ramirez said.

It was a great action shot, the back wheels passing right over the mess that had been the jackal's hind legs. The jackal was already dead, of course, but you couldn't see that or the already drying blood coming out of its mouth because of the angle. You couldn't see the truck's license number either because of the speed the tanker was going, but the number was there, waiting for the Society's computers. It looked like the tanker had just hit it.

"What did they do with the picture?" I asked.

"They took it into the chief's office. I tried to call up

the originals from composing, but the chief had already sent for them *and* your vidcam footage. Then I tried to get you, but I couldn't get past your damned exclusion."

"Are they still in there with the chief?"

"They just left. They're on their way over to your house. The chief told me to tell you he wants 'full cooperation,' which means hand over the negatives and any other film you just took this morning. He told *me* to keep my hands off. No story. Case closed."

"How long ago did they leave?"

"Five minutes. You've got plenty of time to make me a print. Don't highwire it. I'll come pick it up."

"What happened to, 'The last thing I need is trouble with the Society'?"

"It'll take them at least twenty minutes to get to your place. Hide it somewhere the Society won't find it."

"I can't," I said, and listened to her furious silence. "My developer's broken. It just ate my longshot film," I said, and hit the exclusion button again.

"You want to see who hit the jackal?" I said to Katie, and motioned her over to the developer. "One of Phoenix's finest."

She came and stood in front of the screen, looking at the picture. If the Society's computers were really good, they could probably prove the jackal was already dead, but the Society wouldn't keep the film long enough for that. Hunter and Segura had probably already destroyed the highwire copies. Maybe I should offer to run the cartridge sheet through the permanganate bath for them when they got here, just to save time.

I looked at Katie. "It looks guilty as hell, doesn't it?" I said. "Only it isn't." She didn't say anything, didn't move. "It would have killed the jackal if it had hit it. It was going at least ninety. But the jackal was already dead."

She looked across at me.

"The Society would have sent the Amblers to jail. It would have confiscated the house they've lived in for fifteen years for an accident that was nobody's fault. They didn't even see it coming. It just ran right out in front of them."

Katie put her hand up to the screen and touched the jackal's image.

"They've suffered enough," I said, looking at her. It was getting dark. I hadn't turned on any lights, and the red image of the tanker made her nose look sunburned.

"All these years she's blamed him for her dog's death, and he didn't do it," I said. "A Winnebago's a hundred square feet on the inside. That's about as big as this developer, and they've lived inside it for fifteen years, while the lanes got narrower and the highways shut down, hardly enough room to breathe, let alone live, and her blaming him for something he didn't do."

In the ruddy light from the screen she looked sixteen.

"They won't do anything to the driver, not with the tankers hauling thousands of gallons of water into Phoenix every day. Even the Society won't run the risk of a boycott. They'll destroy the negatives and call the case closed. And the Society won't go after the Amblers," I said. "Or you."

I turned back to the developer. "Go," I said, and the image changed. Yucca. Yucca. My forearm. My back. Cups and spoons.

"Besides," I said. "I'm an old hand at shifting the blame." Mrs. Ambler's arm. Mrs. Ambler's back. Open shower door. "Did I ever tell you about Aberfan?"

Katie was still watching the screen, her face pale now from the light blue one hundred percent formica shower stall.

"The Society already thinks the tanker did it. The only one I've got to convince is my editor." I reached across to the phone and took the exclusion off. "Ramirez," I said, "wanta go after the Society?"

Jake's back. Cups, spoons, and Sanka.

"I did," Ramirez said in a voice that could have frozen the Salt River, "but your developer was broken, and you couldn't get me a picture."

Mrs. Ambler and Taco.

I hit the exclusion button again and left my hand on it. "Stop," I said. "Print." The screen went dark, and the print slid out into the tray. "Reduce frame. Permanganate bath by one percent. Follow on screen." I took my hand off. "What's Dolores Chiwere doing these days, Ramirez?"

"She's working investigative. Why?"

I didn't answer. The picture of Mrs. Ambler faded a little, a little more.

"The Society *does* have a link to the lifelines!" Ramirez said, not quite as fast as Hunter, but almost. "That's why you requested your old girlfriend's line, isn't it? You're running a sting."

I had been wondering how to get Ramirez off Katie's trail, and she had done it herself, jumping to conclusions just like the Society. With a little effort, I could convince Katie, too: Do you know why I really came to see you today? To catch the Society. I had to pick somebody the Society couldn't possibly know about from my lifeline, somebody I didn't have any known connection with.

Katie watched the screen, looking like she already half-believed it. The picture of Mrs. Ambler faded some more. Any known connection.

"Stop," I said.

"What about the truck?" Ramirez demanded. "What does it have to do with this sting of yours?"

"Nothing," I said. "And neither does the water board, which is an even bigger bully than the Society. So do what the chief says. Full cooperation. Case closed. We'll get them on lifeline tapping."

She digested that, or maybe she'd already hung up and was calling Dolores Chiwere. I looked at the image of Mrs. Ambler on the screen. It had faded enough to look slightly overexposed but not enough to look tampered with. And Taco was gone.

I looked at Katie. "The Society will be here in another fifteen minutes," I said, "which gives me just enough time to tell you about Aberfan." I gestured at the couch. "Sit down."

She came and sat down. "He was a great dog," I said. "He loved the snow. He'd dig through it and toss it up with his muzzle and snap at the snowflakes, trying to catch them."

Ramirez had obviously hung up, but she would call back if she couldn't track down Chiwere. I put the exclusion back on and went over to the developer. The image of Mrs. Ambler was still on the screen. The bath hadn't affected the detail that much. You could still see the wrinkles, the thin white hair, but the guilt, or blame, the look of loss and love, was gone. She looked serene, almost happy.

"There are hardly any good pictures of dogs," I said. "They lack the necessary muscles to take good pictures, and Aberfan would lunge at you as soon as he saw the camera."

I turned the developer off. Without the light from the screen, it was almost dark in the room. I turned on the overhead.

"There were less than a hundred dogs left in the United States, and he'd already had the newparvo once and nearly died. The only pictures I had of him had been taken when he was asleep. I wanted a picture of Aberfan playing in the snow."

I leaned against the narrow shelf in front of the developer's screen. Katie looked the way she had at the vet's, sitting there with her hands clenched, waiting for me to tell her something terrible.

"I wanted a picture of him playing in the snow, but he always lunged at the camera," I said, "so I let him out in the front yard, and then I sneaked out the side door and went across the road to some pine trees where he wouldn't be able to see me. But he did."

"And he ran across the road," Katie said. "And I hit him."

She was looking down at her hands. I waited for her to look up, dreading what I would see in her face. Or not see.

"It took me a long time to find out where you'd gone,"

she said to her hands. "I was afraid you'd refuse me access to your lifeline. I finally saw one of your pictures in a newspaper, and I moved to Phoenix, but after I got here I was afraid to call you for fear you'd hang up on me."

She twisted her hands the way she had twisted her mittens at the vet's. "My husband said I was obsessed with it, that I should have gotten over it by now, everybody else had, that they were only dogs anyway." She looked up, and I braced my hands against the developer. "He said forgiveness wasn't something somebody else could give you, but I didn't want you to forgive me exactly. I just wanted to tell you I was sorry."

There hadn't been any reproach, any accusation in her face when I told her she was responsible for the extinction of a species that day at the vet's, and there wasn't now. Maybe she didn't have the facial muscles for it, I thought bitterly.

"Do you know why I came to see you today?" I said angrily. "My camera broke when I tried to catch Aberfan. I didn't get any pictures." I grabbed the picture of Mrs. Ambler out of the developer's tray and flung it at her. "Her dog died of newparvo. They left it in the Winnebago, and when they came back, it was dead."

"Poor thing," she said, but she wasn't looking at the picture. She was looking at me.

"She didn't know she was having her picture taken. I thought if I got you talking about Aberfan, I could get a picture like that of you."

And surely now I would see it, the look I had really wanted when I set the eisenstadt down on Katie's kitchen table, the look I still wanted, even though the eisenstadt was facing the wrong way, the look of betrayal the dogs had never given us. Not even Misha. Not even Aberfan. How does it feel to be responsible for the extinction of an entire species?

I pointed at the eisenstadt. "It's not a briefcase. It's a camera. I was going to take your picture without your even knowing it."

She had never known Aberfan. She had never known Mrs. Ambler either, but in that instant before she started to cry she looked like both of them. She put her hand up to her mouth. "Oh," she said, and the love, the loss was there in her voice, too. "If you'd had it then, it wouldn't have happened."

I looked at the eisenstadt. If I had had it, I could have set it on the porch and Aberfan would never have even noticed it. He would have burrowed through the snow and tossed it up with his nose, and I could have thrown snow up in big glittering sprays that he would have leaped at, and it never would have happened. Katie Powell would have driven past, and I would have stopped to wave at her, and she, sixteen years old and just learning to drive, would maybe even have risked taking a mittened hand off the steering wheel to wave back, and Aberfan would have wagged his tail into a blizzard and then barked at the snow he'd churned up.

He wouldn't have caught the third wave. He would have lived to be an old dog, fourteen or fifteen, too old to play in the snow anymore, and even if he had been the last dog in the world I would not have let them lock him up in a cage, I would not have let them take him away. If I had had the eisenstadt.

No wonder I hated it.

It had been at least fifteen minutes since Ramirez called. The Society would be here any minute. "You shouldn't be here when the Society comes," I said, and Katie nodded and smudged the tears off her cheeks and stood up, reaching for her carryit.

"Do you ever take pictures?" she said, shouldering the carryit. "I mean, besides for the papers?"

"I don't know if I'll be taking pictures for them much longer. Photojournalists are becoming an extinct breed."

"Maybe you could come take some pictures of Jana and Kevin. Kids grow up so fast, they're gone before you know it."

"I'd like that," I said. I opened the screen door for her and looked both ways down the street at the darkness. "All clear," I said, and she went out. I shut the screen door between us.

She turned and looked at me one last time with her dear, open face that even I hadn't been able to close. "I miss them," she said.

I put my hand up to the screen. "I miss them, too."

I watched her to make sure she turned the corner and then went back in the living room and took down the picture of Misha. I propped it against the developer so Segura would be able to see it from the door. In a month or so, when the Amblers were safely in Texas and the Society had forgotten about Katie, I'd call Segura and tell him I might be willing to sell it to the Society, and then in a day or so I'd tell him I'd changed my mind. When he came out to try to talk me into it, I'd tell him about Perdita and Beatrix Potter, and he would tell me about the Society.

Chiwere and Ramirez would have to take the credit for the story—I didn't want Hunter putting anything else together—and it would take more than one story to break them, but it was a start.

Katie had left the print of Mrs. Ambler on the couch. I picked it up and looked at it a minute and then fed it into the developer. "Recycle," I said.

I picked up the eisenstadt from the table by the couch and took the film cartridge out. I started to pull the film out to expose it, and then shoved it into the developer instead and turned it on. "Positives, one two three order, five seconds."

I had apparently set the camera on its activator again—there were ten shots or so of the back seat of the Hitori. Vehicles and people. The pictures of Katie were all in shadow. There was a Still Life of Kool-Aid Pitcher with Whale Glass and another one of Jana's toy cars, and some near-black frames that meant Katie had laid the eisenstadt face-down when she brought it to me.

"Two seconds," I said, and waited for the developer to flash the last shots so I could make sure there wasn't anything else on the cartridge and then expose it before the Society got here. All but the last frame was of the darkness that was all the eisenstadt could see lying on its face. The last one was of me.

The trick in getting good pictures is to make people forget they're being photographed. Distract them. Get them talking about something they care about.

"Stop," I said, and the image froze.

Aberfan was a great dog. He loved to play in the snow, and after I had murdered him, he lifted his head off my lap and tried to lick my hand.

The Society would be here any minute to take the longshot film and destroy it, and this one would have to go, too, along with the rest of the cartridge. I couldn't risk Hunter's being reminded of Katie. Or Segura taking a notion to do a print-fix and peel on Jana's toy cars.

It was too bad. The eisenstadt takes great pictures. "Even you'll forget it's a camera," Ramirez had said in her spiel, and that was certainly true. I was looking straight into the lens.

And it was all there, Misha and Taco and Perdita and the look he gave me on the way to the vet's while I stroked his poor head and told him it would be all right, that look of love and pity I had been trying to capture all these years. The picture of Aberfan.

The Society would be here any minute. "Eject," I said, and cracked the cartridge open, and exposed it to the light.

1990
48th Convention
The Hague, Holland

Boobs
by Suzy McKee Charnas

Enter a Soldier. Later: Enter Another
by Robert Silverberg

The Mountains of Mourning
by Lois McMaster Bujold

One of the things that intrigues me most about the science fiction field is how fertile the soil is. You would think, after all these years, that there would be no more stories to tell about robots and spaceships, about aliens and time machines and Mars. Or that such stories would be worn-out imitations of older stories. Instead, they seem as fresh as ever, with new insights and new visions.

It's the same way with the stuff of myth. There have been stories about ghosts and werewolves and vampires since the very beginning of the field with no sign of repetition or decay setting in. Many of these stories achieve their newness by moving old myths into the modern world—sending the vampire to a bloodbank, putting the ghost on board a spaceship—or by giving supernatural events scientific rationale.

Or, as in this deceptively innocent tale of adolescent changes and junior high culture, by finding the truth that lay hidden at the heart of the myth all along.

"Boobs" is not the only work by Suzy McKee Charnas that uses the materials of myth. Her short story, "Unicorn Tapestry," which won the Nebula Award in 1980, and her collection, The Vampire Tapestry, both explore the legend of the vampire. "Boobs" is Charnas's first Hugo.

—Connie Willis

Boobs

by Suzy Mckee Charnas

The thing is, it's like your brain wants to go on thinking about the miserable history mid-term you have to take tomorrow, but your body takes over. And what a body! You can see in the dark and run like the wind and leap parked cars in a single bound.

Of course you pay for it next morning (but it's worth it). I always wake up stiff and sore, with dirty hands and feet and face, and I have to jump in the shower fast so Hilda won't see me like that.

Not that she would know what it was about, but why take chances? So I pretend it's the other thing that's bothering me. So she goes, "Come on, sweetie, everybody gets cramps, that's no reason to go around moaning and groaning. What are you doing, trying to get out of school just because you've got your period?"

If I didn't like Hilda, which I do even though she is only a stepmother instead of my real mother, I would show her something that would keep me out of school forever, and it's not fake, either.

But there are plenty of people I'd rather show that to.

I already showed that dork Billy Linden.

"Hey, Boobs!" he goes, in the hall right outside Homeroom. A lot of kids laughed, naturally, though Rita Frye called him an asshole.

Billy is the one that started it, sort of, because he always started everything, him with his big mouth. At the beginning of term, he came barreling down on me hollering, "Hey, look at Bornstein, something musta happened to her over the summer! What happened, Bornstein? Hey, everybody, look at Boobs Bornstein!"

He made a grab at my chest, and I socked him in the shoulder, and he punched me in the face, which made me dizzy and shocked and made me cry, too, in front of everybody.

I mean, I always used to wrestle and fight with the boys, being that I was strong for a girl. All of a sudden it was different. He hit me hard, to really hurt, and the shock sort of got me in the pit of my stomach and made me feel nauseous, too, as well as mad and embarrassed to death.

I had to go home with a bloody nose and lie with my head back and ice wrapped in a towel on my face and dripping down into my hair.

Hilda sat on the couch next to me and patted me. She goes, "I'm sorry about this, honey, but really, you have to learn it sometime. You're all growing up and the boys are getting stronger than you'll ever be. If you fight with boys, you're bound to get hurt. You have to find other ways to handle them."

To make things worse, the next morning I started to bleed down there, which Hilda had explained carefully to me a couple of times, so at least I knew what was going on. Hilda really tried extra hard without being icky about it, but I hated when she talked about how it was all part of these exciting changes in my body that are so important and how terrific it is to "become a young woman."

Sure. The whole thing was so messy and disgusting, worse than she had said, worse than I could imagine, with these black clots of gunk coming out in a smear of pink blood—I thought I would throw up. That's just the lining of your uterus, Hilda said. Big deal. It was still gross.

And, plus, the *smell*.

Hilda tried to make me feel better, she really did. She said we should "mark the occasion" like primitive people do, so it's something special, not just a nasty thing that just sort of falls on you.

So we decided to put poor old Pinkie away, my stuffed dog that I've slept with since I was three. Pinkie is bald and sort of hard and lumpy, since he got put in the washing machine by mistake, and you would never know he was all soft plush when he was new, or even that he was pink.

Last time my friend Gerry-Anne came over, before the summer, she saw Pinky laying on my pillow and though she didn't say anything, I could tell she was thinking that was kind of babyish. So I'd been thinking about not keeping Pinky around anymore.

Hilda and I made him this nice box lined with pretty scraps from her quilting class, and I thanked him out loud for being my friend for so many years, and we put him up in the closet, on the top shelf.

I felt terrible, but if Gerry-Anne decided I was too babyish to be friends with anymore, I could end up with no friends at all. When you have never been popular since the time you were skinny and fast and everybody wanted you on their team, you have that kind of thing on your mind.

Hilda and Dad made me go to school the next morning so nobody would think I was scared of Billy Linden (which I was) or that I would let him keep me away just by being such a dork.

Everybody kept sneaking funny looks at me and whispering, and I was sure it was because I couldn't help walking funny with the pad between my legs and because they could smell what was happening, which as far as I knew hadn't happened to anybody else in Eight A yet. Just like nobody else in the whole grade had anything real in their stupid training bras except me, thanks a lot.

Anyway I stayed away from everybody as much as I could and wouldn't talk to Gerry-Anne, even, because I was scared she would ask me why I walked funny and smelled bad.

Billy Linden avoided me just like everybody else, except one of his stupid buddies purposely bumped into me so I stumbled into Billy on the lunch-line. Billy turns around and he goes, real loud, "Hey, Boobs, when did you start wearing black and blue make-up?"

I didn't give him the satisfaction of knowing that he had actually broken my nose, which the doctor said. Good thing they don't have to bandage you up for that. Billy would be hollering up a storm about how I had my nose in a sling as well as my boobs.

That night I got up after I was supposed to be asleep and took off my underpants and T-shirt that I sleep in and stood looking at myself in the mirror. I didn't need to turn a light on. The moon was full and it was shining right into my bedroom through the big dormer window.

I crossed my arms and pinched myself hard to sort of punish my body for what it was doing to me.

As if that could make it stop.

No wonder Edie Siler had starved herself to death in the tenth grade! I understood her perfectly. She was trying to keep her body down, keep it normal-looking, thin and strong, like I was too, back when I looked like a person, not a cartoon that somebody would call "Boobs."

And then something warm trickled in a little line down the inside of my leg, and I knew it was blood and I couldn't stand it anymore. I pressed my thighs together and shut my eyes hard, and I did something.

I mean I felt it happening. I felt myself shrink down to a hard core of sort of cold fire inside my bones, and all the flesh part, the muscles and the squishy insides and the skin, went sort of glowing and free-floating, all shining with moonlight, and I felt a sort of shifting and balance-changing going on.

I thought I was fainting on account of my stupid period. So I turned around and threw myself on my bed, only by the time I hit it, I knew something was seriously wrong.

For one thing, my nose and my head were crammed with these crazy, rich sensations that it took me a second to even figure out were smells, they were so much stronger than any smells I'd ever smelled. And they were—I don't know—*interesting* instead of just stinky, even the rotten ones.

I opened my mouth to get the smells a little better, and heard myself panting in a funny way as if I'd been running, which I hadn't, and then there was this long part of my face sticking out and something moving there—my tongue.

I was licking my chops.

Well, there was this moment of complete and utter panic. I tore around the room whining and panting and hearing my toenails clicking on the floorboards, and then I huddled down and crouched in the corner because I was scared Dad and Hilda would hear me and come to find out what was making all this racket.

Because I could hear them. I could hear their bed creak when one of them turned over, and Dad's breath whistling a little in an almost snore, and I could smell them too, each one with a perfectly clear bunch of smells, kind of like those desserts of mixed ice cream they call a medley.

My body was twitching and jumping with fear and energy, and my room—it's a converted attic-space, wide but with a ceiling that's low in places—my room felt like a jail. And plus, I was terrified of catching a glimpse of myself in the mirror. I had a pretty good idea of what I would see, and I didn't want to see it.

Besides, I had to pee, and I couldn't face trying to deal with the toilet in the state I was in.

So I eased the bedroom door open with my shoulder and nearly fell down the stairs trying to work them with four legs and thinking about it, instead of letting my body just do it. I put my hands on the front door to open it, but my hands weren't hands, they were paws with long knobby toes covered with fur, and the toes had thick black claws sticking out of the ends of them.

The pit of my stomach sort of exploded with horror, and I yelled. It came out this wavery "wooo" noise that echoed eerily in my skullbones. Upstairs, Hilda goes, "Jack, what was that?" I bolted for the basement as I heard Dad hit the floor of their bedroom.

The basement door slips its latch all the time, so I just shoved it open and down I went, doing better on the stairs this time because I was too scared to think. I spent the rest of the night down there, moaning to myself (which meant whining through my nose, really) and trotting around rubbing against the walls trying to rub off this crazy shape I had, or just moving around because I couldn't sit still. The place was thick with stinks and these slow-swirling currents of hot and cold air. I couldn't handle all the input.

As for having to pee, in the end I managed to sort of hike my butt up over the edge of the slop-sink by Dad's workbench and let go in there. The only problem was that I couldn't turn the taps on to rinse out the smell because of my paws.

Then about three A.M. I woke up from a doze curled up in a bare place on the floor where the spiders weren't so likely to walk, and I couldn't see a thing or smell anything either, so I knew I was okay again even before I checked and found fingers on my hands again instead of claws.

I zipped upstairs and stood under the shower so long that Hilda yelled at me for using up the hot water when she had a load of wash to do that morning. I was only trying to steam some of the stiffness out of my muscles, but I couldn't tell her that.

It was real weird to just dress and go to school after a night like that. One good thing, I had stopped bleeding after only one day, which Hilda said wasn't so strange for the first time. So it had to be the huge greenish bruise on my face from Billy's punch that everybody was staring at.

That and the usual thing, of course. Well, why not? *They* didn't know I'd spent the night as a wolf.

So Fat Joey grabbed my book bag in the hallway outside science class and tossed it to some kid from Eight
B. I had to run after them to get it back, which of course
was set up so the boys could cheer the jouncing of my
boobs under my shirt.

I was so mad I almost caught Fat Joey, except I was
afraid if I grabbed him, maybe he would sock me like
Billy had.

Dad had told me, Don't let it get you, kid, all boys
are jerks at that age.

Hilda had been saying all summer, Look, it doesn't do
any good to walk around all hunched up with your arms
crossed, you should just throw your shoulders back and
walk like a proud person who's pleased that she's growing
up. You're just a little early, that's all, and I bet the other
girls are secretly envious of you, with their cute little
training bras, for Chrissake, as if there was something
that needed to be *trained*.

It's okay for her, she's not in school, she doesn't
remember what it's like.

So I quit running and walked after Joey until the bell
rang, and then I got my book bag back from the bushes
outside where he threw it. I was crying a little, and I
ducked into the girls' room.

Stacey Buhl was in there doing her lipstick like usual
and wouldn't talk to me like usual, but Rita came bustling
in and said somebody should off that dumb dork Joey,
except of course it was really Billy that put him up to it.
Like usual.

Rita is okay except she's an outsider herself, being that
her kid brother has AIDS, and lots of kids' parents don't
think she should even be in the school. So I don't hang
around with her a lot. I've got enough trouble, and anyway I was late for Math.

I had to talk to somebody, though. After school I told
Gerry-Anne, who's been my best friend on and off since
fourth grade. She was off at the moment, but I found
her in the library and I told her I'd had a weird dream

about being a wolf. She wants to be a psychiatrist like her mother, so of course she listened.

She told me I was nuts. That was a big help.

That night I made sure the back door wasn't exactly closed, and then I got in bed with no clothes on—imagine turning into a wolf in your underpants and T-shirt—and just shivered, waiting for something to happen.

The moon came up and shone in my window, and I changed again, just like before, which is not one bit like how it is in the movies—all struggling and screaming and bones snapping out with horrible cracking and tearing noises, just the way I guess you would imagine it to be, if you knew it had to be done by building special machines to do that for the camera and make it look real: if you were a special effects man, instead of a werewolf.

For me, it didn't have to look real, it was real. It was this melting and drifting thing, which I got sort of excited by it this time. I mean it felt—interesting. Like something I was doing, instead of just another dumb body-mess happening to me because some brainless hormones said so.

I must have made a noise. Hilda came upstairs to the door of my bedroom, but luckily she didn't come in. She's tall, and my ceiling is low for her, so she often talks to me from the landing.

Anyway I'd heard her coming, so I was in my bed with my whole head shoved under my pillow, praying frantically that nothing showed.

I could smell her, it was the wildest thing—her own smell, sort of sweaty but sweet, and then on top of it her perfume, like an ice-pick stuck in my nose. I didn't actually hear a word she said, I was too scared, and also I had this ripply shaking feeling inside me, a high that was only partly terror.

See, I realized all of a sudden, with this big blossom of surprise, that I didn't have to be scared of Hilda, or anybody. I was strong, my wolf-body was strong, and anyhow one clear look at me and she would drop dead.

What a relief, though, when she went away. I was dying to get out from under the weight of the covers, and besides I had to sneeze. Also I recognized that part of the energy roaring around inside me was hunger.

They went to bed—I heard their voices even in their bedroom, though not exactly what they said, which was fine. The words weren't important anymore, I could tell more from the tone of what they were saying.

Like I knew there were going to do it, and I was right. I could hear them messing around right through the walls, which was also something new, and I have never been so embarrassed in my life. I couldn't even put my hands over my ears, because my hands were paws.

So while I was waiting for them to go to sleep, I looked myself over in the big mirror on my closet door.

There was this big wolf head with a long slim muzzle and a thick ruff around my neck. The ruff stood up as I growled and backed up a little.

Which was silly of course, there was no wolf in the bedroom but me. But I was all strung out, I guess, and one wolf, me in my wolf body, was as much as I could handle the idea of, let alone two wolves, me and my reflection.

After that first shock, it was great. I kept turning one way and another for different views.

I was thin, with these long, slender legs but strong, you could see the muscles, and feet a little bigger than I would have picked. But I'll take four big feet over two big boobs any day.

My face was terrific, with jaggedy white ripsaw teeth and eyes that were small and clear and gleaming in the moonlight. The tail was a little bizarre, but I got used to it, and actually it had a nice plumy shape. My shoulders were big and covered with long, glossy-looking fur, and I had this neat coloring, dark on the back and a sort of melting silver on my front and underparts.

The thing was, though, my tongue, hanging out. I had a lot of trouble with that, it looked gross and silly at the same time. I mean, that was *my tongue*, about a foot long and neatly draped over the points of my bottom canines. That was when I realized that I didn't have a whole lot of expressions to use, not with that face, which was more like a mask.

But it was alive, it was my face, those were my own long black lips that my tongue licked.

No doubt about it, this was *me*. I was a werewolf, like in the movies they showed over Halloween weekend. But it wasn't anything like your ugly movie werewolf that's just some guy loaded up with pounds and pounds of make-up. I was *gorgeous*.

I didn't want to just hang around admiring myself in the mirror, though. I couldn't stand being cooped up in that stuffy, smell-crowded room.

When everything settled down and I could hear Dad and Hilda breathing the way they do when they're sleeping, I snuck out.

The dark wasn't very dark to me, and the cold felt sharp like vinegar, but not in a hurting way. Everyplace I went, there were these currents like waves in the air, and I could draw them in through my long wolf nose and roll the smell of them over the back of my tongue. It was like a whole different world, with bright sounds everywhere and rich, strong smells.

And I could run.

I started running because a car came by while I was sniffing at the garbage bags on the curb, and I was really scared of being seen in the headlights. So I took off down the dirt alley between our house and the Morrisons' next door, and holy cow, I could tear along with hardly a sound, I could jump their picket fence without even thinking about it. My back legs were like steel springs and I came down solid and square on four legs with almost no shock at all, let alone worrying about losing my balance or twisting an ankle.

Man, I could run through that chilly air all thick and moisty with smells, I could almost fly. It was like last year, when I didn't have boobs bouncing and yanking in front even when I'm only walking fast.

Just two rows of neat little bumps down the curve of
my belly. I sat down and looked.

I tore open garbage bags to find out about the smells
in them, but I didn't eat anything from them. I wasn't
about to chow down on other people's stale hotdog-ends
and pizza crusts and fat and bones scraped off their
plates and all mixed in with mashed potatoes and stuff.

When I found places where dogs had stopped and
made their mark, I squatted down and pissed there too,
right on top, I just wiped them *out*.

I bounded across that enormous lawn around the Wanscombe place, where nobody but the Oriental gardener
ever sets foot, and walked up the back and over the top
of their BMW, leaving big fat pawprints all over it.
Nobody saw me, nobody heard me, I was a shadow.

Well, except for the dogs, of course.

There was a lot of barking when I went by, real hyster-
ics, which at first I was really scared about. But then I
popped out of an alley up on Ridge Road, where the big
houses are, right in front of about six dogs that run
together. Their owners let them out all night and don't
care if they get hit by a car.

They'd been trotting along with the wind behind them,
checking out all the garbage bags set out for pickup the
next morning. When they saw me, one of them let out
a yelp of surprise, and they all skidded to a stop.

Six of them. I was scared. I growled.

The dogs turned fast, banging into each other in their
hurry, and trotted away.

I don't know what they would have done if they met
a real wolf, but I was something special, I guess.

I followed them.

They scattered and ran.

Well, I ran too, and this was a different kind of running. I mean, I stretched, and I raced, and there was
this joy. I chased one of them.

Zig, zag, this little terrier-kind of dog tried to cut left
and dive under the gate of somebody's front walk, all

without a sound—he was running too hard to yell, and I was happy running quiet.

Just before he could ooze under the gate, I caught up with him and without thinking I grabbed the back of his neck and pulled him off his feet and gave him a shake as hard as I could, from side to side.

I felt his neck crack, the sound vibrated through all the bones of my face.

I picked him up in my mouth, and it was like he hardly weighed a thing. I trotted away holding him up off the ground, and under a bush in Baker's Park I held him down with my paws and I bit into his belly, that was still warm and quivering.

Like I said, I was hungry.

The blood gave me this rush like you wouldn't believe. I stood there a minute looking around and licking my lips, just sort of panting and tasting the taste because I was stunned by it, it was like eating honey or the best chocolate malted you ever had.

So I put my head down and chomped that little dog, like shoving your face into a pizza and inhaling it. God, I was *starved*, so I didn't mind that the meat was tough and rank-tasting after that first wonderful bite. I even licked blood off the ground after, never mind the grit mixed in.

I ate two more dogs that night, one that was tied up on a clothesline in a cruddy yard full of rusted-out car parts down on the South side, and one fat old yellow dog out snuffling around on his own and way too slow. He tasted pretty bad, and by then I was feeling full, so I left a lot.

I strolled around the park, shoving the swings with my big black wolf nose, and I found the bench where Mr. Granby sits and feeds the pigeons every day, never mind that nobody else wants the dirty birds around crapping on their cars. I took a dump there, right where he sits.

Then I gave the setting moon a goodnight, which came out quavery and wild, "Loo-loo-loo!" And I loped toward

home, springing off the thick pads of my paws and letting
my tongue loll out and feeling generally super.

I slipped inside and trotted upstairs, and in my room
I stopped to look at myself in the mirror.

As gorgeous as before, and only a few dabs of blood
on me, which I took time to lick off. I did get a little
worried—I mean, suppose that was it, suppose having
killed and eaten what I'd killed in my wolf shape, I was
stuck in this shape forever? Like, if you wander into a
fairy castle and eat or drink anything, that's it, you can't
ever leave. Suppose when the morning came I didn't
change back?

Well, there wasn't much I could do about that one
way or the other, and to tell the truth, I felt like I
wouldn't mind; it had been worth it.

When I was nice and clean, including licking off my
own bottom which seemed like a perfectly normal and
nice thing to do at the time, I jumped up on the bed,
curled up, and corked right off. When I woke up with
the sun in my eyes, there I was, my own self again.

It was very strange, grabbing breakfast and wearing
my old sweatshirt that wallowed all over me so I didn't
stick out so much, while Hilda yawned and shuffled
around in her robe and slippers and acted like her and
Dad hadn't been doing it last night, which I knew
different.

And plus, it was perfectly clear that she didn't have a
clue about what I had been doing, which gave me a
strange feeling.

One of the things about growing up which they're
careful not to tell you is, you start having more things
you don't talk to your parents about. And I had a doozie.

Hilda goes, "What's the matter, are you off Sugar Pops
now? Honestly, Kelsey, I can't keep up with you! And
why can't you wear something nicer than that old shirt
to school? Oh, I get it: disguise, right?"

She sighed and looked at me kind of sad but smiling,
her hands on her hips. "Kelsey, Kelsey," she goes, "if
only I'd had half of what you've got when I was a girl—I

was flat as an ironing board, and it made me so miserable, I can't tell you."

She's still real thin and neat-looking, so what does she know about it? But she meant well, and anyhow I was feeling so good I didn't argue.

I didn't change my shirt, though.

That night I didn't turn into a wolf. I laid there waiting, but though the moon came up, nothing happened no matter how hard I tried, and after a while I went and looked out the window and realized that the moon wasn't really full anymore, it was getting smaller.

I wasn't so much relieved as sorry. I bought a calendar at the school book sale two weeks later, and I checked the full moon nights coming up and waited anxiously to see what would happen.

Meantime, things rolled along as usual. I got a rash of zits on my chin. I would look in the mirror and think about my wolf-face, that had beautiful sleek fur instead of zits.

Zits and all I went to Angela Durkin's party, and next day Billy Linden told everybody that I went in one of the bedrooms at Angela's and made out with him, which I did not. But since no grown-ups were home and Fat Joey brought grass to the party, most of the kids were stoned and didn't know who did what or where anyhow.

As a matter of fact, Billy once actually did get a girl in Seven B high one time out in his parents' garage, and him and two of his friends did it to her while she was zonked out of her mind, or anyway they said they did, and she was too embarrassed to say anything one way or the other, and a little while later she changed schools.

How I know about it is the same way everybody else does, which is because Billy was the biggest boaster in the whole school, and you could never tell if he was lying or not.

So I guess it wasn't so surprising that some people believed what Billy said about me. Gerry-Anne quit talking to me after that. Meantime Hilda got pregnant.

This turned into a huge discussion about how Hilda

had been worried about her biological clock so she and
Dad had decided to have a kid, and I shouldn't mind, it
would be fun for me and good preparation for being a
mother myself later on, when I found some nice guy and
got married.

Sure. Great preparation. Like Mary O'Hare in my
class, who gets to change her youngest baby sister's dia-
pers all the time, yick. She jokes about it, but you can
tell she really hates it. Now it looked like it was my turn
coming up, as usual.

The only thing that made life bearable was my secret.

"You're laid back today," Devon Brown said to me in
the lunchroom one day after Billy had been specially
obnoxious, trying to flick rolled up pieces of bread from
his table so they would land on my chest. Devon was
sitting with me because he was bad at French, my only
good subject, and I was helping him out with some verbs.
I guess he wanted to know why I wasn't upset because
of Billy picking on me. He goes, "How come?"

"That's a secret," I said, thinking about what Devon
would say if he knew a werewolf was helping him with
his French: *loup. Manger.*

He goes, "What secret?" Devon has freckles and is
actually kind of cute-looking.

"A *secret*," I go, "so I can't tell you, dummy."

He looks real superior and he goes, "Well, it can't be
much of a secret, because girls can't keep secrets, everybody knows that."

Sure, like that kid Sara in Eight B who it turned out
her own father had been molesting her for years, but
she never told anybody until some psychologist caught
on from some tests we all had to take in seventh grade.
Up till then, Sara kept her secret fine.

And I kept mine, marking off the days on the calendar.
The only part I didn't look forward to was having a period
again, which last time came right before the change.

When the time came, I got crampy and more zits
popped out on my face, but I didn't have a period.

I changed, though.

The next morning they were talking in school about a couple of prize miniature Schnauzers at the Wanscombes that had been hauled out of their yard by somebody and killed, and almost nothing left of them.

Well, my stomach turned a little when I heard some kids describing what Mr. Wanscombe had found over in Baker's Park, "the remains," as people said. I felt a little guilty, too, because Mrs. Wanscombe had really loved those little dogs, which somehow I didn't think about at all when I was a wolf the night before, trotting around hungry in the moonlight.

I knew those Schnauzers personally, so I was sorry, even if they were irritating little mutts that made a lot of noise.

But heck, the Wanscombes shouldn't have left them out all night in the cold. Anyhow, they were rich, they could buy new ones if they wanted.

Still and all, though. I mean, dogs are just dumb animals. If they're mean, it's because they're wired that way or somebody made them mean, they can't help it. They can't just decide to be nice, like a person can. And plus, they don't taste so great, I think because they put so much junk in commercial dog-foods—anti-worm medicine and ashes and ground up fish, stuff like that. Ick.

In fact after the second schnauzer I had felt sort of sick and I didn't sleep real well that night. So I was not in a great mood to start with; and that was the day that my new brassiere disappeared while I was in gym. Later on I got passed a note telling me where to find it: stapled to the bulletin board outside the Principal's office, where everybody could see that I was trying a bra with an underwire.

Naturally, it had to be Stacey Buhl that grabbed my bra while I was changing for gym and my back was turned, since she was now hanging out with Billy and hi. friends.

Billy went around all day making bets at the top of his lungs on how soon I would be wearing a D-cup.

Stacey didn't matter, she was just a jerk. Billy mattered.

He had wrecked me in that school forever, with his nasty mind and his big, fat mouth. I was past crying or fighting and getting punched out. I was boiling, I had had enough crap from him, and I had an idea.

I followed Billy home and waited on his porch until his mom came home and she made him come down and talk to me. He stood in the doorway and talked through the screen door, eating a banana and lounging around like he didn't have a care in the world.

So he goes, "Whatcha want, Boobs?"

I stammered a lot, being I was so nervous about telling such big lies, but that probably made me sound more believable.

I told him that I would make a deal with him: I would meet him that night in Baker's Park, late, and take off my shirt and bra and let him do whatever he wanted with my boobs if that would satisfy his curiosity and he would find somebody else to pick on and leave me alone.

"What?" he said, staring at my chest with his mouth open. His voice squeaked and he was practically drooling on the floor. He couldn't believe his good luck.

I said the same thing over again.

He almost came out onto the porch to try it right then and there. "Well, shit," he goes, lowering his voice a lot, "why didn't you say something before? You really mean it?"

I go, "Sure," though I couldn't look at him.

After a minute he goes, "Okay, it's a deal. Listen, Kelsey, if you like it, can we, uh, do it again, you know?"

I go, "Sure. But Billy, one thing: this is a secret, between just you and me. If you tell anybody, if there's one other person hanging around out there tonight—"

"Oh, no," he goes, real fast, "I won't say a thing to anybody, honest. Not a word, I promise!"

Not until afterward, of course, was what he meant, which if there was one thing Billy Linden couldn't do, it was to keep quiet if he knew something bad about another person.

"You're gonna like it, I know you are," he goes,

speaking strictly for himself as usual. "Jeez. I can't believe this!"

But he did, the dork.

I couldn't eat much for dinner that night, I was too
excited, and I went upstairs early to do homework, I told
Dad and Hilda.

Then I waited for the moon, and when it came, I
changed.

Billy was in the park. I caught a whiff of him, very
sweaty and excited, but I stayed cool. I snuck around for
a while, as quiet as I could—which was real quiet—
making sure none of his stupid friends were lurking
around. I mean, I wouldn't have trusted just his promise
for a million dollars.

I passed up half a hamburger lying in the gutter where
somebody had parked for lunch next to Baker's Park. My
mouth watered, but I didn't want to spoil my appetite.
I was hungry and happy, sort of singing inside my own
head, "Shoo, fly, pie, and an apple-pan-dowdie . . ."

Without any sound, of course.

Billy had been sitting on a bench, his hands in his
pockets, twisting around to look this way and that way,
watching for me—for my human self—to come join him.
He had a jacket on, being it was very chilly out.

Which he didn't stop to think that maybe a sane person wouldn't be crazy enough to sit out there and take
off her top leaving her naked skin bare to the breeze.
But that was Billy all right, totally fixed on his own greedy
self and without a single thought for somebody else. I
bet all he could think about was what a great scam this
was, to feel up old Boobs in the park and then crow
about it all over school.

Now he was walking around the park, kicking at the
sprinkler-heads and glancing up every once in a while,
frowning and looking sulky.

I could see he was starting to think that I might stand
him up. Maybe he even suspected that old Boobs was
lurking around watching him and laughing to herself
because he had fallen for a trick. Maybe old Boobs had

even brought some kids from school with her to see what
a jerk he was.

Actually that would have been pretty good, except Billy
probably would have broken my nose for me again, or
worse, if I'd tried it.

"Kelsey?" he goes, sounding mad.

I didn't want him stomping off home in a huff. I
moved up closer, and I let the bushes swish a little
around my shoulders.

He goes, "Hey, Kelse, it's late, where've you been?"

I listened to the words, but mostly I listened to the
little thread of worry flickering in his voice, low and high,
high and low, as he tried to figure out what was going on.

I let out the whisper of a growl.

He stood real still, staring at the bushes, and he goes,
"That you, Kelse? Answer me."

I was wild inside. I couldn't wait another second. I
tore through the bushes and leaped for him, flying.

He stumbled backward with a squawk—"What!"—
jerking his hands up in front of his face, and he was just
sucking in a big breath to yell with when I hit him like
a demo-derby truck.

I jammed my nose past his feeble claws and chomped
down hard on his face.

No sound came out of him except this wet, thick gur-
gle, which I could more taste than hear because the
sound came right into my mouth with the gush of his
blood and the hot mess of meat and skin that I tore away
and swallowed.

He thrashed around, hitting at me, but I hardly felt
anything through my fur. I mean, he wasn't so big and
strong laying there on the ground with me straddling him
all lean and wiry with wolf-muscle. And plus, he was in
shock. I got a strong whiff from below as he let go of
everything right into his pants.

Dogs were barking, but so many people around
Baker's Park have dogs to keep out burglars, and the
dogs make such a racket all the time, that nobody pays

any attention. I wasn't worried. Anyway, I was too busy
to care.

I nosed in under what was left of Billy's jaw and I bit
his throat out.

Now let him go around telling lies about people.

His clothes were a lot of trouble and I really missed
having hands. I managed to drag his shirt out of his belt
with my teeth, though, and it was easy to tear his belly
open. Pretty messy, but once I got in there, it was better
than Thanksgiving dinner. Who would think that somebody as horrible as Billy Linden could taste so *good*?

He was barely moving by then, and I quit thinking
about him as Billy Linden anymore. I quit thinking at
all, I just pushed my head in and pulled out delicious
steaming chunks and ate until I was picking at tidbits,
and everything was getting cold.

On the way home I saw a police car cruising the neighborhood the way they do sometimes. I hid in the shadows
and of course they never saw me.

There was a lot of washing up to do in the morning,
and when Hilda saw my sheets she shook her head and
she goes, "You should be more careful about keeping
track of your period so as not to get caught by surprise."

Everybody in school knew something had happened to
Billy Linden, but it wasn't until the day after that that
they got the word. Kids stood around in little huddles
trading rumors about how some wild animal had chewed
Billy up. I would walk up and listen in and add a really
gross remark or two, like part of the game of thrilling
each other green and nauseous with made-up details to
see who would upchuck first.

Not me, that's for sure. I mean, when somebody went
on about how Billy's whole head was gnawed down to
the skull and they didn't even know who he was except
from the bus pass in his wallet, I got a little urpy. It's
amazing the things people will dream up. But when I
thought about what I had actually done to Billy, I had
to smile.

It felt totally wonderful to walk through the halls without having anybody yelling, "Hey, Boobs!"

Even my social life is looking up. Gerry-Anne is not only talking to me again, she invited me out on a double-date with her. Some guy she met at a party asked her to go to the movies with him next weekend, and he has a friend. They're both from Fawcett Junior High across town, which will be a change. I was nervous when she asked me, but finally I said yes. My first real date!

I am still pretty nervous, to tell the truth. I have to keep promising myself that I will not worry about my chest, I will not be self-conscious, even if the guy stares.

Actually things at school are not completely hunky-dory. Hilda says "That's Life" when I complain about things, and I am beginning to believe her. Fat Joey somehow got to be my lab-partner in Science, and if he doesn't quit trying to grab a feel whenever we have to stand close together to do an experiment, he is going to be sorry.

He doesn't know it, but he's got until the next full moon.

People who never read science fiction always think it's about the future. Actually, it is concerned almost as much with the past, I think because our only clues to what will happen lie in what's happened already. And the past is fascinating in its own right.

Science fiction is the one genre that can wander freely around in the past, exploring it through time travel, as in Jack Finney's Time and Again, *and C. L. Moore and Henry Kuttner's "Vintage Season." It can also bring the past to the present, as in Kit Reed's "Mr. da V," and to the future, as in Nancy Kress's "And Wild for to Hold."*

Or it can as in "Enter a Soldier. Later: Enter Another," bring past and future together in one place. With unlooked-for results.

This is not the only work of Robert Silverberg's to deal with the complicated business of past and future. He has also explored them in his short works: "Many Mansions," "The Assassin," and the ironic "Trips," and in his novel, Up the Line. *"Enter a Soldier" is Silverberg's third Hugo-winning story. He also won for his novellas, "Nightwings," in 1969 and "Gilgamesh in the Outback" in 1987.*

—Connie Willis

Enter a Soldier. Later: Enter Another

by Robert Silverberg

It might be heaven. Certainly it wasn't Spain and he doubted it could be Peru. He seemed to be floating, suspended midway between nothing and nothing. There was a shimmering golden sky far above him and a misty, turbulent sea of white clouds boiling far below. When he looked down he saw his legs and his feet dangling like child's toys above an unfathomable abyss, and the sight of it made him want to puke, but there was nothing in him for the puking. He was hollow. He was made of air. Even the old ache in his knee was gone, and so was the everlasting dull burning in the fleshy part of his arm where the Indian's little arrow had taken him, long ago on the shore of that island of pearls, up by Panama.

It was as if he had been born again, sixty years old but freed of all the harm that his body had experienced and all its myriad accumulated injuries: freed, one might almost say, of his body itself.

"Gonzalo?" he called. "Hernando?"

Blurred dreamy echoes answered him. And then silence.

"Mother of God, am I dead?"

No. No. He had never been able to imagine death.

An end to all striving? A place where nothing moved? A great emptiness, a pit without a bottom? Was this place the place of death, then? He had no way of knowing. He needed to ask the holy fathers about this.

"Boy, where are my priests? Boy?"

He looked about for his page. But all he saw was blinding whorls of light coiling off to infinity on all sides. The sight was beautiful but troublesome. It was hard for him to deny that he had died, seeing himself afloat like this in a realm of air and light. Died and gone to heaven. This is heaven, yes, surely, surely. What else could it be?

So it was true, that if you took the Mass and took the Christ faithfully into yourself and served Him well you would be saved from your sins, you would be forgiven, you would be cleansed. He had wondered about that. But he wasn't ready yet to be dead, all the same. The thought of it was sickening and infuriating. There was so much yet to be done. And he had no memory even of being ill. He searched his body for wounds. No, no wounds. Not anywhere. Strange. Again he looked around. He was alone here. No one to be seen, not his page, nor his brother, nor De Soto, nor the priests, nor anyone. "Fray Marcos! Fray Vicente! Can't you hear me? Damn you, where are you? Mother of God! Holy Mother, blessed among women! Damn you, Fray Vicente, tell me—tell me—"

His voice sounded all wrong: too thick, too deep, a stranger's voice. The words fought with his tongue and came from his lips malformed and lame, not the good crisp Spanish of Estremadura but something shameful and odd. What he heard was like the spluttering foppishness of Madrid or even the furry babble that they spoke in Barcelona; why, he might almost be a Portuguese, so coarse and clownish was his way of shaping his speech.

He said carefully and slowly, "I am the Governor and Captain-General of New Castile."

That came out no better, a laughable noise.

"Adelantado—Alguacil Mayor—Marqués de la Conquista—"

The strangeness of his new way of speech made insults of his own titles. It was like being tongue-tied. He felt streams of hot sweat breaking out on his skin from the effort of trying to frame his words properly; but when he put his hand to his forehead to brush the sweat away before it could run into his eyes he seemed dry to the touch, and he was not entirely sure he could feel himself at all.

He took a deep breath. "I am Francisco Pizarro!" he roared, letting the name burst desperately from him like water breaching a rotten dam.

The echo came back, deep, rumbling, mocking. *Frantheethco. Peetharro.*

That too. Even his own name, idiotically garbled.

"O great God!" he cried. "Saints and angels!"

More garbled noises. Nothing would come out as it should. He had never known the arts of reading or writing; now it seemed that true speech itself was being taken from him. He began to wonder whether he had been right about this being heaven, supernal radiance or no. There was a curse on his tongue; a demon, perhaps, held it pinched in his claws. Was this hell, then? A very beautiful place, but hell nevertheless?

He shrugged. Heaven or hell, it made no difference. He was beginning to grow more calm, beginning to accept and take stock. He knew—had learned, long ago— that there was nothing to gain from raging against that which could not be helped, even less from panic in the face of the unknown. He was here, that was all there was to it—wherever *here* was—and he must find a place for himself, and not this place, floating here between nothing and nothing. He had been in hells before, small hells, hells on Earth. That barren isle called Gallo, where the sun cooked you in your own skin and there was nothing to eat but crabs that had the taste of dog-dung. And that dismal swamp at the mouth of the Rio Biru, where the rain fell in rivers and the trees reached down to cut you like swords. And the mountains he had crossed with his army, where the snow was so cold that it burned, and the air went into your throat like a dagger at every breath. He had come forth from those, and they had been worse than this. Here there was no pain and no danger, here there was only soothing light and a strange absence of all discomfort. He began to move forward. He was walking on air. Look, look, he thought, I am walking on air! Then he said it out loud. "I am walking on air," he announced, and laughed at the way the words emerged from him. "Santiago! Walking on air! But why not? I am Pizarro!" He shouted it with all his might, "Pizarro! Pizarro!" and waited for it to come back to him.

Peetharro. Peetharro.

He laughed. He kept on walking.

Tanner sat hunched forward in the vast sparkling sphere that was the ninth-floor imaging lab, watching the little figure at the distant center of the holotank strut and preen. Lew Richardson, crouching beside him with both hands thrust into the data gloves so that he could feed instructions to the permutation network, seemed almost not to be breathing—seemed to be just one more part of the network, in fact.

But that was Richardson's way, Tanner thought: total absorption in the task at hand. Tanner envied him that. They were very different sorts of men. Richardson lived for his programming and nothing but his programming. It was his grand passion. Tanner had never quite been able to understand people who were driven by grand passions. Richardson was like some throwback to an earlier age, an age when things had really mattered, an age when you were able to have some faith in the significance of your own endeavors.

"How do you like the armor?" Richardson asked. "The armor's very fine, I think. We got it from old engravings. It has real flair."

"Just the thing for tropical climates," said Tanner. "A nice tin suit with matching helmet."

He coughed and shifted about irritably in his seat. The demonstration had been going on for half an hour without anything that seemed to be of any importance happening—just the minuscule image of the bearded man in Spanish armor tramping back and forth across the glowing field—and he was beginning to get impatient.

Richardson didn't seem to notice the harshness in Tanner's voice or the restlessness of his movements. He went on making small adjustments. He was a small man himself, neat and precise in dress and appearance, with faded blond hair and pale blue eyes and a thin, straight mouth. Tanner felt huge and shambling beside him. In theory Tanner had authority over Richardson's research projects, but in fact he always had simply permitted Richardson to do as he pleased. This time, though, it might be necessary finally to rein him in a little.

This was the twelfth or thirteenth demonstration that Richardson had subjected him to since he had begun fooling around with this historical-simulation business. The others all had been disasters of one kind or another, and Tanner expected that this one would finish the same way. And basically Tanner was growing uneasy about the project that he once had given his stamp of approval to, so long ago. It was getting harder and harder to go on believing that all this work served any useful purpose. Why had it been allowed to absorb so much of Richardson's group's time and so much of the lab's research budget for so many months? What possible value was it going to have for anybody? What possible use?

It's just a game, Tanner thought. One more desperate meaningless technological stunt, one more pointless pirouette in a meaningless ballet. The expenditure of vast resources on a display of ingenuity for ingenuity's sake and nothing else: now *there's* decadence for you.

The tiny image in the holotank suddenly began to lose color and definition.

"Uh-oh," Tanner said. "There it goes. Like all the others."

But Richardson shook his head. "This time it's different, Harry."

"You think?"

"We aren't losing him. He's simply moving around in there of his own volition, getting beyond our tracking parameters. Which means that we've achieved the high level of autonomy that we were shooting for."

"Volition, Lew? Autonomy?"

"You know that those are our goals."

"Yes, I know what our goals are supposed to be," said Tanner, with some annoyance. "I'm simply not convinced that a loss of focus is a proof that you've got volition."

"Here," Richardson said. "I'll cut in the stochastic tracking program. He moves freely, we freely follow him." Into the computer ear in his lapel he said, "Give me a gain boost, will you?" He made a quick flicking gesture with his left middle finger to indicate the quantitative level.

The little figure in ornate armor and pointed boots grew sharp again. Tanner could see fine details on the armor, the plumed helmet, the tapering shoulder-pieces, the joints at the elbows, the intricate pommel of his sword. He was marching from left to right in a steady hip-rolling way, like a man who was climbing the tallest mountain in the world and didn't mean to break his stride until he was across the summit. The fact that he was walking in what appeared to be mid-air seemed not to trouble him at all.

"There he is," Richardson said grandly. "We've got him back, all right? The conqueror of Peru, before your very eyes, in the flesh. So to speak."

Tanner nodded. Pizarro, yes, before his very eyes. And he had to admit that what he saw was impressive and even, somehow, moving. Something about the dogged way with which that small armored figure was moving across the gleaming pearly field of the holotank aroused a kind of sympathy in him. That little man was entirely imaginary, but *he* didn't seem to know that, or if he did he wasn't letting it stop him for a moment: he went plugging on, and on and on, as if he intended actually to get somewhere. Watching that, Tanner was oddly captivated by it, and found himself surprised suddenly to discover that his interest in the entire project was beginning to rekindle.

"Can you make him any bigger?" he asked. "I want to see his face."

"I can make him big as life," Richardson said. "Bigger. Any size you like. Here."

He flicked a finger and the hologram of Pizarro expanded instantaneously to a height of about two meters. The Spaniard halted in mid-stride as though he might actually be aware of the imaging change.

That can't be possible, Tanner thought. That isn't a living consciousness out there. Or is it?

Pizarro stood poised easily in mid-air, glowering, shading his eyes as if staring into a dazzling glow. There were brilliant streaks of color in the air all around him, like an aurora. He was a tall, lean man in late middle age with a grizzled beard and a hard, angular face. His lips were thin, his nose was sharp, his eyes were cold, shrewd, keen. It seemed to Tanner that those eyes had come to rest on him, and he felt a chill.

My God, Tanner thought, he's *real*.

It had been a French program to begin with, something developed at the Centre Mundial de la Computation in Lyons about the year 2119. The French had some truly splendid minds working in software in those days. They worked up astounding programs, and then nobody did anything with them. That was *their* version of Century Twenty-Two Malaise.

The French programmers' idea was to use holograms of actual historical personages to dress up the *son et lumière* tourist events at the great monuments of their national history. Not just preprogrammed robot mockups of the old Disneyland kind, which would stand around in front of Notre Dame or the Arc de Triomphe or the Eiffel Tower and deliver canned spiels, but apparent reincarnations of the genuine great ones, who could freely walk and talk and answer questions and make little quips. Imagine Louis XIV demonstrating the fountains of

Versailles, they said, or Picasso leading a tour of Paris museums, or Sartre sitting in his Left Bank cafe exchanging existential *bons mots* with passersby! Napoleon! Joan of Arc! Alexandre Dumas! Perhaps the simulations could do even more than that: perhaps they could be designed so well that they would be able to extend and embellish the achievements of their original lifetimes with new accomplishments, a fresh spate of paintings and novels and works of philosophy and great architectural visions by vanished masters.

The concept was simple enough in essence. Write an intelligencing program that could absorb data, digest it, correlate it, and generate further programs based on what you had given it. No real difficulty there. Then start feeding your program with the collected written works— if any—of the person to be simulated: that would provide not only a general sense of his ideas and positions but also of his underlying pattern of approach to situations, his style of thinking—for *le style*, after all, *est l'homme même*. If no collected works happened to be available, why, find works *about* the subject by his contemporaries, and use those. Next, toss in the totality of the historical record of the subject's deeds, including all significant subsequent scholarly analyses, making appropriate allowances for conflicts in interpretation—indeed, taking advantage of such conflicts to generate a richer portrait, full of the ambiguities and contradictions that are the inescapable hallmarks of any human being. Now build in substrata of general cultural data of the proper period so that the subject has a loam of references and vocabulary out of which to create thoughts that are appropriate to his place in time and space. Stir. *Et voilà!* Apply a little sophisticated imaging technology and you had a simulation capable of thinking and conversing and behaving as though it is the actual self after which it was patterned.

Of course, this would require a significant chunk of computer power. But that was no problem, in a world where 150-gigaflops networks were standard laboratory items and ten-year-olds carried pencil-sized computers with capacities far beyond the ponderous mainframes of their great-great-grandparents' day. No, there was no theoretical reason why the French project could not have succeeded. Once the Lyons programmers had worked out the basic intelligencing scheme that was needed to write the rest of the programs, it all should have followed smoothly enough.

Two things went wrong: one rooted in an excess of ambition that may have been a product of the peculiarly French personalities of the original programmers, and the other having to do with an abhorrence of failure typical of the major nations of the mid-twenty-second century, of which France was one.

The first was a fatal change of direction that the project underwent in its early phases. The King of Spain was coming to Paris on a visit of state; and the programmers decided that in his honor they would synthesize Don Quixote for him as their initial project. Though the intelligencing program had been designed to simulate only individuals who had actually existed, there seemed no inherent reason why a fictional character as well documented as Don Quixote could not be produced instead. There was Cervantes' lengthy novel; there was ample background data available on the milieu in which Don Quixote supposedly had lived; there was a vast library of critical analysis of the book and of the Don's distinctive and flamboyant personality. Why should bringing Don Quixote to life out of a computer be any different from simulating Louis XIV, say, or Moliere, or Cardinal Richelieu? True, they had all existed once, and the knight of La Mancha was a mere figment; but had Cervantes not provided far more detail about Don Quixote's mind and soul than was known of Richelieu, or Molière, or Louis XIV?

Indeed he had. The Don—like Oedipus, like Odysseus, like Othello, like David Copperfield—had come to have a reality far more profound and tangible than that of most people who had indeed actually lived. Such characters as those had transcended their fictional origins.

But not so far as the computer was concerned. It was able to produce a convincing fabrication of Don Quixote, all right—a gaunt bizarre holographic figure that had all the right mannerisms, that ranted and raved in the expectable way, that referred knowledgeably to Dulcinea and Rosinante and Mambrino's helmet. The Spanish king was amused and impressed. But to the French the experiment was a failure. They had produced a Don Quixote who was hopelessly locked to the Spain of the late sixteenth century and to the book from which he had sprung. He had no capacity for independent life and thought—no way to perceive the world that had brought him into being, or to comment on it, or to interact with it. There was nothing new or interesting about that. Any actor could dress up in armor and put on a scraggly beard and recite snatches of Cervantes. What had come forth from the computer, after three years of work, was no more than a predictable reprocessing of what had gone into it, sterile, stale.

Which led the Centre Mundial de la Computation to its next fatal step: abandoning the whole thing. *Zut!* and the project was cancelled without any further attempts. No simulated Picassos, no simulated Napoleons, no Joans of Arc. The Quixote event had soured everyone and no one had the heart to proceed with the work from there. Suddenly it had the taint of failure about it, and France—like Germany, like Australia, like the Han Commercial Sphere, like Brazil, like any of the dynamic centers of the modern world, had a horror of failure. Failure was something to be left to the backward nations or the decadent ones—to the Islamic Socialist Union, say, or the Soviet People's Republic, or to that slumbering giant, the United States of America. So the historic-personage simulation scheme was put aside.

The French thought so little it, as a matter of fact, that after letting it lie fallow for a few years they licensed it to a bunch of Americans, who had heard about it somehow and felt it might be amusing to play with.

*   *   *

"You may really have done it this time," Tanner said.

"Yes. I think we have. After all those false starts."

Tanner nodded. How often had he come into this room with hopes high, only to see some botch, some inanity, some depressing bungle? Richardson had always had an explanation. Sherlock Holmes hadn't worked because he was fictional: that was a necessary recheck of the French Quixote project, demonstrating that fictional characters didn't have the right sort of reality texture to take proper advantage of the program, not enough ambiguity, not enough contradiction. King Arthur had failed for the same reason. Julius Caesar? Too far in the past, maybe; unreliable data, bordering on fiction. Moses? Ditto. Einstein? Too complex, perhaps, for the project in its present level of development: they needed more experience first. Queen Elizabeth I? George Washington? Mozart? We're learning more each time, Richardson insisted after each failure. This isn't black magic we're doing, you know. We aren't necromancers, we're programmers, and we have to figure out how to give the program what it needs.

And now Pizarro.

"Why do you want to work with *him*?" Tanner had asked, five or six months earlier. "A ruthless medieval Spanish imperialist, is what I remember from school. A bloodthirsty despoiler of a great culture. A man without morals, honor, faith—"

"You may be doing him an injustice," said Richardson. "He's had a bad press for centuries. And there are things about him that fascinate me."

"Such as?"

"His drive. His courage. His absolute confidence. The other side of ruthlessness, the good side of it, is a total concentration on your task, an utter unwillingness to be stopped by any obstacle. Whether or not you approve of the things he accomplished, you have to admire a man who—"

"All right," Tanner said, abruptly growing weary of the whole enterprise. "Do Pizarro. Whatever you want."

The months had passed. Richardson gave him vague progress reports, nothing to arouse much hope. But now Tanner stared at the tiny strutting figure in the holotank and the conviction began to grow in him that Richardson finally had figured out how to use the simulation program as it was meant to be used.

"So you've actually re-created him, you think? Someone who lived—what, five hundred years ago?"

"He died in 1541," said Richardson.

"Almost six hundred, then."

"And he's not like the others—not simply a re-creation of a great figure out of the past who can run through a set of pre-programmed speeches. What we've got here, if I'm right, is an artificially generated intelligence which can think for itself in modes other than the ones its programmers think in. Which has more information available to itself, in other words, than we've provided it with. That would be the real accomplishment. That's the fundamental philosophical leap that we were going for when we first got involved with this project. To use the program to give us new programs that are capable of true autonomous thought—a program that can think like Pizarro, instead of like Lew Richardson's idea of some historian's idea of how Pizarro might have thought."

"Yes," Tanner said.

"Which means we won't just get back the expectable, the predictable. There'll be surprises. There's no way to learn anything, you know, except through surprises. The sudden combination of known components into something brand new. And that's what I think we've managed to bring off here, at long last. Harry, it may be the biggest artificial-intelligence breakthrough ever achieved."

Tanner pondered that. Was it so? Had they truly done it?

And if they had—

Something new and troubling was beginning to occur to him, much later in the game than it should have.

Tanner stared at the holographic figure floating in the center of the tank, that fierce old man with the harsh face and the cold, cruel eyes. He thought about what sort of man he must have been—the man after whom this image had been modeled. A man who was willing to land in South America at age fifty or sixty or whatever he had been, an ignorant illiterate Spanish peasant wearing a suit of ill-fitting armor and waving a rusty sword, and set out to conquer a great empire of millions of people spreading over thousands of miles. Tanner wondered what sort of man would be capable of carrying out a thing like that. Now that man's eyes were staring into his own and it was a struggle to meet so implacable a gaze.

After a moment he looked away. His left leg began to quiver. He glanced uneasily at Richardson.

"Look at those eyes, Lew. Christ, they're scary!"

"I know. I designed them myself, from the old prints."

"Do you think he's seeing us right now? Can he do that?"

"All he is is software, Harry."

"He seemed to know it when you expanded the image."

Richardson shrugged. "He's very good software. I tell you, he's got autonomy, he's got volition. He's got an electronic *mind*, is what I'm saying. He may have perceived a transient voltage kick. But there are limits to his perceptions, all the same. I don't think there's any way that he can see anything that's outside the holotank unless it's fed to him in the form of data he can process, which hasn't been done."

"You don't *think*? You aren't sure?"

"Harry. Please."

"This man conquered the entire enormous Incan empire with fifty soldiers, didn't he?"

"In fact I believe it was more like a hundred and fifty."

"Fifty, a hundred fifty, what's the difference? Who knows what you've actually got here? What if you did an even better job than you suspect?"

"What are you saying?"

"What I'm saying is, I'm uneasy all of a sudden. For a long time I didn't think this project was going to produce anything at all. Suddenly I'm starting to think that maybe it's going to produce more than we can handle. I don't want any of your goddamned simulations walking out of the tank and conquering *us*."

Richardson turned to him. His face was flushed, but he was grinning. "Harry, Harry! For God's sake! Five minutes ago you didn't think we had anything at all here except a tiny picture that wasn't even in focus. Now you've gone so far the other way that you're imagining the worst kind of—"

"I see his eyes, Lew. I'm worried that his eyes see me."

"Those aren't real eyes you're looking at. What you see is nothing but a graphics program projected into a holotank. There's no visual capacity there as you understand the concept. His eyes will see you only if I want them to. Right now they don't."

"But you can make them see me?"

"I can make them see anything I want them to see. I created him, Harry."

"With volition. With autonomy."

"After all this time you start worrying *now* about these things?"

"It's my neck on the line if something that you guys on the technical side make runs amok. This autonomy thing suddenly troubles me."

"I'm still the one with the data gloves," Richardson said. "I twitch my fingers and he dances. That's not really Pizarro down there, remember. And that's no Frankenstein monster either. It's just a simulation. It's just so much data, just a bunch of electromagnetic impulses that I can shut off with one movement of my pinkie."

"Do it, then."

"Shut him off? But I haven't begun to show you—"

"Shut him off, and then turn him on," Tanner said.

Richardson looked bothered. "If you say so, Harry."

He moved a finger. The image of Pizarro vanished

from the holotank. Swirling gray mists moved in it for a moment, and then all was white wool. Tanner felt a quick jolt of guilt, as though he had just ordered the execution of the man in the medieval armor. Richardson gestured again, and color flashed across the tank, and then Pizarro reappeared.

"I just wanted to see how much autonomy your little guy really has," said Tanner. "Whether he was quick enough to head you off and escape into some other channel before you could cut his power."

"You really don't understand how this works at all, do you, Harry?"

"I just wanted to see," said Tanner again, sullenly. After a moment's silence he said, "Do you ever feel like God?"

"Like God?"

"You breathed life in. Life of a sort, anyway. But you breathed free will in, too. That's what this experiment is all about, isn't it? All your talk about volition and autonomy? You're trying to re-create a human mind—which means to create it all over again—a mind that can think in its own special way, and come up with its own unique responses to situations, which will not necessarily be the responses that its programmers might anticipate, in fact almost certainly will not be, and which might not be all that desirable or beneficial, either, and you simply have to allow for that risk, just as God, once he gave free will to mankind, knew that He was likely to see all manner of evil deeds being performed by His creations as they exercised that free will—"

"Please, Harry—"

"Listen, is it possible for me to talk with your Pizarro?"

"Why?"

"By way of finding out what you've got there. To get some first-hand knowledge of what the project has accomplished. Or you could say I just want to test the quality of the simulation. Whatever. I'd feel more a part of this thing, more aware of what it's all about in here, if I could have some direct contact with him. Would it be all right if I did that?"

"Yes. Of course."

"Do I have to talk to him in Spanish?"

"In any language you like. There's an interface, after all. He'll think it's his own language coming in, no matter what, sixteenth-century Spanish. And he'll answer you in what seems like Spanish to him, but you'll hear it in English."

"Are you sure?"

"Of course."

"And you don't mind if I make contact with him?"

"Whatever you like."

"It won't upset his calibration, or anything?"

"It won't do any harm at all, Harry."

"Fine. Let me talk to him, then."

There was a disturbance in the air ahead, a shifting, a swirling, like a little whirlwind. Pizarro halted and watched it for a moment, wondering what was coming next. A demon arriving to torment him, maybe. Or an angel. Whatever it was, he was ready for it.

Then a voice out of the whirlwind said, in that same comically exaggerated Castilian Spanish that Pizarro himself had found himself speaking a little while before, "Can you hear me?"

"I hear you, yes. I don't see you. Where are you?"

"Right in front of you. Wait a second. I'll show you." Out of the whirlwind came a strange face that hovered in the middle of nowhere, a face without a body, a lean face, close-shaven, no beard at all, no mustache, the hair cut very short, dark eyes set close together. He had never seen a face like that before.

"What are you?" Pizarro asked. "A demon or an angel?"

"Neither one." Indeed he didn't sound very demonic. "A man, just like you."

"Not much like me, I think. Is a face all there is to you, or do you have a body, too?"

"All you see of me is a face?"

"Yes."

"Wait a second."

"I will wait as long as I have to. I have plenty of time."

The face disappeared. Then it returned, attached to the body of a big, wide-shouldered man who was wearing a long loose gray robe, something like a priest's cassock, but much more ornate, with points of glowing light gleaming on it everywhere. Then the body vanished and Pizarro could see only the face again. He could make no sense out of any of this. He began to understand how the Indians must have felt when the first Spaniards came over the horizon, riding horses, carrying guns, wearing armor.

"You are very strange. Are you an Englishman, maybe?"

"American."

"Ah," Pizarro said, as though that made things better. "An American. And what is that?"

The face wavered and blurred for a moment. There was mysterious new agitation in the thick white clouds surrounding it. Then the face grew steady and said, "America is a country north of Peru. A very large country, where many people live."

"You mean New Spain, which was Mexico, where my kinsman Cortés is Captain-General?"

"North of Mexico. Far to the north of it."

Pizarro shrugged. "I know nothing of those places. Or not very much. There is an island called Florida, yes? And stories of cities of gold, but I think they are only stories. I found the gold, in Peru. Enough to choke on, I found. Tell me this, am I in heaven now?"

"No."

"Then this is hell?"

"Not that, either. Where you are—it's very difficult to explain, actually—"

"I am in America."

"Yes. In America, yes."

"And am I dead?"

There was silence for a moment.

"No, not dead," the voice said uneasily.

"You are lying to me, I think."

"How could we be speaking with each other, if you were dead?"

Pizarro laughed hoarsely. "Are you asking *me*? I understand nothing of what is happening to me in this place. Where are my priests? Where is my page? Send me my brother!" He glared. "Well? Why don't you get them for me?"

"They aren't here. You're here all by yourself, Don Francisco."

"In America. All by myself in your America. Show me your America, then. Is there such a place? Is America all clouds and whorls of light? Where is America? Let me see America. Prove to me that I am in America."

There was another silence, longer than the last. Then the face disappeared and the wall of white cloud began to boil and churn more fiercely than before. Pizarro stared into the midst of it, feeling a mingled sense of curiosity and annoyance. The face did not reappear. He saw nothing at all. He was being toyed with. He was a prisoner in some strange place and they were treating him like a child, like a dog, like—like an Indian. Perhaps this was the retribution for what he had done to King Atahuallpa, then, that fine noble foolish man who had given himself up to him in all innocence, and whom he had put to death so that he might have the gold of Atahuallpa's kingdom.

Well, so be it, Pizarro thought. Atahuallpa accepted all that befell him without complaint and without fear, and so will I. Christ will be my guardian, and if there is no Christ, well, then I will have no guardian, and so be it. So be it.

The voice out of the whirlwind said suddenly, "Look, Don Francisco. This is America."

A picture appeared on the wall of cloud. It was a kind of picture Pizarro had never before encountered or even imagined, one that seemed to open before him like a

gate and sweep him in and carry him along through a
vista of changing scenes depicted in brilliant, vivid bursts
of color. It was like flying high above the land, looking
down on an infinite scroll of miracles. He saw vast cities
without walls, roadways that unrolled like endless skeins
of white ribbon, huge lakes, mighty rivers, gigantic mountains, everything speeding past him so swiftly that he
could scarcely absorb any of it. In moments it all became
chaotic in his mind: the buildings taller than the highest
cathedral spire, the swarming masses of people, the shining metal chariots without beasts to draw them, the stu-
pendous landscapes, the close-packed complexity of it
all. Watching all this, he felt the fine old hunger taking
possession of him again: he wanted to grasp this strange
vast place, and seize it, and clutch it close, and ransack
it for all it was worth. But the thought of that was overwhelming. His eyes grew glassy and his heart began to
pound so terrifyingly that he supposed he would be able
to feel it thumping if he put his hand to the front of his
armor. He turned away, muttering, "Enough. Enough."

The terrifying picture vanished. Gradually the clamor
of his heart subsided.

Then he began to laugh.

"Peru!" he cried. "Peru was nothing, next to your
America! Peru was a hole! Peru was mud! How ignorant
I was! I went to Peru, when there was America, ten
thousand times as grand! I wonder what I could find, in
America." He smacked his lips and winked. Then, chuckling, he said, "But don't be afraid. I won't try to conquer
your America. I'm too old for that now. And perhaps
America would have been too much for me, even before.
Perhaps." He grinned savagely at the troubled staring
face of the short-haired beardless man, the American. "I
really am dead, is this not so? I feel no hunger, I feel
no pain, no thirst, when I put my hand to my body I do
not feel even my body. I am like one who lies dreaming.
But this is no dream. Am I a ghost?"

"Not—exactly."

"Not exactly a ghost! Not exactly! No one with half

the brains of a pig would talk like that. What is that supposed to mean?"

"It's not easy explaining it in words you would understand, Don Francisco."

"No, of course not. I am very stupid, as everyone knows, and that is why I conquered Peru, because I was so very stupid. But let it pass. I am not exactly a ghost, but I am dead all the same, right?"

"Well—"

"I am dead, yes. But somehow I have not gone to hell or even to purgatory but I am still in the world, only it is much later now. I have slept as the dead sleep, and now I have awakened in some year that is far beyond my time, and it is the time of America. Is this not so? Who is king now? Who is pope? What year is this? 1750? 1800?"

"The year 2130," the face said, after some hesitation.

"Ah." Pizarro tugged thoughtfully at his lower lip. "And the king? Who is king?"

A long pause. "Alfonso is his name," said the face.

"Alfonso? The kings of Aragon were called Alfonso. The father of Ferdinand, he was Alfonso. Alfonso V, he was."

"Alfonso XIX is King of Spain now."

"Ah. Ah. And the pope? Who is pope?"

A pause again. Not to know the name of the pope, immediately upon being asked? How strange. Demon or no, this was a fool.

"Pius," said the voice, when some time had passed. "Pius XVI."

"The sixteenth Pius," said Pizarro somberly. "Jesus and Mary, the sixteenth Pius! What has become of me? Long dead, is what I am. Still unwashed of all my sins. I can feel them clinging to my skin like mud, still. And you are a sorcerer, you American, and you have brought me to life again. Eh? Eh? Is that not so?"

"It is something like that, Don Francisco," the face admitted.

"So you speak your Spanish strangely because you no

longer understand the right way of speaking it. Eh? Even I speak Spanish in a strange way, and I speak it in a voice that does not sound like my own. No one speaks Spanish any more, eh? Eh? Only American, they speak. Eh? But you try to speak Spanish, only it comes out stupidly. And you have caused me to speak the same way, thinking it is the way I spoke, though you are wrong. Well, you can do miracles, but I suppose you can't do everything perfectly, even in this land of miracles of the year 2130. Eh? Eh?" Pizarro leaned forward intently. "What do you say? You thought I was a fool, because I don't have reading and writing? I am not so ignorant, eh? I understand things quickly."

"You understand very quickly indeed."

"But you have knowledge of many things that are unknown to me. You must know the manner of my death, for example. How strange that is, talking to you of the manner of my death, but you must know it, eh? When did it come to me? And how? Did it come in my sleep? No, no, how could that be? They die in their sleep in Spain, but not in Peru. How was it, then? I was set upon by cowards, was I? Some brother of Atahuallpa, falling upon me as I stepped out of my house? A slave sent by the Inca Manco, or one of those others? No. No. The Indians would not harm me, for all that I did to them. It was the young Almagro who took me down, was it not, in vengeance for his father, or Juan de Herrada, eh? or perhaps even Picado, my own secretary—no, not Picado, he was my man, always—but maybe Alvarado, the young one, Diego—well, one of those, and it would have been sudden, very sudden or I would have been able to stop them—am I right, am I speaking the truth? Tell me. You know these things. Tell me of the manner of my dying." There was no answer. Pizarro shaded his eyes and peered into the dazzling pearly whiteness. He was no longer able to see the face of the American. "Are you there?" Pizarro said. "Where have you gone? Were you only a dream? American! American! Where have you gone?"

*   *   *

The break in contact was jolting. Tanner sat rigid, hands trembling, lips tightly clamped. Pizarro, in the holotank, was no more than a distant little streak of color now, no larger than his thumb, gesticulating amid the swirling clouds. The vitality of him, the arrogance, the fierce probing curiosity, the powerful hatreds and jealousies, the strength that had come from vast ventures recklessly conceived and desperately seen through to triumph, all the things that were Francisco Pizarro, all that Tanner had felt an instant before—all that had vanished at the flick of a finger.

After a moment or two Tanner felt the shock beginning to ease. He turned toward Richardson.

"What happened?"

"I had to pull you out of there. I didn't want you telling him anything about how he died."

"I don't know how he died."

"Well, neither does he, and I didn't want to chance it that you did. There's no predicting what sort of psychological impact that kind of knowledge might have on him."

"You talk about him as though he's alive."

"Isn't he?" Richardson said.

"If I said a thing like that, you'd tell me that I was being ignorant and unscientific."

Richardson smiled faintly. "You're right. But somehow I trust myself to know what I'm saying when I say that he's alive. I know I don't mean it literally and I'm not sure about you. What did you think of him, anyway?"

"He's amazing," Tanner said. "Really amazing. The strength of him—I could feel it pouring out at me in waves. And his mind! So quick, the way he picked up on everything. Guessing that he must be in the future. Wanting to know what number pope was in office. Wanting to see what America looked like. And the cockiness of him! Telling me that he's not up to the conquest of America, that he might have tried for it instead of Peru a few years earlier, but not now, now he's a little too old for that. Incredible! Nothing could faze him for long, even when he realized that he must have been dead for a long time. Wanting to know how he died, even!" Tanner frowned. "What age did you make him, anyway, when you put this program together?"

"About sixty. Five or six years after the conquest, and a year or two before he died. At the height of his power, that is."

"I suppose you couldn't have let him have any knowledge of his actual death. That way he'd be too much like some kind of a ghost."

"That's what we thought. We set the cutoff at a time when he had done everything that he had set out to do, when he was the complete Pizarro. But before the end. He didn't need to know about that. Nobody does. That's why I had to yank you, you see? In case you knew. And started to tell him."

Tanner shook his head. "If I ever knew, I've forgotten it. How did it happen?"

"Exactly as he guessed: at the hands of his own comrades."

"So he saw it coming."

"At the age we made him, he already knew that a civil war had started in South America, that the conquistadores were quarreling over the division of the spoils. We built that much into him. He knows that his partner Almagro has turned against him and been beaten in battle, and that they've executed him. What he doesn't know, but obviously can expect, is that Almagro's friends are going to break into his house and try to kill him. He's got it all figured out pretty much as it's going to happen. As it *did* happen, I should say."

"Incredible. To be that shrewd."

"He was a son of a bitch, yes. But he was a genius, too."

"Was he, really? Or is it that you made him one when you set up the program for him?"

"All we put in were the objective details of his life, patterns of event and response. Plus an overlay of commentary by others, his contemporaries and later historians familiar with the record, providing an extra dimension of character density. Put in enough of that kind of stuff and apparently they add up to the whole personality. It isn't *my* personality or that of anybody else who worked on this project, Harry. When you put in Pizarro's set of events and responses you wind up getting Pizarro. You get the ruthlessness and you get the brilliance. Put in a different set, you get someone else. And what we've finally seen, this time, is that when we do our work right we get something out of the computer that's bigger than the sum of what we put in."

"Are you sure?"

Richardson said, "Did you notice that he complained about the Spanish that he thought you were speaking?"

"Yes. He said that it sounded strange, that nobody seemed to know how to speak proper Spanish any more. I didn't quite follow that. Does the interface you built speak lousy Spanish?"

"Evidently it speaks lousy sixteenth-century Spanish," Richardson said. "Nobody knows what sixteenth-century Spanish actually sounded like. We can only guess. Apparently we didn't guess very well."

"But how would *he* know? You synthesized him in the first place! If you don't know how Spanish sounded in his time, how would he? All he should know about Spanish, or about anything, is what you put into him."

"Exactly," Richardson said.

"But that doesn't make any sense, Lew!"

"He also said that the Spanish he heard himself speaking was no good, and that his own voice didn't sound right to him either. That we had *caused* him to speak this way, thinking that was how he actually spoke, but we were wrong."

"How could he possibly know what his voice really sounded like, if all he is is a simulation put together by people who don't have the slightest notion of what his voice really—"

"I don't have any idea," said Richardson quietly. "But he *does* know."

"Does he? Or is this just some diabolical Pizarro-like game that he's playing to unsettle us, because *that's* in his character as you devised it?"

"I think he does know," Richardson said.

"Where's he finding it out, then?"

"It's there. We don't know where, but he does. It's somewhere in the data that we put through the permutation network, even if we don't know it and even though we couldn't find it now if we set out to look for it. *He* can find it. He can't manufacture that kind of knowledge by magic, but he can assemble what look to us like seemingly irrelevant bits and come up with new information leading to a conclusion which is meaningful to him. That's what we mean by artificial intelligence, Harry. We've finally got a program that works something like the human brain: by leaps of intuition so sudden and broad that they seem inexplicable and non-quantifiable, even if they really aren't. We've fed in enough stuff so that he can assimilate a whole stew of ostensibly unrelated data and come up with new information. We don't just have a ventriloquist's dummy in that tank. We've got something that thinks it's Pizarro and thinks like Pizarro and knows things that Pizarro knew and we don't. Which means we've accomplished the qualitative jump in artificial intelligence capacity that we set out to achieve with this project. It's awesome. I get shivers down my back when I think about it."

"I do too," Tanner said. "But not so much from awe as fear."

"Fear?"

"Knowing now that he has capabilities beyond those he was programmed for, how can you be so absolutely certain that he can't comandeer your network somehow and get himself loose?"

"It's technically impossible. All he is is electromagnetic impulses. I can pull the plug on him any time I like. There's nothing to panic over here. Believe me, Harry."

"I'm trying to."

"I can show you the schematics. We've got a phenomenal

simulation in that computer, yes. But it's still only a simulation. It isn't a vampire, it isn't a werewolf, it isn't anything supernatural. It's just the best damned computer simulation anyone's ever made."

"It makes me uneasy. *He* makes me uneasy."

"He should. The power of the man, the indomitable nature of him—why do you think I summoned him up, Harry? He's got something that we don't understand in this country any more. I want us to study him. I want us to try to learn what that kind of drive and determination is really like. Now that you've talked to him, now that you've touched his spirit, of course you're shaken up by him. He radiates tremendous confidence. He radiates fantastic faith in himself. That kind of man can achieve anything he wants—even conquer the whole Inca empire with a hundred fifty men, or however many it was. But I'm not frightened of what we've put together here. And you shouldn't be either. We should all be damned proud of it. You as well as the people on the technical side. And you will be, too."

"I hope you're right," Tanner said.

"You'll see."

For a long moment Tanner stared in silence at the holotank, where the image of Pizarro had been.

"Okay," said Tanner finally. "Maybe I'm overreacting. Maybe I'm sounding like the ignoramus layman that I am. I'll take it on faith that you'll be able to keep your phantoms in their boxes."

"We will," Richardson said.

"Let's hope so. All right," said Tanner. "So what's your next move?"

Richardson looked puzzled. "My next move?"

"With this project. Where does it go from here?"

Hesitantly Richardson said, "There's no formal proposal yet. We thought we'd wait until we had approval from you on the initial phase of the work, and then—"

"How does this sound?" Tanner asked. "I'd like to see you start in on another simulation right away."

"Well—yes, yes, of course—"

"And when you've got him worked up, Lew, would it be feasible for you to put him right there in the tank with Pizarro?"

Richardson looked startled. "To have a sort of dialog with him, you mean?"

"Yes."

"I suppose we could do that," Richardson said cautiously. "*Should* do that. Yes. Yes. A very interesting suggestion, as a matter of fact." He ventured an uneasy smile. Up till now Tanner had kept in the background of this project, a mere management functionary, an observer, virtually an outsider. This was something new, his interjecting himself into the planning process, and plainly Richardson didn't know what to make of it. Tanner watched him fidget. After a little pause Richardson said, "Was there anyone particular you had in mind for us to try next?"

"Is that new parallax thing of yours ready to try?" Tanner asked. "The one that's supposed to compensate for time distortion and myth contamination?"

"Just about. But we haven't tested—"

"Good," Tanner said. "Here's your chance. What about trying for Socrates?"

There was billowing whiteness below him, and on every side, as though all the world were made of fleece. He wondered if it might be snow. That was not something he was really familiar with. It snowed once in a great while in Athens, yes, but usually only a light dusting that melted in the morning sun. Of course he had seen snow aplenty when he had been up north in the war, at Potidaea, in the time of Pericles. But that had been long ago; and that stuff, as best he remembered it, had not been much like this. There was no quality of coldness about the whiteness that surrounded him now. It could just as readily be great banks of clouds.

But what would clouds be doing *below* him? Clouds, he thought, are mere vapor, air and water, no substance to them at all. Their natural place was overheard. Clouds that gathered at one's feet had no true quality of cloudness about them.

Snow that had no coldness? Clouds that had no buoyancy? Nothing in this place seemed to possess any quality that was proper to itself in this place, including himself. He seemed to be walking, but his feet touched nothing at all. It was more like moving through air. But how could one move in the air? Aristophanes, in that mercilessly mocking play of his, had sent him floating through the clouds suspended in a basket, and made him say things like, "I am traversing the air and contemplating the sun." That was Aristophanes' way of playing with him, and he had not been seriously upset, though his friends had been very hurt on his behalf. Still, that was only a play.

This felt real, insofar as it felt like anything at all.

Perhaps he was dreaming, and the nature of his dream was that he thought he was really doing the things he had done in Aristophanes' play. What was that lovely line? "I have to suspend my brain and mingle the subtle essence of my mind with this air, which is of the same nature, in order clearly to penetrate the things of heaven." Good old Aristophanes! Nothing was sacred to him! Except, of course, those things that were truly sacred, such as wisdom, truth, virtue. "I would have discovered nothing if I had remained on the ground and pondered from below the things that are above: for the earth by its force attracts the sap of the mind to itself. It's the same way with watercress." And Socrates began to laugh.

He held his hands before him and studied them, the short sturdy fingers, the thick powerful wrists. His hands, yes. His old plain hands that had stood him in good stead all his life, when he had worked as a stonemason as his father had, when he had fought in his city's wars, when he had trained at the gymnasium. But now when he touched them to his face he felt nothing. There should be a chin here, a forehead, yes, a blunt stubby nose, thick lips; but there was nothing. He was touching air.

He could put his hand right through the place where his face should be. He could put one hand against the other, and press with all his might, and feel nothing.

This is a very strange place indeed, he thought.

Perhaps it is that place of pure forms that young Plato liked to speculate about, where everything is perfect and nothing is quite real. Those are ideal clouds all around me, not real ones. This is ideal air upon which I walk. I myself am the ideal Socrates, liberated from my coarse ordinary body. Could it be? Well, maybe so. He stood for a while, considering that possibility. The thought came to him that this might be the life after life, in which case he might meet some of the gods, if there were any gods in the first place, and if he could manage to find them. I would like that, he thought. Perhaps they would be willing to speak with me. Athena would discourse with me on wisdom, or Hermes on speed, or Ares on the nature of courage, or Zeus on—well, whatever Zeus cared to speak on. Of course I would seem to be the merest fool to them, but that would be all right: anyone who expects to hold discourse with the gods as though he were their equal *is* a fool. I have no such illusion. If there are gods at all, surely they are far superior to me in all respects, for otherwise why would men regard them as gods?

Of course he had serious doubts that the gods existed at all. But if they did, it was reasonable to think that they might be found in a place such as this.

He looked up. The sky was radiant with brilliant golden light. He took a deep breath and smiled and set out across the fleecy nothingness of this airy world to see if he could find the gods.

Tanner said, "What do you think now? Still so pessimistic?"

"It's too early to say," said Richardson, looking glum.

"He *looks* like Socrates, doesn't he?"

"That was the easy part. We've got plenty of descriptions of Socrates that came down from people who knew him, the flat wide nose, the bald head, the thick lips, the short neck. A standard Socrates face that everybody recognizes, just as they do Sherlock Holmes, or Don Quixote. So that's how we made him look. It doesn't signify anything important. It's what's going on inside his head that'll determine whether we really have Socrates."

"He seems calm and good-humored as he wanders around in there. The way a philosopher should."

"Pizarro seemed just as much of a philosopher when we turned him loose in the tank."

"Pizarro may *be* just as much of a philosopher," Tanner said. "Neither man's the sort who'd be likely to panic if he found himself in some mysterious place." Richardson's negativism was beginning to bother him. It was as if the two men had exchanged places: Richardson now uncertain of the range and power of his own program, Tanner pushing the way on and on toward bigger and better things.

Bleakly Richardson said, "I'm still pretty skeptical. We've tried the new parallax filters, yes. But I'm afraid we're going to run into the same problem the French did with Don Quixote, and that we did with Holmes and Moses and Caesar. There's too much contamination of the data by myth and fantasy. The Socrates who has come down to us is as much fictional as real, or maybe *all* fictional. For all we know, Plato made up everything we think we know about him, the same way Conan Doyle made up Holmes. And what we're going to get, I'm afraid, will be something second-hand, something lifeless, something lacking in the spark of self-directed intelligence that we're after."

"But the new filters—"

"Perhaps. Perhaps."

Tanner shook his head stubbornly. "Holmes and Don Quixote are fiction through and through. They exist in only one dimension, constructed for us by their authors. You cut through the distortions and fantasies of later readers and commentators and all you find underneath is a made-up character. A lot of Socrates may have been invented by Plato for his own purposes, but a lot wasn't. He really existed. He took an actual part in civic activities in fifth-century Athens. He figures in books by a lot of other contemporaries of his besides Plato's dialogues. That gives us the parallax you're looking for, doesn't it— the view of him from more than one viewpoint?"

"Maybe it does. Maybe not. We got nowhere with Moses. Was *he* fictional?"

"Who can say? All you had to go by was the Bible. And a ton of Biblical commentary, for whatever that was worth. Not much, apparently."

"And Caesar? You're not going to tell me that Caesar wasn't real," said Richardson. "But what we have of him is evidently contaminated with myth. When we synthesized him we got nothing but a caricature, and I don't have to remind you how fast even that broke down into sheer gibberish."

"Not relevant," Tanner said. "Caesar was early in the project. You know much more about what you're doing now. I think this is going to work."

Richardson's dogged pessimism, Tanner decided, must be a defense mechanism, designed to insulate himself against the possibility of a new failure. Socrates, after all, hadn't been Richardson's own choice. And this was the first time he had used these new enhancement methods, the parallax program that was the latest refinement of the process.

Tanner looked at him. Richardson remained silent.

"Go on," Tanner said. "Bring up Pizarro and let the two of them talk to each other. Then we'll find out what sort of Socrates you've conjured up here."

Once again there was a disturbance in the distance, a little dark blur on the pearly horizon, a blotch, a flaw in the gleaming whiteness. Another demon is arriving, Pizarro thought. Or perhaps it is the same one as before, the American, the one who liked to show himself only as a face, with short hair and no beard.

But as this one drew closer Pizarro saw that he was

different from the last, short and stocky, with broad shoulders and a deep chest. He was nearly bald and his thick beard was coarse and unkempt. He looked old, at least sixty, maybe sixty-five. He looked very ugly, too, with bulging eyes and a flat nose that had wide, flaring nostrils, and a neck so short that his oversized head seemed to sprout straight from his trunk. All he wore was a thin, ragged brown robe. His feet were bare.

"You, there," Pizarro called out. "You! Demon! Are you also an American, demon?"

"Your pardon. An Athenian, did you say?"

"*American* is what I said. That's what the last one was. Is that where you come from too, demon? America?"

A shrug. "No, I think not. I am of Athens." There was a curious mocking twinkle in the demon's eyes.

"A Greek? This demon is a Greek?"

"I am of Athens," the ugly one said again. "My name is Socrates, the son of Sophroniscus. I could not tell you what a Greek is, so perhaps I may be one, but I think not, unless a Greek is what you call a man of Athens." He spoke in a slow, plodding way, like one who was exceedingly stupid. Pizarro had sometimes met men like this before, and in his experience they were generally not as stupid as they wanted to be taken for. He felt caution rising in him. "And I am no demon, but just a plain man: very plain, as you can easily see."

Pizarro snorted. "You like to chop words, do you?"

"It is not the worst of amusements, my friend," said the other, and put his hands together behind his back in the most casual way, and stood there calmly, smiling, looking off into the distance, rocking back and forth on the balls of his feet.

"Well?" Tanner said. "Do we have Socrates or not? I say that's the genuine article there."

Richardson looked up and nodded. He seemed relieved and quizzical both at once. "So far so good, I have to say. He's coming through real and true."

"Yes."

"We may actually have worked past the problem of information contamination that ruined some of the earlier simulations. We're not getting any of the signal degradation we encountered then."

"He's some character, isn't he?" Tanner said. "I liked the way he just walked right up to Pizarro without the slightest sign of uneasiness. He's not at all afraid of him."

"Why should he be?" Richardson asked.

"Wouldn't you? If you were walking along through God knows what kind of unearthly place, not knowing where you were or how you got there, and suddenly you saw a ferocious-looking bastard like Pizarro standing in front of you wearing full armor and carrying a sword—" Tanner shook his head. "Well, maybe not. He's Socrates, after all, and Socrates wasn't afraid of anything except boredom."

"And Pizarro's just a simulation. Nothing but software."

"So you've been telling me all along. But Socrates doesn't know that."

"True," Richardson said. He seemed lost in thought a moment. "Perhaps there *is* some risk."

"Huh?"

"If our Socrates is anything like the one in Plato, and he surely ought to be, then he's capable of making a considerable pest of himself. Pizarro may not care for Socrates' little verbal games. If he doesn't feel like playing, I suppose there's a theoretical possibility that he'll engage in some sort of aggressive response."

That took Tanner by surprise. He swung around and said, "Are you telling me that there's some way he can *harm* Socrates?"

"Who knows?" said Richardson. "In the real world one program can certainly crash another one. Maybe one simulation can be dangerous to another one. This is all new territory for all of us, Harry. Including the people in the tank."

The tall grizzled-looking man said, scowling, "You tell me you're an Athenian, but not a Greek. What sense am

I supposed to make of that? I could ask Pedro de Candía, I guess, who is a Greek but not an Athenian. But he's not here. Perhaps you're just a fool, eh? Or you think I am."

"I have no idea what you are. Could it be that you are a god?"

"A *god?*"

"Yes," Socrates said. He studied the other impassively. His face was harsh, his gaze was cold. "Perhaps you are Ares. You have a fierce warlike look about you, and you wear armor, but not such armor as I have ever seen. This place is so strange that it might well be the abode of the gods, and that could be a god's armor you wear, I suppose. If you are Ares, then I salute you with the respect that is due you. I am Socrates of Athens, the stonemason's son."

"You talk a lot of nonsense. I don't know your Ares."

"Why, the god of war, of course! Everyone knows that. Except barbarians, that is. Are you a barbarian, then? You sound like one, I must say—but then, I seem to sound like a barbarian myself, and I've spoken the tongue of Hellas all my life. There are many mysteries here, indeed."

"Your language problem again," Tanner said. "Couldn't you even get classical Greek to come out right? Or are they both speaking Spanish to each other?"

"Pizarro thinks they're speaking Spanish. Socrates thinks they're speaking Greek. And of course the Greek is off. We don't know how *anything* that was spoken before the age of recordings sounded. All we can do is guess."

"But can't you—"

"Shhh," Richardson said.

Pizarro said, "I may be a bastard, but I'm no barbarian, fellow, so curb your tongue. And let's have no more blasphemy out of you either."

"If I blaspheme, forgive me. It is in innocence. Tell me where I trespass, and I will not do it again."

"This crazy talk of gods. Of my being a god. I'd expect a heathen to talk like that, but not a Greek. But maybe you're a heathen kind of Greek, and not to be blamed. It's heathens who see gods everywhere. Do I look like a god to you? I am Francisco Pizarro, of Trujillo in Estremadura, the son of the famous soldier Gonzalo Pizarro, colonel of infantry, who served in the wars of Gonzalo de Córdova whom men call the Great Captain. I have fought some wars myself."

"Then you are not a god but simply a soldier? Good. I too have been a soldier. I am more at ease with soldiers than with gods, as most people are, I would think."

"A soldier? You?" Pizarro smiled. This shabby ordinary little man, more bedraggled-looking than any self-respecting groom would be, a soldier? "In which wars?"

"The wars of Athens. I fought at Potidaea, where the Corinthians were making trouble, and withholding the tribute that was due us. It was very cold there, and the siege was long and bleak, but we did our duty. I fought again some years later at Delium against the Boeotians. Laches was our general then, but it went badly for us, and we did our best fighting in retreat. And then," Socrates said, "when Brasidas was in Amphipolis, and they sent Cleon to drive him out, I—"

"Enough," said Pizarro with an impatient wave of his hand. "These wars are unknown to me." A private soldier, a man of the ranks, no doubt. "Well, then this is the place where they send dead soldiers, I suppose."

"Are we dead, then?"

"Long ago. There's an Alfonso who's king, and a Pius who's pope, and you wouldn't believe their numbers. Pius the Sixteenth, I think the demon said. And the American said also that it is the year 2130. The last year that I can remember was 1539. What about you?"

The one who called himself Socrates shrugged again. "In Athens we use a different reckoning. But let us say, for argument's sake, that we are dead. I think that is very likely, considering what sort of place this seems to be, and how airy I find my body to be. So we have died, and this is the life after life. I wonder: is this a place where virtuous men are sent, or those who were not virtuous? Or do all men go to the same place after death, whether they were virtuous or not? What would you say?"

"I haven't figured that out yet," said Pizarro.

"Well, were you virtuous in your life, or not?"

"Did I sin, you mean?"

"Yes, we could use that word."

"Did I sin, he wants to know," said Pizarro, amazed. "He asks, Was I a sinner? Did I live a virtuous life? What business is that of his?"

"Humor me," said Socrates. "For the sake of the argument, if you will, allow me a few small questions—"

"So it's starting," Tanner said. "You see? You really *did* do it! Socrates is drawing him into a dialog!"

Richardson's eyes were glowing. "He is, yes. How marvelous this is, Harry!"

"Socrates is going to talk rings around him."

"I'm not so sure of that," Richardson said.

"I gave as good as I got," said Pizarro. "If I was injured, I gave injury back. There's no sin in that. It's only common sense. A man does what is necessary to survive and to protect his place in the world. Sometimes I might forget a fast-day, yes, or use the Lord's name in vain—those are sins, I suppose, Fray Vicente was always after me for things like that—but does that make me a sinner? I did my penances as soon as I could find time for them. It's a sinful world and I'm no different from anyone else, so why be harsh on me? Eh? God made me as I am. I'm done in His image. And I have faith in His Son."

"So you are a virtuous man, then?"

"I'm not a sinner, at any rate. As I told you, if ever I sinned I did my contrition, which made it the same as if the sin hadn't ever happened."

"Indeed," said Socrates. "Then you are a virtuous man and I have come to a good place. But I want to be absolutely sure. Tell me again: is your conscience completely clear?"

"What are you, a confessor?"

"Only an ignorant man seeking understanding. Which you can provide, by taking part with me in the exploration. If I have come to the place of virtuous men, then I must have been virtuous myself when I lived. Ease my mind, therefore, and let me know whether there is anything on your soul that you regret having done."

Pizarro stirred uneasily. "Well," he said, "I killed a king."

"A wicked one? An enemy of your city?"

"No. He was wise and kind."

"Then you have reason for regret indeed. For surely that is a sin, to kill a wise king."

"But he was a heathen."

"A what?"

"He denied God."

"He denied his own god?" said Socrates. "Then perhaps it was not so wrong to kill him."

"No. He denied mine. He *preferred* his own. And so he was a heathen. And all his people were heathens, since they followed his way. That could not be. They were at risk of eternal damnation because they followed him. I killed him for the sake of his people's souls. I killed him out of the love of God."

"But would you not say that all gods are the reflection of the one God?"

Pizarro considered that. "In a way, that's true, I suppose."

"And is the service of God not itself godly?"

"How could it be anything but godly, Socrates?"

"And you would say that one who serves his god faithfully according to the teachings of his god is behaving in a godly way?"

Frowning, Pizarro said, "Well—if you look at it that way, yes—"

"Then I think the king you killed was a godly man, and by killing him you sinned against God."

"Wait a minute!"

"But think of it: by serving his god he must also have served yours, for any servant of a god is a servant of the true God who encompasses all our imagined gods."

"No," said Pizarro sullenly. "How could he have been a servant of God? He knew nothing of Jesus. He had no understanding of the Trinity. When the priest offered him the Bible, he threw it to the ground in scorn. He was a heathen, Socrates. And so are you. You don't know anything of these matters at all, if you think that Atahuallpa was godly. Or if you think you're going to get me to think so."

"Indeed I have very little knowledge of anything. But you say he was a wise man, and kind?"

"In his heathen way."

"And a good king to his people?"

"So it seemed. They were a thriving people when I found them."

"Yet he was not godly."

"I told you. He had never had the sacraments, and in fact he spurned them right up until the moment of his death, when he accepted baptism. *Then* he came to be godly. But by then the sentence of death was upon him and it was too late for anything to save him."

"Baptism? Tell me what that is, Pizarro."

"A sacrament."

"And that is?"

"A holy rite. Done with holy water, by a priest. It admits one to Holy Mother Church, and brings forgiveness from sin both original and actual, and gives the gift of the Holy Spirit."

"You must tell me more about these things another time. So you made this good king godly by this baptism? And then you killed him?"

"Yes."

"But he was godly when you killed him. Surely, then, to kill him was a sin."

"He had to die, Socrates!"

"And why was that?" asked the Athenian.

"Socrates is closing in for the kill," Tanner said. "Watch this!"

"I'm watching. But there isn't going to be any kill," said Richardson. "Their basic assumptions are too far apart."

"You'll see."

"Will I?"

Pizarro said, "I've already told you why he had to die. It was because his people followed him in all things. And so they worshipped the sun, because he said the sun was God. Their souls would have gone to hell if we had allowed them to continue that way."

"But if they followed him in all things," said Socrates, "then surely they would have followed him into baptism, and become godly, and thus done that which was pleasing to you and to your god! Is that not so?"

"No," said Pizarro, twisting his fingers in his beard.

"Why do you think that?"

"Because the king agreed to be baptized only after we had sentenced him to death. He was in the way, don't you see? He was an obstacle to our power! So we had to get rid of him. He would never have led his people to the truth of his own free will. That was why we had to kill him. But we didn't want to kill his soul as well as his body, so we said to him, Look, Atahuallpa, we're going to put you to death, but if you let us baptize you we'll strangle you quickly, and if you don't we'll burn you alive and it'll be very slow. So of course he agreed to be baptized, and we strangled him. What choice was there for anybody? He had to die. He still didn't believe the true faith, as we all well knew. Inside his head he was as big a heathen as ever. But he died a Christian all the same."

"A what?"

"A Christian! A Christian! One who believes in Jesus Christ the Son of God!"

"The *son* of God," Socrates said, sounding puzzled. "And do Christians believe in God too, or only his son?"

"What a fool you are!"

"I would not deny that."

"There is God the Father, and God the Son, and then there is the Holy Spirit."

"Ah," said Socrates. "And which one did your Atahuallpa believe in, then, when the strangler came for him?"

"None of them."

"And yet he died a Christian? Without believing in any of your three gods? How is that?"

"Because of the baptism," said Pizarro in rising annoyance. "What does it matter what he believed? The priest sprinkled the water on him! The priest said the words! If the rite is properly performed, the soul is saved regardless of what the man understands or believes! How else could you baptize an infant? An infant understands nothing and believes nothing—but he becomes a Christian when the water touches him!"

"Much of this is mysterious to me," said Socrates. "But I see that you regard the king you killed as godly as well as wise, because he was washed by the water your gods require, and so you killed a good king who now lived in the embrace of your gods because of the baptism. Which seems wicked to me; and so this cannot be the place where the virtuous are sent after death, so it must be that I too was not virtuous, or else that I have misunderstood everything about this place and why we are in it."

"Damn you, are you trying to drive me crazy?" Pizarro roared, fumbling at the hilt of his sword. He drew it and waved it around in fury. "If you don't shut your mouth I'll cut you in thirds!"

"Uh-oh," Tanner said. "So much for the dialectical method."

*　　*　　*

Socrates said mildly, "It isn't my intention to cause you any annoyance, my friend. I'm only trying to learn a few things."

"You are a fool!"

"That is certainly true, as I have already acknowledged several times. Well, if you mean to strike me with your sword, go ahead. But I don't think it'll accomplish very much."

"Damn you," Pizarro muttered. He stared at his sword and shook his head. "No. No, it won't do any good, will it? It would go through you like air. But you'd just stand there and let me try to cut you down, and not even blink, right? Right?" He shook his head. "And yet you aren't stupid. You argue like the shrewdest priest I've ever known."

"In truth I am stupid," said Socrates. "I know very little at all. But I strive constantly to attain some understanding of the world, or at least to understand something of myself."

Pizarro glared at him. "No," he said. "I won't buy this false pride of yours. I have a little understanding of people myself, old man. I'm on to your game."

"What game is that, Pizarro?"

"I can see your arrogance. I see that you believe you're the wisest man in the world, and that it's your mission to go around educating poor sword-waving fools like me. And you pose as a fool to disarm your adversaries before you humiliate them."

"Score one for Pizarro," Richardson said. "He's wise to Socrates' little tricks, all right."

"Maybe he's read some Plato," Tanner suggested.

"He was illiterate."

"That was then. This is now."

"Not guilty," said Richardson. "He's operating on peasant shrewdness alone, and you damned well know it."

"I wasn't being serious," Tanner said. He leaned forward, peering toward the holotank. "God, what an astonishing thing this is, listening to them going at it. They seem absolutely real."

"They are," said Richardson.

"No, Pizarro, I am not wise at all," Socrates said. "But, stupid as I am, it may be that I am not the least wise man who ever lived."

"You think you're wiser than I am, don't you?"

"How can I say? First tell me how wise you are."

"Wise enough to begin my life as a bastard tending pigs and finish it as Captain-General of Peru."

"Ah, then you must be very wise."

"I think so, yes."

"Yet you killed a wise king because he wasn't wise enough to worship God the way you wished him to. Was that so wise of you, Pizarro? How did his people take it, when they found out that their king had been killed?"

"They rose in rebellion against us. They destroyed their own temples and palaces, and hid their gold and silver from us, and burned their bridges, and fought us bitterly."

"Perhaps you could have made some better use of him by *not* killing him, do you think?"

"In the long run we conquered them and made them Christians. It was what we intended to accomplish."

"But the same thing might have been accomplished in a wiser way?"

"Perhaps," said Pizarro grudgingly. "Still, we accomplished it. That's the main thing, isn't it? We did what we set out to do. If there was a better way, so be it. Angels do things perfectly. We were no angels, but we achieved what we came for, and so be it, Socrates. So be it."

"I'd call that one a draw," said Tanner.

"Agreed."

"It's a terrific game they're playing."

"I wonder who we can use to play it next," said Richardson.

"I wonder what we can do with this besides using it to play games," said Tanner.

"Let me tell you a story," said Socrates. "The oracle at Delphi once said to a friend of mine, 'There is no man wiser than Socrates,' but I doubted that very much, and it troubled me to hear the oracle saying something that I knew was so far from the truth. So I decided to look for a man who was obviously wiser than I was. There was a politician in Athens who was famous for his wisdom, and I went to him and questioned him about many things. After I had listened to him for a time, I came to see that though many people, and most of all he himself, thought that he was wise, yet he was not wise. He only imagined that he was wise. So I realized that I must be wiser than he. Neither of us knew anything that was really worthwhile, but he knew nothing and thought that he knew, whereas I neither knew anything nor thought that I did. At least on one point, then, I was wiser than he: I didn't think that I knew what I didn't know."

"Is this intended to mock me, Socrates?"

"I feel only the deepest respect for you, friend Pizarro. But let me continue. I went to other wise men, and they too, though sure of their wisdom, could never give me a clear answer to anything. Those whose reputations for wisdom were the highest seemed to have the least of it. I went to the great poets and playwrights. There was wisdom in their works, for the gods had inspired them, but that did not make *them* wise, though they thought that it had. I went to the stonemasons and potters and other craftsmen. They were wise in their own skills, but most of them seemed to think that that made them wise in everything, which did not appear to be the case. And so it went. I was unable to find anyone who showed true wisdom. So perhaps the oracle was right: that although I am an ignorant man, there is no man wiser than I am. But oracles often are right without there being much value in it, for I think that all she was saying was that no man is wise at all, that wisdom is reserved for the gods. What do you say, Pizarro?"

"I say that you are a great fool, and very ugly besides."

"You speak the truth. So, then, you are wise after all. And honest."

"Honest, you say? I won't lay claim to that. Honesty's a game for fools. I lied whenever I needed to. I cheated. I went back on my word. I'm not proud of that, mind you. It's simply what you have to do to get on in the world. You think I wanted to tend pigs all my life? I wanted gold, Socrates! I wanted power over men! I wanted fame!"

"And did you get those things?"

"I got them all."

"And were they gratifying, Pizarro?"

Pizarro gave Socrates a long look. Then he pursed his lips and spat.

"They were worthless."

"Were they, do you think?"

"Worthless, yes. I have no illusions about that. But still it was better to have had them than not. In the long run nothing has any meaning, old man. In the long run we're all dead, the honest man and the villain, the king and the fool. Life's a cheat. They tell us to strive, to conquer, to gain—and for what? What? For a few years of strutting around. Then it's taken away, as if it had never been. A cheat, I say." Pizarro paused. He stared at his hands as though he had never seen them before. "Did I say all that just now? Did I mean it?" He laughed. "Well, I suppose I did. Still, life is all there is, so you want as much of it as you can. Which means getting gold, and power, and fame."

"Which you had. And apparently have no longer. Friend Pizarro, where are we now?"

"I wish I knew."

"So do I," said Socrates soberly.

"He's real," Richardson said. "They both are. The bugs are out of the system and we've got something spectacu-

lar here. Not only is this going to be of value to scholars,
I think it's also going to be a tremendous entertainment
gimmick, Harry."

"It's going to be much more than that," said Tanner
in a strange voice.

"What do you mean by that?"

"I'm not sure yet," Tanner said. "But I'm definitely on
to something big. It just began to hit me a couple of
minutes ago, and it hasn't really taken shape yet. But it's
something that might change the whole goddamned
world."

Richardson looked amazed and bewildered.

"What the hell are you talking about, Harry?"

Tanner said, "A new way of settling political disputes,
maybe. What would you say to a kind of combat-at-arms
between one nation and another? Like a medieval tournament, so to speak. With each side using champions
that we simulate for them—the greatest minds of all the
past, brought back and placed in competition—" He
shook his head. "Something like that. It needs a lot of
working out, I know. But it's got possibilities."

"A medieval tournament—combat-at-arms, using simulations? Is that what you're saying?"

"Verbal combat. Not actual jousts, for Christ's sake."

"I don't see how—" Richardson began.

"Neither do I, not yet. I wish I hadn't even spoken
of it."

"But—"

"Later, Lew. Later. Let me think about it a little
while more."

"You don't have any idea what this place is?" Pizarro
said.

"Not at all. But I certainly think this is no longer the
world where we once dwelled. Are we dead, then? How
can we say? You look alive to me."

"And you to me."

"Yet I think we are living some other kind of life.

Here, give me your hand. Can you feel mine against yours?"

"No. I can't feel anything."

"Nor I. Yet I see two hands clasping. Two old men standing on a cloud, clasping hands." Socrates laughed. "What a great rogue you are, Pizarro!"

"Yes, of course. But do you know something, Socrates? You are too. A windy old rogue. I like you. There were moments when you were driving me crazy with all your chatter, but you amused me too. Were you really a soldier?"

"When my city asked me, yes."

"For a soldier, you're damned innocent about the way the world works, I have to say. But I guess I can teach you a thing or two."

"Will you?"

"Gladly," said Pizarro.

"I would be in your debt," Socrates said.

"Take Atahuallpa," Pizarro said. "How can I make you understand why I had to kill him? There weren't even two hundred of us, and twenty-four million of them, and his word was law, and once he was gone they'd have no one to command them. So of *course* we had to get rid of him if we wanted to conquer them. And so we did, and then they fell."

"How simple you make it seem."

"Simple is what it was. Listen, old man, he would have died sooner or later anyway, wouldn't he? This way I made his death useful: to God, to the Church, to Spain. And to Francisco Pizarro. Can you understand that?"

"I think so," said Socrates. "But do you think King Atahuallpa did?"

"Any king would understand such things."

"Then he should have killed you the moment you set foot in his land."

"Unless God meant us to conquer him, and allowed him to understand that. Yes. Yes, that must have been what happened."

"Perhaps he is in this place, too, and we could ask him," said Socrates.

Pizarro's eyes brightened. "Mother of God, yes! A good idea! And if he didn't understand, why, I'll try to explain it to him. Maybe you'll help me. You know how to talk, how to move words around and around. What do you say? Would you help me?"

"If we meet him, I would like to talk with him," Socrates said. "I would indeed like to know if he agrees with you on the subject of the usefulness of his being killed by you."

Grinning, Pizarro said, "Slippery, you are! But I like you. I like you very much. Come. Let's go look for Atahuallpa."

The heartland of science fiction has always been stories about life on other planets, from Robert A. Heinlein's Red Planet *and* Farmer in the Sky *to Ray Bradbury's* The Martian Chronicles *to Frank Herbert's* Dune. *These stories have always held the romantic fascination of faraway places, with strange sights and stranger customs, the exotic charm of Samarkand and Shangri-la and far Cathay. Sometimes, there is also the fascination of looking at ourselves, as in this complex story of murder and progress and duty on faraway Barrayar.*

Lois McMaster Bujold leaped into the field feet-first with a Nebula Award and a Hugo nomination for her novel Falling Free *in 1988, only a year after she'd been nominated for Best New Writer. The following year she won the Hugo for "The Mountains of Mourning," later collected in* Borders of Infinity. *She has since won the Best Novel Hugo for* The Vor Game *and for* Barrayar.

—Connie Willis

The Mountains of Mourning
by Lois McMaster Bujold

Miles heard the woman weeping as he was climbing the hill from the long lake. He hadn't dried himself after his swim, as the morning already promised shimmering heat. Lake water trickled cool from his hair onto his naked chest and back, more annoyingly down his legs from his ragged shorts. His leg braces chafed on his damp skin as he pistoned up the faint trail through the scrub, military double-time. His feet squished in his old wet shoes. He slowed curiously as he became conscious of the voices.

The woman's voice grated with grief and exhaustion. "Please, lord, please. All I want is m'justice . . ."

The front gate guard's voice was irritated and embarrassed. "I'm no lord. C'mon, get *up*, woman. Go back to the village and report it at the district magistrate's office."

"I tell you, I just came from there!" The woman did not move from her knees as Miles emerged from the bushes and paused to take in the tableau across the paved road. "The magistrate's not to return for weeks, weeks. I walked four days to get here. I only have a little money. . . ." A desperate hope rose in her voice, and her spine bent and straightened as she scrabbled in her skirt pocket and held out her cupped hands to the guard. "A mark and twenty pence, it's all I have, but—"

The exasperated guard's eye fell on Miles, and he

straightened abruptly, as if afraid Miles might suspect him of being tempted by so pitiful a bribe. "Be off, woman!" he snapped.

Miles quirked an eyebrow, and limped across the road to the main gate. "What's all this about, Corporal?" he inquired easily.

The guard corporal was on loan from Imperial Security, and wore the high-necked dress greens of the Barrayaran Service. He was sweating and uncomfortable in the bright morning light of this southern district, but Miles fancied he'd be boiled before he'd undo his collar on this post. His accent was not local, he was a city man from the capital, where a more-or-less efficient bureaucracy absorbed such problems as the one on her knees before him.

The woman, now, was local and more than local—she had backcountry written all over her. She was younger than her strained voice had at first suggested. Tall, feverred from her weeping, with stringy blonde hair hanging down across a ferret-thin face and protuberant grey eyes. If she were cleaned up, fed, rested, happy and confident, she might achieve a near-prettiness, but she was far from that now, despite her remarkable figure. Lean but full-breasted—no, Miles revised himself as he crossed the road and came up to the gate. Her bodice was all blotched with dried milk leaks, though there was no baby in sight. Only temporarily full-breasted. Her worn dress was factory-woven cloth, but hand-sewn, crude and simple. Her feet were bare, thickly-callused, cracked and sore.

"No problem," the guard assured Miles. "Go *away*," he hissed to the woman.

She lurched off her knees and sat stonily.

"I'll call my sergeant," the guard eyed her warily, "and have her removed."

"Wait a moment," said Miles.

She stared up at Miles from her cross-legged position, clearly not knowing whether to identify him as hope or not. His clothing, what there was of it, offered her no clue as to what he might be. The rest of him was all too plainly displayed. He jerked up his chin and smiled thinly. Too-large head, too-short neck, back thickened with its crooked spine, crooked legs with their brittle bones too-often broken, drawing the eye in their gleaming chromium braces. Were the hill woman standing, the top of his head would barely be even with the top of her shoulder. He waited in boredom for her hand to make the back-country hex sign against evil mutations, but it only jerked and clenched into a fist.

"I must see my Lord Count," she said to an uncertain point halfway between Miles and the guard. "It's my right. My daddy, he died in the Service. It's my right."

"Prime Minister Count Vorkosigan," said the guard stiffly, "is on his country estate to rest. If he were working, he'd be back in Vorbarr Sultana." The guard looked like he wished *he* were back in Vorbarr Sultana.

The woman seized the pause. "You're only a city man. He's *my* count. My right."

"What do you want to see Count Vorkosigan for?" asked Miles patiently.

"Murder," growled the girl/woman. The security guard spasmed slightly. "I want to report a murder."

"Shouldn't you report to your village speaker first?" inquired Miles, with a hand-down gesture to calm the twitching guard.

"I did. He'll do *nothing*." Rage and frustration cracked her voice. "He says it's over and done. He won't write down my accusation, says it's nonsense. It would only make trouble for everybody, he says. I don't care! I want my justice!"

Miles frowned thoughtfully, looking the woman over. The details checked, corroborated her claimed identity, added up to a solid if subliminal sense of authentic truth which perhaps escaped the professionally paranoid security man. "It's true, Corporal," Miles said. "She has a right to appeal, first to the district magistrate, then to the count's court. And the district magistrate won't be back for two weeks."

This sector of Count Vorkosigan's native district had only one overworked district magistrate, who rode a circuit that included the lakeside village of Vorkosigan Surleau but one day a month. Since the region of the Prime Minister's country estate was crawling with Imperial Security when the great lord was in residence, and closely monitored even when he was not, prudent troublemakers took their troubles elsewhere.

"Scan her, and let her in," said Miles. "On my authority."

The guard was one of Imperial Security's best, trained to look for assassins in his own shadow. He now looked scandalized, and lowered his voice to Miles. "Sir, if I let every country lunatic wander the estate at will—"

"I'll take her up. I'm going that way."

The guard shrugged helplessly, but stopped short of saluting; Miles was decidedly not in uniform. The gate guard pulled a scanner from his belt and made a great show of going over the woman. Miles wondered if he'd have been inspired to harass her with a strip-search without Miles's inhibiting presence. When the guard finished demonstrating how alert, conscientious, and loyal he was, he palmed open the gate's lock, entered the transaction, including the woman's retina scan, into the computer monitor, and stood aside in a pose of rather pointed parade rest. Miles grinned at the silent editorial, and steered the bedraggled woman by the elbow through the gates and up the winding drive.

She twitched away from his touch at the earliest opportunity, yet still refrained from superstitious gestures, eyeing him with a strange and hungry curiosity. Time was, such openly repelled fascination with the peculiarities of his body had driven Miles to grind his teeth; now he could take it with a serene amusement only slightly tinged with acid. They would learn, all of them. They would learn.

"Do you serve Count Vorkosigan, little man?" she asked cautiously.

Miles thought about that one a moment. "Yes," he

answered finally. The answer was, after all, true on every
level of meaning but the one she'd asked it. He quelled
the temptation to tell her he was the court jester. From
the look of her, this one's troubles were much worse
than his own.

She had apparently not quite believed in her own
rightful destiny, despite her mulish determination at the
gate, for as they climbed unimpeded toward her goal a
nascent panic made her face even more drawn and pale,
almost ill. "How—how do I talk to him?" she choked.
"Should I curtsey . . . ?" She glanced down at herself as
if conscious for the first time of her own dirt and sweat
and squalor.

Miles suppressed a facetious set-up starting with, *Kneel
and knock your forehead three times on the floor before
speaking, that's what the General Staff does,* and said
instead, "Just stand up straight and speak the truth. Try
to be clear. He'll take it from there. He does not, after
all," Miles's lips twitched, "lack experience."

She swallowed.

A hundred years ago, the Vorkosigans' summer retreat
had been a guard barracks, part of the outlying fortifica-
tions of the great castle on the bluff above the village of
Vorkosigan Surleau. The castle was now a burnt-out ruin,
and the barracks transformed into a comfortable low
stone residence, modernized and re-modernized, artisti-
cally landscaped and bright with flowers. The arrow slits
had been widened into big glass windows overlooking the
lake, and comm link antennae bristled from the roof.
There was a new guard barracks concealed in the trees
downslope, but it had no arrow slits.

A man in the brown-and-silver livery of the Count's
personal retainers exited the residence's front door as
Miles approached with the strange woman in tow. It was
the new man, what was his name? Pym, that was it.

"Where's m'lord Count?" Miles asked him.

"In the upper pavilion, taking breakfast with m'lady."
Pym glanced at the woman, waited on Miles in a posture
of polite inquiry.

"Ah. Well, this woman has walked four days to lay an appeal before the district magistrate's court. The court's not here, but the Count is, so she now proposes to skip the middlemen and go straight to the top. I like her style. Take her up, will you?"

"During *breakfast?*" said Pym.

Miles cocked his head at the woman. "Have you had breakfast?"

She shook her head mutely.

"I thought not." Miles turned his hands palm-out, dumping her, symbolically, on the retainer. "Now, yes."

"My daddy, he died in the Service," the woman repeated faintly. "It's my right." The phrase seemed as much to convince herself as anyone else, now.

Pym was, if not a hill man, district-born. "So it is," he sighed, and gestured her to follow him without further ado. Her eyes widened, as she trailed him around the house, and she glanced back nervously over her shoulder at Miles. "Little man . . . ?"

"Just stand straight," he called to her. He watched her round the corner, grinned, and took the steps two at a time into the residence's main entrance.

After a shave and cold shower, Miles dressed in his own room overlooking the long lake. He dressed with great care, as great as he'd expended on the Service Academy ceremonies and Imperial Review two days ago. Clean underwear, long-sleeved cream shirt, dark green trousers with the side piping. High-collared green tunic tailor-cut to his own difficult fit. New pale blue plastic ensign's rectangles aligned precisely on the collar and poking most uncomfortably into his jaw. He dispensed with the leg braces and pulled on mirror-polished boots to the knee, and swiped a bit of dust from them with his pajama pants, ready-to-hand on the floor where he'd dropped them before going swimming.

He straightened and checked himself in the mirror. His dark hair hadn't even begun to recover from that last cut before the graduation ceremonies. A pale, sharp-featured face, not too much dissipated bag under the grey eyes, nor too bloodshot—alas, the limits of his body compelled him to stop celebrating well before he could hurt himself.

Echoes of the late celebration still boiled up silently in his head, crooking his mouth into a grin. He was on his way now, had his hand clamped firmly around the lowest rung of the highest ladder on Barrayar, Imperial Service itself. There were no giveaways in the Service even for sons of the old Vor. You got what you earned. His brother-officers could be relied on to know that, even if outsiders wondered. He was in position at last to prove himself to all doubters. Up and away and never look down, never look back.

One last look back. As carefully as he'd dressed, Miles gathered up the necessary objects for his task. The white cloth rectangles of his former Academy cadet's rank. The hand-calligraphed second copy, purchased for this purpose, of his new officer's commission in the Barrayaran Imperial Service. A copy of his Academy three-year scholastic transcript on paper, with all its commendations (and demerits). No point in anything but honesty in this next transaction. In a cupboard downstairs he found the brass brazier and tripod, wrapped in its polishing cloth, and a plastic bag of very dry juniper bark. Chemical firesticks.

Out the back door and up the hill. The landscaped path split, right going up to the pavilion overlooking it all, left forking sideways to a garden-like area surrounded by a low fieldstone wall. Miles let himself in by the gate. "Good morning, crazy ancestors," he called, then quelled his humor. It might be true, but lacked the respect due the occasion.

He strolled over and around the graves until he came to the one he sought, knelt, and set up the brazier and tripod, humming. The stone was simple, *General Count Piotr Pierre Vorkosigan,* and the dates. If they'd tried to list all the accumulated honors and accomplishments, they'd have had to go to microprint.

He piled in the bark, the very expensive papers, the cloth bits, a clipped mat of dark hair from that last cut. He set it alight and rocked back on his heels to watch it burn. He'd played a hundred versions of this moment over in his head, over the years, ranging from solemn public orations with musicians in the background, to dancing naked on the old man's grave. He'd settled on this private and traditional ceremony, played straight. Just between the two of them.

"So, Grandfather," he purred at last. "And here we are after all. Satisfied now?"

All the chaos of the graduation ceremonies behind, all the mad efforts of the last three years, all the pain, came to this point; but the grave did not speak, did not say, *Well done; you can stop now.* The ashes spelled out no messages, there were no visions to be had in the rising smoke. The brazier burned down all too quickly. Not enough stuff in it, perhaps.

He stood, and dusted his knees, in the silence and the sunlight. So what had he expected? Applause? Why was he here, in the final analysis? Dancing out a dead man's dreams—who did his Service really serve? Grandfather? Himself? Pale Emperor Gregor? Who cared?

"Well, old man," he whispered, then shouted: "ARE YOU SATISFIED YET?" The echoes rang from the stones.

A throat cleared behind him, and Miles whirled like a scalded cat, heart pounding.

"Uh . . . my lord?" said Pym carefully. "Pardon me, I did not mean to interrupt . . . anything. But the Count your father requires you to attend on him in the upper pavilion."

Pym's expression was perfectly bland. Miles swallowed, and waited for the scarlet heat he could feel in his face to recede. "Quite," he shrugged. "The fire's almost out. I'll clean it up later. Don't . . . let anybody else touch it."

He marched past Pym and didn't look back.

The pavilion was a simple structure of weathered silver wood, open on all four sides to catch the breeze, this morning a few faint puffs from the west. Good sailing on the lake this afternoon, maybe. Only ten days precious home leave left, and much Miles wanted to do, including the trip to Vorbarr Sultana with his cousin Ivan to pick out his new lightflyer. And then his first assignment would be coming through—ship duty, Miles prayed. He'd had to overcome a major temptation, not to ask his father to make sure it was ship duty. He would take whatever assignment fate dealt him, that was the first rule of the game. And win with the hand he was dealt.

The interior of the pavilion was shady and cool after the glare outside. It was furnished with comfortable old chairs and tables, one of which bore the remains of a noble breakfast—Miles mentally marked two lonely-looking oil cakes on a crumb-scattered tray as his own. Miles's mother, lingering over her cup, smiled across the table at him.

Miles's father, casually dressed in an open-throated shirt and shorts, sat in a worn armchair. Aral Vorkosigan was a thick-set, grey-haired man, heavy-jawed, heavy-browed, scarred. A face that lent itself to savage caricature—Miles had seen some, in Opposition press, in the histories of Barrayar's enemies. They had only to draw one lie, to render dull those sharp penetrating eyes, to create everyone's parody of a military dictator.

And how much is he haunted by Grandfather? Miles wondered. He doesn't show it much. But then, he doesn't have to. Admiral Aral Vorkosigan, space master strategist, conquerer of Komarr, hero of Escobar, for sixteen years Imperial Regent and supreme power on Barrayar in all but name. And then he'd capped it, confounded history and all self-sure witnesses and heaped up honor and glory beyond all that had gone before by voluntarily stepping *down* and transferring command smoothly to Emperor Gregor upon his majority. Not that the Prime Ministership hadn't made a dandy retirement from the Regency, and he was showing no signs yet of stepping down from *that*.

And so Admiral Aral's life took General Piotr's like an

overpowering hand of cards, and where did that leave Ensign Miles? Holding two deuces and the joker. He must surely either concede or start bluffing like crazy. . . .

The hill woman sat on a hassock, a half-eaten oil cake clutched in her hands, staring open-mouthed at Miles in all his power and polish. As he caught and returned her gaze her lips pressed closed and her eyes lit. Her expression was strange—anger? Exhilaration? Embarrassment? Glee? Some bizarre mixture of all? *And what did you think I was, woman?*

Being in uniform (showing off his uniform?), Miles came to attention before his father. "Sir?"

Count Vorkosigan spoke to the woman. "That is my son. If I send him as my Voice, would that satisfy you?"

"Oh," she breathed, her wide mouth drawing back in a weird, fierce grin, the most expression Miles had yet seen on her face, "*yes*, my lord."

"Very well. It will be done."

What will be done? Miles wondered warily. The Count was leaning back in his chair, looking satisfied himself, but with a dangerous tension around his eyes hinting that something had aroused his true anger. Not anger at the woman, clearly they were in some sort of agreement, and—Miles searched his conscience quickly—not at Miles himself. He cleared his throat gently, cocking his head and baring his teeth in an inquiring smile.

The Count steepled his hands and spoke to Miles at last. "A most interesting case. I can see why you sent her up."

"Ah . . ." said Miles. What had he got hold of? He'd only greased the woman's way through Security on a quixotic impulse, for God's sake, and to tweak his father at breakfast. ". . . ah?" he continued noncommittally.

Count Vorkosigan's brows rose. "Did you not know?"

"She spoke of a murder, and a marked lack of cooperation from her local authorities about it. Figured you'd give her a lift on to the district magistrate."

The Count settled back still further, and rubbed his

hand thoughtfully across his scarred chin. "It's an infanticide case."

Miles's belly went cold. *I don't want anything to do with this.* Well, that explained why there was no baby to go with the breasts. "Unusual . . . for it to be reported."

"We've fought the old customs for twenty years and more," said the Count. "Promulgated, propagandized . . . In the cities, we've made good progress."

"In the cities," murmured the Countess, "people have access to alternatives."

"But in the backcountry—well—little has changed. We all know what's going on, but without a report, a complaint—and with the family invariably drawing together to protect its own—it's hard to get leverage."

"What," Miles cleared his throat, nodded at the woman, "what was your baby's mutation?"

"The cat's mouth," the woman dabbed at her upper lip to demonstrate. "She had the hole inside her mouth, too, and was a weak sucker, she choked and cried, but she was getting enough, she *was*. . . ."

"Hare-lip," the Count's off-worlder wife murmured half to herself, translating the Barrayaran term to the galactic standard, "and a cleft palate, sounds like. Harra, that's not even a mutation. They had that back on Old Earth. A . . . a normal birth defect, if that's not a contradiction in terms. Not a punishment for our Barrayaran ancestors' pilgrimage through the Fire. A simple operation could have corrected—" Countess Vorkosigan cut herself off. The hill woman was looking anguished.

"I'd heard," the woman said. "My lord had made a hospital to be built at Hassadar. I meant to take her there, when I was a little stronger, though I had no money. Her arms and legs were sound, her head was well-shaped, anybody could see—surely they would have—" her hands clenched and twisted, her voice went ragged, "but Lem killed her first."

A seven-day walk, Miles calculated, from the deep Dendarii Mountains to the lowland town of Hassadar. Reasonable, that a woman newly risen from childbed might delay that hike a few days. An hour's ride in an aircar. . . .

"So one is reported as a murder at last," said Count Vorkosigan, "and we will treat it as exactly that. This is a chance to send a message to the farthest corners of my own district. You, Miles, will be my Voice, to reach where it has not reached before. You will dispense Count's justice upon this man—and not quietly, either. It's time for the practices that brand us as barbarians in galactic eyes to end."

Miles gulped. "Wouldn't the district magistrate be better qualified . . . ?"

The Count smiled slightly. "For this case, I can think of no one better qualified than yourself."

The messenger and the message all in one; *Times have changed.* Indeed. Miles wished himself elsewhere, anywhere—back sweating blood over his final examinations, for instance. He stifled an unworthy wail, *My home leave . . . !*

Miles rubbed the back of his neck. "Who, ah . . . who is it killed your little girl?" *Meaning, who is it I'm expected to drag out, put up against a wall, and shoot?*

"My husband," she said tonelessly, looking at—through—the polished silvery floorboards.

I knew this was going to be messy. . . .

"She cried and cried," the woman went on, "and wouldn't go to sleep, not nursing well—he shouted at me to shut her up—"

"Then?" Miles prompted, sick to his stomach.

"He swore at me, and went to go sleep at his mother's. He said at least a working man could sleep there. I hadn't slept either. . . ."

This guy sounds like a real winner. Miles had an instant picture of him, a bull of a man with a bullying manner—nevertheless, there was something missing in the climax of the woman's story.

The Count had picked up on it too. He was listening with total attention, his strategy-session look, a slit-eyed intensity of thought you could mistake for sleepiness.

That would be a grave mistake. "Were you an eyewitness?" he asked in a deceptively mild tone that put Miles on full alert. "Did you actually see him kill her?"

"I found her dead in the midmorning, lord."

"You went into the bedroom—" Count Vorkosigan led her on.

"We've only got one room." She shot him a look as if doubtful for the first time of his total omniscience. "She had slept, slept at last. I went out to get some brillberries, up the ravine a way. And when I came back . . . I should have taken her with me, but I was so glad she slept at last, didn't want to risk waking her—" Tears leaked from the woman's tightly-closed eyes. "I let her sleep when I came back, I was glad to eat and rest, but I began to get full," her hand touched a breast, "and I went to wake her . . ."

"What, were there no marks on her? Not a cut throat?" asked the Count. That was the usual method for these backcountry infanticides, quick and clean compared to, say, exposure.

The woman shook her head. "Smothered, I think, lord. It was cruel, something cruel. The village Speaker said I must have overlain her, and wouldn't take my plea against Lem. I did not, I did not! She had her own cradle, Lem made it with his own hands when she was still in my belly. . . ." She was close to breaking down.

The Count exchanged a glance with his wife, and a small tilt of his head. Countess Vorkosigan rose smoothly.

"Come, Harra, down to the house. You must wash and rest before Miles takes you home."

The hill woman looked taken aback. "Oh, not in your house, lady!"

"Sorry, it's the only one I've got handy. Besides the guard barracks. The guards are good boys, but you'd make 'em uncomfortable . . ." The Countess eased her out.

"It is clear," said Count Vorkosigan as soon as the women were out of earshot, "that you will have to check out the medical facts before, er, popping off. And I trust

you will also have noticed the little problem with a positive identification of the accused. This could be the ideal
public-demonstration case we want, but not if there's any
ambiguity about it. No bloody mysteries."

"I'm not a coroner," Miles pointed out immediately.
If he could wriggle off this hook. . . .

"Quite. You will take Dr. Dea with you."

Lieutenant Dea was the Prime Minister's physician's
assistant. Miles had seen him around—an ambitious
young military doctor, in a constant state of frustration
because his superior would never let him touch his most
important patient—oh, he was going to be thrilled with
this assignment, Miles predicted morosely.

"He can take his osteo kit with him, too," the Count
went on, brightening slightly, "in case of accidents."

"How economical," said Miles, rolling his eyes. "Look,
uh—suppose her story checks out and we nail this guy.
Do I have to, personally . . . ?"

"One of the liveried men will be your bodyguard.
And—if the story checks—the executioner."

That was only slightly better. "Couldn't we wait for
the district magistrate?"

"Every judgment the district magistrate makes, he
makes in my place. Every sentence his office carries out,
is carried out in my name. Someday, it will be done in
your name. It's time you gained a clear understanding of
the process. Historically, the Vor may be a military caste,
but a Vor lord's duties were never only military ones."

No escape. Damn, damn, damn. Miles sighed. "Right.
Well . . . we could take the aircar, I suppose, and be up
there in a couple of hours. Allow some time to find the
right hole. Drop out of the sky on 'em, make the message
loud and clear . . . be back before bedtime." Get it over
with quickly.

The Count had that slit-eyed look again. "No . . ." he
said slowly, "not the aircar, I don't think."

"No roads for a groundcar, up that far. Just trails." He
added uneasily—surely his father could not be thinking

of—"I don't think I'd cut a very impressive figure of central Imperial authority on foot, sir."

His father glanced up at his crisp dress uniform and smiled slightly. "Oh, you don't do so badly."

"But picture this after three or four days of beating through the bushes," Miles protested. "You didn't see us in Basic. Or smell us."

"I've been there," said the Admiral dryly. "But no, you're quite right. Not on foot. I have a better idea."

My own cavalry troop, thought Miles ironically, turning in his saddle, *just like Grandfather*. Actually, he was pretty sure the old man would have had some acerbic comments about the riders now strung out behind Miles on the wooded trail, once he'd got done rolling on the ground laughing at the equitation being displayed. The Vorkosigan stables had shrunk sadly since the old man was no longer around to take an interest, the polo string sold off, the few remaining ancient and ill-tempered ex-cavalry beasts put permanently out to pasture. The handful of riding horses left were retained for their surefootedness and good manners, not their exotic bloodlines, and kept exercised and gentle for the occasional guest by a gaggle of girls from the village.

Miles gathered his reins, tensed one calf, and shifted his weight slightly, and Fat Ninny responded with a neat half turn and two precise back steps. The thickset roan gelding could not have been mistaken by the most ignorant urbanite for a fiery steed, but Miles adored him, for his dark and liquid eye, his wide velvet nose, his phlegmatic disposition equally unappalled by rushing streams or screaming aircars, but most of all for his exquisite dressage-trained responsiveness. Brains before beauty. Just being around him made Miles calmer, the beast was an emotional blotter, like a purring cat. Miles patted Fat Ninny on the neck. "If anybody asks," he murmured, "I'll tell them your name is Chieftan." Fat Ninny waggled one fuzzy ear, and heaved a wooshing, barrel-chested sigh.

Grandfather had a great deal to do with the unlikely parade Miles now led. The great guerrilla general had poured out his youth in these mountains, fighting the Cetagandan invaders to a standstill and then reversing their tide. Anti-flyer heatless seeker-strikers smuggled in at bloody cost from off-planet had a lot more to do with the final victory than cavalry horses, which, according to Grandfather, had saved his forces through the worst winter of that campaign mainly by being edible. But through retroactive romance, the horse had become the symbol of that struggle.

Miles thought his father was being overly optimistic, if he thought Miles was going to cash in thusly on the old man's residual glory. The guerrilla caches and camps were shapeless lumps of rust and *trees*, dammit, not just weeds and scrub anymore—they had passed some, earlier in today's ride—the men who had fought that war had long since gone to ground for the last time, just like Grandfather. What was he doing here? It was Jump ship duty he wanted, taking him high, high above all this. The future, not the past, held his destiny.

Miles's meditations were interrupted by Dr. Dea's horse, which, taking exception to a branch lying across the logging trail, planted all four feet in an abrupt stop and snorted loudly. Dr. Dea toppled off with a faint cry.

"Hang onto the *reins*," Miles called, and pressed Fat Ninny back down the trail.

Dr. Dea was getting rather better at falling off, he'd landed more-or-less on his feet this time. He made a lunge at the dangling reins, but his sorrel mare shied away from his grab. Dea jumped back as she swung on her haunches and then, realizing her freedom, bounced back down the trail, tail bannering, horse body-language for *Nyah, nyah, ya can't catch me!* Dr. Dea, red and furious, ran swearing in pursuit. She broke into a canter.

"No, no, don't run after her!" called Miles.

"How the hell am I supposed to catch her if I don't run after her?" snarled Dea. The space surgeon was not a happy man. "My medkit's on that bloody beast!"

"How do you think you can catch her if you do?"
asked Miles. "She can run faster than you can."

At the end of the little column, Pym turned his horse
sideways, blocking the trail. "Just wait, Harra," Miles
advised the anxious hill woman in passing. "Hold your
horse still. Nothing starts a horse running faster than
another running horse."

The other two riders were doing rather better. The
woman Harra Csurik sat her horse wearily, allowing it to
plod along without interference, but at least riding on
balance instead of trying to use the reins as a handle like
the unfortunate Dea. Pym, bringing up the rear, was
competent if not comfortable.

Miles slowed Fat Ninny to a walk, reins loose, and
wandered after the mare, radiating an air of calm relaxation. *Who, me? I don't want to catch you. We're just
enjoying the scenery, right. That's it, stop for a bite.* The
sorrel mare paused to nibble at a weed, but kept a wary
eye on Miles's approach.

At a distance just short of starting the mare bolting off
again, Miles stopped Fat Ninny and slid off. He made
no move toward the mare, but instead stood still and
made a great show of fishing in his pockets. Fat Ninny
butted his head against Miles eagerly, and Miles cooed
and fed him a bit of sugar. The mare cocked her ears
with interest. Fat Ninny smacked his lips and nudged for
more. The mare snuffled up for her share. She lipped a
cube from Miles's palm as he slid his other arm quietly
through the loop of her reins.

"Here you go, Dr. Dea. One horse. No running."

"No fair," wheezed Dea, trudging up. "You had sugar
in your pockets."

"Of course I had sugar in my pockets. It's called fore-
sight and planning. The trick of handling horses isn't to
be faster than the horse, or stronger than the horse. That
pits your weakness against his strengths. The trick is to
be smarter than the horse. That pits your strength against
his weakness, eh?"

Dea took his reins. "It's snickering at me," he said suspiciously.

"That's nickering, not snickering," Miles grinned. He tapped Fat Ninny behind his left foreleg, and the horse obediently grunted down onto one knee. Miles clambered up readily to his conveniently-lowered stirrup.

"Does mine do that?" asked Dr. Dea, watching with fascination.

"Sorry, no."

Dea glowered at his horse. "This animal is an idiot. I shall lead it for a while."

As Fat Ninny lurched back to his four feet Miles suppressed a riding-instructorly comment gleaned from his Grandfather's store such as *Be smarter than the horse, Dea.* Though Dr. Dea was officially sworn to Lord Vorkosigan for the duration of this investigation, Space Surgeon Lieutenant Dea certainly outranked Ensign Vorkosigan. To command older men who outranked one called for a certain measure of tact.

The logging road widened out here, and Miles dropped back beside Harra Csurik. Her fierceness and determination of yesterday morning at the gate seemed to be fading even as the trail rose toward her home. Or perhaps it was simply exhaustion catching up with her. She'd said little all morning, been sunk in silence all afternoon. If she was going to drag Miles all the way up to the back of beyond and then wimp out on him . . .

"What, ah, branch of the Service was your father in, Harra?" Miles began conversationally.

She raked her fingers through her hair in a combing gesture more nervousness than vanity. Her eyes looked out at him through the straw-colored wisps like skittish creatures in the protection of a hedge.

"District Militia, m'lord. I don't really remember him, he died when I was real little."

"In combat?"

She nodded. "In the fighting around Vorbarr Sultana, during Vordarian's Pretendership."

Miles refrained from asking which side he had been

swept up on—most footsoldiers had had little choice, and the amnesty had included the dead as well as the living.

"Ah . . . do you have any sibs?"

"No, lord. Just me and my mother left."

A little anticipatory tension eased in Miles's neck. If this judgment indeed drove all the way through to an execution, one misstep could trigger a blood feud among the in-laws. *Not* the legacy of justice the Count intended him to leave behind. So the fewer in-laws involved, the better. "What about your husband's family?"

"He's got seven. Four brothers and three sisters."

"Hm." Miles had a mental flash of an entire team of huge, menacing hill hulks. He glanced back at Pym, feeling a trifle understaffed for his task. He had pointed out this factor to the Count, when they'd been planning this expedition last night.

"The village Speaker and his deputies will be your back-up," the Count had said, "just as for the district magistrate on court circuit."

"What if they don't want to cooperate?" Miles had asked nervously.

"An officer who expects to command Imperial troops," the Count had glinted, "should be able to figure out how to extract cooperation from a backcountry headman."

In other words, his father had decided this was a test, and wasn't going to give him any more clues. Thanks, Dad.

"You have no sibs, lord?" said Harra, snapping him back to the present.

"No. But surely that's known, even in the back-beyond."

"They *say* a lot of things about you," Harra shrugged.

Miles bit down on the morbid question in his mouth like a wedge of raw lemon. He would not ask it, he would not . . . he couldn't help himself. "Like what?" forced out past his stiff lips.

"Everyone knows the Count's son is a mutant." Her eyes flicked defiant-wide. "Some said it came from the off-worlder woman he married. Some said it was from radiation from the wars, or a disease from, um, corrupt practices in his youth among his brother-officers—"

That last was a new one to Miles. His brow lifted.

"—but most say he was poisoned by his enemies."

"I'm glad most have it right. It was an assassination attempt using soltoxin gas, when my mother was pregnant with me. But it's not—" *a mutation,* his thought hiccoughed through the well-worn grooves—how many times had he explained this?—*it's teratogenic, not genetic, I'm not a mutant, not.* . . . What the hell did a fine point of biochemistry matter to this ignorant, bereaved woman? For all practical purposes—for her purposes—he might as well be a mutant. "—important," he finished.

She eyed him sideways, swaying gently in the clop-a-clop rhythm of her mount. "Some said you were born with no legs, and lived all the time in a float chair in Vorkosigan House. Some said you were born with no bones—"

"—and kept in a jar in the basement, no doubt," Miles muttered.

"But Karal said he'd seen you with your grandfather at Hassadar Fair, and you were only sickly and under-sized. Some said your father had got you into the Service, but others said no, you'd gone off-planet to your mother's home and had your brain turned into a computer and your body fed with tubes, floating in a liquid—"

"I knew there'd be a jar turn up in this story somewhere," Miles grimaced. *You knew you'd be sorry you asked, too, but you went and did it anyway.* She was baiting him, Miles realized suddenly. How *dare* she . . . but there was no humor in her, only a sharp-edged watchfulness.

She had gone out, way out on a limb to lay this murder charge, in defiance of family and local authorities alike, in defiance of established custom. And what had her Count given her for a shield and support, going back to face the wrath of all her nearest and dearest? Miles. Could he handle this? She must be wondering indeed. Or would he botch it, cave and cut and run, leaving her to face the whirlwind of rage and revenge alone?

He wished he'd left her weeping at the gate.

The woodland, fruit of many generations of terraforming forestry, opened out suddenly on a vale of brown native scrub. Down the middle of it, through some accident of soil chemistry, ran a half-kilometer-wide swathe of green and pink—feral roses, Miles realized with astonishment as they rode nearer. Earth roses. The track dove into the fragrant mass of them and vanished.

He took turns with Pym, hacking their way through with their Service bush knives. The roses were vigorous and studded with thick thorns, and hacked back with a vicious elastic recoil. Fat Ninny did his part by swinging his big head back and forth and nipping off blooms and chomping them down happily. Miles wasn't sure just how many he ought to let the big roan eat—just because the species wasn't native to Barrayar didn't mean it wasn't poisonous to horses. Miles sucked at his wounds and reflected upon Barrayar's shattered ecological history.

The fifty thousand Firsters from Earth had only meant to be the spearhead of Barrayar's colonization. Then, through a gravitational anomaly, the wormhole jump through which the colonists had come shifted closed, irrevocably and without warning. The terraforming which had begun, so careful and controlled in the beginning, collapsed along with everything else. Imported Earth plant and animal species had escaped everywhere to run wild, as the humans turned their attention to the most urgent problems of survival. Biologists still mourned the mass extinctions of native species that had followed, the erosions and droughts and floods, but really, Miles thought, over the centuries of the Time of Isolation the fittest of both worlds had fought it out to a perfectly good new balance. If it was alive and covered the ground who cared where it came from?

We are all here by accident. Like the roses.

They camped that night high in the hills, and pushed on in the morning to the flanks of the true mountains. They were now out of the region Miles was personally familiar with from his childhood, and he checked Harra's directions frequently on his orbital survey map. They stopped only a few hours short of their goal at sunset of the second day. Harra insisted she could lead them on in the dusk from here, but Miles did not care to arrive after nightfall, unannounced, in a strange place of uncertain welcome.

He bathed the next morning in a stream, and unpacked and dressed carefully in his new officer's Imperial dress greens. Pym wore the Vorkosigan brown-and-silver livery, and pulled the Count's standard on a telescoping aluminum pole from the recesses of his saddlebag and mounted it on his left stirrup. *Dressed to kill,* thought Miles joylessly. Dr. Dea wore ordinary black fatigues and looked uncomfortable. If they constituted a message, Miles was damned if he knew what it was.

They pulled the horses up at midmorning before a two-room cabin set on the edge of a vast grove of sugar maples, planted who-knew-how-many centuries ago but now raggedly marching up the vale by self-seeding. The mountain air was cool and pure and bright. A few chickens stalked and bobbed in the weeds. An algae-choked wooden pipe from the woods dribbled water into a trough, which overflowed into a squishy green streamlet and away.

Harra slid down and smoothed her skirt and climbed the porch. "Karal?" she called. Miles waited high on horseback for the initial contact. Never give up a psychological advantage.

"Harra? Is that you?" came a man's voice from within. He banged open the door and rushed out. "Where have you been, girl? We've been beating the bushes for you! Thought you'd broke your neck in the scrub somewhere—" He stopped short before the three silent men on horseback.

"You wouldn't write down my charges, Karal," said Harra rather breathlessly. Her hands kneaded her skirt. "So I walked to the district magistrate at Vorkosigan Surleau to Speak them myself."

"Oh, girl," Karal breathed regretfully, "that was a *stupid* thing to do ..." His head lowered and swayed, as he stared uneasily at the riders. He was a balding man of maybe sixty, leathery and worn, and his left arm ended in a stump. Another veteran.

"Speaker Serg Karal?" began Miles sternly. "I am the Voice of Count Vorkosigan. I am charged to investigate the crime Spoken by Harra Csurik before the Count's court, namely the murder of her infant daughter Raina. As Speaker of Silvy Vale, you are requested and required to assist me in all matters pertaining to the Count's justice."

At this point Miles ran out of prescribed formalities, and was on his own. That hadn't taken long. He waited. Fat Ninny snuffled. The silver-on-brown cloth of the standard made a few soft snapping sounds, lifted by a vagrant breeze.

"The district magistrate wasn't there," put in Harra, "but the Count was."

Karal was grey-faced, staring. He pulled himself together with an effort, came to a species of attention, and essayed a creaking half-bow. "Who—who are you, sir?"

"Lord Miles Vorkosigan."

Karal's lips moved silently. Miles was no lip reader, but he was pretty sure it came to a dismayed variant of *Oh, shit.* "This is my liveried man Sergeant Pym, and my medical examiner, Lieutenant Dea of the Imperial Service."

"You are my lord Count's son?" Karal croaked.

"The one and only." Miles was suddenly sick of the posing. Surely that was a sufficient first impression. He swung down off Ninny, landing lightly on the balls of his feet. Karal's gaze followed him down, and down. *Yeah, so I'm short. But wait'll you see me dance.* "All right if we water our horses in your trough here?" Miles looped Ninny's reins through his arm and stepped toward it.

"Uh, that's for the people, m'lord," said Karal. "Just a minute and I'll fetch a bucket." He hitched up his baggy trousers and trotted off around the side of the cabin. A minute's uncomfortable silence, then Karal's voice floating faintly, "Where'd you put the goat bucket, Zed?"

Another voice, light and young, "Behind the woodstack, Da." The voices fell to a muffled undertone. Karal came trotting back with a battered aluminum bucket, which he placed beside the trough. He knocked out a wooden plug in the side and a bright stream arced out to splash and fill. Fat Ninny flickered his ears and snuffled and rubbed his big head against Miles, smearing his tunic with red and white horsehairs and nearly knocking him off his feet. Karl glanced up and smiled at the horse, though his smile fell away as his gaze passed on to the horse's owner. As Fat Ninny gulped his drink Miles caught a glimpse of the owner of the second voice, a boy of around twelve who flitted off into the woods behind the cabin.

Karal fell to, assisting Miles and Harra and Pym in securing the horses. Miles left Pym to unsaddle and feed, and followed Karal into his house. Harra stuck to Miles like glue, and Dr. Dea unpacked his medical kit and trailed along. Miles's boots rang loud and unevenly on the wooden floorboards.

"My wife, she'll be back in the nooning," said Karal, moving uncertainly around the room as Miles and Dea settled themselves on a bench and Harra curled up with her arms around her knees on the floor beside the fieldstone hearth. "I'll . . . I'll make some tea, m'lord." He skittered back out the door to fill a kettle at the trough before Miles could say, *No, thank you.* No, let him ease his nerves in ordinary movement. Then maybe Miles could begin to tease out how much of this static was social nervousness and how much was—perhaps—guilty conscience. By the time Karal had the kettle on the coals he was noticeably better controlled, so Miles began.

"I'd prefer to commence this investigation immediately, Speaker. It need not take long."

"It need not . . . take place at all, m'lord. The baby's death was natural—there were no marks on her. She was weakly, she had the cat's mouth, who knows what else was wrong with her? She died in her sleep, or by some accident."

"It is remarkable," said Miles dryly, "how often such accidents happen in this district. My father the Count himself has . . . remarked on it."

"There was no call to drag you up here." Karal looked in exasperation at Harra. She sat silent, unmoved by his persuasion.

"It was no problem," said Miles blandly.

"Truly, m'lord," Karal lowered his voice, "I believe the child might have been overlain. 'S no wonder, in her grief, that her mind rejected it. Lem Csurik, he's a good boy, a good provider. She really doesn't want to do this, her reason is just temporarily overset by her troubles."

Harra's eyes, looking out from her hair-thatch, were poisonously cold.

"I begin to see," Miles's voice was mild, encouraging. Karal brightened slightly. "It all could still be all right. If she will just be patient. Get over her sorrow. Talk to poor Lem. I'm sure he didn't kill the babe. Not rush to something she'll regret."

"I begin to see," Miles let his tone go ice cool, "why Harra Csurik found it necessary to walk four days to get an unbiased hearing. 'You think.' 'You believe.' 'Who knows what?' Not you, it appears. I hear speculation— accusation—innuendo—assertion. I came for *facts*, Speaker Karal. The Count's justice doesn't turn on guesses. It doesn't have to. This isn't the Time of Isolation. Not even in the backbeyond.

"My investigation of the facts will begin now. No judgment will be—rushed into, before the facts are complete. Confirmation of Lem Csurik's guilt or innocence will come from his own mouth, under fast-penta, administered by Dr. Dea before two witnesses—yourself and a deputy of your choice. Simple, clean, and quick." *And maybe I can be on my way out of this benighted hole before sundown.* "I require you, Speaker, to go now and bring Lem Csurik for questioning. Sergeant Pym will assist you."

Karal killed another moment pouring the boiling water into a big brown pot before speaking. "I'm a travelled man, lord. A twenty-year Service man. But most folks here have never been out of Silvy Vale. Interrogation chemistry might as well be magic to them. They might say it was a false confession, got that way."

"Then you and your deputy can say otherwise. This isn't exactly like the good old days, when confessions were extracted under torture, Karal. Besides, if he's as innocent as you *guess*—he'll clear himself, no?"

Reluctantly, Karal went into the adjoining room. He came back shrugging on a faded Imperial Service uniform jacket with a corporal's rank marked on the collar, the buttons of which did not quite meet across his middle anymore. Preserved, evidently, for such official functions. Even as in Barrayaran custom one saluted the uniform, and not the man in it, so might the wrath engendered by an unpopular duty fall on the office and not the individual who carried it out. Miles appreciated the nuance.

Karal paused at the door. Harra still sat wrapped in silence by the hearth, rocking slightly.

"M'lord," said Karal. "I've been Speaker of Silvy Vale for sixteen years now. In all that time nobody has had to go to the district magistrate for a Speaking, not for water rights or stolen animals or swiving or even the time Neva accused Bors of tree piracy over the maple sap. We've not had a blood feud in all that time."

"I have no intention of starting a blood feud, Karal. I just want the facts."

"That's the thing, m'lord. I'm not so in love with facts as I used to be. Sometimes, they bite." Karal's eyes were urgent.

Really, the man was doing everything but stand on his head and juggle cats—one-handed—to divert Miles. How overt was his obstruction likely to get?

"Silvy Vale cannot be permitted to have its own little Time of Isolation," said Miles warningly. "The Count's justice is for everyone, now. Even if they're small. And weakly. And have something wrong with them. And cannot even speak for themselves—*Speaker*."

Karal flinched, white about the lips—point taken, evidently. He trudged away up the trail, Pym following watchfully, one hand loosening the stunner in his holster.

They drank the tea while they waited, and Miles pottered about the cabin, looking but not touching. The hearth was the sole source of heat for cooking and washwater. There was a beaten metal sink for washing up, filled by hand from a covered bucket but emptied through a drainpipe under the porch to join the streamlet running down out of the trough. The second room was a bedroom, with a double bed and chests for storage. A loft held three more pallets; the boy around back had brothers, apparently. The place was cramped, but swept, things put away and hung up.

On a side table sat a government-issue audio receiver, and a second and older military model, opened up, apparently in the process of getting minor repairs and a new power pack. Exploration revealed a drawer full of old parts, nothing more complex than for simple audio sets, unfortunately. Speaker Karal must double as Silvy Vale's comm link specialist. How appropriate. They must pick up broadcasts from the station in Hassadar, maybe the high-power government channels from the capital as well.

No other electricity, of course. Powersat receptors were expensive pieces of precision technology. They would come even here, in time; some communities almost as small, but with strong economic co-ops, already had them. Silvy Vale was obviously still stuck in subsistence-level, and must needs wait till there was enough surplus in the district to gift them, if the surplus was not grabbed off first by some competing want. If only the city of Vorkosigan Vashnoi had not been obliterated by Cetagandan atomics, the whole district could be years ahead, economically. . . .

Miles walked out on the porch and leaned on the rail. Karal's son had returned. Down at the end of the cleared yard Fat Ninny was standing tethered, hip-shot, ears aflop, grunting with pleasure as the grinning boy scratched him vigorously under his halter. The boy looked up to catch Miles watching him, and scooted off fearfully to vanish again in the scrub downslope. "Huh," muttered Miles.

Dr. Dea joined him. "They've been gone a long time. About time to break out the fast-penta?"

"No, your autopsy kit, I should say. I fancy that's what we'll be doing next."

Dea glanced at him sharply. "I thought you sent Pym along to enforce the arrest."

"You can't arrest a man who's not there. Are you a wagering man, Doctor? I'll bet you a mark they don't come back with Csurik. No, hold it—maybe I'm wrong. I hope I'm wrong. Here are three coming back. . . ."

Karal, Pym, and another were marching down the trail. The third was a hulking young man, big-handed, heavy-browed, thick-necked, surly. "Harra," Miles called, "is this your husband?" He looked the part, by God, just what Miles had pictured. And four brothers just like him—only bigger, no doubt. . . .

Harra appeared by Miles's shoulder, and let out her breath. "No, m'lord. That's Alex, the Speaker's deputy."

"Oh." Miles's lips compressed in silent frustration. *Well, I had to give it a chance to be simple.*

Karal stopped beneath him and began a wandering explanation of his emptyhanded state. Miles cut him off with a lift of his eyebrows. "Pym?"

"Bolted, m'lord," said Pym laconically. "Almost certainly warned."

"I agree." He frowned down at Karal, who prudently stood silent. Facts first. Decisions, such as how much deadly force to pursue the fugitive with, second. "Harra. How far is it to your burying place?"

"Down by the stream, lord, at the bottom of the valley. About two kilometers."

"Get your kit, Doctor, we're taking a walk. Karal, fetch a shovel."

"M'lord, surely it isn't needful to disturb the peace of the dead," began Karal.

"It is entirely needful. There's a place for the autopsy report right in the Procedural I got from the district magistrate's office. Where I will file my completed report upon this case when we return to Vorkosigan Surleau. I have permission from the next-of-kin—do I not, Harra?"

She nodded numbly.

"I have the two requisite witnesses, yourself and your," *gorilla*, "deputy, we have the doctor and the daylight—if you don't stand there arguing till sundown. All we need is the shovel. Unless you're volunteering to dig with your hand, Karal." Miles's voice was flat and grating and getting dangerous.

Karal's balding head bobbed in his distress. "The—the father is the legal next-of-kin, while he lives, and you don't have his—"

"Karal," said Miles.

"M'lord?"

"Take care the grave you dig is not your own. You've got one foot in it already."

Karal's hand opened in despair. "I'll ... get the shovel, m'lord."

The mid-afternoon was warm, the air golden and summer-sleepy. The shovel bit with a steady *scrunch-scrunch* through the soil at the hands of Karal's deputy. Downslope, a bright stream burbled away over clean rounded stones. Harra hunkered watching, silent and grim.

When big Alex levered out the little crate—so little!—Sergeant Pym went off for a patrol of the wooded perimeter. Miles didn't blame him. He hoped the soil at that depth had been cool, these last eight days. Alex pried open the box, and Dr. Dea waved him away and took over. The deputy too went off to find something to examine at the far end of the graveyard.

Dea looked the cloth-wrapped bundle over carefully, lifted it out and set it on his tarp laid out on the ground in the bright sun. The instruments of his investigation were arrayed upon the plastic in precise order. He unwrapped the brightly-patterned cloths in their special folds, and Harra crept up to retrieve them, straighten and fold them ready for re-use, then crept back.

Miles fingered the handkerchief in his pocket, ready to hold over his mouth and nose, and went to watch over Dea's shoulder. Bad, but not too bad. He'd seen and smelled worse. Dea, filter-masked, spoke procedurals into his recorder, hovering in the air by his shoulder, and made his examination first by eye and gloved touch, then by scanner.

"Here, my lord," said Dea, and motioned Miles closer. "Almost certainly the cause of death, though I'll run the toxin tests in a moment. Her neck was broken. See here on the scanner where the spinal cord was severed, then the bones twisted back into alignment."

"Karal, Alex," Miles motioned them up to witness; they came reluctantly.

"Could this have been accidental?" said Miles.

"Very remotely possible. The re-alignment had to be deliberate, though."

"Would it have taken long?"

"Seconds only. Death was immediate."

"How much physical strength was required? A big man's or . . ."

"Oh, not much at all. Any adult could have done it, easily."

"Any sufficiently motivated adult." Miles's stomach churned at the mental picture Dea's words conjured up. The little fuzzy head would easily fit under a man's hand. The twist, the muffled cartilaginous crack—if there was one thing Miles knew by heart, it was the exact tactile sensation of breaking bone, oh yes.

"Motivation," said Dea, "is not my department." He paused. "I might note, a careful external examination could have found this. Mine did. An experienced layman—" his eye fell cool on Karal, "paying attention to what he was doing, should not have missed it."

Miles too stared at Karal, waiting.

"Overlain," hissed Harra. Her voice was ragged with scorn.

"M'lord," said Karal carefully, "it's true I suspected the possibility—"

Suspected, hell. You knew.

"But I felt—and still feel, strongly," his eye flashed a wary defiance, "that only more grief would come from a fuss. There was nothing I could do to help the baby at that point. My duties are to the living."

"So are mine, Speaker Karal. As, for example, my duty to the next small Imperial subject in mortal danger from those who should be his or her protectors, for the grave fault of being," Miles flashed an edged smile, "physically different. In Count Vorkosigan's view this is not just a case. This is a test case, fulcrum of a thousand cases. Fuss ..." he hissed the sibilant; Harra rocked to the rhythm of his voice, "you haven't begun to see *fuss* yet."

Karal subsided as if folded.

There followed an hour of messiness yielding mainly negative data; no other bones were broken, the infant's lungs were clear, her gut and bloodstream free of toxins except those of natural decomposition. Her brain held no secret tumors. The defect for which she had died did not extend to spina bifida, Dea reported. Fairly simple plastic surgery would indeed have corrected the cat's mouth, could she somehow have won access to it. Miles wondered what comfort this confirmation was to Harra; cold, at best.

Dea put his puzzle back together, and Harra rewrapped the tiny body in intricate, meaningful folds. Dea cleaned his tools and placed them in their cases and washed his hands and arms and face thoroughly in the stream, for rather a longer time than needed for just hygiene Miles thought, while the gorilla reburied the box.

Harra made a little bowl in the dirt atop the grave and piled in some twigs and bark scraps and a sawed-off strand of her lank hair.

Miles, caught short, felt in his pockets. "I have no offering on me that will burn," he said apologetically.

Harra glanced up, surprised at even the implied offer. "No matter, m'lord." Her little pile of scraps flared briefly and went out, like her infant Raina's life.

But it does matter, thought Miles.

Peace to you, small lady, after our rude invasions. I will give you a better sacrifice, I swear by my word as Vorkosigan. And the smoke of that burning will rise and be seen from one end of these mountains to the other.

Miles charged Karal and Alex straightly with producing Lem Csurik, and gave Harra Csurik a ride home up behind him on Fat Ninny. Pym accompanied them.

They passed a few scattered cabins on the way. At one a couple of grubby children playing in the yard loped alongside the horses, giggling and making hex signs at Miles, egging each other on to bolder displays, until their mother spotted them and ran out and hustled them indoors with a fearful look over her shoulder. In a weird way it was almost relaxing to Miles, the welcome he'd expected, not like Karal's and Alex's strained, self-conscious, careful not-noticing. Raina's life would not have been an easy one.

Harra's cabin was at the head of a long draw, just before it narrowed into a ravine. It seemed very quiet and isolated, in the dappled shade.

"Are you sure you wouldn't rather go stay with your mother?" asked Miles dubiously.

Harra shook her head. She slid down off Ninny, and Miles and Pym dismounted and followed her in.

The cabin was of standard design, a single room with a fieldstone fireplace and a wide roofed front porch. Water apparently came from the rivulet in the ravine. Pym held up a hand and entered first behind Harra, his hand on his stunner. If Lem Csurik had run, might he have run home first? Pym had been making scanner checks of perfectly innocent clumps of bushes all the way here.

The cabin was deserted. Although not long deserted; it did not have the lingering, dusty silence one would expect of eight days mournful disoccupation. The remains of a few hasty meals sat on the sinkboard. The bed was slept-in, rumpled and unmade. A few man's garments were scattered about. Automatically Harra began to move about the room, straightening it up, reasserting her presence, her existence, her worth. If she could not control the events of her life, at least she might control one small room.

The one untouched item was a cradle that sat beside the bed, little blankets neatly folded. Harra had fled for Vorkosigan Surleau just a few hours after the burial.

Miles wandered about the room, checking the view from the windows. "Will you show me where you went to get your brillberries, Harra?"

She led them up the ravine; Miles timed the hike. Pym divided his attention unhappily between the brush and Miles, alert to catch any bone-breaking stumble. After flinching away from about three aborted protective grabs Miles was ready to tell him to go climb a tree. Still, there was a certain understandable self-interest at work here, if Miles broke a leg it would be Pym who'd be stuck with carrying him out.

The brillberry patch was nearly a kilometer up the ravine. Miles plucked a few seedy red berries and ate them absently, looking around, while Harra and Pym waited respectfully. Afternoon sun slanted through green and brown leaves, but the bottom of the ravine was already grey and cool with premature twilight. The brillberry vines clung to the rocks and hung down invitingly, luring one to risk one's neck reaching. Miles resisted their weedy temptations, not being all that fond of brillberries. "If someone called out from your cabin, you couldn't hear them up here, could you?" remarked Miles.

"No, m'lord."

"About how long did you spend picking?"

"About," Harra shrugged, "a basketful."

The woman didn't own a chrono. "An hour, say. And a twenty-minute climb each way. About a two hour time window, that morning. Your cabin was not locked?"

"Just a latch, m'lord."

"Hm."

Method, motive, and opportunity, the district magistrate's Procedural had emphasized. Damn. The method was established, and almost anybody could have used it. The opportunity angle, it appeared, was just as bad. Anyone at all could have walked up to that cabin, done the deed, and departed, unseen and unheard. It was much too late for an aura detector to be of use, tracing the shining ghosts of movements in and out of that room, even if Miles had brought one.

Facts, hah. They were back to motive, the murky workings of men's minds. Anybody's guess.

Miles had, as per the instructions in the district magistrate's Procedural, been striving to keep an open mind about the accused, but it was getting harder and harder to resist Harra's assertions. She'd been proved right about everything so far.

They left Harra re-installed in her little home, going through the motions of order and the normal routine of life as if they could somehow re-create it, like an act of sympathetic magic.

"Are you sure you'll be all right?" Miles asked, gathering Fat Ninny's reins and settling himself in the saddle. "I can't help but think that if your husband's in the area, he could show up here. You say nothing's been taken, so it's unlikely he's been here and gone before we arrived. Do you want someone to stay with you?"

"No, m'lord." She hugged her broom, on the porch. "I'd . . . I'd like to be alone for a while."

"Well . . . all right. I'll, ah, send you a message if anything important happens."

"Thank you, m'lord." Her tone was unpressing, she really did want to be left alone. Miles took the hint.

At a wide place in the trail back to Speaker Karal's, Pym and Miles rode stirrup to stirrup. Pym was still painfully on the alert for boogies in the bushes.

"My lord, may I suggest that your next logical step be to draft all the able-bodied men in the community for a hunt for this Csurik? Beyond doubt, you've established that the infanticide was a murder."

Interesting turn of phrase, Miles thought dryly. *Even Pym doesn't find it redundant. Oh, my poor Barrayar.* "It seems reasonable at first glance, Sergeant Pym, but has it occurred to you that half the able-bodied men in this community are probably relatives of Lem Csurik's?"

"It might have a psychological effect. Create enough disruption, and perhaps someone would turn him in just to get it over with."

"Hm, possibly. Assuming he hasn't already left the area. He could have been halfway to the coast before we were done at the autopsy."

"Only if he had access to transport." Pym glanced at the empty sky.

"For all we know one of his sub-cousins had a rickety lightflyer in a shed somewhere. But . . . he's never been out of Silvy Vale. I'm not sure he'd know how to run, where to go. Well, if he has left the district it's a problem for Imperial Civil Security, and I'm off the hook." *Happy thought.* "But—one of the things that bothers me, a lot, are the inconsistencies in the picture I'm getting of our chief suspect. Have you noticed them?"

"Can't say as I have, m'lord."

"Hm. Where did Karal take you, by the way, to arrest this guy?"

"To a wild area, rough scrub and gullies. Half a dozen men were out searching for Harra. They'd just called off their search and were on their way back when we met up with them. By which I concluded our arrival was no surprise."

"Had Csurik actually been there, and fled, or was Karal just ring-leading you in a circle?"

"I think he'd actually been there, m'lord. The men claimed not, but as you point out they were relatives, and besides, they did not, ah, lie well. They were tense. Karal may begrudge you his cooperation, but I don't think he'll quite dare disobey your direct orders. He is a twenty-year man, after all."

Like Pym himself, Miles thought. Count Vorkosigan's personal guard was legally limited to a ceremonial twenty men, but given his political position their function included very practical security. Pym was typical of their number, a decorated veteran of the Imperial Service who had retired to this elite private force. It was not Pym's fault that when he had joined he had stepped into a dead man's shoes, replacing the late Sergeant Bothari. Did anyone in the universe besides himself miss the deadly and difficult Bothari? Miles wondered sadly.

"I'd like to question *Karal* under fast-penta," said Miles morosely. "He displays every sign of being a man who knows where the body's buried."

"Why don't you, then?" asked Pym logically.

"I may come to that. There is, however, a certain unavoidable degradation in a fast-penta interrogation. If the man's loyal it may not be in our best long-range interest to shame him publicly."

"It wouldn't be in public."

"No, but he would remember being turned into a drooling idiot. I need . . . more information."

Pym glanced back over his shoulder. "I thought you had all the information, by now."

"I have facts. Physical facts. A great big pile of— meaningless, useless facts." Miles brooded. "If I have to fast-penta every backbeyonder in Silvy Vale to get to the bottom of this, I will. But it's not an elegant solution."

"It's not an elegant problem, m'lord," said Pym dryly.

They returned to find Speaker Karal's wife back and in full possession of her home. She was running in frantic circles, chopping, beating, kneading, stoking, and flying upstairs to change the bedding on the three pallets, driving her three sons before her to fetch and run and carry. Dr. Dea, bemused, was following her about trying to slow her down, explaining that they had brought their own tent and food, thank you, and that her hospitality was not required. This produced a most indignant response from Ma Karal.

"My lord's own son come to my house, and I to turn him out in the fields like his horse! I'd be ashamed!" And she returned to her work.

"She seems rather distraught," said Dea, looking over his shoulder.

Miles took him by the elbow and propelled him out onto the porch. "Just get out of her way, Doctor. We're doomed to be Entertained. It's an obligation on both sides. The polite thing to do is sort of pretend we're not here till she's ready for us."

Dea lowered his voice. "It might be better, in light of the circumstances, if we were to eat only our packaged food."

The chatter of a chopping knife, and a scent of herbs and onions, wafted enticingly through the open window. "Oh, I would imagine anything out of the common pot would be all right, wouldn't you?" said Miles. "If anything really worries you, you can whisk it off and check it, I suppose, but—discreetly, eh? We don't want to insult anyone."

They settled themselves in the homemade wooden chairs, and were promptly served tea again by a boy draftee of ten, Karal's youngest. He had apparently already received private instructions in manners from one or the other of his parents, for his response to Miles's deformities was the same flickering covert not-noticing as the adults, not quite as smoothly carried off.

"Will you be sleeping in my bed, m'lord?" he asked. "Ma says we got to sleep on the porch."

"Well, whatever your Ma says, goes," said Miles. "Ah . . . do you like sleeping on the porch?"

"Naw. Last time, Zed kicked me and I rolled off in the dark."

"Oh. Well, perhaps, if we're to displace you, you would care to sleep in our tent by way of trade."

The boy's eyes widened. "Really?"

"Certainly. Why not?"

"Wait'll I tell Zed!" He danced down the steps and

shot away around the side of the house. "Zed, hey,
Zed . . . !"

"I suppose," said Dea, "we can fumigate it, later. . . ."

Miles's lips twitched. "They're no grubbier than you
were at the same age, surely. Or than I was. When I was
permitted." The late afternoon was warm. Miles took off
his green tunic and hung it on the back of his chair, and
unbuttoned the round collar of his cream shirt.

Dea's brows rose. "Are we keeping shopman's hours,
then, m'lord, on this investigation? Calling it quits for
the day?"

"Not exactly." Miles sipped tea thoughtfully, gazing
out across the yard. The trees and treetops fell away
down to the bottom of this feeder valley. Mixed scrub
climbed the other side of the slope. A crested fold, then
the long flanks of a backbone mountain, beyond, rose
high and harsh to a summit still flecked with dwindling
dirty patches of snow.

"There's still a murderer loose out there somewhere,"
Dea pointed out helpfully.

"You sound like Pym." Pym, Miles noted, had finished
with their horses and was taking his scanner for another
walk. "I'm waiting."

"What for?"

"Not sure. The piece of information that will make
sense of all this. Look, there's only two possibilities. Csurik's either innocent or he's guilty. If he's guilty, he's not
going to turn himself in. He'll certainly involve his rela-
tions, hiding and helping him. I can call in reinforce-
ments by comm link from Imperial Civil Security in
Hassadar, if I want to. Any time. Twenty men, plus
equipment, here by aircar in a couple of hours. Create
a circus. Brutal, ugly, disruptive, exciting—could be quite
popular. A manhunt, with blood at the end.

"Of course, there's also the possibility that Csurik's
innocent, but scared. In which case . . ."

"Yes?"

"In which case, there's still a murderer out there."
Miles drank more tea. "I merely note, if you want to

catch something, running after it isn't always the best way."

Dea cleared his throat, and drank his tea too.

"In the meantime, I have another duty to carry out. I'm here to be seen. If your scientific spirit is yearning for something to do to wile away the hours, try keeping count of the number of Vor-watchers that turn up tonight."

Miles's predicted parade began almost immediately. It was mainly women, at first, bearing gifts as to a funeral. In the absence of a comm link system Miles wasn't sure by what telepathy they managed to communicate with each other, but they brought covered dishes of food, flowers, extra bedding, and offers of assistance. They were all introduced to Miles with nervous curtseys, but seldom lingered to chat; apparently a look was all their curiosity desired. Ma Karal was polite, but made it clear that she had the situation well in hand, and set their culinary offerings back of her own.

Some of the women had children in tow. Most of these were sent to play in the woods in back, but a small party of whispering boys sneaked back around the cabin to peek up over the rim of the porch at Miles. Miles had obligingly remained on the porch with Dea, remarking that it was a better view, without saying for whom. For a few moments Miles pretended not to notice his audience, restraining Pym with a hand signal from running them off. *Yes, look well, look your fill,* thought Miles. *What you see is what you're going to get, for the rest of your lives or at any rate mine. Get used to it. . . .* Then he caught Zed Karal's whisper, as self-appointed tour guide to his cohort—"That big one's the one that's come to kill Lem Csurik!"

"Zed," said Miles.

There was an abrupt frozen silence from under the edge of the porch. Even the animal rustlings stopped.

"Come here," said Miles.

To a muted background of dismayed whispers and

nervous giggles, Karal's middle boy slouched warily up on to the porch.

"You three—" Miles's pointing finger caught them in mid-flight, "wait there." Pym added his frown for emphasis, and Zed's friends stood paralyzed, eyes wide, heads lined up at the level of the porch floor as if stuck up on some ancient battlement as a warning to kindred malefactors.

"What did you just say to your friends, Zed?" asked Miles quietly. "Repeat it."

Zed licked his lips. "I jus' said you'd come to kill Lem Csurik, lord." Zed was clearly now wondering if Miles's murderous intent included obnoxious and disrespectful boys as well.

"That is not true, Zed. That is a dangerous lie."

Zed looked bewildered. "But Da—said it."

"What is true, is that I've come to catch the person who killed Lem Csurik's baby daughter. That may be Lem. But it may not. Do you understand the difference?"

"But Harra said Lem did it, and she ought to know, he's her husband and all."

"The baby's neck was broken by someone. Harra thinks Lem, but she didn't see it happen. What you and your friends here have to understand is that I won't make a mistake. I *can't* condemn the wrong person. My own truth drugs won't let me. Lem Csurik has only to come here and tell me the truth to clear himself, if he didn't do it.

"But suppose he did. What should I do with a man who would kill a baby, Zed?"

Zed shuffled. "Well, she was only a mutie . . ." then shut his mouth and reddened, not-looking at Miles.

It was, perhaps, a bit much to ask a twelve-year-old boy to take an interest in any baby, let alone a mutie one . . . *no*, dammit. It wasn't too much. But how to get a hook into that prickly defensive surface? And if Miles couldn't even convince one surly twelve-year-old, how was he to magically transmute a whole District of adults? A rush of despair made him suddenly want to rage. These people were so bloody *impossible*. He checked his temper firmly.

"Your Da was a twenty-year man, Zed. Are you proud that he served the Emperor?"

"Yes, lord." Zed's eyes sought escape, trapped by these terrible adults.

Miles forged on. "Well, these practices—mutie-killing—shame the Emperor, when he stands for Barrayar before the galaxy. I've been out there. I know. They call us all savages, for the crimes of a few. It shames the Count my father before his peers, and Silvy Vale before the District. A soldier gets honor by killing an armed enemy, not a baby. This matter touches my honor as a Vorkosigan, Zed. Besides," Miles's lips drew back on a mirthless grin, and he leaned forward intently in his chair—Zed recoiled as much as he dared—"you will all be astonished at what *only a mutie* can do. *That* I have sworn on my grandfather's grave."

Zed looked more suppressed than enlightened, his slouch now almost a crouch. Miles slumped back in his chair and released him with a weary wave of his hand. "Go play, boy."

Zed needed no urging. He and his companions shot away around the house as though released from springs.

Miles drummed his fingers on the chair arm, frowning into the silence that neither Pym nor Dea dared break.

"These hill-folk are ignorant, lord," offered Pym after a moment.

"These hill-folk are *mine*, Pym. Their ignorance is . . . a shame upon my house." Miles brooded. How had this whole mess become his anyway? He hadn't created it. Historically, he'd only just got here himself. "Their continued ignorance, anyway," he amended in fairness. It still made a burden like a mountain. "Is the message so complex? So difficult? 'You don't have to kill your children anymore.' It's not like we're asking them all to learn—5-Space navigational math." That had been the plague of Miles's last Academy semester.

"It's not easy for them," shrugged Dea. "It's easy for

the central authorities to make the rules, but these people have to live every minute of the consequences. They have so little, and the new rules force them to give their margin to marginal people who can't pay back. The old ways were wise, in the old days. Even now you have to wonder how many premature reforms we can afford, trying to ape the galactics."

And what's your definition of a marginal person, Dea? "But the margin is growing," Miles said aloud. "Places like this aren't up against famine every winter any more. They're not isolated in their disasters, relief can get from one district to another under the Imperial seal . . . we're all getting more connected, just as fast as we can. Besides," Miles paused, and added rather weakly, "perhaps you underestimate them."

Dea's brows rose ironically. Pym strolled the length of the porch, running his scanner in yet another pass over the surrounding scrubland. Miles, turning in his chair to pursue his cooling teacup, caught a slight movement, a flash of eyes, behind the casement-hung front window swung open to the summer air—Ma Karal, standing frozen, listening. For how long? Since he'd called her boy Zed, Miles guessed, arresting her attention. She raised her chin as his eyes met hers, sniffed, and shook out the cloth she'd been holding with a snap. They exchanged a nod. She turned back to her work before Dea, watching Pym, noticed her.

Karal and Alex returned, understandably, around suppertime.

"I have six men out searching," Karal reported cautiously to Miles on the porch, now well on its way to becoming Miles's official HQ. Clearly, Karal had covered ground since midafternoon. His face was sweaty, lined with physical as well as the underlying emotional strain. "But I think Lem's gone into the scrub. It could take days to smoke him out. There's hundreds of places to lie low out there."

Karal ought to know. "You don't think he's gone to

some relative's?" asked Miles. "Surely, if he intends to
evade us for long, he has to take a chance on re-supply,
on information. Will they turn him in when he surfaces?"
"It's hard to say." Karal turned his hand palm-out. "It's
. . . a hard problem for 'em, m'lord."

"Hm."

How long would Lem Csurik hang around out there
in the scrub, anyway? His whole life—his blown-to-bits
life—was all here in Silvy Vale. Miles considered the
contrast. A few weeks ago, Csurik had been a young man
with everything going for him; a home, a wife, a family
on the way, happiness; by Silvy Vale standards, comfort
and security. His cabin, Miles had not failed to note,
though simple, had been kept with love and energy, and
so redeemed from the potential squalor of its poverty.
Grimmer in the winter, to be sure. Now Csurik was a
hunted fugitive, all the little he had torn away in the
twinkling of an eye. With nothing to hold him, would he
run away and keep running? With nothing to run to,
would he linger near the ruins of his life?

The police force available to Miles a few hours away
in Hassadar was an itch in his mind. Was it not time to
call them in, before he fumbled this into a worse mess?
But . . . if he were meant to solve this by a show of force,
why hadn't the Count let him come by aircar on the first
day? Miles regretted that two-and-a-half-day ride. It had
sapped his forward momentum, slowed him down to Silvy
Vale's walking pace, tangled him with time to doubt. Had
the Count foreseen it? What did he know that Miles
didn't? What *could* he know? Dammit, this test didn't
need to be made harder by artificial stumbling blocks, it
was bad enough all on its own. *He wants me to be clever,*
Miles thought morosely. *Worse, he wants me to be seen
to be clever, by everyone here.* He prayed he was not
about to be spectacularly stupid instead.

"Very well, Speaker Karal. You've done all you can for
today. Knock off for the night. Call your men off too.
You're not likely to find anything in the dark."

Pym held up his scanner, clearly about to volunteer

its use, but Miles waved him down. Pym's brows rose, editorially. Miles shook his head slightly.

Karal needed no further urging. He dispatched Alex to call off the night search with torches. He remained wary of Miles. Perhaps Miles puzzled him as much as he puzzled Miles? Dourly, Miles hoped so.

Miles was not sure at what point the long summer evening segued into a party. After supper the men began to drift in, Karal's cronies, Silvy Vale's elders. Some were apparently regulars who shared the evening government news broadcasts on Karal's audio set. Too many names, and Miles daren't forget a one. A group of amateur musicians arrived with their homemade mountain instruments, rather breathless, obviously the band tapped for all the major weddings and wakes in Silvy Vale; this all seemed more like a funeral to Miles every minute.

The musicians stood in the middle of the yard and played. Miles's porch-HQ now became his aristocratic box seat. It was hard to get involved with the music when the audience was all so intently watching him. Some songs were serious, some—rather carefully at first—funny. Miles's spontaneity was frequently frozen in mid-laugh by a faint sigh of relief from those around him; his stiffening froze them in turn, self-stymied like two people trying to dodge each other in a corridor.

But one song was so hauntingly beautiful—a lament for lost love—that Miles was struck to the heart. *Elena....* In that moment, old pain transformed to melancholy, sweet and distant; a sort of healing, or at least the realization that a healing had taken place, unwatched. He almost had the singers stop there, while they were perfect, but feared they might think him displeased. But he remained quiet and inward for a time afterward, scarcely hearing their next offering in the gathering twilight.

At least the piles of food that had arrived all afternoon were thus accounted for, Miles had been afraid Ma Karal and her cronies had expected him to get around that culinary mountain all by himself.

At one point Miles leaned on the rail and glanced down the yard to see Fat Ninny at tether, making more friends. A whole flock of pubescent girls was clustered around him, petting him, brushing his fetlocks, braiding flowers and ribbons in his mane and tail, feeding him tidbits, or just resting their cheeks against his warm silky side. Ninny's eyes were half-closed in smug content.

God, thought Miles jealously, *if I had half the sex-appeal of that bloody horse I'd have more girlfriends than my cousin Ivan.* Miles considered, very briefly, the pros and cons of making a play for some unattached female. The striding lords of old and all that . . . no. There were some kinds of stupid he didn't have to be, and that was definitely one of them. The service he had already sworn to one small lady of Silvy Vale was surely all he could bear without breaking; he could feel the strain of it all around him now, like a dangerous pressure in his bones.

He turned to find Speaker Karal presenting a woman to him, far from pubescent; she was perhaps fifty, lean and little, work-worn. She was carefully clothed in an aging best-dress, her greying hair combed back and bound at the nape of her neck. She bit at her lips and cheeks in quick tense motions, half-suppressed in her self-consciousness.

" 'S Ma Csurik, m'lord. Lem's mother." Speaker Karal ducked his head and backed away, abandoning Miles without aid or mercy—*Come back, you coward!*

"Ma'am," Miles said. His throat was dry. Karal had set him up, dammit, a public play—no, the other guests were retreating out of earshot too, most of them.

"M'lord," said Ma Csurik. She managed a nervous curtsey.

"Uh . . . do sit down." With a ruthless jerk of his chin Miles evicted Dr. Dea from his chair and motioned the hill woman into it. He turned his own chair to face hers. Pym stood behind them, silent as a statue, tight as a wire. Did he imagine the old woman was about to whip a needler-pistol from her skirts? No—it was Pym's job to imagine things like that for Miles, so that Miles might free his whole mind for the problem at hand. Pym was almost as much an object of study as Miles himself. Wisely, he'd been holding himself apart, and would doubtless continue to do so till the dirty work was over.

"M'lord," said Ma Csurik again, and stumbled again to silence. Miles could only wait. He prayed she wasn't about to come unglued and weep on his knees or some damn thing. This was excruciating. *Stay strong, woman,* he urged silently.

"Lem, he . . ." she swallowed, "I'm sure he didn't kill the babe. There's never been any of that in our family. I swear it! He says he didn't, and I believe him."

"Good," said Miles affably. "Let him come say the same thing to me under fast-penta, and I'll believe him too."

"Come away, Ma," urged a lean young man who had accompanied her and now stood waiting by the steps, as if ready to bolt into the dark at a motion. "It's no good, can't you see." He glowered at Miles.

She shot the boy a quelling frown—another of her five sons?—and turned back more urgently to Miles, groping for words. "My Lem. He's only twenty, lord."

"*I'm* only twenty, Ma Csurik," Miles felt compelled to point out. There was another brief impasse.

"Look, I'll say it again," Miles burst out impatiently. "And again, and again, till the message penetrates all the way back to its intended recipient. I *cannot* condemn an innocent person. My truth drugs won't let me. Lem can clear himself. He has only to come in. Tell him, will you? Please?"

She went stony, guarded. "I . . . haven't seen him, m'lord."

"But you might."

She tossed her head. "So? I might not." Her eyes shifted to Pym and away, as if the sight of him burned. The silver Vorkosigan logos embroidered on Pym's collar gleamed in the twilight like animal eyes, moving only with his breathing. Karal was now bringing lighted lamps onto the porch, but keeping his distance still.

"Ma'am," said Miles tightly. "The Count my father has ordered me to investigate the murder of your grand-daughter. If your son means so much to you, how can his child mean so little? Was she . . . your first grandchild?"

Her face was sere. "No, lord. Lem's older sister, she has two. *They're* all right," she added with emphasis.

Miles sighed. "If you truly believe your son is innocent of this crime, you must help me prove it. Or—do you doubt?"

She shifted uneasily. There was doubt in her eyes—she didn't know, blast it. Fast-penta would be useless on her, for sure. As Miles's magic wonder drug, much counted-upon, fast-penta seemed to be having wonderfully little utility in this case so far.

"Come away, Ma," the young man urged again. "It's no good. The mutie lord came up here for a killing. They have to have one. It's a show."

Damn straight, thought Miles acidly. He was a percep-tive young lunk, that one.

Ma Csurik let herself be persuaded away by her angry and embarrassed son plucking at her arm. She paused on the steps, though, and shot bitterly over her shoulder, "It's all so easy for you, isn't it?"

My head hurts, thought Miles.

There was worse to come before the evening ended.

The new woman's voice was grating, low and angry. "Don't you talk down to me, Serg Karal. I got a right for one good look at this mutie lord."

She was tall and stringy and tough. *Like her daughter,* Miles thought. She had made no attempt to freshen up. A faint reek of summer sweat hung about her working dress. And how far had she walked? Her grey hair hung in a switch down her back, a few strands escaping the tie. If Ma Csurik's bitterness had been a stabbing pain behind the eyes, this one's rage was a wringing knot in the gut.

She shook off Karal's attempted restraint and stalked up to Miles in the lamplight. "So."

"Uh ... this is Ma Mattulich, m'lord," Karal introduced her. "Harra's mother."

Miles rose to his feet, managed a short formal nod. "How do you do, madam." He was very conscious of being a head shorter. She had once been of a height with Harra, Miles estimated, but her aging bones were beginning to pull her down.

She merely stared. She was a gum-leaf chewer, by the faint blackish stains around her mouth. Her jaw worked now on some small bit, tiny chomps, grinding too hard. She studied him openly, without subterfuge or the least hint of apology, taking in his head, his neck, his back, his short and crooked legs. Miles had the unpleasant illusion that she saw right through to all the healed cracks in his brittle bones as well. Miles's chin jerked up twice in the twitchy, nervous-involuntary tic that he was sure made him look spastic, before he controlled it with an effort.

"All right," said Karal roughly, "you've seen. Now come away, for God's sake, Mara." His hand opened in apology to Miles. "Mara, she's been pretty distraught over all this, m'lord. Forgive her."

"Your only grandchild," said Miles to her, in an effort to be kind, though her peculiar anguish repelled kindness with a scraped and bleeding scorn. "I understand your distress, ma'am. But there will be justice for little Raina. That I have sworn."

"How can there be justice *now*?" she raged, thick and low. "It's too late—a world too late—for justice, mutie lordling. What use do I have for your damned justice *now*?"

"Enough, Mara!" Karal insisted. His brows drew down and his lips thinned, and he forced her away and escorted her firmly off his porch.

The last lingering remnant of visitors parted for her with an air of respectful mercy, except for two lean teenagers hanging on the fringes who drew away as if avoiding poison. Miles was forced to revise his mental image of the Brothers Csurik. If those two were another sample, there was no team of huge menacing hill hulks after all. They were a team of little skinny menacing hill squirts instead. Not really an improvement, they looked like they could move as fast as striking ferrets if they had to. Miles's lips curled in frustration.

The evening's entertainments ended finally, thank God, close to midnight. Karal's last cronies marched off into the woods by lantern light. The repaired and repowered audio set was carried off by its owner with many thanks to Karal. Fortunately it had been a mature and sober crowd, even somber, no drunken brawls or anything. Pym got the Karal boys settled in the tent, took a last patrol around the cabin, and joined Miles and Dea in the loft. The pallets' stuffing had been spiked with fresh scented native herbs, to which Miles hoped devoutly he was not allergic. Ma Karal had wanted to turn her own bedroom over to Miles's exclusive lordly use, exiling herself and her husband to the porch too, but fortunately Pym had been able to persuade her that putting Miles in the loft, flanked by Dea and himself, was to be preferred from a security standpoint.

Dea and Pym were soon snoring, but sleep eluded Miles. He tossed on his pallet as he turned his ploys of the day, such as they had been, over and over in his mind. Was he being too slow, too careful, too conservative? This wasn't exactly good assault tactics, surprise with a superior force. The view he'd gained of the terrain from Karal's porch tonight had been ambiguous at best.

On the other hand, it did no good to charge off across a swamp, as his fellow cadet and cousin Ivan Vorpatril had demonstrated so memorably once on summer maneuvers. It had taken a heavy hovercab with a crane to crank the six big, strong, healthy, fully field-equipped young men of Ivan's patrol out of the chest-high, gooey black mud. Ivan had got his revenge simultaneously, though, when the cadet "sniper" they had been attacking fell out of his tree and broke his arm while laughing hysterically as they sank slowly and beautifully into the ooze. Ooze that a little guy, with his laser rifle wrapped in his loincloth, could swim across like a frog. The war games umpire had ruled it a draw. Miles rubbed his forearm and grinned in memory, and faded out at last.

Miles awoke abruptly and without transition deep in the night with a sense of something wrong. A faint orange glow shimmered in the blue darkness of the loft. Quietly, so as not to disturb his sleeping companions, he rose on his pallet and peered over the edge into the main room. The glow was coming through the front window.

Miles swung onto the ladder and padded downstairs for a look outdoors. "Pym," he called softly.

Pym shot awake with a snort. "M'lord?" he said, alarmed.

"Come down here. Quietly. Bring your stunner."

Pym was by his side in seconds. He slept in his trousers with his stunner holster and boots by his pillow. "What the hell—?" Pym muttered, looking out too.

The glow was from fire. A pitchy torch, flung to the top of Miles's tent set up in the yard, was burning quietly. Pym lurched toward the door, then controlled his movements as the same realization came to him as had to Miles. Theirs was a Service-issue tent, and its combat-rated synthetic fabric would neither melt nor burn.

Miles wondered if the person who'd heaved the torch had known that. Was this some arcane warning, or a singularly inept attack? If the tent had been ordinary fabric, and Miles in it, the intended result might not have been trivial. Worse with Karal's boys in it—a bursting blossom of flame—Miles shuddered.

Pym loosened his stunner in his holster and stood poised by the front door. "How long?"

"I'm not sure. Could have been burning like that for ten minutes before it woke me."

Pym shook his head, took a slight breath, raised his scanner, and vaulted into the fire-gilded darkness.

"Trouble, m'lord?" Speaker Karal's anxious voice came from his bedroom door.

"Maybe. Wait—" Miles halted him as he plunged for the door. "Pym's running a patrol with a scanner and a stunner. Wait'll he calls the all-clear, I think. Your boys may be safer inside the tent."

Karal came up to the window, caught his breath, and swore.

Pym returned in a few minutes. "There's no one within a kilometer, now," he reported shortly. He helped Karal take the goat bucket and douse the torch. The boys, who had slept through the fire, woke at its quenching.

"I think maybe it was a bad idea to lend them my tent," said Miles from the porch in a choked voice. "I am profoundly sorry, Speaker Karal. I didn't think."

"This should never . . ." Karal was spluttering with anger and delayed fright, "this should never have happened, m'lord. I apologize for . . . for Silvy Vale." He turned helplessly, peering into the darkness. The night sky, star-flecked, lovely, was threatening now.

The boys, once the facts penetrated their sleepiness, thought it was all just great, and wanted to return to the tent and lie in wait for the next assassin. Ma Karal, shrill and firm, herded them indoors instead and made them bed down in the main room. It was an hour before they stopped complaining at the injustice of it and went back to sleep.

Miles, keyed up nearly to the point of gibbering, did not sleep at all. He lay stiffly on his pallet, listening to Dea, who slept breathing heavily, and Pym, feigning sleep for courtesy and scarcely seeming to breathe at all.

Miles was about to suggest to Pym that they give up and go out on the porch for the rest of the night when the silence was shattered by a shrill squeal, enormously loud, pain-edged, from outside.

"The horses!" Miles spasmed to his feet, heart racing, and beat Pym to the ladder. Pym cut ahead of him by dropping straight over the side of the loft into an elastic crouch, and beat him to the door. There, Pym's trained bodyguard's reflexes compelled him to try and thrust

Miles back inside. Miles almost bit him. "Go, dammit! I've got a weapon!"

Pym, good intentions frustrated, swung out the cabin door with Miles on his heels. Halfway down the yard they split to each side as a massive snorting shape loomed out of the darkness and nearly ran them down; the sorrel mare, loose again. Another squeal pierced the night from the lines where the horses were tethered.

"Ninny?" Miles called, panicked. It was Ninny's voice making those noises, the like of which Miles had not heard since the night a shed had burned down at Vorkosigan Surleau with a horse trapped inside. "Ninny!"

Another grunting squeal, and a thunk like someone splitting a watermelon with a mallet. Pym staggered back, inhaling with difficulty, a resonant deep stutter, and tripped to the ground where he lay curled up around himself. Not killed outright, apparently, because between gasps he was managing to swear lividly. Miles dropped to the ground beside him, checked his skull—no, thank God it had been Pym's chest Ninny's hoof had hit with that alarming sound. The bodyguard only had the wind knocked out of him, maybe a cracked rib. Miles more sensibly ran around to the *front* of the horse lines. "Ninny!"

Fat Ninny was jerking his head against his rope, attempting to rear. He squealed again, his white-rimmed eyes gleaming in the darkness. Miles ran to his head. "Ninny, boy! What is it?" His left hand slid up the rope to Ninny's halter, his right stretched to stroke Ninny's shoulder soothingly. Fat Ninny flinched, but stopped trying to rear, and stood trembling. The horse shook his head. Miles's face and chest were suddenly spattered with something hot and dark and sticky.

"Dea!" Miles yelled. *"Dea!"*

Nobody slept through this uproar. Six people tumbled off the porch and down the yard, and not one of them thought to bring a light ... no, the brilliant flare of a cold light sprang from between Dr. Dea's fingers, and Ma Karal was struggling even now to light a lantern.

"Dea, get that damn light over here!" Miles demanded, and stopped to choke his voice back down an octave to its usual carefully-cultivated deeper register.

Dea galloped up and thrust the light toward Miles, then gasped, his face draining. "My lord! Are you shot?" In the flare the dark liquid soaking Miles's shirt glowed suddenly scarlet.

"Not me," Miles said, looking down at his chest in horror. A flash of memory turned his stomach over, cold at the vision of another blood-soaked death, that of the late Sergeant Bothari whom Pym had replaced. Would never replace.

Dea spun. "Pym?"

"He's all right," said Miles. A long inhaling wheeze rose from the grass a few meters off, the exhalation punctuated with obscenities. "But he got kicked by the horse. Get your medkit!" Miles peeled Dea's fingers off the cold light, and Dea dashed back to the cabin.

Miles held the light up to Ninny, and swore in a sick whisper. A huge cut, a third of a meter long and of unknown depth, scored Ninny's glossy neck. Blood soaked his coat and runneled down his foreleg. Miles's fingers touched the wound fearfully; his hands spread on either side, trying to push it closed, but the horse's skin was elastic and it pulled apart and bled profusely as Fat Ninny shook his head in pain. Miles grabbed the horse's nose—"Hold still, boy!" Somebody had been going for Ninny's jugular. And had almost made it; Ninny—tame, petted, friendly, trusting Ninny—would not have moved from the touch until the knife bit deep.

Karal was helping Pym to his feet as Dr. Dea returned. Miles waited while Dea checked Pym over, then called, "Here, Dea!"

Zed, looking quite as horrified as Miles, helped to hold Ninny's head as Dea made inspection of the cut. "I took tests," Dea complained *sotto voce* as he worked. "I beat out twenty-six other applicants, for the honor of becoming the Prime Minister's personal physician. I have practiced the procedures of seventy separate possible medical emergencies, from coronary thrombosis to attempted assassination. Nobody—*nobody*—told me my duties would include sewing up a damned horse's neck in the middle of the night in the middle of a howling wilderness. . . ." But he kept working as he complained, so Miles didn't quash him, but kept gently petting Ninny's nose, and hypnotically rubbing the hidden pattern of his muscles, to soothe and still him. At last Ninny relaxed enough to rest his slobbery chin on Miles's shoulder.

"Do horses get anesthetics?" asked Dea plaintively, holding his medical stunner as if not sure just what to do with it.

"This one does," said Miles stoutly. "You treat him just like a person, Dea. This is the last animal that the Count my grandfather personally trained. He named him. I watched him get born. We trained him together. Grandfather had me pick him up and hold him every day for a week after he was foaled, till he got too big. Horses are creatures of habit, Grandfather said, and take first impressions to heart. Forever after Ninny thought I was bigger than he was."

Dea sighed and made busy with anesthetic stun, cleansing solution, antibiotics, muscle relaxants, and biotic glue. With a surgeon's touch he shaved the edges of the cut and placed the reinforcing net. Zed held the light anxiously.

"The cut is clean," said Dea, "but it will undergo a lot of flexing—I don't suppose it can very well be immobilized, in this position? No, hardly. This should do. If he were a human, I'd tell him to rest at this point."

"He'll be rested," Miles promised firmly. "Will he be all right now?"

"I suppose so. How the devil should I know?" Dea looked highly aggrieved, but his hand sneaked out to recheck his repairs.

"General Piotr," Miles assured him, "would have been very pleased with your work." Miles could hear him in his head now, snorting, *Damned technocrats. Nothing but horse doctors with a more expensive set of toys.*

Grandfather would have loved being proved right. "You, ah . . . never met my grandfather, did you?"

"Before my time, my lord," said Dea. "I've studied his life and campaigns, of course."

"Of course."

Pym had a hand-light now, and was limping with Karal in a slow spiral around the horse lines, inspecting the ground. Karal's eldest boy had recaptured the sorrel mare and brought her back and re-tethered her. Her tether had been torn loose, not cut; had the mysterious attacker's choice of equine victim been random, or calculated? How calculated? Was Ninny attacked as a mere symbol of his master, or had the person known how passionately Miles loved the animal? Was this vandalism, a political statement, or an act of precisely-directed, subtle cruelty?

What have I ever done to you? Miles's thought howled silently to the surrounding darkness.

"They got away, whoever it was," Pym reported. "Out of scanner range before I could breathe again. My apologies, m'lord. They don't seem to have dropped anything on the ground."

There had to have been a knife, at least. A knife, its haft gory with horse blood in a pattern of perfect fingerprints, would have been extremely convenient just now. Miles sighed.

Ma Karal drifted up and eyed Dea's medkit, as he cleaned and re-packed it. "All that," she muttered under her breath, "for a horse. . . ."

Miles refrained, barely, from leaping to a hot defense of the value of this particular horse. How many people in Silvy Vale had Ma Karal seen suffer and die, in her lifetime, for lack of no more medical technology than what Dea was carrying under his arm just now?

Guarding his horse, Miles watched from the porch as dawn crept over the landscape. He had changed his shirt and washed off. Pym was inside getting his ribs taped. Miles sat with his back to the wall and a stunner on his lap as the night mists slowly grew grey. The valley was a grey blur, fog-shrouded, the hills darker rolls of fog beyond. Directly overhead, grey thinned to a paling blue. The day would be fine and hot once the fog burned away.

It was surely time now to call out the troops from Hassadar. This was getting just too weird. His bodyguard was half out of commission—true, it was Miles's horse that had rendered him so, not the mystery attacker. But just because the attacks hadn't been fatal didn't mean they hadn't been intended so. Perhaps a third attack would be brought off more expertly. Practice makes perfect.

Miles felt unstrung with nervous exhaustion. How had he let a mere horse become such a handle on his emotions? Bad, that, almost unbalanced—yet Ninny's was surely one of the truly innocent pure souls Miles had ever known. Miles remembered the other innocent in the case then, and shivered in the damp. *It was cruel, lord, something cruel.* . . . Pym was right, the bushes could be crawling with Csurik assassins right now.

Dammit, the bushes *were* crawling—over there, a movement, a damping wave of branch lashing in recoil from—what? Miles's heart lurched in his chest. He adjusted his stunner to full power, slipped silently off the porch, and began his stalk, crouching low, taking advantage of cover wherever the long grasses of the yard had not been trampled flat by the activities of the last day, and night. Miles froze like a predatory cat as a shape seemed to coalesce out of the mist.

A lean young man, not too tall, dressed in the baggy trousers that seemed to be standard here, stood wearily by the horse lines, staring up the yard at Karal's cabin. He stood so for a full two minutes without moving. Miles held a bead on him with his stunner. If he dared make one move toward Ninny. . . .

The young man walked back and forth uncertainly, then crouched on his heels, still gazing up the yard. He pulled something from the pocket of his loose jacket—Miles's finger tightened on the trigger—but he only put it to his mouth and bit. An apple. The crunch carried clearly in the damp air, and the faint perfume of its juices. He ate about half, then stopped, seeming to have trouble swallowing. Miles checked the knife at his belt, made sure it was loose in its sheath. Ninny's nostrils widened, and he nickered hopefully, drawing the young man's attention. He rose and walked over to the horse.

The blood pulsed in Miles's ears, louder than any other sound. His grip on the stunner was damp and white-knuckled. The young man fed Ninny his apple. The horse chomped it down, big jaw rippling under his skin, then cocked his hip, dangled one hind hoof, and sighed hugely. If he hadn't seen the man eat off the fruit first Miles might have shot him on the spot. It couldn't be poisoned. . . . The man made to pet Ninny's neck, then his hand drew back in startlement as he encountered Dea's dressing. Ninny shook his head uneasily. Miles rose slowly and stood waiting. The man scratched Ninny's ears instead, looked up one last time at the cabin, took a deep breath, stepped forward, saw Miles, and stood stock still.

"Lem Csurik?" said Miles.

A pause, a frozen nod. "Lord Vorkosigan?" said the young man. Miles nodded in turn.

Csurik swallowed. "Vor lord," he quavered, "do you keep your word?"

What a bizarre opening. Miles's brows climbed. Hell, go with it. "Yes. Are you coming in?"

"Yes and no, m'lord."

"Which?"

"A bargain, lord. I must have a bargain, and your word on it."

"If you killed Raina . . ."

"No, lord. I swear it. I didn't."

"Then you have nothing to fear from me."

Lem Csurik's lips thinned. What the devil could this hill man find ironic? How dare he find irony in Miles's confusion? Irony, but no amusement.

"Oh, lord," breathed Csurik, "I wish that were so. But

I have to prove it to Harra. Harra must believe me—you have to make her believe me, lord!"

"You have to make me believe you first. Fortunately, that isn't hard. You come up to the cabin and make that same statement under fast-penta, and I will rule you cleared."

Csurik was shaking his head.

"Why not?" said Miles patiently. That Csurik had turned up at all was strong circumstantial indication of his innocence. Unless he somehow imagined he could beat the drug. Miles would be patient for, oh, three or four seconds at least. Then, by God, he'd stun him, drag him inside, tie him up till he came round, and get to the bottom of this before breakfast.

"The drug—they say you can't hold anything back."

"It would be pretty useless if you could."

Csurik stood silent a moment.

"Are you trying to conceal some lesser crime on your conscience? Is that the bargain you wish to strike? An amnesty? It . . . might be possible. If it's short of another murder, that is."

"No, lord. I've never killed anybody!"

"Then maybe we can deal. Because if you're innocent, I need to know as soon as possible. Because it means my work isn't finished here."

"That's . . . that's the trouble, m'lord." Csurik shuffled, then seemed to come to some internal decision and stood sturdily. "I'll come in and risk your drug. And I'll answer anything about me you want to ask. But you have to promise—swear!—you won't ask me about . . . about anything else. Anybody else."

"Do you know who killed your daughter?"

"Not for sure." Csurik threw his head back defiantly. "I didn't see it. I have guesses."

"I have guesses too."

"That's as may be, lord. Just so's they don't come from my mouth. That's all I ask."

Miles holstered his stunner, and rubbed his chin. "Hm." A very slight smile turned one corner of his lip.

"I admit, it would be more—elegant—to solve this case by reason and deduction than brute force. Even so tender a force as fast-penta."

Csurik's head lowered. "I don't know elegant, lord. But I don't want it to be from my mouth."

Decision bubbled up in Miles, straightening his spine. Yes. He *knew*, now. He had only to run through the proofs, step by chained step. Just like 5-Space math. "Very well. I swear by my word as a Vorkosigan, I shall confine my questions to the facts to which you were an eyewitness. I will not ask you for conjectures about persons or events for which you were not present. There, will that do?"

Csurik bit his lip. "Yes, lord. If you keep your word."

"Try me," suggested Miles. His lips wrinkled back on a vulpine smile, absorbing the implied insult without comment.

Csurik climbed the yard beside Miles as if to an executioner's block. Their entrance created a tableau of astonishment among Karal and his family, clustered around their wooden table, where Dea was treating Pym. Pym and Dea looked rather blanker, till Miles made introduction: "Dr. Dea, get out your fast-penta. Here's Lem Csurik come to talk with us."

Miles steered Lem to a chair. The hill man sat with his hands clenched. Pym, a red and purpling bruise showing at the edges of the white tape circling his chest, took up his stunner and stepped back.

Dr. Dea muttered under his breath to Miles as he got out the hypospray. "How'd you *do* that?"

Miles's hand brushed his pocket. He pulled out a sugar cube and held it up, and grinned through the C of his thumb and finger. Dea snorted, but pursed his lips with reluctant respect.

Lem flinched as the hypospray hissed on his arm, as if he expected it to hurt.

"Count backwards from ten," Dead instructed. By the time Lem reached three, he had relaxed; at zero, he giggled.

"Karal, Ma Karal, Pym, gather round," said Miles. "You are my witnesses. Boys, stay back and stay quiet. No interruptions, please."

Miles ran through the preliminaries, half a dozen questions designed to set up a rhythm and kill time while the fast-penta took full effect. Lem Csurik grinned foolishly, lolling in his chair, and answered them all with sunny good will. Fast-penta interrogation had been part of Miles's military intelligence course at the Service Academy. The drug seemed to be working exactly as advertised, oddly enough.

"Did you return to your cabin that morning, after you spent the night at your parents'?"

"Yes, m'lord," Lem smiled.

"About what time?"

"Midmorning."

Nobody here had a chrono, that was probably as precise an answer as Miles was likely to get. "What did you do when you got there?"

"Called for Harra. She was gone, though. It frightened me that she was gone. Thought she might've run out on me." Lem hiccoughed. "I want my Harra."

"Later. Was the baby asleep?"

"She was. She woke up when I called for Harra. Started crying again. It goes right up your spine."

"What did you do then?"

Lem's eyes widened. "I got no milk. She wanted Harra. There's nothing I could do for her."

"Did you pick her up?"

"No, lord, I let her lay. There was nothing I could do for her. Harra, she'd hardly let me touch her, she was that nervous about her. Told me I'd drop her or something."

"You didn't shake her, to stop her screaming?"

"No, lord, I let her lay. I left to look down the path for Harra."

"Then where did you go?"

Lem blinked. "My sister's. I'd promised to help haul wood for a new cabin. Bella—m'other sister—is getting married, y'see, and—"

He was beginning to wander, as was normal for this drug. "Stop," said Miles. Lem fell silent obediently, swaying slightly in his chair. Miles considered his next question carefully. He was approaching the fine line, here. "Did you meet anyone on the path? Answer yes or no."

"Yes."

Dea was getting excited. "Who? Ask him who!"

Miles held up his hand. "You can administer the antagonist now, Dr. Dea."

"Aren't you going to ask him? It could be vital!"

"I can't. I gave my word. Administer the antagonist now, doctor!"

Fortunately, the confusion of two interrogators stopped Lem's mumbled willing reply to Dea's question. Dea, bewildered, pressed his hypospray against Lem's arm. Lem's eyes, half-closed, snapped open within seconds. He sat up straight and rubbed his arm, and his face.

"Who did you meet on the path?" Dea asked him directly.

Lem's lips pressed tight; he looked for rescue to Miles. Dea looked too. "Why won't you ask him?"

"Because I don't need to," said Miles. "I know precisely who Lem met on the path, and why he went on and not back. It was Raina's murderer. As I shall shortly prove. And—witness this, Karal, Ma Karal—that information did not come from Lem's mouth. Confirm!"

Karal nodded slowly. "I . . . see, m'lord. That was . . . very good of you."

Miles gave him a direct stare, his mouth set in a tight smile. "And when is a mystery no mystery at all?"

Karal reddened, not replying for a moment. Then he said, "You may as well keep on like you're going, m'lord. There's no stopping you now, I suppose."

"No."

Miles sent runners to collect the witnesses, Ma Karal in one direction, Zed in a second, Speaker Karal and his eldest in a third. He had Lem wait with Pym, Dea, and himself. Having the shortest distance to cover, Ma Karal arrived back first, with Ma Csurik and two of her sons in tow.

His mother fell on Lem, embracing him and then looking fearfully over her shoulder at Miles. The younger brothers hung back, but Pym had already moved between them and the door.

"It's all right, Ma," Lem patted her on the back. "Or . . . anyway, I'm all right. I'm clear. Lord Vorkosigan believes me."

She glowered at Miles, still holding Lem's arm. "You didn't let the mutie lord give you that poison drug, did you?"

"Not poison," Miles denied. "In fact, the drug may have saved his life. That damn near makes it a medicine, I'd say. However," he turned toward Lem's two younger brothers, and folded his arms sternly, "I would like to know which of you young morons threw the torch on my tent last night?"

The younger one whitened; the elder, hotly indignant, noticed his brother's expression and cut his denial off in mid-syllable. "You didn't!" he hissed in horror.

"Nobody," said the white one. "Nobody did."

Miles raised his eyebrows. There followed a short, choked silence.

"Well, *nobody* can make his apologies to Speaker and Ma Karal, then," said Miles, "since it was their sons who were sleeping in the tent last night. I and my men were in the loft."

The boy's mouth opened in dismay. The youngest Karal stared at the pale Csurik brother, his age-mate, and whispered importantly, "You, Dono! You idiot, didn't ya know that tent wouldn't burn? It's real Imperial Service issue!"

Miles clasped his hands behind his back, and fixed the Csuriks with a cold eye. "Rather more to the point, it was attempted assassination upon your Count's heir, which carries the same capital charge of treason as an attempt upon the Count himself. Or perhaps Dono didn't think of that?"

Dono was thrown into flummoxed confusion. No need for fast-penta here, the kid couldn't carry off a lie worth a damn. Ma Csurik now had hold of Dono's arm too, without letting go of Lem's; she looked as frantic as a hen with too many chicks, trying to shelter them from a storm.

"I wasn't trying to kill you, lord!" cried Dono.

"What were you trying to do, then?"

"You'd come to kill Lem. I wanted to ... make you go away. Frighten you away. I didn't think anyone would really get hurt—I mean, it was only a tent!"

"You've never seen anything burn down, I take it. Have you, Ma Csurik?"

Lem's mother nodded, lips tight, clearly torn between a desire to protect her son from Miles, and a desire to beat Dono till he bled for his potentially lethal stupidity.

"Well, but for a chance, you could have killed or horribly injured three of your friends. Think on that, please. In the meantime, in view of your youth and ah, apparent mental defectiveness, I shall hold the treason charge. In return, Speaker Karal and your parents shall be responsible for your good behavior in future, and decide what punishment is appropriate."

Ma Csurik melted with relief and gratitude. Dono looked like he'd rather have been shot. His brother poked him, and whispered, "Mental defective!" Ma Csurik slapped the taunter on the side of his head, suppressing him effectively.

"What about your horse, m'lord?" asked Pym.

"I ... do not suspect them of the business with the horse," Miles replied slowly. "The attempt to fire the tent was plain stupidity. The other was ... a different order of calculation altogether."

Zed, who had been permitted to take Pym's horse, returned then with Harra up behind him. Harra entered Speaker Karal's cabin, saw Lem, and stopped with a bitter glare. Lem stood openhanded, his eyes wounded, before her.

"So, lord," Harra said. "You caught him." Her jaw was clenched in joyless triumph.

"Not exactly," said Miles. "He came here and turned himself in. He's made his statement under fast-penta, and cleared himself. Lem did not kill Raina."

Harra turned from side to side. "But I saw he'd been there! He'd left his jacket, and took his good saw and wood planer away with him. I knew he'd been back while I was out! There must be something wrong with your drug!"

Miles shook his head. "The drug worked fine. Your deduction was correct as far as it went, Lem did visit the cabin while you were out. But when he left, Raina was still alive, crying vigorously. It wasn't Lem."

She swayed. "Who, then?"

"I think you know. I think you've been working very hard to deny that knowledge, hence your excessive focus on Lem. As long as you were sure it was Lem, you didn't have to think about the other possibilities."

"But who else would care?" Harra cried. "Who else would bother?"

"Who, indeed?" sighed Miles. He walked to the front window and glanced down the yard. The fog was clearing in the full light of morning. The horses were moving uneasily. "Dr. Dea, would you please get a second dose of fast-penta ready?" Miles turned, paced back to stand before the fireplace, its coals still banked for the night. The faint heat was pleasant on his back.

Dea was staring around, the hypospray in his hand, clearly wondering to whom to administer it. "My lord?" he queried, brows lowering in demand for explanation.

"Isn't it obvious to you, Doctor?" Miles asked lightly.

"*No*, my lord." His tone was slightly indignant.

"Nor to you, Pym?"

"Not . . . entirely, m'lord." Pym's glance, and stunner aim, wavered uncertainly to Harra.

"I suppose it's because neither of you ever met my

grandfather," Miles decided. "He died just about a year before you entered my father's service, Pym. He was born at the very end of the Time of Isolation, and lived through every wrenching change this century has dealt to Barrayar. He was called the last of the Old Vor, but really, he was the first of the new. He changed with the times, from the tactics of horse cavalry to that of flyer squadrons, from swords to atomics, and he changed *successfully*. Our present freedom from the Cetagandan occupation is a measure of how fiercely he could adapt, then throw it all away and adapt again. At the end of his life he was called a conservative, only because so much of Barrayar had streamed past him in the direction he had led, prodded, pushed, and pointed all his life.

"He changed, and adapted, and bent with the wind of the times. Then, in his age—for my father was his youngest and sole surviving son, and did not himself marry till middle-age—in his age, he was hit with me. And he had to change again. And he couldn't.

"He begged for my mother to have an abortion, after they knew more or less what the fetal damage would be. He and my parents were estranged for five years after I was born. They didn't see each other or speak or communicate. Everyone thought my father moved us to the Imperial Residence when he became Regent because he was angling for the throne, but in fact it was because the Count my grandfather denied him the use of Vorkosigan House. Aren't family squabbles jolly fun? Bleeding ulcers run in my family, we give them to each other." Miles strolled back to the window and looked out. Ah, yes. Here it comes.

"The reconciliation was gradual, when it became quite clear there would not be another son," Miles went on. "No dramatic denouement. It helped when the medics got me walking. It was essential that I tested out bright. Most important of all, I never let him see me give up."

Nobody had dared interrupt this lordly monologue, but it was clear from several expressions that the point of it was escaping them. Since half the point was to kill time,

Miles was not greatly disturbed by their failure to track. Footsteps sounded on the wooden porch outside. Pym moved quietly to cover the door with an unobscured angle of fire.

"Dr. Dea," said Miles, sighting through the window, "would you be so kind as to administer that fast-penta to the first person through the door, as they step in?"

"You're not waiting for a volunteer, my lord?"

"Not this time."

The door swung inward, and Dea stepped forward, raising his hand. The hypospray hissed. Ma Mattulich wheeled to face Dea, the skirts of her work dress swirling around her veined calves, hissing in return—"You dare!" Her arm drew back as if to strike him, but slowed in mid-swing and failed to connect as Dea ducked out of her way. This unbalanced her, and she staggered. Speaker Karal, coming in behind, caught her by the arm and steadied her. "You dare!" she wailed again, then turned to see not only Dea but all the other witnesses waiting; Ma Csurik, Ma Karal, Lem, Harra, Pym. Her shoulders sagged, and then the drug cut in and she just stood, a silly smile fighting with anguish for possession of her harsh face.

The smile made Miles ill, but it was the smile he needed. "Sit her down, Dea, Speaker Karal."

They guided her to the chair lately vacated by Lem Csurik. She was fighting the drug desperately, flashes of resistance melting into flaccid docility. Gradually the docility became ascendant, and she sat draped in the chair, grinning helplessly. Miles sneaked a peek at Harra. She stood white and silent, utterly closed.

For several years after the reconciliation Miles had never been left with his grandfather without his personal bodyguard. Sergeant Bothari had worn the Count's livery, but been loyal to Miles alone, the one man dangerous enough—some said, crazy enough—to stand up to the great General himself. There was no need, Miles decided, to spell out to these fascinated people just what interrupted incident had made his parents think Sergeant

Bothari a necessary precaution. Let General Piotr's untarnished reputation serve—Miles, now. As *he* willed. Miles's eyes glinted.

Lem lowered his head. "If I had known—if I had guessed—I wouldn't have left them alone together, m'lord. I thought—Harra's mother would take care of her. I couldn't have—I didn't know *how*—"

Harra did not look at him. Harra did not look at anything.

"Let us conclude this," Miles sighed. Again, he requested formal witness from the crowd in the room, and cautioned against interruptions, which tended to unduly confuse a drugged subject. He moistened his lips and turned to Ma Mattulich.

Again, he began with the standard neutral questions, name, birthdate, parents' names, checkable biographical facts. Ma Mattulich was harder to lull than the cooperative Lem had been, her responses scattered and staccato. Miles controlled his impatience with difficulty. For all its deceptive ease, fast-penta interrogation required skill, skill and patience. He'd got too far to risk a stumble now. He worked his questions up gradually to the first critical ones.

"Were you there, when Raina was born?"

Her voice was low and drifting, dreamy. "The birth came in the night. Lem, he went for Jean the midwife. The midwife's son was supposed to go for me but he fell back to sleep. I didn't get there till morning, and then it was too late. They'd all seen."

"Seen what?"

"The cat's mouth, the dirty mutation. Monsters in us. Cut them out. Ugly little man." This last, Miles realized, was an aside upon himself. Her attention had hung up on him, hypnotically. "Muties make more muties, they breed faster, overrun ... I saw you watching the girls. You want to make mutie babies on clean women, poison us all ..."

Time to steer her back to the main issue. "Were you ever alone with the baby after that?"

"No, Jean she hung around. Jean knows me, she knew what I wanted. None of her damn business. And Harra was always there. Harra must not know. Harra must not . . . why should she get off so soft? The poison must be in her. Must have come from her Da, I lay only with her Da and they were all wrong but the one."

Miles blinked. "What were all wrong?" Across the room Miles saw Speaker Karal's mouth tighten. The headman caught Miles's glance and stared down at his own feet, absenting himself from the proceedings. Lem, his lips parted in absorption, and the rest of the boys were listening with alarm. Harra hadn't moved.

"All my babies," Ma Mattulich said.

Harra looked up sharply at that, her eyes widening.

"Was Harra not your only child?" Miles asked. It was an effort to keep his voice cool, calm; he wanted to shout. He wanted to be gone from here. . . .

"No, of course not. She was my only clean child, I thought. I thought, but the poison must have been hidden in her. I fell on my knees and thanked God when she was born clean, a clean one at last, after so many, so much pain. . . . I thought I had finally been punished enough. She was such a pretty baby, I thought it was over at last. But she must have been mutie after all, hidden, tricksy, sly. . . ."

"How many," Miles choked, "babies did you have?"

"Four, besides Harra my last."

"And you killed all four of them?" Speaker Karal, Miles saw, gave a slow nod to his feet.

"No!" said Ma Mattulich. Indignation broke through the fast-penta wooze briefly. "Two were born dead already, the first one, and the twisted-up one. The one with too many fingers and toes, and the one with the bulgy head, those I cut. Cut out. My mother, she watched over me to see I did it right. Harra, I made it soft for Harra. I did it for her."

"So you have in fact murdered not one infant, but three?" said Miles frozenly. The younger witnesses in the room, Karal's boys and the Csurik brothers, looked horrified. The older ones, Ma Mattulich's contemporaries, who must have lived through the events with her, looked mortified, sharing her shame. Yes, they all must have known.

"Murdered?" said Ma Mattulich. "No! I cut them out. I had to. I had to do the right thing." Her chin lifted proudly, then dropped. "Killed my babies, to please, to please ... I don't know who. And now you call me a murderer? Damn you! What use is your justice to me *now*? I needed it then—where were you *then*?" Suddenly, shockingly, she burst into tears, which wavered almost instantly into rage. "If mine must die then so must hers! Why should she get off so soft? Spoiled her ... I tried my best, I did my best, it's not fair ..."

The fast-penta was not keeping up with this ... no, it was working. Miles decided, but her emotions were too overwhelming. Upping the dose might level her emotional surges, at some risk of respiratory arrest, but it would not elicit any more complete a confession. Miles's belly was trembling, a reaction he trusted he concealed. It had to be completed now.

"Why did you break Raina's neck, instead of cutting her throat?"

"Harra, she must not know," said Ma Mattulich. "Poor baby. It would look like she just died. ..."

Miles eyed Lem, Speaker Karal. "It seems a number of others shared your opinion that Harra should not know."

"I didn't want it to be from my mouth," repeated Lem sturdily.

"I wanted to save her double grief, m'lord," said Karal. "She'd had so much. ..."

Miles met Harra's eyes at that. "I think you all underestimate her. Your excessive tenderness insults both her intelligence and will. She comes from a tough line, that one."

Harra inhaled, controlling her own trembling. She gave Miles a short nod, as if to say *Thank you, little man.* He returned her a slight inclination of the head. *Yes, I understand.*

"I'm not sure yet where justice lies in this case," said Miles, "but this I swear to you, the days of cooperative concealment are over. No more secret crimes in the night. Daylight's here. And speaking of crimes in the night," he turned back to Ma Mattulich, "*was* it you who tried to cut my horse's throat last night?"

"I tried," said Ma Mattulich, calmer now in a wave of fast-penta mellowness, "but it kept rearing up on me."

"Why my *horse?*" Miles could not keep exasperation from his voice, though a calm, even tone was enjoined upon fast-penta interrogators by the training manual.

"I couldn't get at you," said Ma Mattulich simply.

Miles rubbed his forehead. "Retroactive infanticide by proxy?" he muttered.

"You," said Ma Mattulich, and her loathing came through even the nauseating fast-penta cheer, "*you* are the worst. All I went through, all I did, all the grief, and you come along at the end. A mutie made lord over us all, and all the rules changed, betrayed at the end by an off-worlder woman's weakness. You make it all for *nothing*. Hate you. Dirty mutie . . ." her voice trailed off in a drugged mumble.

Miles took a deep breath, and looked around the room. The stillness was profound, and no one dared break it.

"I believe," he said, "that concludes my investigation into the facts of this case."

The mystery of Raina's death was solved.

The problem of justice, unfortunately, remained.

Miles took a walk.

The graveyard, though little more than a crude clearing in the woodland, was a place of peace and beauty in the morning light. The stream burbled endlessly, shifting green shadows and blinding brilliant reflections. The faint breeze that had shredded away the last of the night fog whispered in the trees, and the tiny, short-lived creatures that everyone on Barrayar but biologists called bugs sang and twittered in the patches of native scrub.

"Well, Raina," Miles sighed, "and what do I do now?"

Pym lingered by the borders of the clearing, giving Miles
room. "It's all right," Miles assured the tiny grave, "Pym's
caught me talking to dead people before. He may think
I'm crazy, but he's far too well-trained to say so."

Pym in fact did not look happy, nor altogether well.
Miles felt rather guilty for dragging him out; by rights
the man should be resting in bed, but Miles had desperately needed this time alone. Pym wasn't just suffering
the residual effect of having been kicked by Ninny. He
had been silent ever since Miles had extracted the confession from Ma Mattulich. Miles was unsurprised. Pym
had steeled himself to play executioner to their imagined
hill bully; the substitution of a mad grandmother as his
victim had clearly given him pause. He would obey whatever order Miles gave him, though, Miles had no doubt
of that.

Miles considered the peculiarities of Barrayaran law,
as he wandered about the clearing, watching the stream
and the light, turning over an occasional rock with the
toe of his boot. The fundamental principle was clear;
the spirit was to be preferred over the letter, truth over
technicalities. Precedent was held subordinate to the
judgment of the man on the spot. Alas, the man on the
spot was himself. There was no refuge for him in auto-
mated rules, no hiding behind *the law says* as if the law
were some living overlord with a real Voice. The only
voice here was his own.

And who would be served by the death of that half-
crazed old woman? Harra? The relationship between
mother and daughter had been wounded unto death by
this, Miles had seen that in their eyes, yet still Harra had
no stomach for matricide. Miles rather preferred it that
way, having her standing by his ear crying for bloody
revenge would have been enormously distracting just
now. The obvious justice made a damn poor reward for
Harra's courage in reporting the crime. Raina? Ah. That
was more difficult.

"I'd like to lay the old gargoyle right there at your
feet, small lady," Miles muttered to her. "Is it your

desire? Does it serve you? What *would* serve you?" Was
this the great burning he had promised her?

What judgment would reverberate along the entire
Dendarii mountain range? Should he indeed sacrifice
these people to some larger political statement, regardless of their wants? Or should he forget all that, make
his judgment serve only those directly involved? He
scooped up a stone and flung it full force into the stream.
It vanished invisibly in the rocky bed.

He turned to find Speaker Karal waiting by the edge
of the graveyard. Karal ducked his head in greeting and
approached cautiously.

"So, m'lord," said Karal.

"Just so," said Miles.

"Have you come to any conclusion?"

"Not really." Miles gazed around. "Anything less than
Ma Mattulich's death seems . . . inadequate justice, and
yet . . . I cannot see who her death would serve."

"Neither could I. That's why I took the position I did
in the first place."

"No . . ." said Miles slowly, "no, you were wrong in
that. For one thing, it very nearly got Lem Csurik killed.
I was getting ready to pursue him with deadly force at
one point. It almost·destroyed him with Harra. Truth is
better. Slightly better. At least it isn't a fatal error. Surely
I can do . . . something with it."

"I didn't know what to expect of you, at first," admitted Karal.

Miles shook his head. "I meant to make changes. A
difference. Now . . . I don't know."

Speaker Karal's balding forehead wrinkled. "But we
are changing."

"Not enough. Not fast enough."

"You're young yet, that's why you don't see how much,
how fast. Look at the difference between Harra and her
mother. God—look at the difference between Ma Mattulich and *her* mother. *There* was a harridan." Speaker
Karal shuddered. "I remember her, all right. And yet,
she was not so unusual, in her day. So far from having

to make change. I don't think you could stop it if you tried. The minute we finally get a powersat receptor up here, and get on the comm net, the past will be done and over. As soon as the kids see the future—their future—they will be mad after it. They're already lost to the old ones like Ma Mattulich. The old ones know it, too, don't believe they don't know it. Why d'you think we haven't been able to get at least a small unit up here yet? Not just the cost. The old ones are fighting it. They call it off-planet corruption, but it's really the future they fear."

"There's so much still to be done."

"Oh, yes. We are a desperate people, no lie. But we have hope. I don't think you realize how much you've done, just by coming up here."

"I've done nothing," said Miles bitterly. "Sat around, mostly. And now, I swear, I'm going to end up doing more nothing. And then go home. Hell!"

Speaker Karal pursed his lips, looked at his feet, at the high hills. "You are doing something for us every minute. Mutie lord. Do you think you are invisible?"

Miles grinned wolfishly. "Oh, Karal, I'm a one-man band, I am. I'm a parade."

"As you say, just so. Ordinary people need extraordinary examples. So they can say to themselves, well, if he can do *that*, I can surely do *this*. No excuses."

"No quarter, yes, I know that game. Been playing it all my life."

"I think," said Karal, "Barrayar needs you. To go on being just what you are."

"Barrayar will eat me, if it can."

"Yes," said Karal, his eyes on the horizon, "so it will." His gaze fell to the graves at his feet. "But it swallows us all in the end, doesn't it? You will outlive the old ones."

"Or in the beginning." Miles pointed down. "Don't tell *me* who I'm going to outlive. Tell Raina."

Karal's shoulders slumped. "True. S'truth. Make your judgment, lord. I'll back you."

*   *   *

Miles assembled them all in Karal's yard for his Speaking, the porch now having become his podium. The interior of the cabin would have been impossibly hot and close for this crowd, suffocating with the afternoon sun beating on the roof, though outdoors the light made them squint. They were all here, everyone they could round up, Speaker Karal, Ma Karal, their boys, all the Csuriks, most of the cronies who had attended last night's funereal festivities, men, women, and children. Harra sat apart. Lem kept trying to hold her hand, though from the way she flinched it was clear she didn't want to be touched. Ma Mattulich sat displayed by Miles's side, silent and surly, flanked by Pym and an uncomfortable-looking Deputy Alex.

Miles jerked up his chin, settling his head on the high collar of his dress greens, as polished and formal as Pym's batman's expertise could make him. The Imperial Service uniform that Miles had earned. Did these people know he had earned it, or did they all imagine it a mere gift from his father, nepotism at work? Damn what they thought. He knew. He stood before his people, and gripped the porch rail.

"I have concluded the investigation of the charges laid before the Count's Court by Harra Csurik of the murder of her daughter Raina. By evidence, witness, and her own admissions, I find Mara Mattulich guilty of this murder, she having twisted the infant's neck until it broke, and then attempted to conceal that crime. Even when that concealment placed her son-in-law Lem Csurik in mortal danger from false charges. In light of the helplessness of the victim, the cruelty of the method, and the cowardly selfishness of the attempted concealment, I can find no mitigating excuse for the crime.

"In addition, Mara Mattulich by her own admission testifies to two previous infanticides, some twenty years ago, of her own children. These facts shall be announced by Speaker Karal in every corner of Silvy Vale, until every subject has been informed."

He could feel Ma Mattulich's glare boring into his

back. *Yes, go on and hate me, old woman. I will bury you yet, and you know it.* He swallowed, and continued, the formality of the language a sort of shield before him.

"For this unmitigated crime, the only proper sentence is death. And I so sentence Mara Mattulich. But in light of her age and close relation to the next-most-injured party in the case, Harra Csurik, I choose to hold the actual execution of that sentence. Indefinitely." Out of the corner of his eyes Miles saw Pym let out, very carefully and covertly, a sigh of relief. Harra combed at her straw-colored bangs with her fingers and listened intently.

"But she shall be as dead before the law. All her property, even to the clothes on her back, now belongs to her daughter Harra, to dispose of as she wills. Mara Mattulich may not own property, enter contract, sue for injuries, nor exert her will after death in any testament. She shall not leave Silvy Vale without Harra's permission. Harra shall be given power over her as a parent over a child, or as in senility. In Harra's absence Speaker Karal will be her deputy. Mara Mattulich shall be watched to see she harms no other child.

"Further. She shall die without sacrifice. No one, not Harra nor any other, shall make a burning for her when she goes into the ground at last. As she murdered her future, so her future shall return only death to her spirit. She will die as the childless do, without remembrance."

A low sigh swept the older members of the crowd before Miles. For the first time, Mara Mattulich bent her stiff neck.

Some, Miles knew, would find this only spiritually symbolic. Others would see it as literally lethal, according to the strength of their beliefs. The literal-minded, such as those who saw mutation as a sin to be violently expiated. But even the less superstitious, Miles saw in their faces, found the meaning clear. So.

Miles turned to Ma Mattulich, and lowered his voice. "Every breath you take from this moment on is by my mercy. Every bite of food you eat, by Harra's charity. By charity and mercy—such as you did not give—you shall live. Dead woman."

"Some mercy. Mutie lord." Her growl was low, weary, beaten.

"You get the point," he said through his teeth. He swept her a bow, infinitely ironic, and turned his back on her. "I am the Voice of Count Vorkosigan. This concludes my Speaking."

Miles met Harra and Lem afterwards, in Speaker Karal's cabin.

"I have a proposition for you." Miles controlled his nervous pacing and stood before them. "You're free to turn it down, or think about it for a while. I know you're very tired right now." *As are we all.* Had he really been in Silvy Vale only a day and a half? It seemed like a century. His head ached with fatigue. Harra was red-eyed too. "First of all, can you read and write?"

"Some," Harra admitted. "Speaker Karal taught us some, and Ma Lannier."

"Well, good enough. You wouldn't be starting completely blind. Look. A few years back Hassadar started a teacher's college. It's not very big yet, but it's begun. There are some scholarships. I can swing one your way, if you will agree to live in Hassadar for three years of intense study."

"Me!" said Harra. "I couldn't go to a college! I barely know . . . any of that stuff."

"Knowledge is what you're supposed to have coming out, not going in. Look, they know what they're dealing with in this district. They have a lot of remedial courses. It's true, you'd have to work harder, to catch up with the town-bred and the lowlanders. But I know you have courage, and I know you have will. The rest is just picking yourself up and ramming into the wall again and again until it falls down. You get a bloody forehead, so what? You can do it, I swear you can."

Lem, sitting beside her, looked worried. He captured

her hand again. "Three years?" he said in a small voice. "Gone away?"

"The school stipend isn't that much," said Miles. "But Lem, I understand you have carpenter's skills. There's a building boom going on in Hassadar right now. Hassadar's going to be the next Vorkosigan Vashnoi, I think. I'm certain you could get a job. Between you, you could live."

Lem looked at first relieved, then extremely worried. "But they all use power tools—computers—robots. . . ."

"By no means. And they weren't all born knowing how to use that stuff either. If they can learn it, you can. Besides, the rich pay well for hand-work, unique one-off items, if the quality's good. I can see you get a start, which is usually the toughest moment. After that you should be able to figure it out all right."

"To leave Silvy Vale . . ." said Harra in a dismayed tone.

"Only in order to return. That's the other half of the bargain. I can send a comm unit up here, a small one with a portable power pack that lasts a year. Somebody'd have to hump down to Vorkosigan Surleau to replace it annually, no big problem. The whole set up wouldn't cost much more than oh, a new lightflyer." Such as the shiny red one Miles had coveted in a dealer's showroom in Vorbarr Sultana, very suitable for a graduation present, he had pointed out to his parents. The credit chit was sitting in the top drawer of his dresser in the lake house at Vorkosigan Surleau right now. "It's not a massive project like installing a powersat receptor for the whole of Silvy Vale or anything. The holovid would pick up the educational satellite broadcasts from the capital; set it up in some central cabin, add a couple of dozen lap-links for the kids, and you've got an instant school. All the children would be required to attend, with Speaker Karal to enforce it, though once they'd discovered the holovid you'd probably have to beat them to make them go home. I, ah," Miles cleared his throat, "thought you might name it the Raina Csurik Primary School."

"Oh," said Harra, and began to cry for the first time that grueling day. Lem patted her clumsily. She returned the grip of his hand at last.

"I can send a lowlander up here to teach," said Miles. "I'll get one to take a short-term contract, till you're ready to come back. But he or she won't understand Silvy Vale like you do. Wouldn't understand *why*. You—you already know. You know what they can't teach in any lowland college."

Harra scrubbed her eyes, and looked up—not very far up—at him. "You went to the Imperial Academy."

"I did." His chin jerked up.

"Then I," she said shakily, "can manage . . . Hassadar Teacher's College." The name was awkward in her mouth. At first. "At any rate—I'll try, m'lord."

"I'll bet on you," Miles agreed. "Both of you. Just, ah," a smile sped across his mouth and vanished, "stand up straight and speak the truth, eh?"

Harra blinked understanding. An answering half-smile lit her tired face, equally briefly. "I will. Little man."

Fat Ninny rode home by air the next morning, in a horse van, along with Pym. Dr. Dea went along with his two patients, and his nemesis the sorrel mare. A replacement bodyguard had been sent with the groom who flew the van from Vorkosigan Surleau, who stayed with Miles to help him ride the remaining two horses back down. Well, Miles thought, he'd been considering a camping trip in the mountains with his cousin Ivan as part of his home leave anyway. The liveried man was the laconic veteran Esterhazy, whom Miles had known most of his life; excellent company for a man who didn't want to talk about it, unlike Ivan you could almost forget he was there. Miles wondered if Esterhazy's assignment had been random chance, or a mercy of the Count's. Esterhazy was good with horses.

They camped overnight by the river of roses. Miles walked up the vale in the evening light, desultorily looking for the spring of it; indeed, the floral barrier did seem to peter out a couple of kilometers upstream, merging into slightly less impassable scrub. Miles plucked a rose, checked to make sure that Esterhazy was nowhere in sight, and bit into it curiously. Clearly, he was not a horse. A cut bunch would probably not survive the trip back as a treat for Ninny. Ninny could settle for oats.

Miles watched the evening shadows flowing up along the backbone of the Dendarii range, high and massive in the distance. How small those mountains looked from space! Little wrinkles on the skin of a globe he could cover with his hand, all their crushing mass made invisible. Which was illusory, distance or nearness? Distance, Miles decided. Distance was a damned lie. Had his father known this? Miles suspected so.

He contemplated his urge to throw all his money, not just a lightflyer's worth, at those mountains; to quit it all and go teach children to read and write, to set up a free clinic, a powersat net, or all of these at once. But Silvy Vale was only one of hundreds of such communities buried in these mountains, one of thousands across the whole of Barrayar. Taxes squeezed from this very district helped maintain the very elite military school he'd just spent—how much of their resources in? How much would he have to give back just to make it even, now? He was himself a planetary resource, his training had made him so, and his feet were set on their path.

What God means you to do, Miles's theist mother claimed, could be deduced from the talents he gave you. The academic honors, Miles had amassed by sheer brute work. But the war games, outwitting his opponents, staying one step ahead—a necessity, true, he had no margin for error—the war games had been an unholy joy. War had been no game here once, not so long ago. It might be so again. What you did best, that was what was wanted from you. God seemed to be lined up with the Emperor on that point, at least, if no other.

Miles had sworn his officer's oath to the Emperor less than two weeks ago, puffed with pride at his achievement. In his secret mind he had imagined himself keeping that oath through blazing battle, enemy torture, what-have-you, even while sharing cynical cracks afterwards with Ivan about archaic dress swords and the sort of people who insisted on wearing them.

But in the dark of subtler temptations, those which hurt without heroism for consolation, he foresaw, the Emperor would no longer be the symbol of Barrayar in his heart.

Peace to you, small lady, he thought to Raina. *You've won a twisted poor modern knight, to wear your favor on his sleeve. But it's a twisted poor world we were both born into, that rejects us without mercy and ejects us without consultation. At least I won't just tilt at windmills for you. I'll send in sappers to mine the twirling suckers, and blast them into the sky. . . .*

He knew who he served now. And why he could not quit. And why he must not fail.

1991
49th Convention
Chicago

Bears Discover Fire
by Terry Bisson

The Manamouki
by Mike Resnick

The Hemingway Hoax
by Joe Haldeman

Science fiction people, like everybody else in the known universe, have an overwhelming impulse to put things in categories, including science fiction stories. There's the Invasion from Mars story and the Overpopulation story, the If This Goes On Story and the If We Could Only Go Back and Change Things story, the Machine that Takes Over and the Children with Telepathic Powers, even the Creatures from Mythology that Were Actually Aliens story.

But in science fiction, as in life, there are some things that are simply uncategorizable. This category, known as Stories that Cannot be Categorized, or Misc. (I told you the impulse was overwhelming) contains some of my favorite stories in all of science fiction: "The Light of Other Days" by Bob Shaw and "Morning Child" by Gardner Dozois and R. A. Lafferty's "Continued on Next Rock."

And this story by Terry Bisson, which contains one of the most marvelously haunting images in all of science fiction.

"Bears Discover Fire" is Terry Bisson's first Hugo Award. It also won the Nebula Award and the Theodore Sturgeon Memorial Award for Best Short Story. Bisson is the author of Talking Man, Fire on the Mountain, and Voyage to the Red Planet.

—Connie Willis

Bears Discover Fire
by Terry Bisson

I was driving with my brother, the preacher, and my
nephew, the preacher's son, on I-65 just north of Bowling
Green when we got a flat. It was Sunday night and we
had been to visit Mother at the Home. We were in my
car. The flat caused what you might call knowing groans
since, as the old-fashioned one in my family (so they tell
me), I fix my own tires, and my brother is always telling
me to get radials and quit buying old tires.

But if you know how to mount and fix tires yourself,
you can pick them up for almost nothing.

Since it was a left rear tire, I pulled over left, onto
the median grass. The way my Caddy stumbled to a stop,
I figured the tire was ruined. "I guess there's no need
asking if you have any of that *FlatFix* in the trunk,"
said Wallace.

"Here, son, hold the light," I said to Wallace Jr. He's
old enough to want to help and not old enough (yet) to
think he knows it all. If I'd married and had kids, he's
the kind I'd have wanted.

An old Caddy has a big trunk that tends to fill up like
a shed. Mine's a '56. Wallace was wearing his Sunday
shirt, so he didn't offer to help while I pulled magazines,
fishing tackle, a wooden tool box, some old clothes, a
comealong wrapped in a grass sack, and a tobacco sprayer

out of the way, looking for my jack. The spare looked a little soft.

The light went out. "Shake it, son," I said.

It went back on. The bumper jack was long gone, but I carry a little ¼ ton hydraulic. I finally found it under Mother's old *Southern Livings*, 1978–1986. I had been meaning to drop them at the dump. If Wallace hadn't been along, I'd have let Wallace Jr. position the jack under the axle, but I got on my knees and did it myself. There's nothing wrong with a boy learning to change a tire. Even if you're not going to fix and mount them, you're still going to have to change a few in this life. The light went off again before I had the wheel off the ground. I was surprised at how dark the night was already. It was late October and beginning to get cool. "Shake it again, son," I said.

It went back on but it was weak. Flickery.

"With radials you just don't *have* flats," Wallace explained in that voice he uses when he's talking to a number of people at once; in this case, Wallace Jr. and myself. "And even when you *do*, you just squirt them with this stuff called *FlatFix* and you just drive on. $3.95 the can."

"Uncle Bobby can fix a tire hisself," said Wallace Jr., out of loyalty I presume.

"*Him*self," I said from halfway under the car. If it was up to Wallace, the boy would talk like what Mother used to call "a helot from the gorges of the mountains." But drive on radials.

"Shake that light again," I said. It was about gone. I spun the lugs off into the hubcap and pulled the wheel. The tire had blown out along the sidewall. "Won't be fixing this one," I said. Not that I cared. I have a pile as tall as a man out by the barn.

The light went out again, then came back better than ever as I was fitting the spare over the lugs. "Much better," I said. There was a flood of dim orange flickery light. But when I turned to find the lug nuts, I was surprised to see that the flashlight the boy was holding was dead. The light was coming from two bears at the edge of the trees, holding torches. They were big, three-hundred pounders, standing about five feet tall. Wallace Jr. and his father had seen them and were standing perfectly still. It's best not to alarm bears.

I fished the lug nuts out of the hubcap and spun them on. I usually like to put a little oil on them, but this time I let it go. I reached under the car and let the jack down and pulled it out. I was relieved to see that the spare was high enough to drive on. I put the jack and the lug wrench and the flat into the trunk. Instead of replacing the hubcap, I put it in there too. All this time, the bears never made a move. They just held the torches up, whether out of curiosity or helpfulness, there was no way of knowing. It looked like there may have been more bears behind them, in the trees.

Opening three doors at once, we got into the car and drove off. Wallace was the first to speak. "Looks like bears have discovered fire," he said.

When we first took Mother to the Home, almost four years (forty-seven months) ago, she told Wallace and me she was ready to die. "Don't worry about me, boys," she whispered, pulling us both down so the nurse wouldn't hear. "I've drove a million miles and I'm ready to pass over to the other shore. I won't have long to linger here." She drove a consolidated school bus for thirty-nine years. Later, after Wallace left, she told me about her dream. A bunch of doctors were sitting around in a circle discussing her case. One said, "We've done all we can for her, boys, let's let her go." They all turned their hands up and smiled. When she didn't die that fall, she seemed disappointed, though as spring came she forgot about it, as old people will.

In addition to taking Wallace and Wallace Jr. to see Mother on Sunday nights, I go myself on Tuesdays and Thursdays. I usually find her sitting in front of the TV, even though she doesn't watch it. The nurses keep it on all the time. They say the old folks like the flickering. It soothes them down.

"What's this I hear about bears discovering fire?" she said on Tuesday. "It's true," I told her as I combed her long white hair with the shell comb Wallace had brought her from Florida. Monday there had been a story in the Louisville *Courier-Journal*, and Tuesday one on NBC or CBS Nightly News. People were seeing bears all over the state, and in Virginia as well. They had quit hibernating, and were apparently planning to spend the winter in the medians of the interstates. There have always been bears in the mountains of Virginia, but not here in western Kentucky, not for almost a hundred years. The last one was killed when Mother was a girl. The theory in the *Courier-Journal* was that they were following I-65 down from the forests of Michigan and Canada, but one old man from Allen County (interviewed on nationwide TV) said that there had always been a few bears left back in the hills, and they had come out to join the others now that they had discovered fire.

"They don't hibernate any more," I said. "They make a fire and keep it going all winter."

"I declare," Mother said. "What'll they think of next!" The nurse came to take her tobacco away, which is the signal for bedtime.

Every October, Wallace Jr. stays with me while his parents go to camp. I realize how backward that sounds, but there it is. My brother is a minister (House of the Righteous Way, Reformed), but he makes two thirds of his living in real estate. He and Elizabeth go to a Christian Success Retreat in Florida, where people from all over the country practice selling things to one another. I know what it's like not because they've ever bothered to tell me, but because I've seen the Revolving Equity Success Plan ads late at night on TV.

The schoolbus let Wallace Jr. off at my house on Wednesday, the day they left. The boy doesn't have to pack much of a bag when he stays with me. He has his own room here. As the eldest of our family, I hung onto the old home place near Smiths Grove. It's getting run down, but Wallace Jr. and I don't mind. He has his own room in Bowling Green, too, but since Wallace and Elizabeth move to a different house every three months (part of the Plan), he keeps his .22 and his comics, the stuff that's important to a boy his age, in his room here at the home place. It's the room his dad and I used to share.

Wallace Jr. is twelve. I found him sitting on the back porch that overlooks the interstate when I got home for work. I sell crop insurance.

After I changed clothes, I showed him how to break the bead on a tire two ways, with a hammer and by backing a car over it. Like making sorghum, fixing tires by hand is a dying art. The boy caught on fast, though. "Tomorrow I'll show you how to mount your tire with the hammer and a tire iron," I said.

"What I wish is I could see the bears," he said. He was looking across the field to I-65, where the northbound lanes cut off the corner of our field. From the house at night, sometimes the traffic sounds like a waterfall.

"Can't see their fire in the daytime," I said. "But wait till tonight." That night CBS or NBC (I forget which is which) did a special on the bears, which were becoming a story of nationwide interest. They were seen in Kentucky, West Virginia, Missouri, Illinois (southern), and, of course, Virginia. There have always been bears in Virginia. Some characters there were even talking about hunting them. A scientist said they were heading into the states where there is some snow but not too much, and where there is enough timber in the medians for firewood. He had gone in with a video camera, but his shots were just blurry figures sitting around a fire. Another scientist said the bears were attracted by the berries on a new bush that grew only in the medians of the interstates. He claimed this berry was the first new species in recent history, brought about by the mixing of seeds along the highway. He ate one on TV, making a

face, and called it a "newberry." A climatic ecologist said
that the warm winters (there was no snow last winter in
Nashville, and only one flurry in Louisville) had changed
the bears' hibernation cycle, and now they were able to
remember things from year to year. "Bears may have
discovered fire centuries ago," he said, "but forgot it."
Another theory was that they had discovered (or remembered) fire when Yellowstone burned, several years ago.

The TV showed more guys talking about bears than it
showed bears, and Wallace Jr. and I lost interest. After
the supper dishes were done I took the boy out behind
the house and down to our fence. Across the interstate
and through the trees, we could see the light of the
bears' fire. Wallace Jr. wanted to go back to the house
and get his .22 and go shoot one, and I explained why
that would be wrong. "Besides," I said, "a .22 wouldn't
do much more to a bear than make it mad.

"Besides," I added, "It's illegal to hunt in the
medians."

The only trick to mounting a tire by hand, once you
have beaten or pried it onto the rim, is setting the bead.
You do this by setting the tire upright, sitting on it, and
bouncing it up and down between your legs while the
air goes in. When the bead sets on the rim, it makes a
satisfying "pop." On Thursday, I kept Wallace Jr. home
from school and showed him how to do this until he got
it right. Then we climbed our fence and crossed the field
to get a look at the bears.

In northern Virginia, according to "Good Morning
America," the bears were keeping their fires going all
day long. Here in western Kentucky, though, it was still
warm for late October and they only stayed around the
fires at night. Where they went and what they did in the
daytime, I don't know. Maybe they were watching from
the newberry bushes as Wallace Jr. and I climbed the
government fence and crossed the northbound lanes. I
carried an axe and Wallace Jr. brought his .22, not because he wanted to kill a bear but because a boy likes

to carry some kind of a gun. The median was all tangled with brush and vines under the maple, oaks, and sycamores. Even though we were only a hundred yards from the house, I had never been there, and neither had anyone else that I knew of. It was like a created country. We found a path in the center and followed it down across a slow, short stream that flowed out of one grate and into another. The tracks in the gray mud were the first bear signs we saw. There was a musty but not really unpleasant smell. In a clearing under a big hollow beech, where the fire had been, we found nothing but ashes. Logs were drawn up in a rough circle and the smell was stronger. I stirred the ashes and found enough coals left to start a new flame, so I banked them back the way they had been left.

I cut a little firewood and stacked it to one side, just to be neighborly.

Maybe the bears were watching us from the bushes even then. There's no way to know. I tasted one of the newberries and spit it out. It was so sweet it was sour, just the sort of thing you would imagine a bear would like.

That evening after supper, I asked Wallace Jr. if he might want to go with me to visit Mother. I wasn't surprised when he said "yes." Kids have more consideration than folks give them credit for. We found her sitting on the concrete front porch of the Home, watching the cars go by on I-65. The nurse said she had been agitated all day. I wasn't surprised by that, either. Every fall as the leaves change, she gets restless, maybe the word is hopeful, again. I brought her into the dayroom and combed her long, white hair. "Nothing but bears on TV anymore," the nurse complained, flipping the channels. Wallace Jr. picked up the remote after the nurse left, and we watched a CBS or NBC Special Report about some hunters in Virginia who had gotten their houses torched. The TV interviewed a hunter and his wife whose $117,500 Shenandoah Valley home had burned. She blamed the bears. He didn't blame the bears, but he was suing for compensation from the state since he had a valid hunting license. The state hunting commissioner came on and said that possession of a hunting license didn't prohibit (enjoin, I think, was the word he used) *the hunted* from striking back. I thought that was a pretty liberal view for a state commissioner. Of course, he had a vested interest in not paying off. I'm not a hunter myself.

"Don't bother coming on Sunday," Mother told Wallace Jr. with a wink. "I've drove a million miles and I've got one hand on the gate." I'm used to her saying stuff like that, especially in the fall, but I was afraid it would upset the boy. In fact, he looked worried after we left and I asked him what was wrong.

"How could she have drove a million miles?" he asked. She had told him 48 miles a day for 39 years, and he had worked it out on his calculator to be 336,960 miles.

"Have *driven*," I said. "And it's forty-eight in the morning and forty-eight in the afternoon. Plus there were the football trips. Plus, old folks exaggerate a little." Mother was the first woman school bus driver in the state. She did it every day and raised a family, too. Dad just farmed.

I usually get off the interstate at Smiths Grove, but that night I drove north all the way to Horse Cave and doubled back so Wallace Jr. and I could see the bears' fires. There were not as many as you would think from the TV—one every six or seven miles, hidden back in a clump of trees or under a rocky ledge. Probably they look for water as well as wood. Wallace Jr. wanted to stop, but it's against the law to stop on the interstate and I was afraid the state police would run us off.

There was a card from Wallace in the mailbox. He and Elizabeth were doing fine and having a wonderful time. Not a word about Wallace Jr., but they didn't seem to mind. Like most kids his age, he doesn't really enjoy going places with his parents.

*   *   *

On Saturday afternoon, the Home called my office (Burley Belt Drought & Hail) and left word that Mother was gone. I was on the road. I work Saturdays. It's the only day a lot of part-time farmers are home. My heart literally skipped a beat when I called in and got the message, but only a beat. I had long been prepared. "It's a blessing," I said when I got the nurse on the phone.

"You don't understand," the nurse said. "Not *passed* away, gone. *Ran* away, gone. Your mother has escaped." Mother had gone through the door at the end of the corridor when no one was looking, wedging the door with her comb and taking a bedspread which belonged to the Home. What about her tobacco? I asked. It was gone. That was a sure sign she was planning to stay away. I was in Franklin, and it took me less than an hour to get to the Home on I-65. The nurse told me that Mother had been acting more and more confused lately. Of course they are going to say that. We looked around the grounds, which is only an acre with no trees between the interstate and a soybean field. Then they had me leave a message at the Sheriff's office. I would have to keep paying for her care until she was officially listed as Missing, which would be Monday.

It was dark by the time I got back to the house, and Wallace Jr. was fixing supper. This just involves opening a few cans, already selected and grouped together with a rubber band. I told him his grandmother had gone, and he nodded, saying, "She told us she would be." I called Florida and left a message. There was nothing more to be done. I sat down and tried to watch TV, but there was nothing on. Then, I looked out the back door, and saw the firelight twinkling through the trees across the northbound lane of I-65, and realized I just might know where to find her.

It was definitely getting colder, so I got my jacket. I told the boy to wait by the phone in case the Sheriff called, but when I looked back, halfway across the field, there he was behind me. He didn't have a jacket. I let him catch up. He was carrying his .22, and I made him leave it leaning against our fence. It was harder climbing the government fence in the dark, at my age, than it had been in the daylight. I am sixty-one. The highway was busy with cars heading south and trucks heading north.

Crossing the shoulder, I got my pants cuffs wet on the long grass, already wet with dew. It is actually bluegrass.

The first few feet into the trees it was pitch black and the boy grabbed my hand. Then it got lighter. At first I thought it was the moon, but it was the high beams shining like moonlight into the treetops, allowing Wallace Jr. and me to pick our way through the brush. We soon found the path and its familiar bear smell.

I was wary of approaching the bears at night. If we stayed on the path we might run into one in the dark, but if we went through the bushes we might be seen as intruders. I wondered if maybe we shouldn't have brought the gun.

We stayed on the path. The light seemed to drip down from the canopy of the woods like rain. The going was easy, especially if we didn't try to look at the path but let our feet find their own way.

Then through the trees I saw their fire.

The fire was mostly of sycamore and breech branches, the kind of fire that puts out very little heat or light and lots of smoke. The bears hadn't learned the ins and outs of wood yet. They did okay at tending it, though. A large cinnamon brown northern-looking bear was poking the fire with a stick, adding a branch now and then from a pile at his side. The others sat around in a loose circle on the logs. Most were smaller black or honey bears; one was a mother with cubs. Some were eating berries from a hubcap. Not eating, but just watching the fire, my mother sat among them with the bedspread from the Home around her shoulders.

If the bears noticed us, they didn't let on. Mother patted a spot right next to her on the log and I sat down. A bear moved over to let Wallace Jr. sit on her other side.

The bear smell is rank but not unpleasant, once you get used to it. It's not like a barn smell, but wilder. I leaned over to whisper something to Mother and she shook her head. *It would be rude to whisper around these creatures that don't possess the power of speech,* she let me know without speaking. Wallace Jr. was silent too. Mother shared the bedspread with us and we sat for what seemed hours, looking into the fire.

The big bear tended the fire, breaking up the dry branches by holding one end and stepping on them, like people do. He was good at keeping it going at the same level. Another bear poked the fire from time to time, but the others left it alone. It looked like only a few of the bears knew how to use fire, and were carrying the others along. But isn't that how it is with everything? Every once in a while, a smaller bear walked into the circle of firelight with an armload of wood and dropped it onto the pile. Median wood has a silvery cast, like driftwood.

Wallace Jr. isn't fidgety like a lot of kids. I found it pleasant to sit and stare into the fire. I took a little piece of Mother's *Red Man,* though I don't generally chew. It was no different from visiting her at the Home, only more interesting, because of the bears. There were about eight or ten of them. Inside the fire itself, things weren't so dull, either: little dramas were being played out as fiery chambers were created and then destroyed in a crashing of sparks. My imagination ran wild. I looked around the circle at the bears and wondered what *they* saw. Some had their eyes closed. Though they were gathered together, their spirits still seemed solitary, as if each bear was sitting alone in front of its own fire.

The hubcap came around and we all took some newberries. I don't know about Mother, but I just pretended to eat mine. Wallace Jr. made a face and spit his out. When he went to sleep, I wrapped the bedspread around all three of us. It was getting colder and we were not provided, like the bears, with fur. I was ready to go home, but not Mother. She pointed up toward the canopy of trees, where a light was spreading, and then pointed to herself. Did she think it was angels approaching from on high? It was only the high beams of some southbound truck, but she seemed mighty pleased. Holding her hand, I felt it grow colder and colder in mine.

Wallace Jr. woke me up by tapping on my knee. It was past dawn, and his grandmother had died sitting on the log between us. The fire was banked up and the bears were gone and someone was crashing straight through the woods, ignoring the path. It was Wallace. Two state troopers were right behind him. He was wearing a white shirt, and I realized it was Sunday morning. Underneath his sadness on learning of Mother's death, he looked peeved.

The troopers were sniffing the air and nodding. The bear smell was still strong. Wallace and I wrapped Mother in the bedspread and started with her body back out to the highway. The troopers stayed behind and scattered the bears' fire ashes and flung their firewood away into the bushes. It seemed a petty thing to do. They were like bears themselves, each one solitary in his own uniform.

There was Wallace's Olds 98 on the median, with its radial tires looking squashed on the grass. In front of it there was a police car with a trooper standing beside it, and behind it a funeral home hearse, also an Olds 98.

"First report we've had of them bothering old folks," the trooper said to Wallace. "That's not hardly what happened at all," I said, but nobody asked me to explain. They have their own procedures. Two men in suits got out of the hearse and opened the rear door. That to me was the point at which Mother departed this life. After we put her in, I put my arms around the boy. He was shivering even though it wasn't that cold. Sometimes death will do that, especially at dawn, with the police around and the grass wet, even when it comes as a friend.

We stood for a minute watching the cars pass. "It's a blessing," Wallace said. It's surprising how much traffic there is at 6:22 A.M.

That afternoon, I went back to the median and cut a little firewood to replace what the troopers had flung away. I could see the fire through the trees that night.

I went back two nights later, after the funeral. The fire was going and it was the same bunch of bears, as far as I could tell. I sat around with them a while but it seemed to make them nervous, so I went home. I had taken a handful of newberries from the hubcap, and on Sunday I went with the boy and arranged them on Mother's grave. I tried again, but it's no use, you can't eat them.

Unless you're a bear.

It's been said that the sum total of all human knowledge can be found at a science fiction convention. I believe it. Science fiction fans are experts on all sorts of esoterica, and science fiction writers, whose job it is to be interested in everything, know all about the strangest things: the Titanic *and mating habits of snakes and the history of ballet. I myself am knowledgeable on the subjects of church choirs and the London Blitz, Terry Bisson knows all about Nat Turner's uprising, and Mike Resnick is the resident expert on Theodore Roosevelt and collies. He has written works ranging from* The Soul Eater *(he's also an expert on Melville) to his wonderful Africa books (see the introduction to "Kirinyaga") to* Tales of the Galactic Midway, *and* Will the Last Person to Leave the Planet Please Shut Off the Sun?*

He also knows a great deal about Africa. And, as this beautifully subtle story shows, the tremendous difficulty involved in trying to maintain the status quo.

—Connie Willis

The Manamouki

by Mike Resnick

Many eons ago, the children of Gikuyu, who was himself
the first Kikuyu, lived on the slopes of the holy mountain
Kirinyaga, which men now call Mount Kenya.

There were many serpents on the mountain, but the
sons and grandsons of Gikuyu found them repulsive, and
they soon killed all but one.

Then one day the last serpent entered their village and
killed and ate a young child. The children of Gikuyu
sought out their *mundumugu*—their witch doctor—and
asked him to destroy the menace.

The *mundumugu* rolled the bones and sacrificed a
goat, and finally he created a poison that would kill the
serpent. He slit open the belly of another goat, and
placed the poison inside it, and left it beneath a tree,
and the very next day the serpent swallowed the goat
and died.

"Now," said the *mundumugu*, "you must cut the serpent into one hundred pieces and scatter them on the
holy mountain, so that no demon can breathe life back
into its body."

The children of Gikuyu did as they were instructed,
and scattered the hundred pieces of the serpent across
the slopes of Kirinyaga. But during the night, each piece
came to life and became a new serpent, and soon the
Kikuyu were afraid to leave their *bomas*.

The *mundumugu* ascended the mountain, and when he neared the highest peak, he addressed Ngai.

"We are besieged by serpents," he said. "If you do not slay them, then the Kikuyu shall surely die as a people."

"I made the serpent, just as I made the Kikuyu and all other things," answered Ngai, who sat on His golden throne atop Kirinyaga. "And anything that I made, be it a man or a serpent or a tree or even an idea, is not repellent in My eyes. I will save you this one time, because you are young and ignorant, but you must never forget that you cannot destroy that which you find repulsive—for if you try to destroy it, it will always return one hundred times greater than before."

This is one of the reasons why the Kikuyu chose to till the soil rather than hunt the beasts of the jungle like the Wakamba, or make war on their neighbors like the Maasai, for they had no wish to see that which they destroyed return to plague them. It is a lesson taught by every *mundumugu* to his people, even after we left Kenya and emigrated to the terraformed world of Kirinyaga.

In the entire history of our tribe, only one *mundumugu* ever forgot the lesson that Ngai taught atop the holy mountain on that distant day.

And that *mundumugu* was myself.

When I awoke, I found hyena dung within the thorn enclosure of my *boma*. That alone should have warned me that the day carried a curse, for there is no worse omen. Also the breeze, hot and dry and filled with dust, came from the west, and all good winds come from the east.

It was the day that our first immigrants were due to arrive. We had argued long and hard against allowing any newcomers to settle on Kirinyaga, for we were dedicated to the old ways of our people, and we wanted no outside influences corrupting the society that we had created. But our charter clearly stated that any Kikuyu who pledged to obey our laws and make the necessary payments to the Eutopian Council could emigrate from

Kenya, and after postponing the inevitable for as long as we could, we finally agreed to accept Thomas Nkobe and his wife.

Of all the candidates for immigration, Nkobe had seemed the best. He had been born in Kenya, had grown up in the shadow of the holy mountain, and after going abroad for his schooling, had returned and run the large farm his family had purchased from one of the last European residents. Most important of all, he was a direct descendant of Jomo Kenyatta, the great Burning Spear of Kenya, who had led us to independence.

I trudged out across the hot, arid savannah to the tiny landing field at Haven to greet our new arrivals, accompanied only by Ndemi, my youthful assistant. Twice buffalo blocked our path, and once Ndemi had to hurl some stones to frighten a hyena away, but eventually we reached our destination, only to discover that the Maintenance ship which was carrying Nkobe and his wife had not yet arrived. I squatted down in the shade of an acacia tree, and a moment later Ndemi crouched down beside me.

"They are late," he said, peering into the cloudless sky. "Perhaps they will not come at all."

"They will come," I said. "The signs all point to it."

"But they are bad signs, and Nkobe may be a good man."

"There are many good men," I replied. "Not all of them belong on Kirinyaga."

"You are worried, Koriba?" asked Ndemi as a pair of crested cranes walked through the dry, brittle grass.

"I am concerned," I said.

"Why?"

"Because I do not know why he wants to live here."

"Why shouldn't he?" asked Ndemi, picking up a dry twig and methodically breaking it into tiny pieces. "Is it not Utopia?"

"There are many different notions of Utopia," I replied. "Kirinyaga is the Kikuyus'."

"And Nkobe is a Kikuyu, so this is where he belongs," said Ndemi decisively.

"I wonder."

"Why?"

"Because he is almost forty years old. Why did he wait so long to come here?"

"Perhaps he could not afford to come sooner."

I shook my head. "He comes from a very wealthy family."

"They have many cattle?" asked Ndemi.

"Many," I said.

"And goats?"

I nodded.

"Will he bring them with him?"

"No. He will come empty-handed, as we all did." I paused, frowning. "Why would a man who owned a large farm and had many tractors and men to do his work turn his back on all that he possessed? That is what troubles me."

"You make it sound like the way he lived on Earth was better," said Ndemi.

"Not better, just different."

He paused for a moment. "Koriba, what *is* a tractor?"

"A machine that does the work of many men in the fields."

"It sounds truly wonderful," offered Ndemi.

"It makes deep wounds in the ground and stinks of gasoline," I said, making no effort to hide my contempt.

We sat in silence for another moment. Then the Maintenance ship came into view, its descent creating a huge cloud of dust and causing a great screeching and squawking by the birds and monkeys in the nearby trees.

"Well," I said, "we shall soon have our answer."

I remained in the shade until the ship had touched down and Thomas Nkobe and his wife emerged from its interior. He was a tall, well-built man dressed in casual Western clothes; she was slender and graceful, her hair elegantly braided, her khaki slacks and hunting jacket exquisitely tailored.

"Hello!" said Nkobe in English as I approached him. "I was afraid we might have to find our way to the village ourselves."

"*Jambo,*" I replied in Swahili. "Welcome to Kirinyaga."

"*Jambo,*" he amended, switching to Swahili. "Are you Koinnage?"

"No," I answered. "Koinnage is our paramount chief. You will live in his village."

"And you are?"

"I am Koriba," I said.

"He is the *mundumugu,*" added Ndemi proudly. "I am Ndemi." He paused. "Someday I will be a *mundumugu* too."

Nkobe smiled down at him. "I'm sure you will." Suddenly he remembered his wife. "And this is Wanda."

She stepped forward, smiled, and extended her hand. "A true *mundumugu!*" she said in heavily-accented Swahili. "I'm thrilled to meet you!"

"I hope you will enjoy your new life on Kirinyaga," I said, shaking her hand.

"Oh, I'm certain I will," she replied enthusiastically, as the ship disgorged their baggage and promptly took off again. She looked around at the dry savannah, and saw a trio of maribou storks and a jackal patiently waiting for a hyena to finish gorging itself on the wildebeest calf it had killed earlier in the morning. "I love it already!" She paused, then added confidentially, "I'm really the one who got Tom to agree to come here."

"Oh?"

She nodded her head. "I just couldn't stand what Kenya has become. All those factories, all that pollution! Ever since I learned about Kirinyaga, I've wanted to move here, to come back to Nature and live the way we were meant to live." She inhaled deeply. "Smell that air, Tom! It will add ten years to your life."

"You don't have to sell me any more," he said with a smile. "I'm here, aren't I?"

I turned to Wanda Nkobe. "You yourself are not Kikuyu, are you?"

"I am now," she replied. "Ever since I married Tom. But to answer your question, no, I was born and raised in Oregon."

"Oregon?" repeated Ndemi, brushing some flies away from his face with his hand.

"That's in America," she explained. She paused. "By the way, why are we speaking Swahili rather than Kikuyu?"

"Kikuyu is a dead language," I said. "Most of our people no longer know it."

"I had rather hoped it would still be spoken here," she said, obviously disappointed. "I've been studying it for months."

"If you had moved to Italy, you would not speak Latin," I replied. "We still use a few Kikuyu words, just as the Italians use a few Latin words."

She was silent for a moment, then shrugged. "At least I'll have the opportunity to improve my Swahili."

"I am surprised that you are willing to forgo the amenities of America for Kirinyaga," I said, studying her closely.

"I was willing years ago," she answered. "It was Tom who had to be convinced, not me." She paused. "Besides, I gave up most of those so-called amenities when I left America and moved to Kenya."

"Even Kenya has certain luxuries," I noted. "We have no electricity here, no running water, no—"

"We camp out whenever we can," she said, and I placed a hand on Ndemi's shoulder before he could chide her for interrupting the *mundumugu*. "I'm used to roughing it."

"But you have always had a home to return to."

She stared at me, an amused smile on her face. "Are you trying to talk me out of moving here?"

"No," I replied. "But I wish to point out that nothing is immutable. Any member of our society who is unhappy and wishes to leave need only inform Maintenance of the fact and a ship will arrive at Haven an hour later."

"Not us," she said. "We're in for the long haul."

"The long haul?" I repeated.

"She means that we're here to stay," explained Nkobe, putting an arm around his wife's shoulders.

A hot breeze sent the dust swirling around us.

"I think I should take you to the village," I said, shielding my eyes. "You are doubtless tired and will wish to rest."

"Not at all," said Wanda Nkobe. "This is a brand-new world. I want to look around." Her gaze fell upon Ndemi, who was staring at her intently. "Is something wrong?" she asked.

"You are very strong and sturdy," said Ndemi approvingly. "That is good. You will bear many children."

"I certainly hope not," she said. "If there's one thing Kenya has more than enough of, it's children."

"This is not Kenya," said Ndemi.

"I will find other ways to contribute to the society."

Ndemi studied her for a moment. "Well," he said at last, "I suppose you can carry firewood."

"I'm glad I meet with your approval," she said.

"But you will need a new name," continued Ndemi. "Wanda is a European name."

"It is just a name," I said. "Changing it will not make her more of a Kikuyu."

"I have no objection," she interjected. "I'm starting a new life; I *ought* to have a new name."

I shrugged. "Which name will you take as your own?"

She smiled at Ndemi. "You choose one," she said.

He furrowed his brow for a long moment, then looked up at her. "My mother's sister, who died in childbirth last year, was named Mwange, and now there is no one in the village of that name."

"Then Mwange it shall be," she said. "Mwange wa Ndemi."

"But I am not your father," said Ndemi.

She smiled at him. "You are the father of my new name."

Ndemi puffed his chest up proudly.

"Well, now that *that's* settled," said Nkobe, "what about our luggage?"

"You will not need it," I said.

"Yes we will," said Mwange.

"You were told to bring nothing of Kenya with you."

"I've brought some *kikois* that I made myself," she said. "Surely that must be permissible, since I will be expected to weave my own fabrics and make my own clothes on Kirinyaga."

I considered her explanation for a moment, then nodded my consent. "I will send one of the village children for the bags."

"It's not that heavy," said Nkobe. "I can carry it myself."

"Kikuyu men do not fetch and carry," said Ndemi.

"What about Kikuyu women?" asked Mwange, obviously reluctant to leave the luggage behind.

"They carry firewood and grain, not bags of clothing," responded Ndemi. "*Those,*" he said, pointing contemptuously toward the two leather bags, "are for children."

"Then we might as well start walking," said Mwange. "There are no children here."

Ndemi beamed with pride and strutted forward.

"Let Ndemi go first," I said. "His eyes are young and clear. He will be able to see any snakes or hyenas hiding in the tall grass."

"Do you have poisonous snakes here?" asked Nkobe.

"A few."

"Why don't you kill them?"

"Because this is not Kenya," I replied.

I walked directly behind Ndemi, and Nkobe and Mwange followed us, remarking upon the scenery and the animals to each other. After about half a mile we came to an impala ram standing directly in our path.

"Isn't he beautiful?" whispered Mwange. "Look at the horns on him!"

"I wish I had my camera with me!" said Nkobe.

"We do not permit cameras on Kirinyaga," I said.

"I know," said Nkobe. "But to be perfectly honest, I

can't see how something as simple as a camera could be a corrupting influence to your society."

"To have a camera, one needs film, and one must therefore have a factory that manufactures both cameras and films. To develop the film, one needs chemicals, and then one must find a place to dump those chemicals that haven't been used. To print the pictures, one needs photographic paper, and we have barely enough wood to burn in our fires." I paused. "Kirinyaga supplies us with all of our desires. That is why we came here."

"Kirinyaga supplies you with all of your *needs*," said Mwange. "That is not quite the same thing."

Suddenly Ndemi stopped walking and turned to her.

"This is your first day here, so you are to be forgiven your ignorance," he explained. "But no *manamouki* may argue with the *mundumugu*."

"*Manamouki?*" she repeated. "What is a *manamouki?*"

"*You* are," said Ndemi.

"I've heard that word before," said Nkobe. "I think it means *wife*."

"You are wrong," I said. "A *manamouki* is a female."

"You mean a woman?" asked Mwange.

I shook my head. "*Any* female property," I said. "A woman, a cow, a sow, a bitch, a ewe."

"And Ndemi thinks I'm some kind of property?"

"You are Nkobe's *manamouki*," said Ndemi.

She considered it for a moment, then shrugged with amusement. "What the hell," she said in English. "If Wanda was only a name, *manamouki* is only a word. I can live with it."

"I hope so," I replied in Swahili, "for you will have to."

She turned to me. "I know we are the first immigrants to come to Kirinyaga, and that you must have your doubts about us—but this is the life I've always wanted. I'm going to be the best damned *manamouki* you ever saw."

"I hope so," I said, but I noticed that the wind still blew from the west.

*   *   *

I introduced Nkobe and Mwange to their neighbors, showed them their *shamba* where they would grow their food, pointed out their six cattle and ten goats and recommended that they lock them in their *boma* at night to protect them from the hyenas, told them how to reach the river to procure water, and left them at the entrance to their hut. Mwange seemed enthused about everything, and was soon engaged in animated conversation with the women who came by to look at her strange outfit.

"She is very nice," commented Ndemi as I walked through the fields, blessing the scarecrows. "Perhaps the omens you read were wrong."

"Perhaps," I said.

He stared at me. "But you do not think so."

"No."

"Well, *I* like her," he said.

"That is your right."

"Do you dislike her, then?"

I paused as I considered my answer.

"No," I said at last. "I fear her."

"But she is just a *manamouki*!" he protested. "She can do no harm."

"Under the proper circumstances, anything can do harm."

"I do not believe it," said Ndemi.

"Do you doubt your *mundumugu's* word?" I asked.

"No," he said uncomfortably. "If you say something, then it must be true. But I cannot understand how."

I smiled wryly. "That is because you are not yet a *mundumugu.*"

He stopped and pointed to a spot some three hundred yards away, where a group of impala does were grazing.

"Can even *they* do harm?" he asked.

"Yes."

"But how?" he asked, frowning. "When danger appears, they do not confront it, but run away from it. Ngai has not blessed them with horns, so they cannot defend themselves. They are not large enough to destroy our crops. They cannot even kick an enemy, as can the zebra. I do not understand."

"I shall tell you the tale of the Ugly Buffalo, and then you will understand," I said.

Ndemi smiled happily, for he loved stories above all things, and I led him to the shade of a thorn tree, where we both squatted down, facing each other.

"One day a cow buffalo was wandering through the savannah," I began. "The hyenas had recently taken her first calf, and she was very sad. Then she came upon a newborn impala, whose mother had been killed by hyenas that very morning.

" 'I would like to take you home with me,' said the buffalo, 'for I am very lonely, and have much love in my heart. But you are not a buffalo.'

" 'I, too, am very lonely,' said the impala. 'And if you leave me here, alone and unprotected, I surely will not survive the night.'

" 'There is a problem,' said the buffalo. 'You are an impala, and we are buffalo. You do not belong with us.'

" 'I will become the best buffalo of all,' promised the impala. 'I will eat what you eat, drink what you drink, go where you go.'

" 'How can you become a buffalo? You cannot even grow horns.'

" 'Then I will wear the branches of a tree upon my head.'

" 'You do not wallow in the mud to protect your skin from parasites,' noted the buffalo.

" 'Take me home with you and I will cover myself with more mud than any other buffalo,' said the impala.

"For every objection the buffalo raised, the impala had an answer, and finally the buffalo agreed to take the impala back with her. Most of the members of the herd thought that the impala was the ugliest buffalo they had ever seen"—Ndemi chuckled at that—"but because the impala tried so hard to act like a buffalo, they allowed her to remain.

"Then one day a number of young buffalo were grazing some distance from the herd, and they came to a deep mud wallow that blocked their way.

" 'We must return to the herd,' said one of the young buffalo.

" 'Why?' asked the impala. 'There is fresh grass on the other side of the wallow.'

" 'Because we have been warned that a deep wallow such as this can suck us down beneath the surface and kill us.'

" 'I do not believe it,' said the impala, and, bolder than her companions, she walked out to the center of the mud wallow.

" 'You see?' she said. 'I have not been sucked beneath the surface. It is perfectly safe.'

"Soon three of the young buffalo ventured out across the mud wallow, and each in turn was sucked beneath the surface and drowned.

" 'It is the ugly buffalo's fault,' said the king of the herd. 'It was she who told them to cross the mud wallow.'

" 'But she meant no harm,' said her foster mother. 'And what she told them was true: the wallow was safe for her. All she wants is to live with the herd and be a buffalo; please do not punish her.'

"The king was blessed with more generosity than wisdom, and so he forgave the ugly buffalo.

"Then, a week later, the ugly buffalo, who could leap as high as a tall bush, jumped up in the air and saw a pack of hyenas lurking in the grass. She waited until they were almost close enough to catch her, and then cried out a warning. All the buffalo began running, but the hyenas were able to catch the ugly buffalo's foster mother, and they pulled her down and killed her.

"Most of the other buffalo were grateful to the ugly buffalo for warning them, but during the intervening week there had been a new king, and this one was wiser than the previous one.

" 'It is the ugly buffalo's fault,' he said.

" 'How can it be her fault?' asked one of the older buffalo. 'It was she who warned us of the hyenas.'

" 'But she only warned you when it was too late,' said the king. 'Had she warned you when she first saw the hyenas, her mother would still be among us. But she forgot that we cannot run as fast as she can, and so her mother is dead.'

"And the new king, though his heart was sad, decreed that the ugly buffalo must leave the herd, for there is a great difference between *being* a buffalo and *wanting* to be a buffalo."

I leaned back against the tree, my story completed.

"Did the ugly buffalo survive?" asked Ndemi.

I shrugged and brushed a crawling insect from my forearm. "That is another story."

"She meant no harm."

"But she caused harm nonetheless."

Ndemi traced patterns in the dirt with his finger as he considered my answer, then looked up at me. "But if she had not been with the herd, the hyenas would have killed her mother anyway."

"Perhaps."

"Then it was not her fault."

"If I fall asleep against this tree, and you see a black mamba slithering through the grass toward me, and you make no attempt to wake me, and the mamba kills me, would you be to blame for my death?" I asked.

"Yes."

"Even though it would certainly have killed me had you not been here?"

Ndemi frowned. "It is a difficult problem."

"Yes, it is."

"The mud wallow was much easier," he said. "That was surely the ugly buffalo's fault, for without her urging, the other buffalo would never have entered it."

"That is true," I said.

Ndemi remained motionless for a few moments, still wrestling with the nuances of the story.

"You are saying that there are many different ways to cause harm," he announced.

"Yes."

"And that it takes wisdom to understand who is to blame, for the foolish king did not recognize the harm of the ugly buffalo's action, while the wise king knew that she was to blame for her inaction."

I nodded my head.

"I see," said Ndemi.

"And what has this to do with the *manamouki*?" I asked.

He paused again. "If harm comes to the village, you must use your wisdom to decide whether Mwange, who wants nothing more than to be a Kikuyu, is responsible for it."

"That is correct," I said, getting to my feet.

"But I still do not know what harm she can do."

"Neither do I," I answered.

"Will you know it when you see it?" he asked. "Or will it seem like a good deed, such as warning the herd that hyenas are near?"

I made no reply.

"Why are you silent, Koriba?" asked Ndemi at last.

I sighed heavily. "Because there are some questions that even a *mundumugu* cannot answer."

Ndemi was waiting for me, as usual, when I emerged from my hut five mornings later.

"*Jambo*, Koriba," he said.

I grunted a greeting and walked over to the fire that he had built, sitting cross-legged next to it until it removed the chill from my aging bones.

"What is today's lesson?" he asked at last.

"Today I will teach you how to ask Ngai for a fruitful harvest," I answered.

"But we did that last week."

"And we will do it next week, and many more weeks as well," I answered.

"When will I learn how to make ointments to cure the sick, or how to turn an enemy into an insect so that I may step on him?"

"When you are older," I said.

"I am already old."

"And more mature."

"How will you know when I am more mature?" he persisted.

"I will know because you will have gone an entire month without asking about ointments or magic, for patience is one of the most important virtues a *mundumugu* can possess." I got to my feet. "Now take my gourds to the river and fill them with water," I said, indicating two empty water gourds.

"Yes, Koriba," he said dejectedly.

While I was waiting for him, I went into my hut, activated my computer, and instructed Maintenance to make a minor orbital adjustment that would bring rain and cooler air to the western plains.

This done, I slung my pouch around my neck and went back out into my *boma* to see if Ndemi had returned, but instead of my youthful apprentice, I found Wambu, Koinnage's senior wife, waiting for me, bristling with barely controlled fury.

"*Jambo*, Wambu," I said.

"*Jambo*, Koriba," she replied.

"You wish to speak to me?"

She nodded. "It is about the Kenyan woman."

"Oh?"

"Yes," said Wambu. "You must make her leave!"

"What has Mwange done?" I asked.

"I am the senior wife of the paramount chief, am I not?" demanded Wambu.

"That is true."

"She does not treat me with the respect that is my due."

"In what way?" I asked.

"In *all* ways!"

"For example?"

"Her *khanga* is much more beautiful than mine. The colors are brighter, the designs more intricate, the fabric softer."

"She wove her *khanga* on her own loom, in the old way," I said.

"What difference does *that* make?" snapped Wambu.

I frowned. "Do you wish me to make her give you the *khanga*?" I asked, trying to understand her rage.

"No!"

"Then I do not understand," I said.

"You are no different than Koinnage!" she said, obviously frustrated that I could not comprehend her complaint. "You may be a *mundumugu*, but you are still a man!"

"Perhaps if you told me more," I suggested.

"Kibo was as silly as a child," she said, referring to Koinnage's youngest wife, "but I was training her to be a good wife. Now she wants to be like the Kenyan woman."

"But the Kenyan woman," I said, using her terminology, "wants to be like *you*."

"She cannot be like me!" Wambu practically shouted at me. "I am Koinnage's senior wife!"

"I mean that she wants to be a member of the village."

"Impossible!" scoffed Wambu. "She speaks of many strange things."

"Such as?"

"It does not matter! You must make her leave!"

"For wearing a pretty *khanga* and making a good impression on Kibo?" I said.

"Bah!" she snapped. "You are just like Koinnage! You pretend not to understand, but you know she must go!"

"I truly do not understand," I said.

"You are *my mundumugu*, not hers. I will pay you two fat goats to place a *thahu* on her."

"I will not place a curse on Mwange for the reasons you gave me," I said firmly.

She glared at me for a long moment, then spat on the ground, turned on her heel and walked back down the winding path to the village, muttering furiously to herself, practically knocking Ndemi down as he returned with my water gourds.

I spent the next two hours instructing Ndemi in the

harvest prayer, then told him to go into the village and bring Mwange back. An hour later Mwange, resplendent in her *khanga,* climbed up my hill, accompanied by Ndemi, and entered my *boma.*

"*Jambo,*" I greeted her.

"*Jambo,* Koriba," she replied. "Ndemi says that you wish to speak to me."

I nodded. "That is true."

"The other women seemed to think I should be frightened."

"I cannot imagine why," I said.

"Perhaps it is because you can call down the lightning, and change hyenas into insects, and kill your enemies from miles away," suggested Ndemi helpfully.

"Perhaps," I said.

"Why have you sent for me?" asked Mwange.

I paused for a moment, trying to think of how best to approach the subject. "There is a problem with your clothing," I said at last.

"But I am wearing a *khanga* that I wove on my own loom," she said, obviously puzzled.

"I know," I responded. "But the quality of the fabric and the subtlety of the colors, have caused a certain . . ." I searched for the proper word.

"Resentment?" she suggested.

"Precisely," I answered, grateful that she so quickly comprehended the situation. "I think it would be best if you were to weave some less colorful garments."

I half-expected her to protest, but she surprised me by agreeing immediately.

"Certainly," she said. "I have no wish to offend my neighbors. May I asked who objected to my *khanga?*"

"Why?"

"I'd like to make her a present of it."

"It was Wambu," I said.

"I should have realized the effect my clothing would have. I am truly sorry, Koriba."

"Anyone may make a mistake," I said. "As long as it is corrected, no lasting harm will be done."

"I hope you're right," she said sincerely.

"He is the *mundumugu*," said Ndemi. "He is always right."

"I don't want the women to be resentful of me," continued Mwange. "Perhaps I could find some way to show my good intentions." She paused. "What if I were to offer to teach them to speak Kikuyu?"

"No *manamouki* may be a teacher," I explained. "Only the chiefs and the *mundumugu* may instruct our people."

"That's not very efficient," she said. "It may very well be that someone besides yourself and the chiefs has something to offer."

"It is possible," I agreed. "Now let me ask you a question."

"What is it?"

"Did you come to Kirinyaga to be efficient?"

She sighed. "No," she admitted. She paused for a moment. "Is there anything else?"

"No."

"Then I think I'd better go back and begin weaving my new fabric."

I nodded my approval, and she walked back down the long, winding path to the village.

"When I become *mundumugu*," said Ndemi, watching her retreating figure, "I will not allow any *manamoukis* to argue with *me*."

"A *mundumugu* must also show understanding," I said. "Mwange is new here, and has much to learn."

"About Kirinyaga?"

I shook my head. "About *manamoukis*."

Life proceeded smoothly and uneventfully for almost six weeks, until just after the short rains. Then one morning, just as I was preparing to go down into the village to bless the scarecrows, three of the women came up the path to my *boma*.

There was Sabo, the widow of old Kadamu, and Bori, the second wife of Sabana, and Wambu.

"We must speak with you, *mundumugu*," said Wambu.

I sat down, cross-legged, in front of my hut, and waited for them to seat themselves opposite me.

"You may speak," I said.

"It is about the Kenyan woman," said Wambu.

"Oh?" I said. "I thought the problem was solved."

"It is not."

"Did she not present you with her *khanga* as a gift?" I asked.

"Yes."

"You are not wearing it," I noted.

"It does not fit," said Wambu.

"It is only a piece of cloth," I said. "How can it not fit?"

"It does not fit," she repeated adamantly.

I shrugged. "What is this new problem?"

"She flaunts the traditions of the Kikuyu," said Wambu.

I turned to the other women. "Is this true?" I asked.

Sabo nodded. "She is a married woman, and she has not shaved her head."

"And she keeps flowers in her hut," added Bori.

"It is not the custom for Kenyan women to shave their heads," I replied. "I will instruct her to do so. As for the flowers, they are not in violation of our laws."

"But *why* does she keep them?" persisted Bori.

"Perhaps she thinks they are pleasing to the eye," I suggested.

"But now my daughter wants to grow flowers, and she answers with disrespect when I tell it her is more important to grow food to eat."

"And now the Kenyan woman has made a throne for her husband, Nkobe," put in Sabo.

"A throne?" I repeated.

"She put a back and arms on his sitting stool," said Sabo. "What man besides a chief sits upon a throne? Does she think Nkobe will replace Koinnage?"

"*Never!*" snarled Wambu.

"And she has made another throne for herself," continued Sabo. "Even Wambu does not sit atop a throne."

"These are not thrones, but chairs," I said.

"Why can she not use stools, like all the other members of the village?" demanded Sabu.

"I think she is a witch," said Wambu.

"Why do you say that?" I asked.

"Just look at her," said Wambu. "She has seen the long rains come and go thirty-five times, and yet her back is not bent, and her skin is not wrinkled, and she has all her teeth."

"Her vegetables grow better than ours," added Sabo, "and yet she spends less time planting and tending to them than we do." She paused. "I think she *must* be a witch."

"And although she carries with her the worst of all *thahus*, that of barrenness, she acts as if she is not cursed at all," said Bori.

"And her new garments are still more beautiful than ours," muttered Sabo sullenly.

"That is true," agreed Bori. "Now Sabana is displeased with me because his *kikoi* is not so bright and soft as Nkobe's."

"And my daughters all want thrones instead of sitting stools," added Sabo. "I tell them that we have scarely enough wood for the fire, and they say that this is more important. She has turned their heads. They no longer respect their elders."

"The young women all listen to her, as if *she* were the wife of a chief instead of a barren *manamouki*," complained Wambu. "You must send her away, Koriba."

"Are you giving me an order, Wambu?" I asked softly, and the other two women immediately fell silent.

"She is an evil witch, and she must go," insisted Wambu, her outrage overcoming her fear of disobeying her *mundumugu*.

"She is not a witch," I said, "for if she were, then I, your *mundumugu*, would certainly know it. She is just a *manamouki* who is trying to learn our ways, and who, as you note, carries the terrible *thahu* of barrenness with her."

"If she is less than a witch, she is still more than a *manamouki*," said Sabo.

"More in what way?" I asked.

"Just more," she answered with a sullen expression.

Which totally summed up the problem.

"I will speak to her again," I said.

"And you will make her shave her head?" demanded Wambu.

"Yes."

"And remove the flowers from her hut?"

"I will discuss it."

"Perhaps you can tell Nkobe to beat her from time to time," added Sabo. "Then she would not act so much like a chief's wife."

"I feel very sorry for him," said Bori.

"For Nkobe?" I asked.

Bori nodded. "To be cursed with such a wife, and further, to have no children."

"He is a good man," agreed Sabo. "He deserves better than the Kenyan woman."

"It is my understanding that he is perfectly happy with Mwange," I said.

"That is all the more reason to pity him, for being so foolish," said Wambu.

"Have you come here to talk about Mwange or Nkobe?" I asked.

"We have said what we have come to say," replied Wambu, getting to her feet. "You must do something, *mundumugu*."

"I will look into the matter," I said.

She walked down the path to the village, followed by Sabo. Bori, her back bent from carrying firewood all her life, her stomach distended from producing three sons and five daughters, all but nine of her teeth missing, her legs permanently bowed from some childhood disease, Bori, who had seen but thirty-four long rains, stood before me for a moment.

"She really *is* a witch, Koriba," she said. "You have only to look at her to know it."

Then she, too, left my hill and returned to the village.

Once again I summoned Mwange to my *boma*.

She came up the path with the graceful stride of a young girl, lithe and lean and filled with energy.

"How old are you, Mwange?" I asked as she approached me.

"Thirty-eight," she replied. "I usually tell people that I'm thirty-five, though," she added with a smile. She stood still for a moment. "Is that why you asked me to come here? To talk about my age?"

"No," I said. "Sit down, Mwange."

She seated herself on the dirt by the ashes of my morning fire, and I squatted across from her.

"How are you adjusting to your new life on Kirinyaga?" I asked at last.

"Very well," she said enthusiastically. "I've made many friends, and I find that I don't miss the amenities of Kenya at all."

"Then you are happy here?"

"Very."

"Tell me about your friends."

"Well, my closest friend is Kibo, Koinnage's youngest wife, and I have helped Sumi and Kalena with their gardens, and—"

"Have you no friends among the older women?" I interrupted.

"Not really," she admitted.

"Why should that be?" I asked. "They are women of your own age."

"We don't seem to have anything to talk about."

"Do you find them unfriendly?" I asked.

She considered the question. "Ndemi's mother has always been very kind to me. The others could be a little friendlier, I suppose, but I imagine that's just because most of them are senior wives and are very busy running their households."

"Did it ever occur to you that there could be some other reason why they are not friendly?" I suggested.

"What are you getting at?" she asked, suddenly alert.

"There is a problem," I said.

"Oh?"

"Some of the older women resent your presence."

"Because I'm an immigrant?" she asked.

I shook my head. "No."

"Then why?" she persisted, genuinely puzzled.

"It is because we have a very rigid social order here, and you have not yet fit in."

"I thought I was fitting in very well," she said defensively.

"You were mistaken."

"Give me an example."

I looked at her. "You know that Kikuyu wives must shave their heads, and yet you have not done so."

She sighed and touched her hair. "I know," she replied. "I've been meaning to, but I'm very fond of it. I'll shave my head tonight." She seemed visibly relieved. "Is that what this is all about?"

"No," I said. "That is merely an outward sign of the problem."

"Then I don't understand."

"It is difficult to explain," I said. "Your *khangas* are more pleasing to the eye than theirs. Your garden grows better. You are as old as Wambu, but appear younger than her daughters. In their minds, these things set you apart from them and make you more than a *manamouki*. The corollary, which they have not yet voiced but must surely feel, is that if you are somehow *more*, then this makes them somehow *less*."

"What do you expect me to do?" she asked. "Wear rags and let my gardens go to seed?"

"No," I said. "I do not expect that."

"Then what can I do?" she continued. "You're telling me that they feel threatened because I am competent." She paused. "*You* are a competent man, Koriba. You have been schooled in Europe and America, you can

read and write and work a computer. And yet I notice
that you feel no need to hide your talents."

"I am a *mundumugu*," I said. "I live alone on my hill,
removed from the village, and I am viewed with awe and
fear by my people. This is the function of a *mundumugu*.
It is not the function of a *manamouki*, who must live
in the village and find her place in the social order of
the tribe."

"That's what I am trying to do," she said in frustration.

"Do not try so hard."

"If you're not telling me to be incompetent, then I
still don't understand."

"One does not fit in by being different," I said. "For
example, I know that you bring flowers into your house.
Doubtless they are fragrant and pleasing to the eye, but
no other woman in the village decorates her hut with
flowers."

"That's not true," she said defensively. "Sumi does."

"If so, then she does it because *you* do it," I pointed
out. "Can you see that this is even more threatening to
the older women than if you alone kept flowers, for it
challenges their authority?"

She stared at me, trying to comprehend.

"They have spent their entire lives achieving their positions within the tribe," I continued, "and now you have
come here and taken a position entirely outside of their
order. We have a new world to populate: You are barren,
but far from feeling shame or grief, you act as though
this is not a terrible *thahu*. Such an attitude is contrary
to their experience, just as decorating your house with
flowers or creating *khangas* with intricate patterns is contrary to their experience, and thus they feel threatened."

"I still don't see what I can do about it," she protested.
"I gave my original *khangas* to Wambu, but she refuses
to wear them. And I have offered to show Bori how to
get a greater yield from her gardens, but she won't
listen."

"Of course not," I replied. "Senior wives will not
accept advice from a *manamouki*, any more than a chief

would accept advice from a newly circumcised young man. You must simply"—here I switched to English, for there is no comparable term in Swahili—"maintain a low profile. If you do so, in time the problems will go away."

She paused for a moment, considering what I had told her.

"I'll try," she said at last.

"And if you *must* do something that will call attention to yourself," I continued, reverting to Swahili, "try to do it in a way that will not offend."

"I didn't even know I *was* offending," she said. "How am I to avoid it if I'm calling attention to myself?"

"There are ways," I answered. "Take, for example, the chair that you built."

"Tom has had back spasms for years," she said. "I built the chair because he couldn't get enough support from a stool. Am I supposed to let my husband suffer because some of the women don't believe in chairs?"

"No," I said. "But you can tell the younger women that Nkobe ordered you to build the chair, and thus the stigma will not be upon you."

"Then it will be upon him."

I shook my head. "Men have far greater leeway here than women. There will be no stigma upon him for ordering his *manamouki* to see to his comfort." I paused long enough for the thought to sink in. "Do you understand?"

She sighed. "Yes."

"And you will do as I suggest?"

"If I'm to live in peace with my neighbors, I suppose I must."

"There is always an alternative," I said.

She shook her head vigorously. "I've dreamed of a place like this all my life, and nobody is going to make me leave it now that I'm here. I'll do whatever I have to do."

"Good," I said, getting to my feet to signify that the interview was over. "Then the problem will soon be solved."

But, of course, it wasn't.

*   *   *

I spent the next two weeks visiting a neighboring village whose chief had died quite suddenly. He had no sons and no brothers, and the line of succession was in doubt. I listened to all the applicants to the throne, discussed the situation with the Council of Elders until there was unanimity, presided at the ceremony that installed the new chief in his ceremonial robes and headdress, and finally returned to my own village.

As I climbed the path to my *boma*, I saw a female figure sitting just outside my hut. I drew closer and saw that it was Shima, Ndemi's mother.

"*Jambo*, Koriba," she said.

"*Jambo*, Shima," I responded.

"You are well, I trust."

"As well as an old man can feel after walking for most of the day," I responded, sitting down opposite her. I looked around my *boma*. "I do not see Ndemi."

"I sent him to the village for the afternoon, because I wished to speak to you alone."

"Does this concern Ndemi?" I asked.

She shook her head. "It is about Mwange."

I sighed wearily. "Proceed."

"I am not like the other women, Koriba," she began. "I have always been good to Mwange."

"So she has told me."

"Her ways do not bother me," she continued. "After all, someday I shall be the mother of the *mundumugu*, and while there can be many senior wives, there can be only one *mundumugu* and one *mundumugu's* mother."

"This is true," I said, waiting for her to get to the point of her visit.

"Therefore, I have befriended Mwange, and have shown her many kindnesses, and she has responded in kind."

"I am pleased to hear it."

"And because I have befriended her," continued Shima, "I have felt great compassion for her, because as you know she carries the *thahu* of barrenness. And it seemed to me that, since Nkobe is such a wealthy man, that he should take another wife to help Mwange with the work on the *shamba* and to produce sons and daughters." She paused. "My daughter Shuni, as you know, will be circumcised before the short rains come, and so I approached Mwange as a friend, and as the mother of the future *mundumugu,* to suggest that Nkobe pay the bride price for Shuni." Here she paused again, and frowned. "She got very mad and yelled at me. You must speak to her, Koriba. A rich man like Nkobe should not be forced to live with only a barren wife."

"Why do you keep calling Nkobe a rich man?" I asked. "His *shamba* is small, and he has only six cattle."

"His family is rich," she stated. "Ndemi told me that they have many men and machines to do their planting and harvesting."

Thank you for nothing, little Ndemi, I thought irritably. Aloud I said: "All that is back on Earth. Here Nkobe is a poor man."

"Even if he is poor," said Shima, "he will not remain poor, for grain and vegetables grow for Mwange as for no one else, as if this is Ngai's blessing to make up for His *thahu* of barrenness." She stared at me. "You must talk to her, Koriba. This would be a good thing. Shuni is very obedient and hard-working, and she already likes Mwange very much. We will not demand a large bride price, for we know that the *mundumugu's* family will never go hungry."

"Why did you not wait for Nkobe to approach you, as is the custom?" I asked.

"I thought if I explained my idea to Mwange, she would see the wisdom of it and speak to Nkobe herself, for he listens to her more than most husbands listen to their wives, and surely the thought of a fertile woman who would share her chores would appeal to her."

"Well, you have presented your idea to her," I said. "Now it is up to Nkobe to make the offer or choose not to."

"But she says that she will permit him to marry no

one else," answered Shima, more puzzled than outraged, "as if a *manamouki* could stop her husband from buying another wife. She is ignorant of our ways, Koriba, and for this reason you must speak with her. You must point out that she should be grateful to have another woman with whom to speak and share the work, and she should not want Nkobe to die without having fathered any children, just because *she* has been cursed." She hesitated for a moment, and then concluded: "And you should remind her that Shuni will someday be sister to the *mundumugu*."

"I am glad that you are so concerned about Mwange's future," I said at last.

She caught the trace of sarcasm in my voice.

"Is it so wrong to be concerned about my little Shuni as well?" she demanded.

"No," I admitted. "No, it is not wrong."

"Oh!" said Shima, as if she had suddenly remembered something important. "When you speak to Mwange, remind her that she is named for my sister."

"I do not intend to speak to Mwange at all."

"Oh?"

"No," I said. "As you yourself pointed out, this is not her concern. I will speak to Nkobe."

"And you will mention Shuni?" she persisted.

"I will speak to Nkobe," I answered noncommittally.

She got to her feet and prepared to leave.

"You can do me a favor, Shima," I said.

"Oh?"

I nodded. "Have Ndemi come to my *boma* immediately. I have many tasks for him to do here."

"How can you be sure, since you have only just returned?"

"I am sure," I said adamantly.

She looked across my *boma*, still the protective mother. "I can see no chores that have been left undone."

"Then I will find some," I said.

*   *   *

I went down to the village in the afternoon, for old Siboki needed ointments to keep the pain from his joints, and Koinnage had asked me to help him settle a dispute between Njoro and Sangora concerning the ownership of a calf that their jointly owned cow had just produced.

When I had finished my business there, I placed charms on some of the scarecrows, and then, in midafternoon, I walked over to Nkobe's *shamba*, where I found him herding his cattle.

"*Jambo*, Koriba!" he greeted me, waving his hand.

"*Jambo*, Nkobe," I replied, approaching him.

"Would you like to come into my hut for some *pombe*?" he offered. "Mwange just brewed it yesterday."

"Thank you for the offer, but I do not care to drink warm *pombe* on a hot afternoon like this."

"It's actually quite cool," he said. "She buries the gourd in the ground to keep it that way."

"Then I will have some," I acquiesced, falling into step beside him as he drove his cattle toward his *boma*.

Mwange was waiting for us, and she invited us into the cool interior of the hut and poured our *pombe* for us, then began to leave, for *manamoukis* do not listen to the conversation of men.

"Stay here, Mwange," I said.

"You're sure?" she said.

"Yes."

She shrugged and sat on the floor, with her back propped up against a wall of the hut.

"What brings you here, Koriba?" asked Nkobe, sitting gingerly upon his chair, and I could see that his back was troubling him. "You have not paid us a visit before."

"The *mundumugu* rarely visits those who are healthy enough to visit him," I replied.

"Then this is a special occasion," said Nkobe.

"Yes," I replied, sipping my *pombe*. "This is a special occasion."

"What is it this time?" asked Mwange warily.

"What do you mean, 'this time'?" said Nkobe sharply.

"There have been some minor problems," I answered, "none of which concern you."

"Anything that affects Mwange concerns me," responded Nkobe. "I am not blind or deaf, Koriba. I know that the older women have refused to accept her—and I'm getting more than a little bit angry about it. She has gone out of her way to fit in here, and has met them more than halfway."

"I did not come here to discuss Mwange with you," I said.

"Oh?" he said suspiciously.

"Are you saying we have a problem that concerns *him*?" demanded Mwange.

"It concerns both of you," I replied. "That is why I have come here."

"All right, Koriba—what is it?" said Nkobe.

"You have made a good effort to fit into the community and to live as a Kikuyu, Nkobe," I said. "And yet there is one more thing that you will be expected to do, and it is this that I have come to discuss with you."

"And what is that?"

"Sooner or later, you will be expected to take another wife."

"I knew it!" said Mwange.

"I'm very happy with the wife I have," said Nkobe with unconcealed hostility.

"That may be," I said, draining the last of my *pombe*, "but you have no children, and as Mwange gets older she will need someone to help her with her duties."

"Now you listen to me!" snapped Nkobe. "I came here because I thought it would make Mwange happy. So far she's been ostracized and shunned and gossiped about, and now you're telling me that I have to take another wife into my house so that Mwange can keep being spat on by the other women? We don't need this, Koriba! I was just as happy on my farm in Kenya. I can go back there any time I want."

"If that is the way you feel, then perhaps you should return to Kenya," I said.

"Tom," said Mwange, staring at him, and he fell silent.

"It is true that you do not have to stay," I continued. "But you are Kikuyus, living on a Kikuyu world, and if you do stay, you will be expected to act as Kikuyus."

"There's no law that says a Kikuyu man must take a second wife," said Nkobe sullenly.

"No, there is no such law," I admitted. "Nor is there a law that says a Kikuyu man must father children. But these are our traditions, and you will be expected to abide by them."

"To hell with them!" he muttered in English.

Mwange laid a restraining hand on his arm. "There is a coterie of young warriors who live beyond the forest," she said. "Why don't *they* marry some of the young women? Why should the men of the village monopolize them all?"

"They cannot afford wives." I said. "That is why they live alone."

"That's *their* problem," said Nkobe.

"I've made many sacrifices in the name of communal harmony," said Mwange, "but this is asking too much, Koriba. We are happy just the way we are, and we intend to stay this way."

"You will not remain happy."

"What does that mean?" she demanded.

"Next month is the circumcision ritual," I said. "When it is over, there will be many girls eligible for marriage, and since you are barren, it is only reasonable to suppose that a number of families will suggest that Nkobe pay the bride price for their daughters. He may refuse once, he may refuse twice, but if he continues to refuse, he will offend most of the village. They will assume that because he comes from Kenya he feels their women are not good enough for him, and they will be further offended by the fact that he refuses to have children with which to populate our empty planet."

"Then I'll explain my reasons to them," said Nkobe.

"They will not understand," I answered.

"No, they will not understand," agreed Mwange unhappily.

"Then they will have to learn to live with it," said Nkobe firmly.

"And you will have to learn to live with silence and animosity," I said. "Is this the life you envisioned when you came to Kirinyaga?"

"Of course not!" snapped Nkobe. "But nothing can make me—"

"We will think about it, Koriba," interrupted Mwange.

Nkobe turned to his wife, stunned. "What are you saying?"

"I am saying that we will think about it," repeated Mwange.

"That is all that I ask," I said, getting to my feet and walking to the door of the hut.

"You demand a lot, Koriba," said Mwange bitterly.

"I demand nothing," I replied. "I merely suggest."

"Coming from the *mundumugu*, is there a difference?"

I did not answer her, because in truth there was no difference whatsoever.

"You seem unhappy, Koriba," said Ndemi.

He had just finished feeding my chickens and my goats, and now he sat down beside me in the shade of my acacia tree.

"I am," I said.

"Mwange," he said, nodding his head.

"Mwange," I agreed.

Two weeks had passed since I had visited her and Nkobe.

"I saw her this morning, when I went to the river to fill your gourds," said Ndemi. "She, too, seems unhappy."

"She is," I said. "And there is nothing that I can do about it."

"But you are the *mundumugu*."

"I know."

"You are the most powerful of men," continued Ndemi. "Surely you can put an end to her sorrow."

I sighed. "The *mundumugu* is both the most powerful
and the weakest of men. In Mwange's case, I am the
weakest."

"I do not understand."

"The *mundumugu* is the most powerful of men when
it comes to interpreting the law," I said. "But he is also
the weakest of men, for it is he, of all men, who must
be bound by that law, no matter what else happens." I
paused. "I should allow her to be what she can be,
instead of being merely a *manamouki*. And failing that,
I should make her leave Kirinyaga and return to Kenya."
I sighed again. "But she must behave like a *manamouki*
if she is to have a life here, and she has broken no law
that would allow me to force her to leave."

Ndemi frowned. "Being a *mundumugu* can be more
difficult than I thought."

I smiled at him and placed a hand upon his head.
"Tomorrow I will begin to teach you to make the ointments that cure the sick."

"Really?" he said, his face brightening.

I nodded. "Your last statement tells me that you are
no longer a child."

"I have not been a child for many rains," he protested.

"Do not say any more," I told him with a wry smile,
"or we will do more harvest prayers instead."

He immediately fell silent, and I looked out across the
distant savannah, where a swirling tower of dust raced
across the arid plain, and wondered, for perhaps the
thousandth time, what to do about Mwange.

How long I sat thus, motionless, I do not know, but
eventually I felt Ndemi tugging at the blanket I had
wrapped around my shoulders.

"Women," he whispered.

"What?" I said, not comprehending.

"From the village," he said, gesturing toward the path
that led to my *boma*.

I looked where he indicated and saw four of the village
women approaching. There was Wambu, and Sabo, and

Bori, and with them this time was Morina, the second wife of Kimoda.

"Should I leave?" asked Ndemi.

I shook my head. "If you are to become a *mundumugu*, it is time you started listening to a *mundumugu's* problems."

The four women stopped perhaps ten feet away from me.

"*Jambo*," I said, staring at them.

"The Kenyan witch must leave!" said Wambu.

"We have been through this before," I said.

"But now she has broken the law," said Wambu.

"Oh?" I said. "In what way?"

Wambu grabbed Morina by the arm and shoved her even closer to me. "Tell him," she said triumphantly.

"She has bewitched my daughter," said Morina, obviously uneasy in my presence.

"How has Mwange bewitched your daughter?" I asked.

"My Muri was a good, obedient child," said Morina. "She always helped me grind the grain, and she dutifully cared for her two younger brothers when I was working in the fields, and she never left the thorn gate open at night so that hyenas could enter our *boma* and kill our goats and cattle." She paused, and I could see that she was trying very hard not to cry. "All she could talk about since the last long rains was her forthcoming circumcision ceremony, and who she hoped would pay the bride price for her. She was a perfect daughter, a daughter any mother would be proud of." Now a tear trickled down her cheek. "And then the Kenyan woman came, and Muri spent her time with her, and now—" suddenly the single tear became a veritable flood "—now she tells me that she refuses to be circumcised. She will never marry and she will die a barren old woman!"

Morina could speak no more, and began beating her breasts with her clenched fists.

"That is not all," added Wambu. "The reason Muri does not wish to be circumcised is because the Kenyan woman herself has not been circumcised. And yet the

Kenyan woman has married a Kikuyu man, and has tried to live among us as his *manamouki*." She glared at me. "She has broken the law, Koriba! We must cast her out!"

"I am the *mundumugu*," I replied sternly. "I will decide what must be done."

"You *know* what must be done!" said Wambu furiously.

"That is all," I said. "I will hear no more."

Wambu glared at me, but did not dare to disobey me, and finally, turning on her heel, she stalked back down the path to the village, followed by Sabo and the still-wailing Morina.

Bori stood where she was for an extra moment, then turned to me.

"It is as I told you before, Koriba," she said, almost apologetically. "She really *is* a witch."

Then she, too, began walking back to the village.

"What will you do, Koriba?" asked Ndemi.

"The law is clear," I said wearily. "No uncircumcised woman may live with a Kikuyu man as his wife."

"Then you will make her leave Kirinyaga?"

"I will offer her a choice," I said, "and I will hope that she chooses to leave."

"It is too bad," said Ndemi. "She has tried very hard to be a good *manamouki*."

"I know," I said.

"Then why is Ngai visiting her with such unhappiness?"

"Because sometimes trying is not enough."

We stood at Haven—Mwange, Nkobe, and I—awaiting the Maintenance ship's arrival.

"I am truly sorry that things did not work out," I said sincerely.

Nkobe glared at me, but said nothing.

"It didn't have to end this way," said Mwange bitterly.

"We had no choice," I said. "If we are to create our Utopia here on Kirinyaga, we must be bound by its rules."

"The fact that a rule exists does not make it right,

Koriba," she said. "I gave up almost everything to live here, but I will not let them mutilate me in the name of some foolish custom."

"Without our traditions, we are not Kikuyu, but only Kenyans who live on another world," I pointed out.

"There is a difference between tradition and stagnation, Koriba," she said. "If you stifle every variation in taste and behavior in the name of the former, you achieve only the latter." She paused. "I would have been a good member of the community."

"But a poor *manamouki*," I said. "The leopard may be a stealthy hunter and fearsome killer, but he does not belong among a pride of lions."

"Lions and leopards have been extinct for a long time, Koriba," she said. "We are talking about human beings, not animals, and no matter how many rules you make and no matter how many traditions you invoke, you cannot make all human beings think and feel and act alike."

"It's coming," announced Nkobe as the Maintenance ship broke through the thin cloud cover.

"*Kwaheri*, Nkobe," I said, extending my hand.

He looked contemptuously at my hand for a moment, then turned his back and continued watching the Maintenance ship.

I turned to Mwange.

"I tried, Koriba," she said. "I really did."

"No one ever tired harder," I said. "*Kwaheri*, Mwange."

She stared at me, her face suddenly an emotionless mask.

"Good-bye, Koriba," she said in English. "And my name is Wanda."

The next morning Shima came to me to complain that Shuni had rejected the suitor that had been arranged for her.

Two days later Wambu complained to me that Kibo, Koinnage's youngest wife, had decorated her hut with colorful ribbons, and was beginning to let her hair grow.

And the morning after that, Kimi, who had only one son, announced that she wanted no more children.

"I thought it had ended," I said with a sigh as I watched Sangora, Kimi's distressed husband, walk back down the path to the village.

"That is because you made a mistake, Koriba."

"Why do you say that?"

"You believed the wrong story," answered Ndemi with the confidence of youth.

"Oh?"

He nodded. "You believed the story about the Ugly Buffalo."

"And which story should I have believed?"

"The story of the *mundumugu* and the serpent."

"Why do you think one story is more worthy of belief than the other?" I asked him.

"Does not the story of the *mundumugu* and the serpent tell us that we cannot be rid of that which Ngai created simply because we find it repugnant or unsettling?"

"That is true," I said.

Ndemi smiled and held up three fingers. "Shuni, Kibo, Kimi," he said, counting them off. "Three serpents have returned already. There are ninety-seven yet to come."

And suddenly I had the awful premonition that he was right.

Science fiction is the literature of possibilities, so it was inevitable that it would not only explore what might happen in this world, but also what might happen (or already have happened) in worlds just like ours except for a lost battle or a missed opportunity or a moment's hesitation: wheels within wheels.

These "alternate history" stories have varied as much as the worlds they posit, exploring political possibilities, as in Ward Moore's classic Bring the Jubilee and Kim Stanley Robinson's "The Lucky Strike," and personal ones, as in Robert Silverberg's "Trips," and sometimes even touching on the impossible, as in Alfred Bester's "The Men Who Murdered Mohammed," in which a man tries, without success, to get rid of his wife.

In the story that follows, Joe Haldeman brings all of these possibilities, and impossibilities, together in a wonderful story about parallel timestreams and misplaced manuscripts and inevitability.

Joe Haldeman is a three-time Hugo recipient, winning for his devastating war novel, The Forever War, in 1976, his short story, "Tricentennial," in 1977, and "The Hemingway Hoax." "The Hemingway Hoax" also won the Nebula Award, as did The Forever War. Haldeman is the author of Mindbridge, the excellent Worlds novels, and "Zero-Gee," the very first story to explore the possibilities of sex in freefall.

—Connie Willis

The Hemingway Hoax

by Joe Haldeman

1. The Torrents of Spring

Our story begins in a rundown bar in Key West, not so many years from now. The bar is not the one Hemingway drank at, nor yet the one that claims to be the one he drank at, because they are both too expensive and full of tourists. This bar, in a more interesting part of town, is a Cuban place. It is neither clean nor well-lighted, but has cold beer and good strong Cuban coffee. Its cheap prices and rascally charm are what bring together the scholar and the rogue.

Their first meeting would be of little significance to either at the time, though the scholar, John Baird, would never forget it. John Baird was not capable of forgetting anything.

Key West is lousy with writers, mostly poor writers, in one sense of that word or the other. Poor people did not interest our rogue, Sylvester Castlemaine, so at first he didn't take any special note of the man sitting in the corner scribbling on a yellow pad. Just another would-be writer, come down to see whether some of Papa's magic would rub off. Not worth the energy of a con.

But Castle's professional powers of observation caught at a detail or two and focused his attention. The man was wearing jeans and a faded flannel shirt, but his shoes were expensive Italian loafers. His beard had been trimmed by a barber. He was drinking Heineken. The pen he was scribbling with was a fat Mont Blanc Diplomat, two hundred bucks on the hoof, discounted. Castle got his cup of coffee and sat at a table two away from the writer.

He waited until the man paused, set the pen down, took a drink. "Writing a story?" Castle said.

The man blinked at him. "No ... just an article." He put the cap on the pen with a crisp snap. "An article about stories. I'm a college professor."

"Publish or perish," Castle said.

The man relaxed a bit. "Too true." He riffled through the yellow pad. "This won't help much. It's not going anywhere."

"Tell you what ... bet you a beer it's Hemingway or Tennessee Williams."

"Too easy." He signaled the bartender. "Dos cervezas. Hemingway, the early stories. You know his work?"

"Just a little. We had to read him in school—*The Old Man and the Fish?* And then I read a couple after I got down here." He moved over to the man's table. "Name's Castle."

"John Baird." Open, honest expression; not too promising. You can't con somebody unless he thinks he's conning you. "Teach up at Boston."

"I'm mostly fishing. Shrimp nowadays." Of course Castle didn't normally fish, not for things in the sea, but the shrimp part was true. He'd been reduced to heading shrimp on the Catalina for five dollars a bucket. "So what about these early stories?"

The bartender set down the two beers and gave Castle a weary look.

"Well . . . they don't exist." John Baird carefully poured the beer down the side of his glass. "They were stolen. Never published."

"So what can you write about them?"

"Indeed. That's what I've been asking myself." He took a sip of the beer and settled back. "Seventy-four years ago they were stolen. December 1922. That's really what got me working on them; thought I would do a paper, a monograph, for the seventy-fifth anniversary of the occasion."

It sounded less and less promising, but this was the first imported beer Castle had had in months. He slowly savored the bite of it.

"He and his first wife, Hadley, were living in Paris. You know about Hemingway's early life?"

"Huh uh. Paris?"

"He grew up in Oak Park, Illinois. That was kind of a prissy, self-satisfied suburb of Chicago."

"Yeah, I been there."

"He didn't like it. In his teens he sort of ran away from home, went down to Kansas City to work on a newspaper.

"World War I started, and like a lot of kids, Hemingway couldn't get into the army because of bad eyesight, so he joined the Red Cross and went off to drive ambulances in Italy. Take cigarettes and chocolate to the troops.

"That almost killed him. He was just doing his cigarettes-and-chocolate routine and an artillery round came in, killed the guy next to him, tore up another, riddled Hemingway with shrapnel. He claims then that he picked up the wounded guy and carried him back to the trench, in spite of being hit in the knee by a machine-gun bullet."

"What do you mean, 'claims'?"

"You're too young to have been in Vietnam."

"Yeah."

"Good for you. I was hit in the knee by a machine-gun bullet myself, and went down on my ass and didn't get up for five weeks. He didn't carry anybody one step."

"That's interesting."

"Well, he was always rewriting his life. We all do it. But it seemed to be a compulsion with him. That's one thing that makes Hemingway scholarship challenging."

Baird poured the rest of the beer into his glass. "Anyhow, he actually was the first American wounded in Italy, and they made a big deal over him. He went back to Oak Park a war hero. He had a certain amount of success with women."

"Or so he says?"

"Right, God knows. Anyhow, he met Hadley Richardson, an older woman but quite a number, and they had a steamy courtship and got married and said the hell with it, moved to Paris to live a sort of Bohemian life while Hemingway worked on perfecting his art. That part isn't bullshit. He worked diligently and he did become one of the best writers of his era. Which brings us to the lost manuscripts."

"Do tell."

"Hemingway was picking up a little extra money doing journalism. He'd gone to Switzerland to cover a peace conference for a news service. When it was over, he wired Hadley to come join him for some skiing.

"This is where it gets odd. On her own initiative, Hadley packed up all of Ernest's work. All of it. Not just the typescripts, but the handwritten first drafts and the carbons."

"That's like a Xerox?"

"Right. She packed them in an overnight bag, then packed her own suitcase. A porter at the train station, the Gare de Lyon, put them aboard for her. She left the train for a minute to find something to read—and when she came back, they were gone."

"Suitcase and all?"

"No, just the manuscripts. She and the porter searched up and down the train. But that was it. Somebody had seen the overnight bag sitting there and snatched it. Lost forever."

That did hold a glimmer of professional interest. "That's funny. You'd think they'd get a note then, like 'If you ever want to see your stories again, bring a million bucks to the Eiffel Tower' sort of thing."

"A few years later, that might have happened. It didn't take long for Hemingway to become famous. But at the time, only a few of the literary intelligentsia knew about him."

Castle shook his head in commiseration with the long-dead thief. "Guy who stole 'em probably didn't even read English. Dumped 'em in the river."

John Baird shivered visibly. "Undoubtedly. But people have never stopped looking for them. Maybe they'll show up in some attic someday."

"Could happen." Wheels turning.

"It's happened before in literature. Some of Boswell's diaries were recovered because a scholar recognized his handwriting on an old piece of paper a merchant used to wrap a fish. Hemingway's own last book, he put together from notes that had been lost for thirty years. They were in a couple of trunks in the basement of the Ritz, in Paris." He leaned forward, excited. "Then after he died, they found another batch of papers down here, in a back room in Sloppy Joe's. It could still happen."

Castle took a deep breath. "It could be made to happen, too."

"Made to happen?"

"Just speakin', you know, in theory. Like some guy who really knows Hemingway, suppose he makes up some stories that're like those old ones, finds some seventy-five-year-old paper and an old, what do you call them, not a word processor—"

"Typewriter."

"Whatever. Think he could pass 'em off for the real thing?"

"I don't know if he could fool me," Baird said, and tapped the side of his head. "I have a freak memory: eidetic, photographic. I have just about every word Hemingway ever wrote committed to memory." He looked slightly embarrassed. "Of course that doesn't make me an expert in the sense of being able to spot a phony. I just wouldn't have to refer to any texts."

"So take yourself, you know, or somebody else who spent all his life studyin' Hemingway. He puts all he's got into writin' these stories—he knows the people who are gonna be readin' 'em; knows what they're gonna look for. And he hires like an expert forger to make the pages look like they came out of Hemingway's machine. So could it work?"

Baird pursed his lips and for a moment looked professorial. Then he sort of laughed, one syllable through his nose. "Maybe it could. A man did a similar thing when I was a boy, counterfeiting the memoirs of Howard Hughes. He made millions."

"Millions?"

"Back when that was real money. Went to jail when they found out, of course."

"And the money was still there when he got out."

"Never read anything about it. I guess so."

"So the next question is, how much stuff are we talkin' about? How much was in that old overnight bag?"

"That depends on who you believe. There was half a novel and some poetry. The short stories, there might have been as few as eleven or as many as thirty."

"That'd take a long time to write."

"It would take forever. You couldn't just 'do' Hemingway; you'd have to figure out what the stories were about, then reconstruct his early style—do you know how many Hemingway scholars there are in the world?"

"Huh uh. Quite a few."

"Thousands. Maybe ten thousand academics who know enough to spot a careless fake."

Castle nodded, cogitating. "You'd have to be real careful. But then you wouldn't have to do all the short stories and poems, would you? You could say all you found was the part of the novel. Hell, you could sell that as a book."

The odd laugh again. "Sure you could. Be a fortune in it."

"How much? A million bucks?"

"A million . . . maybe. Well, sure. The last new Hemingway made at least that much, allowing for inflation. And he's more popular now."

Castle took a big gulp of beer and set his glass down decisively. "So what the hell are we waiting for?"

Baird's bland smile faded. "You're serious?"

2. in our time

Got a ripple in the Hemingway channel.

Twenties again?

No, funny, this one's in the 1990s. See if you can track it down?

Sure. Go down to the armory first and—

Look—no bloodbaths this time. You solve one problem and start ten more.

Couldn't be helped. It's no tea party, twentieth century America.

Just use good judgment. That Ransom guy. . . .

Manson. Right. That was a mistake.

3. A Way You'll Never Be

You can't cheat an honest man, as Sylvester Castlemaine well knew, but then again, it never hurts to find out just how honest a man is. John Baird refused his scheme, with good humor at first, but when Castle persisted, his refusal took on a sarcastic edge; maybe a tinge of outrage. He backed off and changed the subject, talking for a half-hour about commercial fishing around Key West, and then said he had to run. He slipped his business card into John's shirt pocket on the way out. (Sylvester Castlemaine, Consultant, it claimed.)

John left the place soon, walking slowly through the afternoon heat. He was glad he hadn't brought the bicycle; it was pleasant to walk in the shade of the big aromatic trees, a slight breeze on his face from the Gulf side.

One could do it. One could. The problem divided itself

into three parts: writing the novel fragment, forging the manuscript, and devising a suitable story about how one had uncovered the manuscript.

The writing part would be the hardest. Hemingway is easy enough to parody—one fourth of the take-home final he gave in English 733 was to write a page of Hemingway pastiche, and some of his graduate students did a credible job—but parody was exactly what one would not want to do.

It had been a crucial period in Hemingway's development, those three years of apprenticeship the lost manuscripts represented. Two stories survived, and they were maddeningly dissimilar. "My Old Man," which had slipped down behind a drawer, was itself a pastiche, reading like pretty good Sherwood Anderson, but with an O. Henry twist at the end—very unlike the bleak understated quality that would distinguish the stories that were to make Hemingway's reputation. The other, "Up in Michigan," had been out in the mail at the time of the loss. It was a lot closer to Hemingway's ultimate style, a spare and, by the standards of the time, pornographic description of a woman's first sexual experience.

John riffled through the notes on the yellow pad, a talismanic gesture, since he could have remembered any page with little effort. But the sight of the words and the feel of the paper sometimes helped him think.

One would not do it, of course. Except perhaps as a mental exercise. Not to show to anybody. Certainly not to profit from.

You wouldn't want to use "My Old Man" as the model, certainly; no one would care to publish a pastiche of a pastiche of Anderson, now undeservedly obscure. So "Up in Michigan." And the first story he wrote after the loss, "Out of Season," would also be handy. That had a lot of the true Hemingway strength.

You wouldn't want to tackle the novel fragment, of course, not just as an exercise, over a hundred pages. . . .

Without thinking about it, John dropped into a familiar fugue state as he walked through the rundown neighborhood, his freak memory taking over while his body ambled along on autopilot. This is the way he usually remembered pages. He transported himself back to the Hemingway collection at the JFK Library in Boston, last November, snow swirling outside the big picture windows overlooking the harbor, the room so cold he was wearing coat and gloves and could see his breath. They didn't normally let you wear a coat up there, afraid you might squirrel away a page out of the manuscript collection, but they had to make an exception because the heat pump was down.

He was flipping through the much-thumbed Xerox of Carlos Baker's interview with Hadley, page 52: "Stolen suitcase," Baker asked; "lost novel?"

The typescript of her reply appeared in front of him, more clear than the cracked sidewalk his feet negotiated: "This novel was a knock-out, about Nick, up north in Michigan—hunting, fishing, all sorts of experiences—stuff on the order of "Big Two-Hearted River," with more action. Girl experiences well done, too." With an enigmatic addition, evidently in Hadley's handwriting, "Girl experiences too well done."

That was interesting. John hadn't thought about that, since he'd been concentrating on the short stories. Too well done? There had been a lot of talk in the eighties about Hemingway's sexual ambiguity—*gender* ambiguity, actually—could Hadley have been upset, sixty years after the fact, remembering some confidence that Hemingway had revealed to the world in that novel; something girls knew that boys were not supposed to know? Playful pillow talk that was filed away for eventual literary exploitation?

He used his life that way. A good writer remembered everything and then forgot it when he sat down to write, and reinvented it so the writing would be more real than the memory. Experience was important, but imagination was more important.

Maybe I would be a better writer, John thought, if I could learn how to forget. For about the tenth time today, like any day, he regretted not having tried to succeed as a writer, while he still had the independent income. Teaching and research had fascinated him when he was younger, a rich boy's all-consuming hobbies, but the end of this fiscal year would be the end of the monthly checks from the trust fund. So the salary from Boston University wouldn't be mad money any more, but rent and groceries in a city suddenly expensive.

Yes, the writing would be the hard part. Then forging the manuscript, that wouldn't be easy. Any scholar would have access to copies of thousands of pages that Hemingway typed before and after the loss. Could one find the typewriter Hemingway had used? Then duplicate his idiosyncratic typing style—a moment's reflection put a sample in front of him, spaces before and after periods and commas. . . .

He snapped out of the reverie as his right foot hit the first step on the back staircase up to their rented flat. He automatically stepped over the fifth step, the rotted one, and was thinking about a nice tall glass of iced tea as he opened the screen door.

"Scorpions!" his wife screamed, two feet from his face.

"What?"

"We have scorpions!" Lena grabbed his arm and hauled him to the kitchen.

"Look!" She pointed at the opaque plastic skylight. Three scorpions, each about six inches long, cast sharp silhouettes on the milky plastic. One was moving.

"My word."

"Your *word!*" She struck a familiar pose, hands on hips, and glared up at the creatures. "What are we going to do about it?"

"We could name them."

"John."

"I don't know." He opened the refrigerator. "Call the bug man."

"The bug man was just here yesterday. He probably flushed them out."

He poured a glass of cold tea and dumped two

envelopes of artificial sweetener into it. "I'll talk to Julio about it. But you know they've been there all along. They're not bothering anybody."

"They're bothering the hell out of me!"

He smiled. "Okay. I'll talk to Julio." He looked into the oven. "Thought about dinner?"

"Anything you want to cook, sweetheart. I'll be damned if I'm going to stand there with three . . . poisonous . . . arthropods staring down at me."

"Poised to jump," John said, and looked up again. There were only two visible now, which made his skin crawl.

"Julio wasn't home when I first saw them. About an hour ago."

"I'll go check." John went downstairs and Julio, the landlord, was indeed home, but was not impressed by the problem. He agreed that it was probably the bug man, and they would probably go back to where they came from in a while, and gave John a flyswatter.

John left the flyswatter with Lena, admonishing her to take no prisoners, and walked a couple of blocks to a Chinese restaurant. He brought back a few boxes of takeout, and they sat in the living room and wielded chopsticks in silence, listening for the pitter-patter of tiny feet.

"Met a real live con man today." He put the business card on the coffee table between them.

"Consultant?" she read.

"He had a loony scheme about counterfeiting the missing stories." Lena knew more about the missing stories than 98 percent of the people who Hemingway'ed for a living. John liked to think out loud.

"Ah, the stories," she said, preparing herself.

"Not a bad idea, actually, if one had a larcenous nature." He concentrated for a moment on the slippery Moo Goo Gai Pan. "Be millions of bucks in it."

He was bent over the box. She stared hard at his bald spot. "What exactly did he have in mind?"

"We didn't bother to think it through in any detail, actually. You go and find. . . ." He got the slightly wall-eyed look that she knew meant he was reading a page of a book a thousand miles away. "Yes. A 1921 Corona portable, like the one Hadley gave him before they were married. Find some old paper. Type up the stories. Take them to Sotheby's. Spend money for the rest of your life. That's all there is to it."

"You left out jail."

"A mere detail. Also the writing of the stories. That could take weeks. Maybe you could get arrested first, write the stories in jail, and then sell them when you got out."

"You're weird, John."

"Well. I didn't give him any encouragement."

"Maybe you should've. A few million would come in handy next year."

"We'll get by."

"'We'll get by.' You keep saying that. How do you know? You've never had to 'get by.'"

"Okay, then. We won't get by." He scraped up the last of the fried rice. "We won't be able to make the rent and they'll throw us out on the street. We'll live in a cardboard box over a heating grate. You'll have to sell your body to keep me in cheap wine. But we'll be happy, dear." He looked up at her, mooning. "Poor but happy."

"Slap-happy." She looked at the card again. "How do you know he's a con man?"

"I don't know. Salesman type. Says he's in commercial fishing now, but he doesn't seem to like it much."

"He didn't say anything about any, you know, criminal stuff he'd done in the past?"

"Huh uh. I just got the impression that he didn't waste a lot of time mulling over ethics and morals." John held up the Mont Blanc pen. "He was staring at this, before he came over and introduced himself. I think he smelled money."

Lena stuck both chopsticks into the half-finished carton of boiled rice and set it down decisively. "Let's ask him over."

"He's a sleaze, Lena. You wouldn't like him."

THE HEMINGWAY HOAX   355

"I've never met a real con man. It would be fun."

He looked into the darkened kitchen. "Will you cook something?"

She followed his gaze, expecting monsters. "If you stand guard."

4. Romance is Dead
subtitle
The Hell it is

"Be a job an' a half," Castle said, mopping up residual spaghetti sauce with a piece of garlic bread. "It's not like your Howard Hughes guy, or Hitler's notebooks."

"You've been doing some research," John's voice was a little slurred. He'd bought a half-gallon of Portuguese wine, the bottle wrapped in straw like cheap Chianti, the wine not quite that good. If you could get past the first couple of glasses, it was okay. It had been okay to John for some time now.

"Yeah, down to the library. The guys who did the Hitler notebooks, hell, nobody'd ever seen a real Hitler notebook; they just studied his handwriting in letters and such, then read up on what he did day after day. Same with the Howard Hughes, but that was even easier, because most of the time nobody knew what the hell Howard Hughes was doing anyhow. Just stayed locked up in that room."

"The Hughes forgery nearly worked, as I recall," John said. "If Hughes himself hadn't broken silence. . . ."

"Ya gotta know that took balls. 'Scuse me, Lena." She waved a hand and laughed. "Try to get away with that while Hughes was still alive."

"How did the Hitler people screw up?" she asked.

"Funny thing about that one was how many people they fooled. Afterwards everybody said it was a really lousy fake. But you can bet that before the newspapers bid millions of dollars on it, they showed it to the best

Hitler-ologists they could find, and they all said it was real."

"Because they wanted it to be real," Lena said.

"Yeah. But one of the pages had some chemical in it that wouldn't be in paper before 1945. That was kinda dumb."

"People would want the Hemingway stories to be real," Lena said quietly, to John.

John's gaze stayed fixed on the center of the table, where a few strands of spaghetti lay cold and drying in a plastic bowl. "Wouldn't be honest."

"That's for sure," Castle said cheerily. "But it ain't exactly armed robbery, either."

"A gross misuse of intellectual . . . intellectual. . . ."

"It's past your bedtime, John," Lena said. "We'll clean up." John nodded and pushed himself away from the table and walked heavily into the bedroom.

Lena didn't say anything until she heard the bed-springs creak. "He isn't always like this," she said quietly.

"Yeah. He don't act like no alky."

"It's been a hard year for him." She refilled her glass. "Me, too. Money."

"That's bad."

"Well, we knew it was coming. He tell you about the inheritance?"

Castle leaned forward. "Huh uh."

"He was born pretty well off. Family had textile mills up in New Hampshire. John's grandparents died in an auto accident in the forties and the family sold off the mills—good timing, too. They wouldn't be worth much today.

"Then John's father and mother died in the sixties, while he was in college. The executors set up a trust fund that looked like it would keep him in pretty good shape forever. But he wasn't interested in money. He even joined the army, to see what it was like."

"Jesus."

"Afterwards, he carried a picket sign and marched against the war—you know, Vietnam.

"Then he finished his Ph.D. and started teaching. The trust fund must have been fifty times as much as his salary, when he started out. It was still ten times as much, a couple of years ago."

"Boy . . . howdy." Castle was doing mental arithmetic and algebra with variables like Porsches and fast boats.

"But he let his sisters take care of it. He let them re-invest the capital."

"They weren't too swift?"

"They were idiots! They took good solid blue-chip stocks and tax-free municipals, too 'boring' for them, and threw it all away gambling on commodities." She grimaced. "*Pork* bellies? I finally had John go to Chicago and come back with what was left of his money. There wasn't much."

"You ain't broke, though."

"Damned near. There's enough income to pay for insurance and eventually we'll be able to draw on an IRA. But the cash payments stop in two months. We'll have to live on John's salary. I suppose I'll get a job, too."

"What you ought to get is a typewriter."

Lena laughed and slouched back in her chair. "That would be something."

"You think he could do it? I mean if he would, do you think he could?"

"He's a good writer." She looked thoughtful. "He's had some stories published, you know, in the literary magazines. The ones that pay four or five free copies."

"Big deal."

She shrugged. "Pays off in the long run. Tenure. But I don't know whether being able to write a good literary story means that John could write a good Hemingway imitation."

"He knows enough, right?"

"Maybe he knows too much. He might be paralyzed by his own standards." She shook her head. "In some ways he's an absolute nut about Hemingway. Obsessed, I mean. It's not good for him."

"Maybe writing this stuff would get it out of his system."

She smiled at him. "You've got more angles than a protractor."

"Sorry; I didn't mean to—"

"No." She raised both hands. "Don't be sorry; I like it. I like you, Castle. John's a good man but sometimes he's too good."

He poured them both more wine. "Nobody ever accused me of that."

"I suspect not." She paused. "Have you ever been in trouble with the police? Just curious."

"Why?"

"Just curious."

He laughed. "Nickel and dime stuff, when I was a kid. You know, jus' to see what you can get away with." He turned serious. "Then I pulled two months' hard time for somethin' I didn't do. Wasn't even in town when it happened."

"What was it?"

"Armed robbery. Then the guy came back an' hit the same god-damned store! I mean, he was one sharp cookie. He confessed to the first one and they let me go."

"Why did they accuse you in the first place?"

"Used to think it was somebody had it in for me. Like the clerk who fingered me." He took a sip of wine. "But hell. It was just dumb luck. And dumb cops. The guy was about my height, same color hair, we both lived in the neighborhood. Cops didn't want to waste a lot of time on it. Jus' chuck me in jail."

"So you do have a police record?"

"Huh uh. Girl from the ACLU made sure they wiped it clean. She wanted me to go after 'em for what, false arrest an' wrongful imprisonment. I just wanted to get out of town."

"It wasn't here?"

"Nah. Dayton, Ohio. Been here eight, nine years."

"That's good."

"Why the third degree?"

She leaned forward and patted the back of his hand. "Call it a job interview, Castle. I have a feeling we may be working together."

"Okay." He gave her a slow smile. "Anything else you want to know?"

5. The Doctor and the Doctor's Wife

John trudged into the kitchen the next morning, ignored the coffeepot, and pulled a green bottle of beer out of the fridge. He looked up at the skylight. Four scorpions, none of them moving. Have to call the bug man today.

Red wine hangover, the worst kind. He was too old for this. Cheap red wine hangover. He eased himself into a soft chair and carefully poured the beer down the side of the glass. Not too much noise, please.

When you drink too much, you ought to take a couple of aspirin, and some vitamins, and all the water you can hold, before retiring. If you drink too much, of course, you don't remember to do that.

The shower turned off with a bass clunk of plumbing. John winced and took a long drink, which helped a little. When he heard the bathroom door open he called for Lena to bring the aspirin when she came out.

After a few minutes she brought it out and handed it to him. "And how is Dr. Baird today?"

"Dr. Baird needs a doctor. Or an undertaker." He shook out two aspirin and washed them down with the last of the beer. "Like your outfit."

She was wearing only a towel around her head. She simpered and struck a dancer's pose and spun daintily around. "Think it'll catch on?"

"Oh my yes." At thirty-five, she still had the trim model's figure that had caught his eye in the classroom, fifteen years before. A safe, light tan was uniform all over her body, thanks to liberal sunblock and the private sunbathing area on top of the house—private except for the

helicopter that came low overhead every weekday at 1:15.
She always tried to be there in time to wave at it. The
pilot had such white teeth. She wondered how many
sunbathers were on his route.

She undid the towel and rubbed her long blonde hair
vigorously. "Thought I'd cool off for a few minutes before
I got dressed. Too much wine, eh?"

"Couldn't you tell from my sparkling repartee last
night?" He leaned back, eyes closed, and rolled the cool
glass back and forth on his forehead.

"Want another beer?"

"Yeah. Coffee'd be smarter, though."

"It's been sitting all night."

"Pay for my sins." He watched her swivel lightly into
the kitchen and, more than ever before, felt the difference in their ages. Seventeen years; he was half again as
old as she. A young man would say the hell with the
hangover, go grab that luscious thing and carry her back
to bed. The organ that responded to this meditation was
his stomach, though, and it responded very audibly.

"Some toast, too. Or do you want something fancier?"

"Toast would be fine." Why was she being so nice?
Usually if he drank too much, he reaped the whirlwind
in the morning.

"Ugh." She saw the scorpions. "Five of them now."

"I wonder how many it will hold before it comes crashing down. Scorpions everywhere, stunned. Then angry."

"I'm sure the bug man knows how to get rid of them."

"In Africa they claimed that if you light a ring of fire
around them with gasoline or lighter fluid, they go crazy,
run amok, stinging themselves to death in their frenzies.
Maybe the bug man could do that."

"Castle and I came up with a plan last night. It's kinda
screwy but it might just work."

"Read that in a book called *Jungle Ways*. I was eight
years old and believed every word of it."

"We figured out a way that it would be legal. Are
you listening?"

"Uh huh. Let me have real sugar and some milk."

She poured some milk in a cup and put it in the microwave to warm. "Maybe we should talk about it later."

"Oh no. Hemingway forgery. You figured out a way to make it legal. Go ahead. I'm all ears."

"See, you tell the publisher first off what it is, that you wrote it and then had it typed up to look authentic."

"Sure, be a big market for that."

"In fact, there could be. You'd have to generate it, but it could happen." The toast sprang up and she brought it and two cups of coffee into the living room on a tray. "See, the bogus manuscript is only one part of a book."

"I don't get it." He tore the toast into strips, to dunk in the strong Cuban coffee.

"The rest of the book is in the nature of an exegesis of your own text."

"If that con man knows what exegesis is, then I can crack a safe."

"That part's my idea. You're really writing a book *about* Hemingway. You use your own text to illustrate various points—'I wrote it this way instead of that way because. . . .'"

"It would be different," he conceded. "Perhaps the second most egotistical piece of Hemingway scholarship in history. A dubious distinction."

"You could write it tongue-in-cheek, though. It could be really amusing, as well as scholarly."

"God, we'd have to get an unlisted number, publishers calling us night and day. Movie producers. Might sell ten copies, if I bought nine."

"You really aren't getting it, John. You don't have a particle of larceny in your heart."

He put a hand on his heart and looked down. "Ventricles, auricles. My undying love for you, a little heartburn. No particles."

"See, you tell the publisher the truth . . . but the publisher doesn't have to tell the truth. Not until publication day."

"Okay. I still don't get it."

She took a delicate nibble of toast. "It goes like this. They print the bogus Hemingway up into a few copies of bogus bound galleys. Top secret."

"My exegesis carefully left off."

"That's the ticket. They send it out to a few selected scholars, along with Xeroxes of a few sample manuscript pages. All they say, in effect, is 'Does this seem authentic to you? Please keep it under your hat, for obvious reasons.' Then they sit back and collect blurbs."

"I can see the kind of blurbs they'd get from Scott or Mike or Jack, for instance. Some variation of 'What kind of idiot do you think I am?'"

"Those aren't the kind of people you send it to, dope! You send it to people who think they're experts, but aren't. Castle says this is how the Hitler thing almost worked—they knew better than to show it to historians in general. They showed it to a few people and didn't quote the ones who thought it was a fake. Surely you can come up with a list of people who would be easy to fool."

"Any scholar could. Be a different list for each one; I'd be on some of them."

"So they bring it out on April Fool's Day. You get the front page of the New York *Times Book Review. Publishers Weekly* does a story. Everybody wants to be in on the joke. Bestseller list, here we come."

"Yeah, sure, but you haven't thought it through." He leaned back, balancing the coffee cup on his slight pot belly. "What about the guys who give us the blurbs, those second-rate scholars? They're going to look pretty bad."

"We did think of that. No way they could sue, not if the letter accompanying the galleys is carefully written. It doesn't have to say—"

"I don't mean getting sued. I mean I don't want to be responsible for hurting other people's careers—maybe wrecking a career, if the person was too extravagant in his endorsement, and had people looking for things to use against him. You know departmental politics. People go down the chute for less serious crimes than making an ass of yourself and your institution in print."

She put her cup down with a clatter. "You're always thinking about other people. Why don't you think about yourself for a change?" She was on the verge of tears. "Think about *us*."

"All right, let's do that. What do you think would happen to my career at BU if I pissed off the wrong people with this exercise? How long do you think it would take me to make full professor? Do you think BU would make a full professor out of a man who uses his specialty to pull vicious practical jokes?"

"Just do me the favor of thinking about it. Cool down and weigh the pluses and minuses. If you did it with the right touch, your department would love it—and God, Harry wants to get rid of the chairmanship so bad he'd give it to an axe murderer. You know you'll make full professor about thirty seconds before Harry hands you the keys to the office and runs."

"True enough." He finished the coffee and stood up in a slow creak. "I'll give it some thought. Horizontally." He turned toward the bedroom.

"Want some company?"

He looked at her for a moment. "Indeed I do."

6. in our time

Back already?

Need to find a meta-causal. One guy seems to be generating the danger flag in various timelines. John Baird, who's a scholar in some of them, a soldier in some, and a rich playboy in a few. He's always a Hemingway nut, though. He does something that starts off the ripples in '95, '96, '97; depending on which timeline you're in—but I can't seem to get close to it. There's something odd about him, and it doesn't have to do with Hemingway specifically.

But he's definitely causing the eddy?

Has to be him.

All right. Find a meta-causal that all the doom lines have in common, and forget about the others. Then go talk to him.

There'll be resonance—

But who cares? Moot after A.D. 2006.

That's true. I'll hit all the doom lines at once, then: neutralize the meta-causal, then jump ahead and do some spot checks.

Good. And no killing this time.

I understand. But—

You're too close to 2006. Kill the wrong person and the whole thing could unravel.

Well, there are differences of opinion. We would certainly feel it if the world failed to come to an end in those lines.

As you say, differences of opinion. My opinion is that you better not kill anybody or I'll send you back to patrol the fourteenth century again.

Understood. But I can't guarantee that I can neutralize the meta-causal without eliminating John Baird.

Fourteenth century. Some people love it. Others think it was nasty, brutish, and long.

7. A Clean, Well-Lighted Place

Most of the sleuthing that makes up literary scholarship takes place in settings either neutral or unpleasant. Libraries' old stacks, attics metaphorical and actual; dust and silverfish, yellowed paper and fading ink. Books and letters that appear in card files but not on shelves.

Hemingway researchers have a haven outside of Boston, the Hemingway Collection at the University of Massachusetts's John F. Kennedy Library. It's a triangular room with one wall dominated by a picture window that looks over Boston Harbor to the sea. Comfortable easy chairs surrounded a coffee table, but John had never seen them in use; work tables under the picture window provided realistic room for computer and clutter. Skins from animals the Hemingways had dispatched in Africa snarled up from the floor, and one wall was dominated by Hemingway memorabilia and photographs. What made the room Nirvana, though, was row upon row of boxes containing tens of thousand of Xerox pages of Hemingway correspondence, manuscripts, clippings— everything from a boyhood shopping list to all extant versions of every short story and poem and novel.

John liked to get there early so he could claim one of the three computers. He snapped it on, inserted a CD, and typed in his code number. Then he keyed in the database index and started searching.

The more commonly requested items would appear on screen if you asked for them—whenever someone requested a physical copy of an item, an electronic copy automatically was sent into the database—but most of the things John needed were obscure, and he had to haul down the letter boxes and physically flip through them, just like some poor scholar inhabiting the first nine tenths of the twentieth century.

Time disappeared for him as he abandoned his notes and followed lines of instinct, leaping from letter to manuscript to note to interview, doing what was in essence the opposite of the scholar's job: a scholar would normally be trying to find out what these stories had been about. John instead was trying to track down every reference that might restrict what he himself could write about, simulating the stories.

The most confining restriction was the one he'd first remembered, walking away from the bar where he'd met Castle. The one-paragraph answer that Hadley had given to Carlos Baker about the unfinished novel; that it was a Nick Adams story about hunting and fishing up in Michigan. John didn't know anything about hunting and most of his fishing experience was limited to watching a bobber and hoping it wouldn't go down and break his train of thought.

There was the one story that Hemingway had left unpublished, "Boys and Girls Together," mostly clumsy self-parody. It covered the right period and the right activities, but using it as a source would be sensitive business, tip-toeing through a minefield. Anyone looking for a fake would go straight there. Of course John could go up to the Michigan woods and camp out, see things for himself and try to re-create them in the Hemingway style. Later, though. First order of business was to make sure there was nothing in this huge collection that would torpedo the whole project—some postcard where Hemingway said "You're going to like this novel because it has a big scene about cleaning fish."

The short stories would be less restricted in subject matter. According to Hemingway, they'd been about growing up in Oak Park and Michigan and the battlefields of Italy.

That made him stop and think. The one dramatic experience he shared with Hemingway was combat—fifty years later, to be sure, in Vietnam, but the basic situations couldn't have changed that much. Terror, heroism, cowardice. The guns and grenades were a little more streamlined, but they did the same things to people. Maybe do a World War I story as a finger exercise, see whether it would be realistic to try a longer growing-up-in-Michigan pastiche.

He made a note to himself about that on the computer, oblique enough not to be damning, and continued the eyestraining job of searching through Hadley's correspondence, trying to find some further reference to the lost novel—damn!

Writing to Ernest's mother, Hadley noted that "the taxi driver broke his typewriter" on the way to the Constantinople conference—did he get it fixed, or just chuck it? A quick check showed that the typeface of his manuscripts did indeed change after July 1924. So they'd never be able to find it. There were typewriters in Hemingway shrines in Key West, Billings, Schruns; the initial plan had been to find which was the old Corona, then locate an identical one and have Castle arrange a swap.

So they would fall back on Plan B. Castle had claimed to be good with mechanical things, and thought if they could find a 1921 Corona, he could tweak the keys around so they would produce a convincing manuscript— lower-case "s" a hair low, "e" a hair high, and so forth.

How he could be so sure of success without ever having seen the inside of a manual typewriter, John did not know. Nor did he have much confidence.

But it wouldn't have to be a perfect simulation, since they weren't out to fool the whole world, but just a few reviewers who would only see two or three Xeroxed pages. He could probably do a close enough job. John put it out of his mind and moved on to the next letter.

But it was an odd coincidence for him to think about Castle at that instant, since Castle was thinking about him. Or at least asking.

8. The Coming Man

"How was he when he was younger?"

"He never was younger." She laughed and rolled around inside the compass of his arms to face him. "Than you, I mean. He was in his mid-thirties when we met. You can't be much over twenty-five."

He kissed the end of her nose. "Thirty this year. But I still get carded sometimes."

"I'm a year older than you are. So you have to do anything I say."

"So far so good." He'd checked her wallet when she'd gone into the bathroom to insert the diaphragm, and knew she was thirty-five. "Break out the whips and chains now?"

"Not till next week. Work up to it slowly." She pulled away from him and mopped her front with the sheet. "You're good at being slow."

"I like being asked to come back."

"How 'bout tonight and tomorrow morning?"

"If you feed me lots of vitamins. How long you think he'll be up in Boston?"

"He's got a train ticket for Wednesday. But he said he might stay longer if he got onto something."

Castle laughed. "Or into something. Think he might have a girl up there? Some student like you used to be?"

"That would be funny. I guess it's not impossible." She covered her eyes with the back of her hand. "The wife is always the last to know."

They both laughed. "But I don't think so. He's a sweet guy but he's just not real sexy. I think his students see him as kind of a favorite uncle."

"You fell for him once."

"Uh huh. He had all of his current virtues plus a full head of hair, no pot belly—and, hm, what am I forgetting?"

"He was hung like an elephant?"

"No, I guess it was the millions of dollars. That can be pretty sexy."

9. Wanderings

It was a good thing John liked to nose around obscure neighborhoods shopping; you couldn't walk into any old K-Mart and pick up a 1921 Corona portable. In fact, you couldn't walk into any typewriter shop in Boston and find one, not any. Nowadays they all sold self-contained word processors, with a few dusty electrics in the back room. A few had fancy manual typewriters from Italy or Switzerland; it had been almost thirty years since the American manufacturers had made a machine that wrote without electronic help.

He had a little better luck with pawnshops. Lots of Smith-Coronas, a few L.C. Smiths, and two actual Coronas that might have been old enough. One had too large a typeface and the other, although the typeface was the same as Hemingway's, was missing a couple of letters: Th quick b own fox jump d ov th lazy dog. The challenge of writing a convincing Hemingway novel without using the letters "e" and "r" seemed daunting. He bought the machine anyhow, thinking they might ultimately have two or several broken ones that could be concatenated into one reliable machine.

The old pawnbroker rang up his purchase and made change and slammed the cash drawer shut. "Now you don't look to me like the kind of man who would hold it against a man who. . . ." He shrugged. "Well, who sold you something and then suddenly remembered that there was a place with lots of those somethings?"

"Of course not. Business is business."

"I don't know the name of the guy or his shop; I think he calls it a museum. Up in Brunswick, Maine. He's got a thousand old typewriters. He buys, sells, trades. That's the only place I know of you might find one with the missing whatever-you-call-ems."

"Fonts." He put the antique typewriter under his arm—the handle was missing—and shook the old man's hand. "Thanks a lot. This might save me weeks."

With some difficulty John got together packing materials and shipped the machine to Key West, along with Xeroxes of a few dozen pages of Hemingway's typed copy and a note suggesting Castle see what he could do. Then he went to the library and found a Brunswick telephone directory. Under "Office Machines & Supplies" was listed Crazy Tom's Typewriter Museum and Sales Emporium. John rented a car and headed north.

The small town had rolled up its sidewalks by the time he got there. He drove past Crazy Tom's and pulled into the first motel. It had a neon VACANCY sign but the innkeeper had to be roused from a deep sleep. He took John's credit card number and directed him to Room 14 and pointedly turned on the NO sign. There were only two other cars in the motel lot.

John slept late and treated himself to a full "trucker's" breakfast at the local diner: two pork chops and eggs and hash browns. Then he worked off ten calories by walking to the shop.

Crazy Tom was younger than John had expected, thirtyish with an unruly shock of black hair. A manual typewriter lay upside-down on an immaculate work table, but most of the place was definitely maculate. Thousands of peanut shells littered the floor. Crazy Tom was eating them compulsively from a large wooden bowl. When he saw John standing in the doorway, he offered some. "Unsalted," he said. "Good for you."

John crunched his way over the peanut-shell carpet. The only light in the place was the bare bulb suspended over the work table, though two unlit high-intensity lamps were clamped on either side of it. The walls were floor-to-ceiling gloomy shelves holding hundreds of typewriters, mostly black.

"Let me guess," the man said as John scooped up a handful of peanuts. "You're here about a typewriter."

"A specific one. A 1921 Corona portable."

"Ah." He closed his eyes in thought. "Hemingway. His first. Or I guess the first after he started writing. A '27 Corona, now, that'd be Faulkner."

"You got a lot of calls for them?"

"Couple times a year. People hear about this place and see if they can find one like the master used, whoever the master is to them. Sympathetic magic and all that. But you aren't a writer."

"I've had some stories published."

"Yeah, but you look too comfortable. You do something else. Teach school." He looked around in the gloom. "Corona Corona." The he sang the six syllables to the tune of "Corina, Corina." He walked a few steps into the darkness and returned with a small machine and set it on the table. "Newer than 1920 because of the way it says 'Corona' here. Older than 1927 because of the tab set-up." He found a piece of paper and a chair. "Go on, try it."

John typed out a few quick foxes and aids to one's party. The typeface was identical to the one on the machine Hadley had given Hemingway before they'd been married. The up-and-down-displacements of the letters were different, of course, but Castle should be able to fix that once he'd practiced with the back-up machine.

John cracked a peanut. "How much?"

"What you need it for?"

"Why is that important?"

"It's the only one I got. Rather rent it than sell it." He didn't look like he was lying, trying to push the price up. "A thousand to buy, a hundred a month to rent."

"Tell you what, then. I buy it, and if it doesn't bring me luck, you agree to buy it back at a pro ratum. My one thousand dollars minus ten percent per month."

Crazy Tom stuck out his hand. "Let's have a beer on it."

"Isn't it a little early for that?"

"Not if you eat peanuts all morning." He took two long-necked Budweisers from a cooler and set them on paper towels on the table. "So what kind of stuff you write?"

"Short stories and some poetry." The beer was good after the heavy greasy breakfast. "Nothing you would've seen unless you read magazines like *Iowa Review* and *Triquarterly*."

"Oh yeah. Foldouts of Gertrude Stein and H.D. I might've read your stuff."

"John Baird."

He shook his head. "Maybe. I'm no good with names."

"If you recognized my name from *The Iowa Review* you'd be the first person who ever had."

"I was right about the Hemingway connection?"

"Of course."

"But you don't write like Hemingway for no *Iowa Review*. Short declarative sentences, truly this truly that."

"No, you were right about the teaching, too. I teach Hemingway up at Boston University."

"So that's why the typewriter? Play show and tell with your students?"

"That, too. Mainly I want to write some on it and see how it feels."

From the back of the shop, a third person listened to the conversation with great interest. He, it, wasn't really a "person," though he could look like one: he had never been born and he would never die. But then he didn't really exist, not in the down-home pinch-yourself-ouch! way that you and I do.

In another way, he did *more* than exist, since he could slip back and forth between places you and I don't even have words for.

He was carrying a wand that could be calibrated for heart attack, stroke, or metastasized cancer on one end; the other end induced a kind of aphasia. He couldn't use it unless he materialized. He walked toward the two men, making no crunching sounds on the peanut shells because he weighed less than a thought. He studied John Baird's face from about a foot away.

"I guess it's a mystical thing, though I'm uncomfortable with that word. See whether I can get into his frame of mind."

"Funny thing," Crazy Tom said; "I never thought of him typing out his stories. He was always sitting in some café writing in notebooks, piling up saucers."

"You've read a lot about him?" That would be another reason not to try the forgery. This guy comes out of the woodwork and says "I sold John Baird a 1921 Corona portable."

"Hell, all I do is read. If I get two customers a day, one of 'em's a mistake and the other just wants directions. I've read all of Hemingway's fiction and most of the journalism and I think all of the poetry. Not just the *Querschnitt* period; the more interesting stuff."

The invisible man was puzzled. Quite obviously John Baird planned some sort of Hemingway forgery. But then he should be growing worried over this man's dangerous expertise. Instead, he was radiating relief.

What course of action, inaction? He could go back a few hours in time and steal this typewriter, though he would have to materialize for that, and it would cause suspicions. And Baird could find another. He could kill one or both of them, now or last week or next, but that would mean duty in the fourteenth century for more than forever— when you exist out of time, a century of unpleasantness is long enough for planets to form and die.

He wouldn't have been drawn to this meeting if it were not a strong causal nexus. There must be earlier ones, since John Baird did not just stroll down a back street in this little town and decide to change history by buying a typewriter. But the earlier ones must be too weak, or something was masking them.

Maybe it was a good timeplace to get John Baird alone and explain things to him. Then use the wand on him. But no, not until he knew exactly what he was preventing. With considerable effort of will and expenditure of something like energy, he froze time at this instant and traveled to a couple of hundred adjacent realities that were all in this same bundle of doomed timelines.

In most of them, Baird was here in Crazy Tom's Typewriter Museum and Sales Emporium. In some, he was in a similar place in New York. In two, he was back in the Hemingway collection. In one, John Baird didn't exist: the whole planet was a lifeless blasted cinder. He'd known about that timeline; it had been sort of a dry run.

"He did both," John then said in most of the timelines. "Sometimes typing, sometimes fountain pen or pencil. I've seen the rough draft of his first novel. Written out in a stack of seven French schoolkids' copybooks." He looked around, memory working. A red herring wouldn't hurt. He'd never come across a reference to any other specific Hemingway typewriter, but maybe this guy had. "You know what kind of machine he used in Key West or Havana?"

Crazy Tom pulled on his chin. "Nope. Bring me a sample of the typing and I might be able to pin it down, though. And I'll keep an eye out—got a card?"

John took out a business card and his checkbook. "Take a check on a Boston bank?"

"Sure. I'd take one on a Tierra del Fuego bank. Who'd stiff you on a seventy-year-old typewriter?" Sylvester Castlemaine might, John thought. "I've had this business almost twenty years," Tom continued; "not a single bounced check or bent plastic."

"Yeah," John said. "Why would a crook want an old typewriter?" The invisible man laughed and went away.

10. Banal Story

Dear Lena & Castle,

Typing this on the new/old machine to give you an idea about what has to be modified to mimic EH's: abcdefghijklmnopqrstuvwxyz ABCDEFGHIJKL MNOPQRSTUVWXYZ 234567890,./ "#$%_&'()*?

Other mechanical things to think about—

1. Paper -- One thing that made people suspicious about the Hitler forgery is that experts know that old paper smells old. And of course there was that fatal chemical-composition error that clinched it.

As we discussed, my first thought was that one of us would have to go to Paris and nose around in old attics and so forth, trying to find either a stack of 75-year-old paper or an old blank book we could cut pages out of. But in the JFK Library collection I found out that EH actually did bring some American-made paper along with him. A lot of

the rough draft of <u>in our time</u> -- written in Paris
a year or two after our "discovery"-- was typed on
the back of 6x7" stationery from his parents' vacation place in Windemere, Xerox enclosed. It
should be pretty easy to duplicate on a hand
press, and of course it will be a lot easier to find
75-year-old American paper. One complication,
unfortunately, is that I haven't really seen the
paper; only a Xerox of the pages. Have to come up
with some pretext to either visit the vault or have
a page brought up, so I can check the color of the
ink, memorize the weight and deckle of the paper,
check to see how the edges are cut . . .

I'm starting to sound like a real forger. In
for a penny, though, in for a pound. One of the
critics who's sent the fragment might want to
see the actual document, and compare it with
the existing Windemere pages.

2. Inks. This should not be a problem. Here's
a recipe for typewriter ribbon ink from a 1918
book of commercial formulas:

8 oz. lampblack

4 oz. gum arabic

1 quart methylated spirits

That last one is wood alcohol. The others

ought to be available in Miami if you can't find
them on the Rock.

Aging the ink on the paper gets a little
tricky. I haven't been able to find anything
about it in the libraries around here; no FORG-
ERY FOR FUN & PROFIT. May check in New York before coming back.

(If we don't find anything, I'd suggest bak-
ing it for a few days at a temperature low
enough not to greatly affect the paper, and then
interleaving it with blank sheets of the old
paper and pressing them together for a few days,
to restore the old smell, and further absorb
the residual ink solvents.)

Toyed with the idea of actually allowing the
manuscript to mildew somewhat, but that might
get out of hand and actually destroy some of it --
or for all I know we'd be employing a species of
mildew that doesn't speak French. Again, thinking
like a true forger, which may be a waste of time
and effort, but I have to admit is kind of fun.
Playing cops and robbers at my age.

Well, I'll call tonight. Miss you, Lena.

Your partner in crime,

John.

11. A Divine Gesture

When John returned to his place in Boston, there was a message on his answering machine: "John, this is Nelson Van Nuys. Harry told me you were in town. I left something in your box at the office and I strongly suggest you take it before somebody else does. I'll be out of town for a week, but give me a call if you're here next Friday. You can take me and Doris out to dinner at Panache."

Panache was the most expensive restaurant in Cambridge. Interesting. John checked his watch. He hadn't planned to go to the office, but there was plenty of time to swing by on his way to returning the rental car. The train didn't leave for another four hours.

Van Nuys was a fellow Hemingway scholar and sometimes drinking buddy who taught at Brown. What had he brought ninety miles to deliver in person, rather than mail? He was probably just in town and dropped by. But it was worth checking.

No one but the secretary was in the office, noontime, for which John was obscurely relieved. In his box were three interdepartmental memos, a textbook catalog, and a brown cardboard box that sloshed when he picked it up. He took it all back to his office and closed the door.

The office made him feel a little weary, as usual. He wondered whether they would be shuffling people around again this year. The department liked to keep its professors in shape by having them haul tons of books and files up and down the corridor every couple of years.

He glanced at the memos and pitched them, irrelevant since he wasn't teaching in the summer, and put the catalog in his briefcase. Then he carefully opened the cardboard box.

It was a half-pint Jack Daniel's bottle, but it didn't have bourbon in it. A cloudy greenish liquid. John unscrewed the top and with the sharp Pernod tang the memory came back: He and Van Nuys had wasted half an afternoon in Paris years ago, trying to track down a source of true absinthe. So he had finally found some.

Absinthe. Nectar of the gods, ruination of several generations of French artists, students, workingmen—outlawed in 1915 for its addictive and hallucinogenic qualities. Where had Van Nuys found it?

He screwed the top back on tightly and put it back in the box and put the box in his briefcase. If its effect really was all that powerful, you probably wouldn't want to drive under its influence. In Boston traffic, of course, a little lane weaving and a few mild collisions would go unnoticed.

Once he was safely on the train, he'd try a shot or two of it. It couldn't be all that potent. Child of the sixties, John had taken LSD, psilocybin, ecstasy, and peyote, and remembered with complete accuracy the quality of each drug's hallucinations. The effects of absinthe wouldn't be nearly as extreme as its modern successors. But it was probably just as well to try it first in a place where unconsciousness or Steve Allen imitations or speaking in tongues would go unremarked.

He turned in the rental car and took a cab to South Station rather than juggle suitcase, briefcase, and typewriter through the subway system. Once there, he nursed a beer through an hour of the Yankees murdering the Red Sox, and then rented a cart to roll his burden down to track 3, where a smiling porter installed him aboard the *Silver Meteor*, its range newly extended from Boston to Miami.

He had loved the train since his boyhood in Washington. His mother hated flying and so they often clickety-clacked from place to place in the snug comfort of first-class compartments. Eidetic memory blunted his enjoyment of the modern Amtrak version. This compartment was as large as the ones he had read and done puzzles in, forty years before—amazing and delighting his mother with his proficiency in word games—but the smell of good old leather was gone, replaced by plastic, and the fittings that had been polished brass were chromed steel now. On the middle of the red plastic seat was a Hospitality Pak, a plastic box encased in plastic wrap that contained a wedge of indestructible "cheese food," as if cheese had to eat, a small plastic bottle of cheap California wine, a plastic glass to contain it, and an apple, possibly not plastic.

John hung up his coat and tie in the small closet provided beside where the bed would fold down, and for a few minutes he watched with interest as his fellow passengers and their accompaniment hurried or ambled to their cars. Mostly old people, of course. Enough young ones, John hoped, to keep the trains alive a few decades more.

"Mr. Baird?" John turned to face a black porter, who bowed slightly and favored him with a blinding smile of white and gold. "My name is George, and I will be at your service as far as Atlanta. Is everything satisfactory?"

"Doing fine. But if you could find me a glass made of glass and a couple of ice cubes, I might mention you in my will."

"One minute, sir." In fact, it took less than a minute. That was one aspect, John had to admit, that had improved in recent years: The service on Amtrak in the sixties and seventies had been right up there with Alcatraz and the Hanoi Hilton.

He closed and locked the compartment door and carefully poured about two ounces of the absinthe into the glass. Like Pernod, it turned milky on contact with the ice.

He swirled it around and breathed deeply. It did smell much like Pernod, but with an acrid tang that was probably oil of wormwood. An experimental sip: the wormwood didn't dominate the licorice flavor, but it was there.

"Thanks, Nelson," he whispered, and drank the whole thing in one cold fiery gulp. He set down the glass and the train began to move. For a weird moment that seemed hallucinatory, but it always did, the train starting off so smoothly and silently.

For about ten minutes he felt nothing unusual, as the

train did its slow tour of Boston's least attractive back-yards. The conductor who checked his ticket seemed like a normal human being, which could have been a hallucination.

John knew that some drugs, like amyl nitrite, hit with a swift slap, while others creep into your mind like careful infiltrators. This was the way of absinthe; all he felt was a slight alcohol buzz, and he was about to take another shot, when it subtly began.

There were *things* just at the periphery of his vision, odd things with substance, but somehow without shape, that of course moved away when he turned his head to look at them. At the same time a whispering began in his ears, just audible over the train noise, but not intelligible, as if in a language he had heard before but not understood. For some reason the effects were pleasant, though of course they could be frightening if a person were not expecting weirdness. He enjoyed the illusions for a few minutes, while the scenery outside mellowed into woodsy suburbs, and the visions and voices stopped rather suddenly.

He poured another ounce and this time diluted it with water. He remembered the sad woman in "Hills Like White Elephants" lamenting that everything new tasted like licorice, and allowed himself to wonder what Hemingway had been drinking when he wrote that curious story.

Chuckling at his own—what? Effrontery?—John took out the 1921 Corona and slipped a sheet of paper into it and balanced it on his knees. He had earlier thought of the first two lines of the WWI pastiche; he typed them down and kept going:

```
The dirt on the sides of the trenches was never

completely dry in the morning. If Nick could find

an old newspaper he would put it between his chest

and the dirt when he went out to lean on the side
```

of the trench and wait for the light. First light
was the best time. You might have luck and see a
muzzle flash. But patience was better than luck.
Wait to see a helmet or a head without a helmet.

Nick looked at the enemy line through a rectangular box of wood that went through the trench
at about ground level. The other end of the box was
covered by a square of gauze the color of dirt.
A person looking directly at it might see the muzzle flash when Nick fired through the box. But
with luck, the flash would be the last thing he saw.

Nick had fired through the gauze six times,
perhaps killing three enemy, and the gauze now
had a ragged hole in the center.

Okay, John thought, he'd be able to see slightly better
through the hole in the center but staring that way would
reduce the effective field of view, so he would deliber-
ately try to look to one side or the other. How to type
that down in a simple way? Someone cleared his throat.

John looked up from the typewriter. Sitting across
from him was Ernest Hemingway, the weathered, wise
Hemingway of the famous Karsh photograph.

"I'm afraid you must not do that," Hemingway said.

John looked at the half-full glass of absinthe and
looked back. Hemingway was still there. "Jesus Christ,"
he said.

"It isn't the absinthe." Hemingway's image rippled and
he became the handsome teenager who had gone to war,
the war John was writing about. "I am quite real. In a
way, I am more real than you are." As it spoke it aged:

the mustachioed leading-man-handsome Hemingway of
the twenties; the slightly corpulent, still magnetic media
hero of the thirties and forties; the beard turning white,
the features hard and sad and then twisting with impo-
tence and madness, and then a sudden loud report and
the cranial vault exploding, the mahogany veneer of the
wall splashed with blood and brains and imbedded chips
of skull. There was a strong smell of cordite and blood.
The almost headless corpse shrugged, spreading its
hands. "I can look like anyone I want." The mess disappeared and it became the young Hemingway again.

John slumped and stared.

"This thing you just started must never be finished.
This Hemingway pastiche. It will ruin something very
important."

"What could it ruin? I'm not even planning to—"

"Your plans are immaterial. If you continue with this
project it will profoundly affect the future."

"You're from the future?"

"I'm from the future and the past and other temporalities that you can't comprehend. But all you need to know
is that you must not write this Hemingway story. If you
do, I or someone like me will have to kill you."

It gestured and a wand the size of a walking stick, half
black and half white, appeared in its hand. It tapped
John's knee with the white end. There was a slight tingle.

"Now you won't be able to tell anybody about me, or
write anything about me down. If you try to talk about
me, the memory will disappear—and reappear moments
later, along with the knowledge that I will kill you if you
don't cooperate." It turned into the bloody corpse again.
"Understood?"

"Of course."

"If you behave, you will never have to see me again."
It started to fade.

"Wait. What do you really look like?"

"This. . . ." For a few seconds John stared at an ebony
presence deeper than black, at once points and edges
and surfaces and volume and hints of further dimensions.

"You can't really see or know," a voice whispered inside his head. He reached into the blackness and jerked his hand back, rimed with frost and numb. The thing disappeared.

He stuck his hand under his armpit and feeling returned. That last apparition was the unsettling one. He had Hemingway's appearance at every age memorized, and had seen the corpse in his mind's eye often enough. A drug could conceivably have brought them all together and made up this fantastic demand—which might actually be nothing more than a reasonable side of his nature trying to make him stop wasting time on this silly project.

But that thing. His hand was back to normal. Maybe a drug could do that, too; make your hand feel freezing. LSD did more profound things than that. But not while arguing about a manuscript.

He considered the remaining absinthe. Maybe take another big blast of it and see whether ol' Ernie comes back again. Or no—there was a simpler way to check.

The bar was four rocking and rolling cars away, and bouncing his way from wall to window helped sober John up. When he got there, he had another twinge for the memories of the past. Stained formica tables. No service; you had to go to a bar at the other end. Acrid with cigarette fumes. He remembered linen tablecloths and endless bottles of Coke with the names of cities from everywhere stamped on the bottom and, when his father came along with them, the rich sultry smoke of his Havanas. The fat Churchills from Punch that emphysema stopped just before Castro could. "A Coke, please." He wondered which depressed him more, the red can or the plastic cup with miniature ice cubes.

The test. It was not in his nature to talk to strangers on public conveyances. But this was necessary. There was a man sitting alone who looked about John's age, a Social-Security bound hippy with wire-rimmed John Lennon glasses, white hair down to his shoulders, bushy grey beard. He nodded when John sat down across from him, but didn't say anything. He sipped beer and looked blankly out at the gathering darkness.

"Excuse me," John said, "but I have a strange thing to ask you."

The man looked at him. "I don't mind strange things. But please don't try to sell me anything illegal."

"I wouldn't. It may have something to do with a drug, but it would be one I took."

"You do look odd. You tripping?"

"Doesn't feel like it. But I may have been . . . slipped something." He leaned back and rubbed his eyes. "I just talked to Ernest Hemingway."

"The writer?"

"In my roomette, yeah."

"Wow. He must be pretty old."

"He's dead! More than thirty years."

"Oh wow. Now that is something weird. What he say?"

"You know what a pastiche is?"

"French pastry?"

"No, it's when you copy . . . when you create an imitation of another person's writing. Hemingway's, in this case."

"Is that legal? I mean, with him dead and all."

"Sure it is, as long as you don't try to foist it off as Hemingway's real stuff."

"So what happened? He wanted to help you with it?"

"Actually, no . . . he said I'd better stop."

"Then you better stop. You don't fuck around with ghosts." He pointed at the old brass bracelet on John's wrist. "You in the 'Nam."

"Sixty-eight," John said. "Hue."

"Then you oughta know about ghosts. You don't fuck with ghosts."

"Yeah." What he'd thought was aloofness in the man's eyes, the set of his mouth, was aloneness, something slightly different. "You okay?"

"Oh yeah. Wasn't for a while, then I got my shit together." He looked out the window again, and said something weirdly like Hemingway: "I learned to take it

a day at a time. The day you're in's the only day that's
real. The past is shit and the future, hell, some day your
future's gonna be that you got no future. So fuck it, you
know? One day at a time."

John nodded. "What outfit were you in?"

"Like I say, man, the past is shit. No offense?"

"No, that's okay." He poured the rest of his Coke over
the ice and stood up to go.

"You better talk to somebody about those ghosts. Some
kinda shrink, you know? It's not that they're not real.
But just you got to deal with 'em."

"Thanks. I will." John got a little more ice from the
barman and negotiated his way down the lurching corridor back to his compartment, trying not to spill his drink
while also juggling fantasy, reality, past, present,
memory. . . .

He opened the door and Hemingway was there, drinking his absinthe. He looked up with weary malice. "Am
I going to have to kill you?"

What John did next would have surprised Castlemaine,
who thought he was a nebbish. He closed the compartment door and sat down across from the apparition.
"Maybe you can kill me and maybe you can't."

"Don't worry, I can."

"You said I wouldn't be able to talk to anyone about
you. But I just walked down to the bar car and did."

"I know. That's why I came back."

"So if one of your powers doesn't work, maybe another
doesn't. At any rate, if you kill me you'll never find out
what went wrong."

"That's very cute, but it doesn't work." It finished off
the absinthe and then ran a finger around the rim of the
glass, which refilled out of nowhere.

"You're making assumptions about causality that are
necessarily naïve, because you can't perceive even half
the dimensions that you inhabit."

"Nevertheless, you haven't killed me yet."

"And assumptions about my 'psychology' that are

absurd. I am no more a human being than you are a paramecium."

"I'll accept that. But I would make a deal with a paramecium if I thought I could gain an advantage from it."

"What could you possibly have to deal with, though?"

"I know something about myself that you evidently don't, that enables me to overcome your don't-talk restriction. Knowing that might be worth a great deal to you."

"Maybe something."

"What I would like in exchange is, of course, my life, and an explanation of why I must not do the Hemingway pastiche. Then I wouldn't do it."

"You wouldn't do it if I killed you, either."

John sipped his Coke and waited.

"All right. It goes something like this. There is not just one universe, but actually uncountable zillions of them. They're all roughly the same size and complexity as this one, and they're all going off in a zillion different directions, and it is one hell of a job to keep things straight."

"You do this by yourself? You're God?"

"There's not just one of me. In fact, it would be meaningless to assign a number to us, but I guess you could say that altogether, we are God ... and the Devil, and the Cosmic Puppet master, and the Grand Unification Theory, the Great Pumpkin and everything else. When we consider ourselves as a group, let me see, I guess a human translation of our name would be the Spacio-Temporal Adjustment Board."

"STAB?"

"I guess that is unfortunate. Anyhow, what STAB does is more the work of a scalpel than a knife." The Hemingway scratched its nose, leaving the absinthe suspended in mid-air. "Events are supposed to happen in certain ways, in certain sequences. You look at things happening and say cause-and-effect, or coincidence, or golly, that couldn't have happened in a million years—but you don't even have a clue. Don't even try to think about it. It's like an ant trying to figure out General Relativity."

"It wouldn't have a clue. Wouldn't know where to start."

The apparition gave him a sharp look and continued. "These universes come in bundles. Hundreds of them, thousands, that are pretty much the same. And they affect each other. Resonate with each other. When something goes wrong in one, it resonates and screws up all of them."

"You mean to say that if I write a Hemingway pastiche, hundreds of universes are going to go straight to hell?"

The apparition spread its hands and looked to the ceiling. "Nothing is simple. The only thing that's simple is that nothing is simple.

"I'm a sort of literature specialist. American literature of the nineteenth and twentieth centuries. Usually. Most of my timespace is taken up with guys like Hemingway, Teddy Roosevelt, Heinlein, Bierce. Crane, Spillane, Twain."

"Not William Dean Howells?"

"Not him or James or Carver or Coover or Cheever or any of those guys. If everybody gave me as little trouble as William Dean Howells I could spend most of my timespace on a planet where the fishing was good."

"Masculine writers?" John said. "But not all hairy-chested macho types."

"I'll give you an A–on that one. They're writers who have an accumulating effect on the masculine side of the American national character. There's no one word for it, though it is a specific thing: individualistic, competence-worshiping, short-term optimism and long-term existentialism. 'There may be nothing after I die but I sure as hell will do the job right while I'm here, even though I'm surrounded by idiots.' You see the pattern?"

"Okay. And I see how Hemingway fits in. But how could writing a pastiche interfere with it?"

"That's a limitation I have. I don't know specifically. I do know that the accelerating revival of interest in Hemingway from the seventies through the nineties is vitally important. In the Soviet Union as well as the United States. For some reason, I can feel your pastiche interfering with it." He stretched out the absinthe glass into a yard-long amber crystal, and it changed into the black-

and-white cane. The glass reappeared in the drink holder
by the window. "Your turn."

"You won't kill me after you hear what I have to say?"

"No. Go ahead."

"Well . . . I have an absolutely eidetic memory. Everything I've ever seen—or smelled or tasted or heard or
touched, or even dreamed—I can instantly recall.

"Every other memory freak I've read about was limited—numbers, dates, calendar tricks, historical details—
and most of them were *idiots savants*. I have at least
normal intelligence. But from the age of about three, I
have never forgotten anything."

The Hemingway smiled congenially. "Thank you.
That's exactly it." It fingered the black end of the cane,
clicking something. "If you had the choice, would you
rather die of a heart attack, stroke, or cancer?"

"That's it?" The Hemingway nodded. "Well, you're
human enough to cheat. To lie."

"It's not something you could understand. Stroke?"

"It might not work."

"We're going to find out right now." He lowered the
cane.

"Wait! What's death? Is there . . . anything I should
do, anything you know?"

The rod stopped, poised an inch over John's knee. "I
guess you just end. Is that so bad?"

"Compared to not ending, it's bad."

"That shows how little you know. I and the ones like
me can never die. If you want something to occupy your
last moment, your last thought, you might pity me."

John stared straight into his eyes. "*Fuck* you."

The cane dropped. A fireball exploded in his head.

12. Marriage is a Dangerous Game

"We'll blackmail him." Castle and Lena were together
in the big antique bathtub, in a sea of pink foam, her
back against his chest.

"Sure," she said. " 'If you don't let us pass this manuscript off as the real thing, we'll tell everybody you faked it.' Something wrong with that, but I can't quite put my finger on it."

"Here, I'll put mine on it."

She giggled. "Later. What do you mean, blackmail?"

"Got it all figured out. I've got this friend Pansy, she used to be a call girl. Been out of the game seven, eight years; still looks like a million bucks."

"Sure. We fix John up with this hooker—"

"Call girl isn't a hooker. We're talkin' class."

"In the first place, John wouldn't pay for sex. He did that in Vietnam and it still bothers him."

"Not talkin' about pay. Talkin' about fallin' in love. While she meanwhile fucks his eyeballs out."

"You have such a turn of phrase, Sylvester. Then while his eyeballs are out, you come in with a camera."

"Yeah, but you're about six steps ahead."

"Okay, step two; how do we get them together? Church social?"

"She moves in next door." There was another upstairs apartment, unoccupied. "You and me and Julio are conveniently somewhere else when she shows up with all these boxes and that big flight of stairs."

"Sure, John would help her. But that's his nature; he'd help her if she were an ugly old crone with leprosy. Carry a few boxes, sit down for a cup of coffee, maybe. But not jump into the sack."

"Okay, you know John." His voice dropped to a husky whisper and he cupped her breasts. "But I know men, and I know Pansy . . . and Pansy could give a hard-on to a corpse."

"Sure, and then fuck his eyeballs out. They'd come out easier."

"What?"

"Never mind. Go ahead."

"Well . . . look. Do you know what a call girl does?"

"I suppose you call her up and say you've got this eyeball problem."

"Enough with the eyeballs. What she does, she works for like an escort service. That part of it's legal. Guy comes into town, business or maybe on vacation, he calls up the service and they ask what kind of companion he'd like. If he says, like, give me some broad with a tight ass, can suck the chrome off a bumper hitch—the guy says like 'I'm sorry, sir, but this is not that kind of a service.' But mostly the customers are pretty hip to it, they say, oh, a pretty young blonde who likes to go dancing."

"Meanwhile they're thinking about bumper hitches and eyeballs."

"You got it. So it starts out just like a date, just the guy pays the escort service like twenty bucks for getting them together. Still no law broken."

"Now about one out of three, four times, that's it. The guy knows what's going on but he don't get up the nerve to ask, or he really doesn't know the score, and it's like a real dull date. I don't think that happened much with Pansy."

"In the normal course of things, though, the subject of bumper hitches comes up."

"Uh huh, but not from Pansy. The guy has to pop the question. That way if he's a cop it's, what, entrapment."

"Do you know whether Pansy ever got busted?"

"Naw. Mainly the cops just shake down the hookers, just want a blowjob anyhow. This town, half of 'em want a blowjob from *guys*.

"So they pop the question and Pansy blushes and says for you, I guess I could. Then, on the way to the motel or wherever she says, you know, I wouldn't ask this if we weren't really good friends, but I got to make a car payment by tomorrow, and I need like two hundred bucks before noon tomorrow?"

"And she takes MasterCard and Visa."

"No, but she sure as hell knows where every bank machine in town is. She even writes up an I.O.U." Castle laughed. "Told me a guy from Toledo's holdin' five grand of I.O.U.'s from her."

"All right, but that's not John. She could suck the chrome off his eyeballs and he still wouldn't be interested in her if she didn't know Hemingway from hummingbirds."

Castle licked behind her ear, a weird gesture that made her shiver. "That's the trump card. Pansy reads like a son of a bitch. She's got like a thousand books. So this morning I called her up and asked about Hemingway."

"And?"

"She's read them all."

She nodded slowly. "Not bad, Sylvester. So we promote this love affair and sooner or later you catch them in the act. Threaten to tell me unless John accedes to a life of crime."

"Think it could work? He wouldn't say hell, go ahead and tell her?"

"Not if I do my part . . . starting tomorrow. I'm the best, sweetest, lovingest wife in this sexy town. Then in a couple of weeks Pansy comes into his life, and there he is, luckiest man alive. Best of both worlds. Until you accidently catch them *in flagrante delicioso.*"

"So to keep both of you, he goes along with me."

"It might just do it. It might just." She slowly levered herself out of the water and smoothed the suds off her various assets.

"Nice."

"Bring me that bumper hitch, Sylvester. Hold on to your eyeballs."

13. In Another Country

John woke up with a hangover of considerable dimension. The diluted glass of absinthe was still in the drink holder by the window. It was just past dawn, and a verdant forest rushed by outside. The rails made a steady hum; the car had a slight rocking that would have been pleasant to a person who felt well.

A porter knocked twice and inquired after Mr. Baird. "Come in," John said. A short white man, smiling, brought in coffee and Danish.

"What happened to George?"

"Pardon me, sir? George who?"

John rubbed his eyes. "Oh, of course. We must be past Atlanta."

"No, sir." The man's smile froze as his brain went into nutty-passenger mode. "We're at least two hours from Atlanta."

"George . . . is a tall black guy with gold teeth who—"

"Oh, you mean George Mason, sir. He does do this car, but he picks up the train in Atlanta, and works it to Miami and back. He hasn't had the northern leg since last year."

John nodded slowly and didn't ask what year it was. "I understand." He smiled up and read the man's nametag. "I'm sorry, Leonard. Not at my best in the morning." The man withdrew with polite haste.

Suppose that weird dream had not been a dream. The Hemingway creature had killed him—the memory of the stroke was awesomely strong and immediate—but all that death amounted to was slipping into another universe where George Mason was on a different shift. Or perhaps John had gone completely insane.

The second explanation seemed much more reasonable.

On the tray underneath the coffee, juice, and Danish was a copy of *USA Today*, a paper John normally avoided because, although it had its comic aspects, it didn't have any funnies. He checked the date, and it was correct. The news stories were plausible—wars and rumors of war—so at least he hadn't slipped into a dimension where Martians ruled an enslaved earth or Barry Manilow was president. He turned to the weather map and stopped dead.

Yesterday the country was in the middle of a heat wave that had lasted weeks. It apparently had ended overnight. The entry for Boston, yesterday, was "72/58/sh." But it hadn't rained and the temperature had been in the nineties.

He went back to the front page and began checking

news stories. He didn't normally pay much attention to the news, though, and hadn't seen a paper in several days. They'd canceled their *Globe* delivery for the six weeks in Key West and he hadn't been interested enough to go seek out a newsstand.

There was no mention of the garbage collectors' strike in New York; he'd overheard a conversation about that yesterday. A long obituary for a rock star he was sure had died the year before.

An ad for DeSoto automobiles. That company had gone out of business when he was a teen-ager.

Bundles of universes, different from each other in small ways. Instead of dying, or maybe because of dying, he had slipped into another one. What would be waiting for him in Key West?

Maybe John Baird.

He set the tray down and hugged himself, trembling. Who or what was he in this universe? All of his memories, all of his personality, were from the one he had been born in. What happened to the John Baird that was born in this one? Was he an associate professor in American Literature at Boston University? Was he down in Key West wrestling with a paper to give at Nairobi—or working on a forgery? Or was he a Fitzgerald specialist snooping around the literary attics of St. Paul, Minnesota?

The truth came suddenly. Both John Bairds were in this compartment, in this body. And the body was slightly different.

He opened the door to the small washroom and looked in the mirror. His hair was a little shorter, less grey, beard better trimmed.

He was less paunchy and ... something felt odd. There was feeling in his thigh. He lowered his pants and there was no scar where the sniper bullet had opened his leg and torn up the nerves there.

That was the touchstone. As he raised his shirt, the parallel memory flooded in. Puckered round scar on the abdomen; in this universe the sniper had hit a foot

higher—and instead of the convalescent center in Cam
Ranh Bay, the months of physical therapy and then back
into the war, it had been peritonitis raging; surgery in
Saigon and Tokyo and Walter Reed, and no more army.

But slowly they converged again. Amherst and U.
Mass.—perversely using the G.I. Bill in spite of his access
to millions—the doctorate on *The Sun Also Rises* and
the instructorship at B.U., meeting Lena and virtuously
waiting until after the semester to ask her out. Sex on
the second date, and the third . . . but there they verged
again. This John Baird hadn't gone back into combat to
have his midsection sprayed with shrapnel from an American grenade that bounced off a tree; never had dozens
of bits of metal cut out of his dick—and in the ensuing
twenty-five years had made more use of it. Girl friends
and even one disastrous homosexual encounter with a
stranger. As far as he knew, Lena was in the dark about
this side of him; thought that he had remained faithful
other than one incident seven years after they married.
He knew of one affair she had had with a colleague, and
suspected more.

The two Johns' personalities and histories merged, separate but one, like two vines from a common root, climbing a single support.

Schizophrenic but not insane.

John looked into the mirror and tried to address his
new or his old self—John A, John B. There were no such
people. There was suddenly a man who had existed in
two separate universes and, in a way, it was no more
profound than having lived in two separate houses.

The difference being that nobody else knows there is
more than one house.

He moved over to the window and set his coffee in
the holder; picked up the absinthe glass and sniffed it,
considered pouring it down the drain, but then put it in
the other holder, for possible future reference.

Posit this: is it more likely that there are bundles of
parallel universes prevailed over by a Hemingway lookalike with a magic cane, or that John Baird was exposed

to a drug that he had never experienced before and it had had an unusually disorienting effect?

He looked at the paper. He had not hallucinated two weeks of drought. The rock star had been dead for some time. He had not seen a DeSoto in twenty years, and that was a hard car to miss. Tailfins that had to be registered as lethal weapons.

But maybe if you take a person who remembers every trivial thing, and zap his brain with oil of wormwood, that is exactly the effect: perfectly recalled things that never actually happened.

The coffee tasted repulsive. John put on a fresh shirt and decided not to shave and headed for the bar car. He bought the last imported beer in the cooler and sat down across from the long-haired white-bearded man who had an earring that had escaped his notice before, or hadn't existed in the other universe.

The man was staring out at the forest greening by. "Morning," John said.

"How do." The man looked at him with no sign of recognition.

"Did we talk last night?"

He leaned forward. "What?"

"I mean did we sit in this car last night and talk about Hemingway and Vietnam and ghosts?"

He laughed. "You're on somethin', man. I been on this train since two in the mornin' and ain't said boo to nobody but the bartender."

"You were in Vietnam?"

"Yeah, but that's over; that's shit." He pointed at John's bracelet. "What, you got ghosts from over there?"

"I think maybe I have."

He was suddenly intense. "Take my advice, man; I been there. You got to go talk to somebody. Some shrink. Those ghosts ain't gonna go 'way by themself."

"It's not that bad."

"It ain't the ones you killed." He wasn't listening. "Fuckin' dinks, they come back but they don't, you know, they just stand around." He looked at John and tears came so hard they actually spurted from his eyes. "It's your fuckin' friends, man, they all died and they come back now. . . ." He took a deep breath and wiped his face. "They used to come back every night. That like you?" John shook his head, helpless, trapped by the man's grief. "Every fuckin' night, my old lady, finally she said you go to a shrink or go to hell." He fumbled with the button on his shirt pocket and took out a brown plastic prescription bottle and stared at the label. He shook out a capsule. "Take a swig?" John pushed the beer over to him. He washed the pill down without touching the bottle to his lips.

He sagged back against the window. "I musta not took the pill last night, sometimes I do that. Sorry." He smiled weakly. "One day at a time, you know? You get through the one day. Fuck the rest. Sorry." He leaned forward again suddenly and put his hand on John's wrist. "You come outa nowhere and I lay my fuckin' trip on you. You don' need it."

John covered the hand with his own. "Maybe I do need it. And maybe I didn't come out of nowhere." He stood up. "I will see somebody about the ghosts. Promise."

"You'll feel better. It's no fuckin' cure-all but you'll feel better."

"Want the beer?"

He shook his head. "Not supposed to."

"Okay." John took the beer and they waved at each other and he started back.

He stopped in the vestibule between cars and stood in the rattling roar of it, looking out the window at the flashing green blur. He put his forehead against the cool glass and hid the blur behind the dark red of his eyelids.

Were there actually a zillion of those guys each going through a slightly different private hell? Something he rarely asked himself was "What would Ernest Hemingway have done in this situation?"

He'd probably have the sense to leave it to Milton.

14. The Dangerous Summer

Castle and Lena met him at the station in Miami and they drove back to Key West in Castle's old pick-up. The drone of the air-conditioner held conversation to a minimum, but it kept them cool, at least from the knees down.

John didn't say anything about his encounter with the infinite, or transfinite, not wishing to bring back that fellow with the cane just yet. He did note that the two aspects of his personality hadn't quite become equal partners yet, and small details of this world kept surprising him. There was a monorail being built down to Pigeon Key, where Disney was digging an underwater park. Gasoline stations still sold Regular. Castle's car radio picked up TV as well as AM/FM, but sound only.

Lena sat between the two men and rubbed up against John affectionately. That would have been remarkable for John-one and somewhat unusual for John-two. It was a different Lena here, of course; one who had had more of a sex life with John, but there was something more than that, too. She was probably sleeping with Castle, he thought, and the extra attention was a conscious or unconscious compensation, or defense.

Castle seemed a little harder and more serious in this world than the last, not only from his terse moodiness in the pickup, but from recollections of parallel conversations. John wondered how shady he actually was; whether he'd been honest about his police record.

(He hadn't been. In this universe, when Lena had asked him whether he had ever been in trouble with the police, he'd answered a terse "no." In fact, he'd done eight hard years in Ohio for an armed robbery he hadn't committed—the real robber hadn't been so stupid, here—and he'd come out of prison bitter, angry, an actual criminal. Figuring the world owed him one, a week after getting out he stopped for a hitchhiker on a lonely country road, pulled a gun, walked him a few yards off the road into a field of high corn, and shot him pointblank at the base of the skull. It didn't look anything like the movies.)

(He drove off without touching the body, which a farmer's child found two days later. The victim turned out to be a college student who was on probation for dealing—all he'd really done was buy a kilo of green and make his money back by selling bags to his friends, and one enemy—so the papers said **DRUG DEALER FOUND SLAIN IN GANGLAND-STYLE KILLING** and the police pursued the matter with no enthusiasm. Castle was in Key West well before the farmer's child smelled the body, anyhow.)

As they rode along, whatever Lena had or hadn't done with Castle was less interesting to John than what *he* was planning to do with her. Half of his self had never experienced sex, as an adult, without the sensory handicaps engendered by scar tissue and severed nerves in the genitals, and he was looking forward to the experience with relish that was obvious, at least to Lena. She encouraged him in not-so-subtle ways, and by the time they crossed the last bridge into Key West, he was ready to tell Castle to pull over at the first bush.

He left the typewriter in Castle's care and declined help with the luggage. By this time Lena was smiling at his obvious impatience; she was giggling by the time they were momentarily stalled by a truculent door key; laughed her delight as he carried her charging across the room to the couch, then clawing off a minimum of clothing and taking her with fierce haste, wordless, and keeping her on a breathless edge he drifted the rest of the clothes off her and carried her into the bedroom, where they made so much noise Julio banged on the ceiling with a broomstick.

They did quiet down eventually, and lay together in a puddle of mingled sweat, panting, watching the fan push the humid air around. "Guess we both get to sleep in the wet spot," John said.

"No complaints." She raised up on one elbow and traced a figure eight on his chest. "You're full of surprises tonight, Dr. Baird."

"Life is full of surprises."

"You should go away more often—or at least come back more often."

"It's all that Hemingway research. Makes a man out of you."

"You didn't learn this in a book," she said, gently taking his penis and pantomiming a certain motion.

"I did, though; an anthropology book." In another universe. "It's what they do in the Solomon Islands."

"Wisdom of Solomon," she said, lying back. After a pause: "They have anthropology books at JFK?"

"Uh, no." He remembered he didn't own that book in this universe. "Browsing at Wordsworth's."

"Hope you bought the book."

"Didn't have to." He gave her a long slow caress. "Memorized the good parts."

On the other side of town, six days later, she was in about the same position on Castle's bed, and even more exhausted.

"Aren't you overdoing the loving little wifey bit? It's been a week."

She exhaled audibly. "What a week."

"Missed you." He nuzzled her and made an unsubtle preparatory gesture.

"No, you don't." She rolled out of bed. "Once is plenty." She went to the mirror and ran a brush through her damp hair. "Besides, it's not me you missed. You missed *it*." She sat at the open window, improving the neighborhood's scenery. "*It's* gonna need a Teflon lining installed."

"Old boy's feelin' his oats?"

"Not feeling *his* anything. God, I don't know what's gotten into him. Four, five times a day; six."

"Screwed, blewed, and tattooed. You asked for it."

"As a matter of fact, I didn't. I haven't had a chance to start my little act. He got off that train with an erection, and he still has it. No woman would be safe around him. Nothing wet and concave would be safe."

"So does that mean it's a good time to bring in Pansy? Or is he so stuck on you he wouldn't even notice her?"

She scowled at the brush, picking hair out of it. "Actually, Castle, I was just about to ask you the same thing. Relying on your well-known expertise in animal behavior."

"Okay." He sat up. "I say we oughta go for it. If he's a walkin' talkin' hard-on like you say . . . Pansy'd pull him like a magnet. You'd have to be a fuckin' monk not to want Pansy."

"Like Rasputin."

"Like who?"

"Never mind." She went back to the brush. "I guess, I guess one problem is that I really am enjoying the attention. I guess I'm not too anxious to hand him over to this champion sexpot."

"Aw, Lena—"

"Really. I do love him in my way, Castle. I don't want to lose him over this scheme."

"You're not gonna lose him. Trust me. You catch him dickin' Pansy, get mad, forgive him. Hell, you'll have him wrapped around your finger."

"I guess. You make the competition sound pretty formidable."

"Don't worry. She's outa there the next day."

"Unless she winds up in love with him. That would be cute."

"He's almost twice her age. Besides, she's a whore. Whores don't fall in love."

"They're women, Castle. Women fall in love."

"Yeah, sure. Just like on TV."

She turned away from him; looked out the window. "You really know how to make a woman feel great, you know?"

"Come on." He crossed over and smoothed her hair. She turned around but didn't look up. "Don't run yourself down, Lena. You're still one hell of a piece of ass."

"Thanks." She smiled into his leer and grabbed him. "If you weren't such a poet I'd trade you in for a vibrator."

15. In Praise of His Mistress

Pansy was indeed beautiful, even under normal conditions; delicate features, wasp waist combined with generous secondary sexual characteristics. The conditions under which John first saw her were calculated to maximize sexiness and vulnerability. Red nylon running shorts, tight and very short, and a white sleeveless T-shirt from a local bar that was stamped LAST HETEROSEXUAL IN KEY WEST—all clinging to her golden skin with a healthy sweat, the cloth made translucent enough to reveal no possibility of underwear.

John looked out the screen door and saw her at the other door, struggling with a heavy box while trying to make the key work. "Let me help you," he said through the screen, and stepped across the short landing to hold the box while she got the door open.

"You're too kind." John tried not to stare as he handed the box back. Pansy, of course, was relieved at his riveted attention. It had taken days to set up this operation, and would take more days to bring it to its climax, so to speak, and more days to get back to normal. But she did owe Castle a big favor and this guy seemed nice enough. Maybe she'd learn something about Hemingway in the process.

"More to come up?" John asked.

"Oh, I couldn't ask you to help. I can manage."

"It's okay. I was just goofing off for the rest of the day."

It turned out to be quite a job, even though there was only one load from a small rented truck. Most of the load was uniform and heavy boxes of books, carefully labeled LIT A-B, GEN REF, ENCY 1-12, and so forth. Most of her furniture, accordingly, was cinder blocks and boards, the standard student bookshelf arrangement.

John found out that despite a couple of dozen boxes marked LIT, Pansy hadn't majored in literature, but rather Special Education; during the school year, she taught third grade at a school for the retarded in Key Largo. She didn't tell him about the several years she'd spent as a call girl, but if she had, John might have seen a connection that Castle would never have made—that the driving force behind both of the jobs was the same, charity. The more-or-less easy forty dollars an hour for going on a date and then having sex was a factor, too, but she really did like making lonely men feel special, and had herself felt more like a social worker than a woman of easy virtue. And the hundreds of men who had fallen for her, for love or money, weren't responding only to her cheerleader's body. She had a sunny disposition and a natural, artless way of concentrating on a man that made him for a while the only man in the world.

John would not normally be an easy conquest. Twenty years of facing classrooms full of coeds had given him a certain wariness around attractive young women. He also had an impulse toward faithfulness, Lena having suddenly left town, her father ill. But he was still in the grip of the weird overweening horniness that had animated him since inheriting this new body and double-image personality. If Pansy had said "Let's do it," they would be doing it so soon that she would be wise to unwrap the condom before speaking. But she was being as indirect as her nature and mode of dress would allow.

"Do you and your wife always come down here for the summer?"

"We usually go somewhere. Boston's no fun in the heat."

"It must be wonderful in the fall."

And so forth. It felt odd for Pansy, probably the last time she would ever seduce a man for reasons other than personal interest. She wanted it to be perfect. She wanted John to have enough pleasure in her to compensate for the embarrassment of their "accidental" exposure, and whatever hassle his wife would put him through afterwards.

She was dying to know why Castle wanted him set up, but he refused to tell. How Castle ever met a quiet,

kindly gentleman like John was a mystery, too—she had
met some of Castle's friends, and they had other virtues.

Quiet and kindly, but horny. Whenever she contrived,
in the course of their working together, to expose a nip-
ple or a little beaver, he would turn around to adjust
himself, and blush. More like a teenager, discovering his
sexuality, than a middle-aged married man.

He was a pushover, but she didn't want to make it too
easy. After they had finished putting the books up on
shelves, she said thanks a million; I gotta go now, spend-
ing the night house-sitting up in Islamorada. You and
your wife come over for dinner tomorrow? Oh, then
come on over yourself. No, that's all right, I'm a big girl.
Roast beef okay? See ya.

Driving away in the rented truck, Pansy didn't feel
especially proud of herself. She was amused at John's
sexiness and looking forward to trying it out. But she
could read people pretty well, and sensed a core of deep
sadness in John. Maybe it was from Vietnam; he hadn't
mentioned it, but she knew what the bracelet meant.

Whatever the problem, maybe she'd have time to help
him with it—before she had to turn around and add to it.

Maybe it would work out for the best. Maybe the
problem was with his wife, and she'd leave, and he could
start over. . . .

Stop kidding yourself. Just lay the trap, catch him,
deliver him. Castle was not the kind of man you want
to disappoint.

16. Fiesta

She had baked the roast slowly with wine and fruit
juice, along with dried apricots and apples plumped in
port wine, seasoned with cinnamon and nutmeg and car-
damom. Onions and large cubes of acorn squash sim-
mered in the broth. She served new potatoes steamed
with parsley and dressed Italian style, with garlicky olive
oil and a splash of vinegar. Small Caesar salad and air-

light *pan de agua*, the Cuban bread that made you forget every other kind of bread.

The way to a man's heart, her mother had contended, was through his stomach, and although she was accustomed to aiming rather lower, she thought it was probably a good approach for a long-time married man suddenly forced to fend for himself. That was exactly right for John. He was not much of a cook but he was an accomplished eater.

He pushed the plate away after three helpings. "God, I'm such a pig. But that was irresistible."

"Thank you." She cleared the table slowly, accepting John's offer to help. "My mother's 'company' recipe. So you think Hadley might have just thrown the stories away, and made up the business about the train?"

"People have raised the possibility. There she was, eight years older than this handsome hubby—with half the women on the Left Bank after him, at least in her mind—and he's starting to get published, starting to build a reputation. . . ."

"She was afraid he was going to 'grow away' from her? Or did they have that expression back then?"

"I think she was afraid he would start making money from his writing. She had an inheritance, a trust fund from her grandfather, that paid over two thousand a year. That was plenty to keep the two of them comfortable in Paris. Hemingway talked poor in those days, starving artist, but he lived pretty well."

"He probably resented it, too. Not making the money himself."

"That would be like him. Anyhow, if she chucked the stories to ensure his dependency, it backfired. He was still furious thirty years later—three wives later. He said the stuff had been 'fresh from the mint,' even if the writing wasn't so great, and he was never able to reclaim it."

She opened a cabinet and slid a bottle out of its burlap bag, and selected two small glasses. "Sherry?" He said why not? and they moved into the living room.

The living room was mysteriously devoid of chairs, so they had to sit together on the small couch. "You don't actually think she did it."

"No." John watched her pour the sherry. "From what I've read about her, she doesn't seem at all calculating. Just a sweet gal from St. Louis who fell in love with a cad."

"Cad. Funny old-fashioned word."

John shrugged. "Actually, he wasn't really a cad. I think he sincerely loved every one of his wives . . . at least until he married them."

They both laughed. "Of course it could have been something in between," Pansy said, "I mean, she didn't actually throw away the manuscripts, but she did leave them sitting out, begging to be stolen. Why did she leave the compartment?"

"That's one screwy aspect of it. Hadley herself never said, not on paper. Every biographer seems to come up with a different reason: she went to get a newspaper, she saw some people she recognized and stepped out to talk with them, wanted some exercise before the long trip . . . even Hemingway had two different versions—she went out to get a bottle of Evian water or to buy something to read. That one pissed him off, because she did have an overnight bag full of the best American writing since Mark Twain."

"How would you have felt?"

"Felt?"

"I mean, you say you've written stories, too. What if somebody, your wife, made a mistake and you lost everything?"

He looked thoughtful. "It's not the same. In the first place, it's just a hobby with me. And I don't have that much that hasn't been published—when Hemingway lost it, he lost it for good. I could just go to a university library and make new copies of everything."

"So you haven't written much lately?"

"Not stories. Academic stuff."

"I'd love to read some of your stories."

"And I'd love to have you read them. But I don't have any here. I'll mail you some from Boston."

She nodded, staring at him with a curious intensity. "Oh hell," she said, and turned her back to him. "Would you help me with this?"

"What?"

"The zipper." She was wearing a clingy white summer dress. "Undo the zipper a little bit."

He slowly unzipped it a few inches. She did it the rest of the way, stood up and hooked her thumbs under the shoulder straps and shrugged. The dress slithered to the floor. She wasn't wearing anything else.

"You're blushing." Actually, he was doing a good imitation of a beached fish. She straddled him, sitting back lightly on his knees, legs wide, and started unbuttoning his shirt.

"Uh," he said.

"I just get impatient. You don't mind?"

"Uh . . . no?"

17. On Being Shot Again

John woke up happy but didn't open his eyes for nearly a minute, holding on to the erotic dream of the century. Then he opened one eye and saw it hadn't been a dream: the tousled bed in the strange room, unguents and sex toys on the nightstand, the smell of her hair on the other pillow. A noise from the kitchen; coffee and bacon smells.

He put on pants and went into the living room to pick up the shirt where it had dropped. "Good morning, Pansy."

"Morning, stranger." She was wearing a floppy terry-cloth bathrobe with the sleeves rolled up to her elbows. She turned the bacon carefully with a fork. "Scrambled eggs okay?"

"Marvelous." He sat down at the small table and poured himself a cup of coffee. "I don't know what to say."

She smiled at him. "Don't say anything. It was nice."

"More than nice." He watched her precise motions behind the counter. She broke the eggs one-handed, two at a time, added a splash of water to the bowl, plucked some chives from a windowbox and chopped them with a small Chinese cleaver, rocking it in a staccato chatter; scraped them into the bowl, and followed them with a couple of grinds of pepper. She set the bacon out on a paper towel, with another towel to cover. Then she stirred the eggs briskly with the fork and set them aside. She picked up the big cast-iron frying pan and poured off a judicious amount of grease. Then she poured the egg mixture into the pan and studied it with alertness.

"Know what I think?" John said.

"Something profound?"

"Huh-uh. I think I'm in a rubber room someplace, hallucinating the whole thing. And I hope they never cure me."

"I think you're a butterfly who's dreaming he's a man. I'm glad I'm in your dream." She slowly stirred and scraped the eggs with a spatula.

"You like older men?"

"One of them." She looked up, serious. "I like men who are considerate . . . and playful." She returned to the scraping. "Last couple of boyfriends I had were all dick and no heart. Kept to myself the last few months."

"Glad to be of service."

"You could rent yourself out as a service." She laughed. "You must have been impossible when you were younger."

"Different." Literally.

She ran hot water into a serving bowl, then returned to her egg stewardship. "I've been thinking."

"Yes?"

"The lost manuscript stuff we were talking about last night, all the different explanations." She divided the egg into four masses and turned each one. "Did you ever read any science fiction?"

"No. Vonnegut."

"The toast." She hurriedly put four pieces of bread in the toaster. "They write about alternate universes. Pretty much like our own, but different in one way or another. Important or trivial."

"What, uh, what silliness."

She laughed and poured the hot water out of the serving bowl, and dried it with a towel. "I guess maybe. But what if ... what if all of those versions were equally true? In different universes. And for some reason they all came together here." She started to put the eggs into the bowl when there was a knock on the door.

It opened and Ernest Hemingway walked in. Dapper, just twenty, wearing the Italian army cape he'd brought back from the war. He pointed the black and white cane at Pansy. "Bingo."

She looked at John and then back at the Hemingway. She dropped the serving bowl; it clattered on the floor without breaking. Her knees buckled and she fainted dead away, executing a half-turn as she fell so that the back of her head struck the wooden floor with a loud thump and the bathrobe drifted open from the waist down.

The Hemingway stared down at her frontal aspect. "Sometimes I wish I were human," it said. "Your pleasures are intense. Simple, but intense." It moved toward her with the cane.

John stood up. "If you kill her—"

"Oh?" It cocked an eyebrow at him. "What will you do?"

John took one step toward it and it waved the cane. A waist-high brick wall surmounted by needle-sharp spikes appeared between them. It gestured again and an impossible moat appeared, deep enough to reach down well into Julio's living room. It filled with water and a large crocodile surfaced and rested its chin on the parquet floor, staring at John. It yawned teeth.

The Hemingway held up its cane. "The white end. It doesn't kill, remember?" The wall and moat disappeared and the cane touched Pansy lightly below the navel. She twitched minutely but continued to sleep. "She'll have a headache," it said. "And she'll be somewhat confused by the uncommunicatable memory of having seen me. But that will all fade, compared to the sudden tragedy of having her new lover die here, just sitting waiting for his breakfast."

"Do you enjoy this?"

"I love my work. It's all I have." It walked toward him, footfalls splashing as it crossed where the moat had been. "You have not personally helped, though. Not at all."

It sat down across from him and poured coffee into a mug that said ON THE SIXTH DAY GOD CREATED MAN—SHE MUST HAVE HAD PMS.

"When you kill me this time, do you think it will 'take'?"

"I don't know. It's never failed before." The toaster made a noise. "Toast?"

"Sure." Two pieces appeared on his plate; two on the Hemingway's. "Usually when you kill people they stay dead?"

"I don't kill that many people." It spread margarine on its toast; gestured, and marmalade appeared. "But when I do, yeah. They die all up and down the Omniverse, every timespace. All except you." He pointed toast at John's toast. "Go ahead. It's not poison."

"Not my idea of a last meal."

The Hemingway shrugged. "What would you like?"

"Forget it." He buttered the toast and piled marmalade on it, determined out of some odd impulse to act as if nothing unusual were happening. Breakfast with Hemingway, big deal.

He studied the apparition and noticed that it was somewhat translucent, almost like a traditional TV ghost. He could barely see a line that was the back of the chair, bisecting its chest below shoulderblade level. Was this something new? There hadn't been too much light in the train; maybe he had just failed to notice it before.

"A penny for your thoughts."

He didn't say anything about seeing through it. "Has it occurred to you that maybe you're not *supposed* to kill me? That's why I came back?"

The Hemingway chuckled and admired its nails. "That's a nearly content-free assertion."

"Oh really." He bit into the toast. The marmalade was strong, pleasantly bitter.

"It presupposes a higher authority, unknown to me, that's watching over my behavior, and correcting me when I do wrong. Doesn't exist, sorry."

"That's the oldest one in the theologian's book." He set down the toast and kneaded his stomach; shouldn't eat something so strong first thing in the morning. "You can only *assert* the nonexistence of something; you can't prove it."

"What you mean is *you* can't." He held up the cane and looked at it. "The simplest explanation is that there's something wrong with the cane. There's no way I can test it; if I kill the wrong person there's hell to pay up and down the Omniverse. But what I can do is kill you without the cane. See whether you come back again, some timespace."

Sharp, stabbing pains in his stomach now. "Bastard." Heart pounding slow and hard: shirt rustled in time to its spasms.

"Cyanide in the marmalade. Gives it a certain *frisson*, don't you think?"

He couldn't breathe. His heart pounded once, and stopped. Vicious pain in his left arm, then paralysis. From an inch away, he could just see the weave of the white tablecloth. It turned red and then black.

18. The Sun Also Rises

From blackness to brilliance: the morning sun pouring through the window at a flat angle. He screwed up his face and blinked.

Suddenly smothered in terrycloth, between soft breasts. "John, John."

He put his elbow down to support himself, uncomfortable on the parquet floor, and looked up at Pansy. Her face was wet with tears. He cleared his throat. "What happened?"

"You, you started putting on your foot and . . . you just fell over. I thought. . . ."

John looked down over his body, hard ropy muscle and deep tan under white body hair, the puckered bullet wound a little higher on the abdomen. Left leg ended in a stump just above the ankle.

Trying not to faint. His third past flooding back. Walking down a dirt road near Kontum, the sudden loud bang of the mine and he pitched forward, unbelievable pain, rolled over and saw his bloody boot yards away; grey, jagged shinbone sticking through the bloody smoking rag of his pants leg, bright crimson splashing on the dry dust, loud in the shocked silence; another bloodstain spreading between his legs, the deep mortal pain there—and he started to buck and scream and two men held him while the medic took off his belt and made a tourniquet and popped morphine through the cloth and unbuttoned his fly and slowly worked his pants down: penis torn by shrapnel, scrotum ripped open in a bright red flap of skin, bloody grey-blue egg of a testicle separating, rolling out. He fainted, then and now.

And woke up with her lips against his, her breath sweet in his lungs, his nostrils pinched painfully tight. He made a strangled noise and clutched her breast.

She cradled his head, panting, smiling through tears, and kissed him lightly on the forehead. "Will you stop fainting now?"

"Yeah. Don't worry." Her lips were trembling. He put a finger on them. "Just a longer night than I'm accustomed to. An overdose of happiness."

The happiest night of his life, maybe of three lives. Like coming back from the dead.

"Should I call a doctor?"

"No. I faint every now and then." Usually at the gym, from pushing too hard. He slipped his hand inside the terrycloth and covered her breast. "It's been ... do you know how long it's been since I ... did it? I mean ... three times in one night?"

"About six hours." She smiled. "And you can say 'fuck.' I'm no schoolgirl."

"I'll say." The night have been an escalating progression of intimacies, gymnastics, accessories. "Had to wonder where a sweet girl like you learned all that."

She looked away, lips pursed, thoughtful. With a light fingertip she stroked the length of his penis and smiled when it started to uncurl. "At work."

"What?"

"I was a prostitute. That's where I learned the tricks. Practice makes perfect."

"Prostitute. Wow."

"Are you shocked? Outraged?"

"Just surprised." That was true. He respected the sorority and was grateful to it for having made Vietnam almost tolerable, an hour or so at a time. "But now you've got to do something really mean. I could never love a prostitute with a heart of gold."

"I'll give it some thought." She shifted. "Think you can stand up?"

"Sure." She stood and gave him her hand. He touched it but didn't pull; rose in a smooth practiced motion, then took one hop and sat down at the small table. He started strapping on his foot.

"I've read about those new ones," she said, "the permanent kind."

"Yeah; I've read about them, too. Computer interface, graft your nerves onto sensors." He shuddered. "No, thanks. No more surgery."

"Not worth it for the convenience?"

"Being able to wiggle my toes, have my foot itch? Besides, the VA won't pay for it." That startled John as he said it: here, he hadn't grown up rich. His father had spent all the mill money on a photocopy firm six months before Xerox came on the market. "You say you 'were' a prostitute. Not any more?"

"No, that was the truth about teaching. Let's start this egg thing over." She picked up the bowl she had dropped in the other universe. "I gave up whoring about seven years ago." She picked up an egg, looked at it, set it down. She half-turned and stared out the kitchen window. "I can't do this to you."

"You . . . can't do what?"

"Oh, lie. Keep lying." She went to the refrigerator. "Want a beer?"

"Lying? No, no thanks. What lying?"

She opened a beer, still not looking at him. "I like you, John. I really like you. But I didn't just . . . spontaneously fall into your arms." She took a healthy swig and started pouring some of the bottle into a glass.

"I don't understand."

She walked back, concentrating on pouring the beer, then sat down gracelessly. She took a deep breath and let it out, staring at his chest. "Castle put me up to it."

"Castle?"

She nodded. "Sylvester Castlemaine, boy wonder."

John sat back stunned. "But you said you don't do that anymore," he said without too much logic. "Do it for money."

"Not for money," she said in a flat, hurt voice.

"I should've known. A woman like you wouldn't want. . . ." He made a gesture that dismissed his body from the waist down.

"You do all right. Don't feel sorry for yourself." Her face showed a pinch of regret for that, but she plowed on. "If it were just the obligation, once would have been enough. I wouldn't have had to fuck and suck all night long to win you over."

"No," he said, "that's true. Just the first moment, when you undressed. That was enough."

"I owe Castle a big favor. A friend of mine was going to be prosecuted for involving a minor in prostitution. It was a set-up, pure and simple."

"She worked for the same outfit you did?"

"Yeah, but this was free-lance. I think it was the escort service that set her up, sort of delivered her and the man in return for this or that."

She sipped at the beer. "Guy wanted a three-way. My friend had met this girl a couple of days before at the bar where she worked part-time ... she looked old enough; said she was in the biz."

"She was neither?"

"God knows. Maybe she got caught as a juvie and made a deal. Anyhow, he'd just slipped it to her and suddenly cops comin' in the windows. Threw the book at him. 'Two inches, twenty years,' my friend said. He was a county commissioner somewhere, with enemies. Almost dragged my friend down with him. I'm *sorry*." Her voice was angry.

"Don't be," John said, almost a whisper. "It's understandable. Whatever happens, I've got last night."

She nodded. "So two of the cops who were going to testify got busted for possession, cocaine. The word came down and everybody remembered the woman was somebody else."

"So what did Castle want you to do? With me?"

"Oh, whatever comes natural—or *un*-natural, if that's what you wanted. And later be doing it at a certain time and place, where we'd be caught in the act."

"By Castle?"

"And his trusty little VCR. Then I guess he'd threaten to show it to your wife, or the university."

"I wonder. Lena ... she knows I've had other women."

"But not lately."

"No. Not for years."

"It might be different now. She might be starting to feel, well, insecure."

"Any woman who looked at you would feel insecure."

She shrugged. "That could be part of it. Could it cost you your job, too?"

"I don't see how. It would be awkward, but it's not as if you were one of my students—and even that happens,

without costing the guy his job." He laughed. "Poor old
Larry. He had a student kiss and tell, and had to run
the Speakers' Committee for four or five years. Got allergic to wine and cheese. But he made tenure."

"So what is it?" She leaned forward. "Are you an
addict or something?"

"Addict?"

"I mean how come you even *know* Castle? He didn't
pick your name out of a phone book and have me come
seduce you, just to see what would happen."

"No, of course not."

"So? I confess, you confess."

John passed a hand over his face and pressed the other
hand against his knee, bearing down to keep the foot
from tapping. "You don't want to be involved."

"What do you call last night, Spin the Bottle? I'm
involved!"

"Not the way I mean. It's illegal."

"Oh golly. Not really."

"Let me think." John picked up their dishes and
limped back to the sink. He set them down there and
fiddled with the straps and pad that connected the foot
to his stump, then poured himself a cup of coffee and
came back, not limping.

He sat down slowly and blew across the coffee. "What
it is, is that *Castle* thinks there's a scam going on. He's
wrong. I've taken steps to ensure that it couldn't work."
His foot tapped twice.

"You think. You hope."

"No. I'm sure. Anyhow, I'm stringing Castle along
because I need his expertise in a certain matter."

" 'A certain matter,' yeah. Sounds wholesome."

"Actually, that part's not illegal."

"So tell me about it."

"Nope. Still might backfire."

She snorted. "You know what might *back*fire. Fucking
with Castle."

"I can take care of him."

"You don't know. He may be more dangerous than you think he is."

"He talks a lot."

"You men." She took a drink and poured the rest of the bottle into the glass. "Look, I was at a party with him, couple of years ago. He was drunk, got into a little coke, started babbling."

"In vino veritas?"

"Yeah, and Coke is It. But he said he'd killed three people, strangers, just to see what it felt like. He liked it. I more than halfway believe him."

John looked at her silently for a moment, sorting out his new memories of Castle. "Well . . . he's got a mean streak. I don't know about murder. Certainly not over this thing."

"Which is?"

"You'll have to trust me. It's not because of Castle that I can't tell you." He remembered her one universe ago, lying helpless while the Hemingway lowered its cane onto her nakedness. "Trust me?"

She studied the top of the glass, running her finger around it. "Suppose I do. Then what?"

"Business as usual. You didn't tell me anything. Deliver me to Castle and his video camera; I'll try to put on a good show."

"And when he confronts you with it?"

"Depends on what he wants. He knows I don't have much money." John shrugged. "If it's unreasonable, he can go ahead and show the tape to Lena. She can live with it."

"And your department head?"

"He'd give me a medal."

19. in our time

So it wasn't the cane. He ate enough cyanide to kill a horse, but evidently only in one universe.

You checked the next day in all the others?

All 119. He's still dead in the one where I killed him on the train—

That's encouraging.

—but there's no causal resonance in the others.

Oh, but there is some resonance. He remembered you in the universe where you poisoned him. Maybe in all of them.

That's impossible.

Once is impossible. Twice is a trend. A hundred and twenty means something is going on that we don't understand.

What I suggest—

No. You can't go back and kill them all one by one.

If the wand had worked the first time, they'd all be dead anyhow. There's no reason to think we'd cause more of an eddy by doing them one at a time.

It's not something to experiment with. As you well know.

I don't know how we're going to solve it otherwise.

Simple. Don't kill him. Talk to him again. He may be getting frightened, if he remembers both times he died.

Here's an idea. What if someone else killed him?

I don't know. If you just hired someone—made him a direct agent of your will—it wouldn't be any different from the cyanide. Maybe as a last resort. Talk to him again first.

All right. I'll try.

20. Of Wounds and Other Causes

Although John found it difficult to concentrate, trying not to think about Pansy, this was the best time he would have for the foreseeable future to summon the Hemingway demon and try to do something about exorcising it. He didn't want either of the women around if the damned thing went on a killing spree again. They might just do as he did, and slip over into another reality—as unpleasant as that was, it was at least living—but the Hemingway had said otherwise. There was no reason to suspect it was not the truth.

Probably the best way to get the thing's attention was to resume work on the Hemingway pastiche. He decided to rewrite the first page to warm up, typing it out in Hemingway's style:

ALONG WITH YOUTH

1. Mitraigliatrice

The dirt on the side of the trench was
never dry in the morning . If Fever could find a
dry newspaper he could put it between his chest
and the dirt when he went out to lean on the
side of the trench and wait for the light . First
light was the best time . You might have luck
and see a muzzle flash to aim at . But patience was
better than luck . Wait to see a helmet or a
head without a helmet .

Fever looked at the enemy trench line
through a rectangular box of wood that pushed
through the trench wall at about ground level.
The other end of the box was covered with a
square of gauze the color of dirt . A man looking
directly at it might see the muzzle flash when
Fever fired through the box . But with luck , the
flash would be the last thing he saw .

Fever had fired through the gauze six times . He'd potted at least three Austrians . Now the gauze had a ragged hole in the center . One bullet had come in the other way , an accident , and chiseled a deep gouge in the floor of the wooden box . Fever knew that he would be able to see the splinters sticking up before he could see any detail at the enemy trench line.

That would be maybe twenty minutes . Fever wanted a cigarette . There was plenty of time to go down in the bunker and light one . But it would fox his night vision . Better to wait .

Fever heard movement before he heard the voice . He picked up one of the grenades on the plank shelf to his left and his thumb felt the ring on the cotter pin . Someone was crawling in front of his position . Slow crawling but not too quiet . He slid his left forefinger through the ring and waited .

-----Help me, came a strained whisper .

Fever felt his shoulders tense . Of course many Austrians could speak Italian .

-----I am wounded . Help me . I can go no farther .

-----What is your name and unit , Fever whispered through the box .

-----Jean-Franco Dante . Four forty-seventh.

That was the unit that had taken such a beating at the evening show . -----At first light they will kill me .

-----All right . But I'm coming over with a grenade in my hand . If you kill me , you die as well .

-----I will commend this logic to your superior officer . Please hurry .

Fever slid his rifle into the wooden box and eased himself to the top of the trench . He took the grenade out of his pocket and carefully worked the pin out , the arming lever held secure . He kept the pin around his finger so he could replace it .

He inched his way down the slope , guided by the man's whispers . After a few minutes his probing hand found the man's shoulder . -----Thank God . Make haste , now .

The soldier's feet were both shattered by a mine . He would have to be carried .

-----Don't cry out, Fever said . This will hurt .

-----No sound , the soldier said . And
when Fever raised him up onto his back there
was only a breath . But his canteen was loose .
It fell on a rock and made a loud hollow
sound .

Firecracker pop above them and the night
was all glare and bobbing shadow . A big
machine-gun opened up rong, cararong, rong ,
rong . Fever headed for the parapet above as
fast as he could but knew it was hopeless . He saw
dirt spray twice to his right and then felt the
thud of the bullet into the Italian , who said
" Jesus " as if only annoyed , and they almost
made it then but on the lip of the trench a hard
snowball hit Fever behind the kneecap and
they both went down in a tumble . They fell two
yards to safety but the Italian was already
dead .

Fever had sprained his wrist and hurt his
nose falling and they hurt worse than the bullet . But he couldn't move his toes and he knew
that must be bad . Then it started to hurt .

A rifleman closed the Italian's eyes and
with the help of another clumsy one dragged
Fever down the trench to the medical bunker . It

hurt awfully and his shoe filled up with blood
and he puked . They stopped to watch him puke and
then dragged him the rest of the way .

The surgeon placed him between two kero-
sene lanterns . He removed the puttee and shoe
and cut the bloody pants leg with a straight
razor . He rolled Fever onto his stomach and
had four men hold him down while he probed for the
bullet . The pain was great but Fever was in-
sulted enough by the four men not to cry out . He
heard the bullet clink into a metal dish . It
sounded like the canteen .

"That's a little too pat, don't you think?" John turned
around and there was the Hemingway, reading over his
shoulder. " 'It sounded like the canteen,' indeed." Khaki
army uniform covered with mud and splattered with
bright blood. Blood dripped and pooled at its feet.

"So shoot me. Or whatever it's going to be this time.
Maybe I'll rewrite the line in the next universe."

"You're going to run out soon. You only exist in eight
more universes."

"Sure. And you've never lied to me." John turned back
around and stared at the typewriter, tensed.

The Hemingway sighed. "Suppose we talk, instead."

"I'm listening."

The Hemingway walked past him toward the kitchen.
"Want a beer?"

"Not while I'm working."

"Suit yourself." It limped into the kitchen, out of sight,
and John heard it open the refrigerator and pry the top off
of a beer. It came back out as the five-year-old Hemingway,

dressed up in girl's clothing, both hands clutching an incongruous beer bottle. It set the bottle on the end table and crawled up onto the couch with childish clumsiness.

"Where's the cane?"

"I knew it wouldn't be necessary this time," it piped. "It occurs to me that there are better ways to deal with a man like you."

"Do tell." John smiled. "What is 'a man like me'? One on whom your cane for some reason doesn't work?"

"Actually, what I was thinking of was curiosity. That is supposedly what motivates scholars. You *are* a real scholar, not just a rich man seeking legitimacy?"

John looked away from the ancient eyes in the boy's face. "I've sometimes wondered myself. Why don't you cut to the chase, as we used to say. A few universes ago."

"I've done spot-checks on your life through various universes," the child said. "You're always a Hemingway buff, though you don't always do it for a living."

"What else do I do?"

"It's probably not healthy for you to know. But all of you are drawn to the missing manuscripts at about this time, the seventy-fifth anniversary."

"I wonder why that would be."

The Hemingway waved the beer bottle in a disarmingly mature gesture. "The Omniverse is full of threads of coincidence like that. They have causal meaning in a dimension you can't deal with."

"Try me."

"In a way, that's what I want to propose. You will drop this dangerous project at once, and never resume it. In return, I will take you back in time, back to the Gare de Lyon on December 14, 1921."

"Where I will see what happens to the manuscripts."

Another shrug. "I will put you on Hadley's train, well before she said the manuscripts were stolen. You will be able to observe for an hour or so, without being seen. As you know, some people have theorized that there never was a thief; never was an overnight bag; that Hadley simply threw the writings away. If that's the case, you won't see anything dramatic. But the absence of the overnight bag would be powerful indirect proof."

John looked skeptical. "You've never gone to check it out for yourself?"

"If I had, I wouldn't be able to take you back. I can't exist twice in the same timespace, of course."

"How foolish of me. Of course."

"Is it a deal?"

John studied the apparition. The couch's plaid upholstery showed through its arms and legs. It did appear to become less substantial each time. "I don't know. Let me think about it a couple of days."

The child pulled on the beer bottle and it stretched into a long amber stick. It turned into the black-and-white cane. "We haven't tried cancer yet. That might be the one that works." It slipped off the couch and sidled toward John. "It does take longer and it hurts. It hurts 'awfully.'"

John got out of the chair. "You come near me with that and I'll dropkick you into next Tuesday."

The child shimmered and became Hemingway in his mid-forties, a big-gutted barroom brawler. "Sure you will, Champ." It held out the cane so that the tip was inches from John's chest. "See you around." It disappeared with a barely audible pop, and a slight breeze as air moved to fill its space.

John thought about that as he went to make a fresh cup of coffee. He wished he knew more about science. The thing obviously takes up space, since its disappearance caused a vacuum, but there was no denying that it was fading away.

Well, not fading. Just becoming more transparent. That might not affect its abilities. A glass door is as much of a door as an opaque one, if you try to walk through it.

He sat down on the couch, away from the manuscript so he could think without distraction. On the face of it, this offer by the Hemingway was an admission of defeat. An admission, at least, that it couldn't solve its problem by killing him over and over. That was comforting. He would just as soon not die again, except for the one time.

But maybe he should. That was a chilling thought. If he made the Hemingway kill him another dozen times, another hundred . . . what kind of strange creature would he become? A hundred overlapping autobiographies, all perfectly remembered? Surely the brain has a finite capacity for storing information. Or maybe it wasn't finite, at least in his case—but that was logically absurd. There are only so many cells in a brain. Of course he might be "wired" in some way to the John Bairds in all the other universes he had inhabited.

And what would happen if he died in some natural way, not dispatched by an inter-dimensional assassin? Would he still slide into another identity? That was a lovely prospect: sooner or later he would be 130 years old, on his deathbed, dying every fraction of a second for the rest of eternity.

Or maybe the Hemingway wasn't lying, this time, and he had only eight lives left. In context, the possibility was reassuring.

The phone rang; for a change, John was grateful for the interruption. It was Lena, saying her father had come home from the hospital, much better, and she thought she could come on home day after tomorrow. Fine, John said, feeling a little wicked; I'll borrow a car and pick you up at the airport. Don't bother, Lena said; besides, she didn't have a flight number yet.

John didn't press it. If, as he assumed, Lena was in on the plot with Castle, she was probably here in Key West, or somewhere nearby. If she had to buy a ticket to and from Omaha to keep up her end of the ruse, the money would come out of John's pocket.

He hung up and, on impulse, dialed her parents' number. Her father answered. Putting on his professorial tone, he said he was Maxwell Perkins, Blue Cross claims adjuster, and he needed to know the exact date when Mr. Monaghan entered the hospital for this recent confinement. He said you must have the wrong guy; I haven't been inside a hospital in twenty years, knock on wood. Am I not speaking to John Franklin Monaghan? No, this is John *Frederick* Monaghan. Terribly sorry, natural mistake. That's okay; hope the other guy's okay, goodbye, good night, sir.

So tomorrow was going to be the big day with Pansy. To his knowledge, John hadn't been watched during sex for more than twenty years, and never by a disinterested, or at least dispassionate, observer. He hoped that knowing they were being spied upon wouldn't affect his performance. Or knowing that it would be the last time.

A profound helpless sadness settled over him. He knew that the last thing you should do, in a mood like this, was go out and get drunk. It was barely noon, anyhow. He took enough money out of his wallet for five martinis, hid the wallet under a couch cushion, and headed for Duval Street.

21. Dying, Well or Badly

John had just about decided it was too early in the day to get drunk. He had polished off two martinis in Sloppy Joe's and then wandered uptown because the tourists were getting to him and a band was setting up, depressingly young and cheerful. He found a grubby bar he'd never noticed before, dark and smoky and hot. In the other universes it was a yuppie boutique. Three Social Security drunks were arguing politics almost loudly enough to drown out the game show on the television. It seemed to go well with the headache and sour stomach he'd reaped from the martinis and the walk in the sun. He got a beer and some peanuts and a couple of aspirin from the bartender, and sat in the farthest booth with a copy of the local classified-ad newspaper. Somebody had obscurely carved FUCK ANARCHY into the tabletop.

Nobody else in this world knows what anarchy *is*, John thought, and the helpless anomie came back, intensified somewhat by drunken sentimentality. What he would

give to go back to the first universe and undo this all by
just not. . . .

Would that be possible? The Hemingway was willing to
take him back to 1921; why not back a few weeks? Where the
hell was that son of a bitch when you needed him, it,
whatever.

The Hemingway appeared in the booth opposite him,
an Oak Park teenager smoking a cigarette. "I felt a kind
of vibration from you. Ready to make your decision?"

"Can the people at the bar see you?"

"No. And don't worry about appearing to be talking
to yourself. A lot of that goes on around here."

"Look. Why can't you just take me back to a couple
of weeks before we met on the train, back in the first
universe? I'll just. . . ." The Hemingway was shaking its
head slowly. "You can't."

"No. As I explained, you already exist there—"

"You said that *you* couldn't be in the same place twice.
How do you know I can't?"

"How do you know you can't swallow that piano? You
just can't."

"You thought I couldn't talk about you, either; you thought
your stick would kill me. I'm not like normal people."

"Except in that alcohol does nothing for your
judgment."

John ate a peanut thoughtfully. "Try this on for size.
At 11:46 on June 3, a man named Sylvester Castlemaine
sat down in Dos Hermosas and started talking with me
about the lost manuscripts. The forgery would never have
occurred to me if I hadn't talked to him. Why don't you
go back and keep him from going into that cafe? Or just
go back to 11:30 and kill him."

The Hemingway smiled maliciously. "You don't like
him much."

"It's more fear than like or dislike." He rubbed his
face hard, remembering. "Funny how things shift around.
He was kind of likeable the first time I met him. Then
you killed me on the train and in the subsequent universe, he became colder, more serious. Then you killed

me in Pansy's apartment and in this universe, he has turned mean. Dangerously mean, like a couple of men I knew in Viet Nam. The ones who really love the killing. Like you, evidently."

It blew a chain of smoke rings before answering. "I don't 'love' killing, or anything else. I have a complex function and I fulfill it, because that is what I do. That sounds circular because of the limitations of human language.

"I can't go killing people right and left just to see what happens. When a person dies at the wrong time it takes forever to clean things up. Not that it wouldn't be worth it in your case. But I can tell you with certainty that killing Castlemaine would not affect the final outcome."

"How can you say that? He's responsible for the whole thing." John finished off most of his beer and the Hemingway touched the mug and it refilled. "Not poison?"

"Wouldn't work," it said morosely. "I'd gladly kill Castlemaine any way you want—cancer of the penis is a possibility—if there was even a fighting chance that it would clear things up. The reason I know it wouldn't is that I am not in the least attracted to that meeting. There's no probability nexus associated with it, the way there was with your buying the Corona or starting the story on the train, or writing it down here. You may think that you would never have come up with the idea for the forgery on your own, but you're wrong."

"That's preposterous."

"Nope. There are universes in this bundle where Castle isn't involved. You may find that hard to believe, but your beliefs aren't important."

John nodded noncommittally and got his faraway remembering look. "You know . . . reviewing in my mind all the conversations we've had, all five of them, the only substantive reason you've given me not to write this pastiche, and I quote, is that 'I or someone like me will have to kill you.' Since that doesn't seem to be possible, why don't we try some other line of attack?"

It put out the cigarette by squeezing it between thumb

and forefinger. There was a smell of burning flesh. "All right, try this: give it up or I'll kill Pansy. Then Lena."

"I've thought of that, and I'm gambling that you won't, or can't. You had a perfect opportunity a few days ago—maximum dramatic effect—and you didn't do it. Now you say it's an awfully complicated matter."

"You're willing to gamble with the lives of the people you love?"

"I'm gambling with a lot. Including them." He leaned forward. "Take me into the future instead of the past. Show me what will happen if I succeed with the Hemingway hoax. If I agree that it's terrible, I'll give it all up and become a plumber."

The old, wise Hemingway shook a shaggy head at him. "You're asking me to please fix it so you can swallow a piano. I can't. Even I can't go straight to the future and look around; I'm pretty much tied to your present and past until this matter is cleared up."

"One of the first things you said to me was that you were from the future. And the past. And 'other temporalities,' whatever the hell that means. You were lying then?"

"Not really." It sighed. "Let me force the analogy. Look at the piano."

John twisted half around. "Okay."

"You can't eat it—but after a fashion, I can." The piano suddenly transformed itself into a piano-shaped mountain of cold capsules, which immediately collapsed and rolled all over the floor. "Each capsule contains a pinch of sawdust or powdered ivory or metal, the whole piano in about a hundred thousand capsules. If I take one with each meal, I will indeed eat the piano, over the course of the next three hundred-some years. That's not a long time for me."

"That doesn't prove anything."

"It's not a *proof*; it's a demonstration." It reached down and picked up a capsule that was rolling by, and popped it into its mouth. "One down, 99,999 to go. So how many ways could I eat this piano?"

"Ways?"

"I mean I could have swallowed any of the hundred thousand first. Next I can choose any of the remaining 99,999. How many ways can—"

"That's easy. One hundred thousand factorial. A huge number."

"Go to the head of the class. It's ten to the godzillionth power. That represents the number of possible paths—the number of futures—leading to this one guaranteed, pre-ordained event: my eating the piano. They are all different, but in terms of whether the piano gets eaten, their differences are trivial.

"On a larger scale, every possible trivial action that you or anybody else in this universe takes puts us into a slightly different future than would have otherwise existed. An overwhelming majority of actions, even seemingly significant ones, make no difference in the long run. All of the futures bend back to one central, unifying event—except for the ones that you're screwing up!"

"So what is this big event?"

"It's impossible for you to know. It's not important, anyhow." Actually, it would take a rather cosmic viewpoint to consider the event unimportant: the end of the world.

Or at least the end of life on Earth. Right now there were two earnest young politicians, in the United States and Russia, who on 11 August 2006 would be President and Premier of their countries. On that day, one would insult the other beyond forgiveness, and a button would be pushed, and then another button, and by the time the sun set on Moscow, or rose on Washington, there would be nothing left alive on the planet at all—from the bottom of the ocean to the top of the atmosphere; not a cockroach, not a paramecium, not a virus, and all because there are some things a man just doesn't have to take, not if he's a real man.

Hemingway wasn't the only writer who felt that way, but he was the one with the most influence on this generation. The apparition who wanted John dead or at least not typing didn't know exactly what effect his pastiche was going to have on Hemingway's influence, but it was going to be decisive and ultimately negative. It would prevent or at least delay the end of the world in a whole bundle of universes, which would put a zillion adjacent realities out of kilter, and there would be hell to pay all up and down the Omniverse. Many more people than six billion would die—and it's even possible that all of Reality would unravel, and collapse back to the Primordial Hiccup from whence it came.

"If it's not important, then why are you so hell-bent on keeping me from preventing it? I don't believe you."

"*Don't* believe me, then!" At an imperious gesture, all the capsules rolled back into the corner and reassembled into a piano, with a huge crashing chord. None of the barflies heard it. "I should think you'd cooperate with me just to prevent the unpleasantness of dying over and over."

John had the expression of a poker player whose opponent has inadvertently exposed his hole card. "You get used to it," he said. "And it occurs to me that sooner or later I'll wind up in a universe that I really like. This one doesn't have a hell of a lot to recommend it." His foot tapped twice and then twice again.

"No," the Hemingway said. "It will get worse each time."

"You can't know that. This has never happened before."

"True so far, isn't it?"

John considered it for a moment. "Some ways. Some ways not."

The Hemingway shrugged and stood up. "Well. Think about my offer." The cane appeared. "Happy cancer." It tapped him on the chest and disappeared.

The first sensation was utter tiredness, immobility. When he strained to move, pain slithered through his muscles and viscera, and stayed. He could hardly breathe, partly because his lungs weren't working and partly because there was something in the way. In the mirror beside the booth he looked down his throat and saw a large white mass, veined, pulsing. He sank back into the cushion and waited. He remembered the young wounded Hemingway writing his parents from the hospital with ghastly cheerfulness: "If I should have died it would have been very easy for me. Quite the easiest thing I ever did." I don't know, Ernie; maybe it gets harder with practice. He felt something tear open inside and hot stinging fluid trickled through his abdominal cavity. He wiped his face and a patch of necrotic skin came off with a terrible smell. His clothes tightened as his body swelled.

"Hey buddy, you okay?" The bartender came around in front of him and jumped. "Christ, Harry, punch nine-one-one!"

John gave a slight ineffectual wave. "No rush," he croaked.

The bartender cast his eyes to the ceiling. "Always on my shift?"

22. Death in the Afternoon

John woke up behind a dumpster in an alley. It was high noon and the smell of fermenting garbage was revolting. He didn't feel too well in any case; as if he'd drunk far too much and passed out behind a dumpster, which was exactly what had happened in this universe.

In this universe. He stood slowly to a quiet chorus of creaks and pops, brushed himself off, and staggered away from the malefic odor. Staggered, but not limping—he had both feet again, in this present. There was a hand-sized numb spot at the top of his left leg where a .51 caliber machine gun bullet had missed his balls by an inch and ended his career as a soldier.

And started it as a writer. He got to the sidewalk and stopped dead. This was the first universe where he wasn't a college professor. He taught occasionally—sometimes creative writing; sometimes Hemingway—but it was only a hobby now, and a nod toward respectability.

He rubbed his fringe of salt-and-pepper beard. It cov-

ered the bullet scar there on his chin. He ran his tongue
along the metal teeth the army had installed thirty years
ago. Jesus. Maybe it does get worse every time. Which
was worse, losing a foot or getting your dick sprayed with
shrapnel, numb from severed nerves, plus bullets in the
leg and face and arm? If you knew there was a Pansy in
your future, you would probably trade a foot for a whole
dick. Though she had done wonders with what was left.

Remembering furiously, not watching where he was
going, he let his feet guide him back to the oldsters' bar
where the Hemingway had showed him how to swallow
a piano. He pushed through the door and the shock of
air conditioning brought him back to the present.

Ferns. Perfume. Lacy underthings. An epicene sales
clerk sashayed toward him, managing to look worried
and determined at the same time. His nose was pierced,
decorated with a single diamond button. "Si-i-r," he said
in a surprisingly deep voice, "may I *help* you?"

Crotchless panties. Marital aids. The bar had become
a store called The French Connection. "Guess I took a
wrong turn. Sorry." He started to back out.

The clerk smiled. "Don't be shy. Everybody needs
*some*thing here."

The heat was almost pleasant in its heavy familiarity.
John stopped at a convenience store for a sixpack of
greenies and walked back home.

An interesting universe; much more of a divergence
than the other had been. Reagan had survived the Hinck-
ley assassination and actually went on to a second term.
Bush was elected rather than succeeding to the presi-
dency, and the country had not gone to war in Nicaragua.
The Iran/Contra scandal nipped it in the bud.

The United States was actually cooperating with the
Soviet Union in a flight to Mars. There were no DeSotos.
Could there be a connection?

And in this universe he had actually met Ernest
Hemingway.

Havana, 1952. John was eight years old. His father, a
doctor in this universe, had taken a break from the New

England winter to treat his family to a week in the tropics. John got a nice sunburn the first day, playing on the beach while his parents tried the casinos. The next day they made him stay indoors, which meant tagging along with his parents, looking at things that didn't fascinate eight-year-olds.

For lunch they went to La Florida, on the off chance that they might meet the famous Ernest Hemingway, who supposedly held court there when he was in Havana.

To John it was a huge dark cavern of a place, full of adult smells. Cigar smoke, rum, beer, stale urine. But Hemingway was indeed there, at the end of the long dark wood bar, laughing heartily with a table full of Cubans.

John was vaguely aware that his mother resembled some movie actress, but he couldn't have guessed that that would change his life. Hemingway glimpsed her and then stood up and was suddenly silent, mouth open. Then he laughed and waved a huge arm. "Come on over here, daughter."

The three of them rather timidly approached the table, John acutely aware of the careful inspection his mother was receiving from the silent Cubans. "Take a look, Mary," he said to the small blond woman knitting at the table, "The Kraut."

The woman nodded, smiling, and agreed that John's mother looked just like Marlene Dietrich ten years before. Hemingway invited them to sit down and have a drink, and they accepted with an air of genuine astonishment. He gravely shook John's hand, and spoke to him as he would to an adult. Then he shouted to the bartender in fast Spanish, and in a couple of minutes his parents had huge daiquiris and he had a Coke with a wedge of lime in it, tropical and grown-up. The waiter also brought a tray of boiled shrimp. Hemingway even ate the head and tails, crunching loudly, which impressed John more than any Nobel Prize. Hemingway might have agreed, since he hadn't received one, and Faulkner had.

For more than an hour, two Cokes, John watched as his parents sat hypnotized in the aura of Hemingway's

famous charm. He put them at ease with jokes and stories and questions—for the rest of his life John's father
would relate how impressed he was with the sophistica-
tion of Hemingway's queries about cardiac medicine—
but it was obvious even to a child that they were in awe,
electrified by the man's presence.

Later that night John's father asked him what he
thought of Mr. Hemingway. Forty-four years later, John
of course remembered his exact reply: "He has fun all
the time. I never saw a grown-up who plays like that."

Interesting. That meeting was where his eidetic memory started. He could remember a couple of days before
it pretty well, because they had still been close to the
surface. In other universes, he could remember back well
before grade school. It gave him a strange feeling. All of
the universes were different, but this was the first one
where the differentness was so tightly connected to
Hemingway.

He was flabby in this universe, fat over old tired muscle, like Hemingway at his age, perhaps, and he felt a
curious anxiety that he realized was a real *need* to have
a drink. Not just desire, not thirst. If he didn't have a
drink, something very very bad would happen. He knew
that was irrational. Knowing didn't help.

John carefully mounted the stairs up to their apartment, stepping over the fifth one, also rotted in this universe. He put the beer in the refrigerator and took from
the freezer a bottle of icy vodka—that was different—and
poured himself a double shot and knocked it back, medicine drinking.

That spiked the hangover pretty well. He pried the
top off a beer and carried it into the living room,
thoughtful as the alcoholic glow radiated through his
body. He sat down at the typewriter and picked up the
air pistol, a fancy Belgian target model. He cocked it and
with a practiced two-handed grip aimed at a paper target
across the room. The pellet struck less than half an
inch low.

All around the room the walls were pocked from

where he'd fired at roaches, and once a scorpion. Very Hemingwayish, he thought; in fact, most of the ways he was different from the earlier incarnations of himself were in Hemingway's direction.

He spun a piece of paper into the typewriter and made a list:

```
              EH & me --

-- both had doctor fathers


-- both forced into music lessons


-- in high school wrote derivative stuff that

didn't show promise


-- Our war wounds were evidently similar in se-

verity and location. Maybe my groin one was

worse; army doctor there said that in Korea (and

presumably WWI), without helicopter dustoff,

I would have been dead on the battlefield. (Hav-

ing been wounded in the kneecap and foot my-

self, I know that H's story about carrying the

wounded guy on his back is unlikely. It was a

month before I could put any stress on the knee.)

He mentioned genital wounds, possibly simi-

lar to mine, in a letter to Bernard Baruch, but

there's nothing in the Red Cross report about

them.
```

But in both cases, being wounded and surviving was the central experience of our youth. Touching death.

-- We each wrote the first draft of our first novel in six weeks (but his was better and more ambitious).

-- Both had unusual critical success from the beginning.

-- Both shy as youngsters and gregarious as adults.

-- Always loved fishing and hiking and guns; I loved the bullfight from my first corrida, but may have been influenced by H's books.

-- Spain in general

--have better women than we deserve

-- drink too much

-- hypochondria

-- accident proneness

-- a tendency toward morbidity

-- One difference. I will never stick a shotgun
in my mouth and pull the trigger. Leaves too
much of a mess.

He looked up at the sound of the cane tapping. The
Hemingway was in the Karsh wise-old-man mode, but
was nearly transparent in the bright light that streamed
from the open door. "What do I have to do to get your
attention?" it said. "Give you cancer again?"

"That was pretty unpleasant."

"Maybe it will be the last." It half sat on the arm of
the couch and spun the cane around twice. "Today is a
big day. Are we going to Paris?"

"What do you mean?"

"Something big happens today. In every universe
where you're alive, this day glows with importance. I
assume that means you've decided to go along with me.
Stop writing this thing in exchange for the truth about
the manuscripts."

As a matter of fact, he had been thinking just that.
Life was confusing enough already, torn between his
erotic love for Pansy and the more domestic, but still
deep, feeling for Lena ... writing the pastiche was kind
of fun, but he did have his own fish to fry. Besides, he'd
come to truly dislike Castle, even before Pansy had told
him about the set-up. It would be fun to disappoint him.

"You're right. Let's go."

"First destroy the novel." In this universe, he'd completed seventy pages of the Up-in-Michigan novel.

"Sure." John picked up the stack of paper and threw
it into the tiny fireplace. He lit it several places with a
long barbecue match, and watched a month's work go
up in smoke. It was only a symbolic gesture, anyhow; he
could retype the thing from memory if he wanted to.

"So what do I do? Click my heels together three times
and say 'There's no place like the Gare de Lyon'?"

"Just come closer."

John took three steps toward the Hemingway and suddenly fell up down sideways—

It was worse than dying. He was torn apart and scattered throughout space and time, being nowhere and everywhere, everywhen, being a screaming vacuum forever—

Grit crunched underfoot and coalsmoke was choking thick in the air. It was cold. Gray Paris skies glowed through the long skylights, through the complicated geometry of the black steel trusses that held up the high roof. Bustling crowds chattering French. A woman walked through John from behind. He pressed himself with his hands and felt real.

"They can't see us," the Hemingway said. "Not unless I will it."

"That was awful."

"I hoped you would hate it. That's how I spend most of my timespace. Come on." They walked past vendors selling paper packets of roasted chestnuts, bottles of wine, stacks of baguettes and cheeses. There were strange resonances as John remembered the various times he'd been here more than a half-century in the future. It hadn't changed much.

"There she is." The Hemingway pointed. Hadley looked worn, tired, dowdy. She stumbled, trying to keep up with the porter who strode along with her two bags. John recalled that she was just recovering from a bad case of the grippe. She'd probably still be home in bed if Hemingway hadn't sent the telegram urging her to come to Lausanne because the skiing was so good, at Chamby.

"Are there universes where Hadley doesn't lose the manuscripts?"

"Plenty of them," the Hemingway said. "In some of them he doesn't sell 'My Old Man' next year, or anything else, and he throws all the stories away himself. He gives up fiction and becomes a staff writer for the Toronto *Star*. Until the Spanish Civil War; he joins the Abraham Lincoln Battalion and is killed driving an ambulance. His only effect on American literature is one paragraph in *The Autobiography of Alice B. Toklas*."

"But in some, the stories actually do see print?"

"Sure, including the novel, which is usually called *Along With Youth*. There." Hadley was mounting the steps up into a passenger car. There was a microsecond of agonizing emptiness, and they materialized in the passageway in front of Hadley's compartment. She and the porter walked through them.

"*Merci*," she said, and handed the man a few sou. He made a face behind her back.

"*Along With Youth?*" John said.

"It's a pretty good book, sort of prefiguring *A Farewell To Arms*, but he does a lot better in universes where it's not published. *The Sun Also Rises* gets more attention."

Hadley stowed both the suitcase and the overnight bag under the seat. Then she frowned slightly, checked her wristwatch, and left the compartment, closing the door behind her.

"Interesting," the Hemingway said. "So she didn't leave it out in plain sight, begging to be stolen."

"Makes you wonder," John said "This novel. Was it about World War I?"

"The trenches in Italy," the Hemingway said.

A young man stepped out of the shadows of the vestibule, looking in the direction Hadley took. Then he turned around and faced the two travelers from the future.

It was Ernest Hemingway. He smiled. "Close your mouth, John. You'll catch flies." He opened the door to the compartment, picked up the overnight bag, and carried it into the next car.

John recovered enough to chase after him. He had disappeared.

The Hemingway followed. "What *is* this?" John said. "I thought you couldn't be in two timespaces at once."

"That wasn't me."

"It sure as hell wasn't the real Hemingway. He's in Lausanne with Lincoln Steffens."

"Maybe he is and maybe he isn't."

"He knew my *name!*"

"That he did." The Hemingway was getting fainter as John watched.

"Was he another one of you? Another STAB agent?"

"No. Not possible." It peered at John. "What's happening to you?"

Hadley burst into the car and ran right through them, shouting in French for the conductor. She was carrying a bottle of Evian water.

"Well," John said, "that's what—"

The Hemingway was gone. John just had time to think *Marooned in 1922?* when the railroad car and the Gare de Lyon dissolved in an inbursting cascade of black sparks and it was no easier to handle the second time, spread impossibly thin across all those light years and millennia, wondering whether it was going to last forever this time, realizing that it did anyhow, and coalescing with an impossibly painful *snap:*

Looking at the list in the typewriter. He reached for the Heineken; it was still cold. He set it back down. "God," he whispered. "I hope that's that."

The situation called for higher octane. He went to the freezer and took out the vodka. He sipped the gelid syrup straight from the bottle, and almost dropped it when out of the corner of his eye he saw the overnight bag.

He set the open bottle on the counter and sleepwalked over to the dining room table. It was the same bag, slightly beat up, monogrammed EHR, Elizabeth Hadley Richardson. He opened it and inside was a thick stack of manila envelopes.

He took out the top one and took it and the vodka bottle back to his chair. His hands were shaking. He opened the folder and stared at the familiar typing.

ERNEST M. HEMINGWAY

ONE – EYE   FOR   MINE

Fever stood up . In the moon light he could so see blood starting on his hands . His pants were torn at the knee and he knew it would be bleeding there too . He watched the lights of the caboose disappear in the trees where the track curved .

That lousy crut of a brakeman . He would get him someday some day .

scuffed
Fever knocked off the end of a tie and sat down to pick the cinders out of his hands and knee . He could use some water . The brakeman had his canteen .

He could smell a campfire . He wondered if it would be smart fo go find it . He knew about the wolves , the human kind that lived along the rails and the disgusting things they liked . He wasn 't afraid of them but you didn 't look for trouble .

You don 't have to look for trouble , his father would say . Trouble will find you . His father didn 't tell him about wolves , though, or about women .

There was a noise in the brush . Fever
stood up and slipped his hand around the horn
grip of the fat Buck clasp knife in his pocket .

The screen door creaked open and he looked up to
see Pansy walk in with a strange expression on her face.
Lena followed, looking even stranger. Her left eye was
swollen shut and most of that side of her face was bruised
blue and brown.

He stood up, shaking with the sudden collision of emotions. "What the hell—"

"Castle," Pansy said. "He got outta hand."

"Real talent for understatement." Lena's voice was
tightly controlled but distorted.

"He went nuts. Slappin' Lena around. Then he started
to rummage around in a closet, rave about a shotgun,
and we split."

"I'll call the police."

"We've already been there," Lena said. "It's all over."

"Of course. We can't work with—"

"No, I mean, he's a *criminal*. He's wanted in Missis-
sippi for second-degree murder. They went to arrest him,
hold him for extradition. So no more Hemingway hoax."

"What Hemingway?" Pansy said.

"We'll tell you all about it," Lena said, and pointed at
the bottle. "A little early, don't you think? You could at
least get us a couple of glasses."

John went into the kitchen, almost floating with vodka
buzz and anxious confusion. "What do you want with it?"
Pansy said oh-jay and Lena said ice. Then Lena
screamed.

He turned around and there was Castle standing in
the door, grinning. He had a pistol in his right hand and
a sawed-off shotgun in his left.

"You cunts," he said. "You fuckin' cunts. Go to the
fuckin' cops."

There was a butcher knife in the drawer next to the

refrigerator, but he didn't think Castle would stand idly by and let him rummage for it. Nothing else that might serve as a weapon, except the air pistol. Castle knew that it wouldn't do much damage.

He looked at John. "You three're gonnna be my hostages. We're gettin' outta here, lose 'em up in the Everglades. They'll have a make on my pickup, though."

"We don't have a car," John said.

"I *know* that, asshole! There's a Hertz right down on One. You go rent one and don't try nothin' cute. I so much as *smell* a cop, I blow these two cunts away."

He turned back to the women and grinned crookedly, talking hard-guy through his teeth. "Like I did those two they sent, the spic and the nigger. They said somethin' about comin' back with a warrant to look for the shotgun and I was just bein' as nice as could be, I said hell, come on in, don't need no warrant. I got nothin' to hide, and when they come in I take the pistol from the nigger and kill the spic with it and shoot the nigger in the balls. You shoulda heard him. Some nigger. Took four more rounds to shut him up."

Wonder if that means the pistol is empty, John thought. He had Pansy's orange juice in his hand. It was an old-fashioned Smith & Wesson .357 Magnum six-shot, but from this angle he couldn't tell whether it had been reloaded. He could try to blind Castle with the orange juice.

He stepped toward him. "What kind of car do you want?"

"Just a *car*, damn it. Big enough." A siren whooped about a block away. Castle looked wary. "Bitch. You told 'em where you'd be."

"No," Lena pleaded. "We didn't tell them anything."

"Don't do anything stupid," John said.

Two more sirens, closer. "I'll show you *stupid!*" He raised the pistol towards Lena. John dashed the orange juice in his face.

It wasn't really like slow motion. It was just that John didn't miss any of it. Castle growled and swung around and in the cylinder's chambers John saw five copper-jacketed slugs. He reached for the gun and the first shot shattered his hand, blowing off two fingers, and struck the right side of his chest. The explosion was deafening and the shock of the bullet was like being hit simultaneously in the hand and chest with baseball bats. He rocked, still on his feet, and coughed blood spatter on Castle's face. He fired again, and the second slug hit him on the other side of the chest, this time spinning him half around. Was somebody screaming? Hemingway said it felt like an icy snowball, and that was pretty close, except for the inside part, your body saying Well, time to close up shop. There was a terrible familiar radiating pain in the center of his chest, and John realized that he was having a totally superfluous heart attack. He pushed off from the dinette and staggered toward Castle again. He made a grab for the shotgun and Castle emptied both barrels into his abdomen. He dropped to his knees and then fell over on his side. He couldn't feel anything. Things started to go dim and red. Was this going to be the last time?

Castle cracked the shotgun and the two spent shells flew up in an arc over his shoulder. He took two more out of his shirt pocket and dropped one. When he bent over to pick it up, Pansy leaped past him. In a swift motion that was almost graceful—it came to John that he had probably practiced it over and over, acting out fantasies—he slipped both shells into their chambers and closed the gun with a flip of the wrist. The screen door was stuck. Pansy was straining at the knob with both hands. Castle put the muzzles up to the base of her skull and pulled one trigger. Most of her head covered the screen or went through the hole the blast made. The crown of her skull, a bloody bowl, bounced off two walls and went spinning into the kitchen. Her body did a spastic little dance and folded, streaming.

Lena was suddenly on his back, clawing at his face. He spun and slammed her against the wall. She wilted like a rag doll and he hit her hard with the pistol on the way down. She unrolled at his feet, out cold, and with his mouth wide open laughing silently he lowered the shotgun and blasted her pointblank in the crotch. Her body jack-knifed and John tried with all his will not to die but blackness crowded in and the last thing he saw was that evil grin as Castle reloaded again, peering out the window, presumably at the police.

It wasn't the terrible sense of being spread infinitesimally thin over an infinity of pain and darkness; things had just gone black, like closing your eyes. If this is death, John thought, there's not much to it.

But it changed. There was a little bit of pale light, some vague figures, and then colors bled into the scene, and after a moment of disorientation he realized he was still in the apartment, but apparently floating up by the ceiling. Lena was conscious again, barely, twitching, staring at the river of blood that pumped from between her legs. Pansy looked unreal, headless but untouched from the neck down, lying in a relaxed, improbable posture like a knocked-over department store dummy, blood still spurting from a neck artery out through the screen door.

His own body was a mess, the abdomen completely excavated by buckshot. Inside the huge wound, behind the torn coils of intestine, the shreds of fat and gristle, the blood, the shit, he could see sharp splintered knuckles of backbone. Maybe it hadn't hurt so much because the spinal cord had been severed in the blast.

He had time to be a little shocked at himself for not feeling more. Of course most of the people he'd known who had died did die this way, in loud spatters of blood and brains. Even after thirty years of the occasional polite heart attack or stroke carrying off friend or acquaintance, most of the dead people he knew had died in the jungle.

He had been a hero there, in this universe. That would have surprised his sergeants in the original one. Congressional Medal of Honor, so called, which hadn't hurt the sales of his first book. Knocked out the NVA machine-gun emplacement with their own satchel charge, then hauled the machine-gun around and wiped out their mortar and command squads. He managed it all with bullet wounds in the face and triceps. Of course without the bullet wounds he wouldn't have lost his cool and charged the machine-gun emplacement, but that wasn't noted in the citation.

A pity there was no way to trade the medals in—melt them down into one big fat bullet and use it to waste that crazy motherfucker who was ignoring the three people he'd just killed, laughing like a hyena while he shouted obscenities at the police gathering down below.

Castle fires a shot through the lower window and then ducks and a spray of automatic-weapon fire shatters the upper window, filling the air with a spray of glass; bullets and glass fly painlessly through John where he's floating and he hears them spatter into the ceiling and suddenly everything is white with plaster dust—it starts to clear and he is much closer to his body, drawing down closer and closer; he merges with it and there's an instant of blackness and he's looking out through human eyes again.

A dull noise and he looked up to see hundreds of shards of glass leap up from the floor and fly to the window; plaster dust in billows sucked up into bullet holes in the ceiling, which then disappeared.

The top windowpane re-formed as Castle uncrouched, pointed the shotgun, then jerked forward as a blossom of yellow flame and white smoke rolled back into the barrel.

His hand was whole, the fingers restored. He looked down and saw rivulets of blood running back into the hole in his abdomen, then individual drops; then it closed and the clothing restored itself; then one of the holes in his chest closed up and then the other.

The clothing was unfamiliar. A tweed jacket in this weather? His hands had turned old, liver spots forming as he watched. Slow like a plant growing, slow like the moon turning, thinking slowly too, he reached up and felt the beard, and could see out of the corner of his eye that it was white and long. He was too fat, and a belt buckle bit painfully into his belly. He sucked in and pried out and looked at the buckle, yes, it was old brass and said GOTT MIT UNS, the buckle he'd taken from a dead German so long ago. The buckle Hemingway had taken.

John got to one knee. He watched fascinated as the stream of blood gushed back into Lena's womb, disappearing as Castle grinning jammed the barrels in between her legs, flinched, and did a complicated dance in reverse (while Pansy's decapitated body writhed around and jerked upright); Lena, sliding up off the floor, leaped up between the man's back and the wall, then fell off and ran backwards as he flipped the shotgun up to the back of Pansy's neck and seeming gallons of blood and tissue came flying from every direction to assemble themselves into the lovely head and face, distorted in terror as she jerked awkwardly at the door and then ran backwards, past Castle as he did a graceful pirouette, unloading the gun and placing one shell on the floor, which flipped up to his pocket as he stood and put the other one there.

John stood up and walked through some thick resistance toward Castle. Was it *time* resisting him? Everything else was still moving in reverse: Two empty shotgun shells sailed across the room to snick into the weapon's chambers; Castle snapped it shut and wheeled to face John—

But John wasn't where he was supposed to be. As the shotgun swung around, John grabbed the barrels—hot!— and pulled the pistol out of Castle's waistband. He lost his grip on the shotgun barrels just as he jammed the pistol against Castle's heart and fired. A spray of blood from all over the other side of the room converged on Castle's back and John felt the recoil sting of the Magnum just as the shotgun muzzle cracked hard against his teeth, mouthful of searing heat then blackness forever, back in the featureless infinite timespace hell that the Hemingway had taken him to, forever, but in the next instant, a new kind of twitch, a twist. . . .

23. The Time Exchanged

What does that mean, you "lost" him?

We were in the railroad car in the Gare de Lyon, in the normal observation mode. This entity that looked like Hemingway walked up, greeted us, took the manuscripts, and disappeared.

Just like that.

No. He went into the next car. John Baird ran after him. Maybe that was my mistake. I translated instead of running.

That's when you lost him.

Both of them. Baird disappeared, too. Then Hadley came running in—

Don't confuse me with Hadleys. You checked the adjacent universes.

All of them, yes. I think they're all right.

Think?

Well . . . I can't quite get to that moment. When I disappeared. It's as if I were still there for several more seconds, so I'm excluded.

And John Baird is still there?

Not by the time I can insert myself. Just Hadley running around—

No Hadleys. No Hadleys. So naturally you went back to 1996.

Of course. But there is a period of several minutes there from which I'm excluded as well. When I can finally insert myself, John Baird is dead.

Ah.

In every doomline, he and Castlemaine have killed each other. John is lying there with his head blown off, Castle next to him with his heart torn out from a pointblank pistol shot, with two very distraught women screaming while police pile in through the door. And this.

The overnight bag with the stories.

I don't think anybody noticed it. With Baird dead, I could spot-check the women's futures; neither of them mentions the bag. So perhaps the mission is accomplished.

Well, Reality is still here. So far. But the connection

between Baird and this Hemingway entity is disturbing. That Baird is able to return to 1996 without your help is *very* disturbing. He has obviously taken on some of your characteristics, your abilities, which is why you're excluded from the last several minutes of his life.

I've never heard of that happening before.

It never has. I think that John Baird is no more human than you and I.

Is?

I suspect he's still around somewhen.

24. Islands in the Stream

and the unending lightless desert of pain becomes suddenly one small bright spark and then everything is dark red and a taste, a bitter taste, Hoppe's No. 9 gun oil and the twin barrels of the fine Boss pigeon gun cold and oily on his tongue and biting hard against the roof of his mouth; the dark red is light on the other side of his eyelids, sting of pain before he bumps a tooth and opens his eyes and mouth and lowers the gun and with shaking hands unloads—no, *dis*-loads—both barrels and walks backwards, shuffling in the slippers, slumping, stopping to stare out into the Idaho morning dark, helpless tears coursing up from the snarled white beard, walking backwards down the stairs with the shotgun heavily cradled in his elbow, backing into the storeroom and replacing it in the rack, then back up the stairs and slowly put the keys there in plain sight on the kitchen windowsill, a bit of mercy from Miss Mary, then sit and stare at the cold bad coffee as it warms back to one acid sip—

A tiny part of the mind saying *wait! I am John Baird it is 1996*

and back to a spiritless shower, numb to the needle spray, and cramped constipation and a sleep of no ease; an evening with Mary and George Brown tiptoeing around the blackest of black-ass worse and worse each day, only one thing to look forward to

got to throw out an anchor

faster now, walking through the Ketchum woods like a jerky cartoon in reverse, fucking FBI and IRS behind every tree, because you sent Ezra that money, felt sorry for him because he was crazy, what a fucking joke, should have finished the Cantos and shot himself.

effect preceding cause but I can read or hear scraps of thought somehow speeding to a blur now, driving in reverse hundreds of miles per hour back from Ketchum to Minnesota, the Mayo Clinic, holding the madness in while you talk to the shrink, promise not to hurt myself have to go home and write if I'm going to beat this, figuring what he wants to hear, then the rubber mouthpiece and smell of your own hair and flesh slightly burnt by the electrodes then deep total blackness

sharp stabs of thought sometimes stretching

hospital days blur by in reverse, cold chrome and starch white, a couple of mouthfuls of claret a day to wash down the pills that seem to make it worse and worse

what will happen to me when he's born?

When they came back from Spain was when he agreed to the Mayo Clinic, still all beat up from the plane crashes six years before in Africa, liver and spleen shot to hell, brain too, nerves, can't write or can't stop: all day on one damned sentence for the Kennedy book but a hundred thousand fast words, pure shit, for the bullfight article. Paris book okay but stuck. Great to find the trunks in the Ritz but none of the stuff Hadley lost.

Here it stops. A frozen tableau:

Afternoon light slanting in through the tall cloudy windows of the Cambon bar, where he had liberated, would liberate, the hotel in August 1944. A good large American-style martini gulped too fast in the excitement. The two small trunks unpacked and laid out item by item. Hundreds of pages of notes that would become the Paris book. But nothing before '23, of course. *the manuscripts*

The novel and the stories and the poems still gone. One moment nailed down with the juniper sting of the martini and then time crawling rolling flying backwards again— *no control?*

Months blurring by, Madrid Riviera Venice feeling sick and busted up, the plane wrecks like a quick one-two punch brain and body, blurry sick even before them at the Finca Vigia, can't get a fucking thing done after the Nobel Prize, journalists day and night, the prize bad luck and bullshit anyhow but need the $35,000

damn, had to shoot Willie, cat since the boat-time before the war, but winged a burglar too, same gun, just after the Pulitzer, now that was all right

slowing down again—Havana—the Floridita—

Even Mary having a good time, and the Basque jai alai players too though they don't know much English, most of them, interesting couple of civilians, the doctor and the Kraut lookalike, but there's something about the boy that makes it hard to take my eyes off him, looks like someone I guess, another round of Papa Dobles, that boy, what is it about him? and then the first round, with lunch, and things speeding up to a blur again.

out on the Gulf a lot, enjoying the triumph of *The Old Man and the Sea*, the easy good-paying work of providing fishing footage for the movie, and then back into 1951, the worst year of his life that far, weeks of grudging conciliation, uncontrollable anger, and black-ass depression from the poisonous critical slime that followed *Across the River*, bastards gunning for him, Harold Ross dead, mother Grace dead, son Gregory a dope addict hip-deep into the dianetics horseshit, Charlie Scribner dead but first declaring undying love for that asshole Jones

most of the forties an anxious blur, Cuba Italy Cuba France Cuba China found Mary kicked Martha out, thousand pages on the fucking *Eden* book wouldn't come together Bronze Star better than Pulitzer

Martha a chromeplated bitch in Europe but war is swell otherwise, liberating the Ritz, grenades rifles pistols and bomb runs with the RAF, China boring compared to it and the Q-ship runs off Cuba, hell, maybe the bitch was right for once, just kid stuff and booze

marrying the bitch was the end of my belle epoch, easy to see from here, the thirties all sunshine Key West Spain Key West Africa Key West, good hard writing with Pauline holding down the store, good woman but sorry I had to

sorry I had to divorce

stopping

Walking Paris streets after midnight:

I was never going to throw back at her losing the manuscripts. Told Steffens that would be like blaming a human for the weather, or death. These things happen. Nor say anything about what I did the night after I found out she really had lost them. But this one time we got to shouting and I think I hurt her. Why the hell did she have to bring the carbons what the hell did she think carbons were for stupid stupid stupid and she crying and she giving me hell about Pauline Jesus any woman who could fuck up Paris for you could fuck up a royal flush

it slows down around the manuscripts or me—

golden years the mid-twenties everything clicks Paris Vorarlburg Paris Schruns Paris Pamplona Paris Madrid Paris Lausanne

couldn't believe she actually

most of a novel dozens of poems stories sketches— *contes*, Kitty called them by God woman you show me your *conte* and I'll show you mine

so drunk that night I know better than to drink that much absinthe so drunk I was half crawling going up the stairs to the apartment I saw weird I saw God I saw *I saw myself standing there on the fourth landing with Hadley's goddamn bag*

I waited almost an hour, that seemed like no time or all time, and when he, when I, when he came crashing up the stairs he blinked twice, then I walked through me groping, shook my head without looking back and managed to get the door unlocked

flying back through the dead winter French country-
side, standing in the bar car fighting hopelessness to Had-
ley crying so hard she can't get out what was wrong with
Steffens standing gaping like a fish in a bowl

twisting again, painlessly inside-out, I suppose through
various dimensions, seeing the man's life as one complex
chord of beauty and purpose and ugliness and chaos, my
life on one side of the Moebius strip, consistent through
its fading forty-year span, starting, *starting*, here:

the handsome young man sits on the floor of the apartment holding himself, rocking racked with sobs, one
short manuscript crumpled in front of him, the room a
mess with drawers pulled out, their contents scattered
on the floor, it's like losing an arm a leg (a foot a testicle),
it's like losing your youth and along with youth

with a roar he stands up, eyes closed fists clenched,
wipes his face dry and stomps over to the window

breathes deeply until he's breathing normally

strides across the room, kicking a brassiere out of his
way

stands with his hand on the knob and thinks this:

life can break you but you can grow back strong at
the broken places

and goes out slamming the door behind him, somewhat conscious of having been present at his own birth.

With no effort I find myself standing earlier that day in the
vestibule of a train. Hadley is walking away, tired, looking for
a vendor. I turn and confront two aspects of myself.

"Close your mouth, John. You'll catch flies."

They both stand paralyzed while I slide open the door
and pull the overnight bag from under the seat. I walk
away and the universe begins to tingle and sparkle.

I spend forever in the black void between timespaces.
I am growing to enjoy it.

I appear in John Baird's apartment and set down the
bag. I look at the empty chair in front of the old typewriter, the green beer bottle sweating cold next to it, and
John Baird appears, looking dazed, and I have business
elsewhere, elsewhen. A train to catch. I'll come back for

the bag in twelve minutes or a few millennia, after the bloodbath that gives birth to us all.

25. A Moveable Feast

He wrote the last line and set down the pencil and read over the last page sitting on his hands for warmth. He could see his breath. Celebrate the end with a little heat.

He unwrapped the bundle of twigs and banked them around the pile of coals in the brazier. Crazy way to heat a room but it's France. He cupped both hands behind the stack and blew gently. The coals glowed red and then orange and with the third breath the twigs smoldered and a small yellow flame popped up. He held his hands over the fire, rubbing the stiffness out of his fingers, enjoying the smell of the birch as it cracked and spit.

He put a fresh sheet and carbon into the typewriter and looked at his penciled notes. Final draft? Worth a try:

```
Ernest H. Hemingway,

74 rue du Cardinal Lemoine,

Paris, France
```

```
+ +    U P   I N   M I C H I G A N    + +

    Jim Gilmore came to Horton's Bay from

Canada. He bought the blacksmith shop from

old man Hortom
```

Shit, a typo. He flinched suddenly, as if struck, and shook his head to clear it. What a strange sensation to come out of nowhere. A sudden cold stab of grief. But larger somehow than grief for a person.

Grief for everybody, maybe. For being human.

From a typo?

He went to the window and opened it in spite of the cold. He filled his lungs with the cold damp air and looked around the familiar orange and grey mosaic of chimney pots and tiled roofs under the dirty winter Paris sky.

He shuddered and eased the window back down and returned to the heat of the brazier. He had felt it before, exactly that huge and terrible feeling. But where?

For the life of him he couldn't remember.